SEE YOU AT THE Summit

a novel

JORDYN TAYLOR

GALLERY BOOKS
NEW YORK AMSTERDAM/ANTWERP LONDON
TORONTO SYDNEY/MELBOURNE NEW DELHI

Gallery Books
An Imprint of Simon & Schuster, LLC
1230 Avenue of the Americas
New York, NY 10020

First Gallery Books trade paperback edition January 2026

Manufactured in the United States of America

10 9 8 7 6 5 4 3 2 1

Library of Congress Control Number: 2025942356

ISBN 978-1-6682-0329-3
ISBN 978-1-6682-0330-9 (ebook)

Praise for Jordyn Taylor

"Jordyn Taylor has range, y'all, and she proved it once again."

—*Cosmopolitan* on *Wicked Darlings*

"Twisty, thrilling, and absolutely addictive."

—*People* on *Wicked Darlings*

"Smartly written . . . a feminist mystery that'll keep the reader glued."

—*Women's Health* on *The Revenge Game*

"A whip-smart (and low-key hilarious!) mystery with a pitch-perfect protagonist."

—Jessica Goodman, *New York Times* bestselling author, on *The Revenge Game*

"An empowering and timely feminist mystery."

—*Kirkus Reviews* on *The Revenge Game*

"A highly readable mystery about toxic masculinity and the friendships that exist within and in spite of it."

—*Booklist* on *The Revenge Game*

"A binge-worthy page-turner that will leave readers asking themselves, 'What would I have done?'"

—*Bulletin of the Center for Children's Books* on *Don't Breathe a Word*

"An expertly plotted boarding school mystery."

—*Kirkus Reviews* on *Don't Breathe a Word*

ALSO BY JORDYN TAYLOR

The Paper Girl of Paris

Don't Breathe a Word

The Revenge Game

Wicked Darlings

The Rebel Girls of Rome

To anyone worried they're too much or not enough,

this book is for you.

(Also, you're perfect.)

SEE YOU AT THE *Summit*

CHAPTER 1

SIMONE FELT LIKE HER CHEST WAS going to implode from the enormity of what she'd just posted on the internet. Was it possible to die of sheer panic? She could have googled it, except that would mean looking at her phone, and *that* would only increase her chances of a panic-induced death, if such a thing were indeed possible. Also, her fingers were frozen.

She could have taken the streetcar to the Queen subway station. Realistically, she *should* have taken the streetcar, if only to avoid showing up to work on her first day looking like she'd just come off a ski run. But on this particular morning, she hadn't wanted to cram herself in with other commuters any more than she needed to. Too claustrophobic.

Tugging the zipper of her parka as high as it would go, she leaned into the frigid January wind whipping down Queen Street. The icy gusts had already frozen her damp ginger curls solid, and while the cold definitely stung, it wasn't the only reason her eyes were watering.

Simone pictured her parents learning the news. They were

currently doing the snowbird thing and spending the winter at their condo on Florida's Gulf Coast. She had just been down there over the holidays with them, as well as her two older brothers and her brothers' wives and children. Simone, who was turning thirty this year, had been the only unpartnered adult—as her mother had pointed out numerous times.

Right now, Kathy Whitaker was probably perched on her balcony in a matching loungewear set, sipping green tea with lemon and nibbling a slice of toast with a translucently thin layer of cream cheese. Simone's recently retired father, George, was likely on the driving range already, warming up for today's round of golf with his buddies. George didn't have an Instagram account and could barely be counted on to see text messages, so he'd hear Simone's news through Kathy, who perused the app daily to keep tabs on her social circle. When Kathy saw the post, she'd be absolutely mortified, but the only signs of her disapproval would be narrowed eyes, a clenched jaw, and a sharp, sucked-in jet of air through flared nostrils. Hardly a dramatic shift from her typical demeanor—at least to the untrained eye. She'd take a sip of tea to force down her distaste, which would stay inside her forever, festering, and lash out when Simone least expected it.

Simone remembered when she got her ear cartilage pierced in university. The first time Kathy saw it in person, she cloaked her disgust in a sort of compliment: "You don't think it distracts from your natural beauty, darling?" As if Kathy really cared about promoting "natural beauty." Once Simone hit puberty, Kathy would bring her along to get their legs waxed, their eyebrows threaded, their curls straightened, their fair skin spray-tanned before vacations and special events. When it came to the cartilage piercing, Simone suspected she knew Kathy's *real* concern, the one her mother hadn't expressed aloud: that Simone had deviated from the narrow road Kathy had paved for her, from the version of womanhood that was considered acceptable at the family's country clubs in Toronto and Naples. Case in point: When the piercing got infected six months later and Simone was forced to take it out, Kathy let out a sigh of relief and said, "Oh, thank *God*. I always thought that thing was so trashy, Simone. Men won't want to date you with all that crap hanging off your ears."

Simone gritted her teeth. No one had wanted to date her with or without the cartilage piercing, and she couldn't blame them. She'd been the one with the secret buried deep within her bones.

That is, until now. Now, her secret was live on Instagram. Uncontained. Spreading.

"New year, new me," she whispered into the wind, somewhat deliriously, before boarding the subway at Queen, riding it two stops north to College, and walking the rest of the way to the Village. She'd workshopped the post until two in the morning, then lain awake spiraling about it until her alarm had gone off at six thirty. Simone desperately needed caffeine. On Church, across the street from the large rainbow-striped building that was her new place of work, she ducked into a coffee shop and ordered enough cold brew to kill a horse.

"Big day today?" asked the guy who'd made her drink, nodding at the cup.

Actually, yes! I just came out as bisexual after a lifetime of pretending to be straight! Besides the fact that it would have been a massive overshare, Simone still wasn't used to saying the word out loud: *bisexual*. Just *thinking* it made her equal parts excited and downright terrified. "First day of work," she told the barista.

"You got this," he said.

Simone wasn't sure about that, but she thanked him anyway.

She'd been so nervous about coming out that she'd barely given thought to her new job as marketing project manager at the soon-to-open Rainbow Museum. In her interview, the founder, Frankie Marlow, had explained, "We're not so much a museum as we are an immersive, multisensory museum *experience*—dedicated to celebrating, amplifying, and giving back to the 2SLGBTQIA+ community." Simone quickly gathered that "immersive, multisensory museum experience" was fancy start-up-speak for "an array of fun photo ops with loose educational tie-ins and an expansive gift shop," but she hadn't chosen the Rainbow Museum for its cultural prestige. She'd chosen it because a) she'd just been laid off from her project manager job at an educational technology start-up and required money in order to live; and b) she'd been determined to come out, and starting a job at Toronto's new Capital of Queerness in the heart of the historic Gay Village seemed like an effective way to hold herself accountable.

Cold brew in hand, she crossed the street. She'd interviewed for the job over Zoom, since the building had been a full-on construction zone before the holidays. Now that they were just one month away from the Rainbow Museum's grand opening, Simone was able to walk through the front entrance and see the space in real life.

She smelled warm, earthy sawdust with sharp notes of wallpaper glue and fresh paint, and she was instantly transported to the scene shop in the theater where she'd been forced to perform in dance recitals as a girl. She didn't know the first thing about carpentry, but she'd always wished she could work backstage instead of performing in front of an audience. That was the reason she'd gone for a career in project management: She wasn't a big ideas person, but she was *great* at making sure other people's big ideas were executed smoothly.

Simone was surprised to find no color at all in the lobby, the walls and ticket booth plastered with black-and-white shots of the city. The only clue to the magic that lay beyond was a jet-black sliding door with a blinking neon sign that said ENTER HERE in delicate rainbow letters. She approached the sign, and with a smooth whir, the door slid open for the dramatic reveal.

Wide-eyed, Simone stepped into a dazzlingly bright and colorful atrium. In the center of the room was a ball pit with rainbow-colored balls, and shiny plastic slides that looked like rainbows arcing out of fluffy white clouds. There seemed to be other rooms branching off the atrium, but the archways were hung with thick sheets of plastic that blocked her view. Apparently, there was still plenty of work to be done.

Frankie—who in addition to being the museum's founder was also its CEO . . . and her new boss—had said he'd meet her here at nine o'clock to give her the tour. She was early, as always. No matter how hard she tried to be on time, she was inevitably the first one to show up to dinner parties, the friend who held down the spot at the bar when everyone else was running late.

Unable to wait any longer, she pulled out her phone and tapped the screen. There was a whole *stack* of text notifications. Cautiously, she scrolled through them. Two of her childhood friends, Laney and Mira, had said they'd seen the post and were proud of her; they wanted to celebrate at their next catch-up brunch. Her university friends had revived their long-dormant group chat with a slew of celebratory memes. There was even a "Congratulations!" from her favorite Pilates instructor at the gym.

Relief rippled through her—until she saw the text message

from Kathy. It was only two words, but they were arguably the most ominous two words a parent could text their child: "Call me."

It could only mean one thing:

Her mother had seen the news.

Simone glanced at the time in the corner of her screen. She still had fifteen minutes before she had to meet Frankie. She could call Kathy now, get through the first of what were sure to be many excruciating conversations about her newly revealed identity, and have a ready-made excuse to wrap things up early. She frantically looked around for somewhere private, her eyes landing on the nearest archway covered by a sheet of plastic. She hurried over and flung out an arm to sweep the plastic aside.

Simone's hand collided with something hard on the other side of the sheet—something that gave way, making her gasp. She heard the creaking of wood, followed by a deep male voice shouting, "NO!"

Then came an earsplitting, ground-rattling crash. Followed by another creak, and another crash. On it went, like dominoes falling, until finally the cacophony stopped, and all Simone could hear was the deep voice letting out a roar of fury and frustration.

It would have been easy to skitter away and avoid blame—no one had seen her, after all—but she couldn't just ruin someone's day and then leave them to pick up the pieces. Though she dreaded what lay on the other side, she swept the sheet back and surveyed the damage she'd caused.

She'd assumed it would be bad.

But not *this* bad.

The room was designed like a larger-than-life garden out of *Alice in Wonderland*, with spindly metal flowers that stretched up to the high ceiling. The walls were covered in artificial moss, the concrete floor painted a rich forest green. In the center of the room—the star of the show—was a supersize dragonfly made of wood, its slender abdomen at least ten feet long. Only one of its wings was attached: a work of art in and of itself, with intricately carved veins. The remaining three wings, which had presumably been leaning against the wall next to the archway, were now lying in pieces at Simone's feet. A man wearing brown canvas pants and a tool belt stood at the other end of the wreckage, wincing as he clutched his wrist with the opposite hand.

"I am so, *so* sorry," she squeaked. Then she noticed the rivulet of blood trickling from his wrist to his elbow and gasped. "Here, take this." Frantically, she yanked the damp napkin off her cold-brew cup and raced toward him. Simone was so focused on the man's injury that she failed to pay attention to her own feet, and she stepped on a piece of wing. Delicate wooden veins that had miraculously survived the fall now crunched and snapped under the heel of her boot. Simone stumbled. As she stumbled, she squeezed her plastic cup. As she squeezed her plastic cup, the lid shot off. And as the lid shot off, her entire vat of cold brew arced through the air, landing squarely in the center of the man's white T-shirt.

"WHAT THE *ACTUAL* FUCK?!" he yelled, lunging backward and wrenching the front of the soaking-wet shirt off his skin. His glare hit Simone as she staggered to a stop. He was a few inches north of six feet, and he looked to be in his early thirties, with hazel eyes and tousled mahogany-brown hair that spilled onto his forehead and curled around his ears. His nose and cheekbones were lightly dusted with freckles, his square jaw cloaked in stubble. The fact that he was objectively very attractive made Simone even more embarrassed than she already was. At this point, she would have gladly welcomed death by panic-induced chest implosion.

"Let me help you," she insisted, rushing over and dabbing at whatever she could reach: his bleeding wrist; his cold-brew-soaked shirt—

He jerked his arm away from her. "Jesus Christ! What is wrong with you? Can you not put that filthy napkin on my open cut?"

"Sorry," she said quickly, crumpling the paper and shoving it in her pocket. She let out a shaky laugh. "I'm useless."

"Yes, you've made that abundantly clear," he said. Instead of being offended, Simone was relieved they had something to agree on.

She launched into another string of apologies, until the man silenced her with a stare that could have cut glass. Up close, Simone noticed that his eyes were strikingly unusual. His irises were gray around the outside, with a burst of greenish gold in the center. Like moss on a rock. Simone would have appreciated them more if they weren't smoldering with so much dislike. She desperately wanted to smooth things over. "Please, tell me what I can do—*anything*."

His glare became even sharper than before. Meanwhile, his wet shirt was clinging to his abs—yet another part of his body she would have appreciated more under different circumstances. "You can leave me alone so I can deal with the month's worth of work you just ruined."

"A . . . *month*?" Simone felt like she was going to be sick (although she'd definitely reached the quota of fluid she could expel in this man's vicinity).

"Believe it or not, some people put actual hard work into the things they care about." His gaze faltered for a second before hardening again. "Why don't you go back to your fancy desk job and leave the lowly manual labor to me?"

The words hit Simone like a slap in the face. What did he think, that she was waltzing through life? That she'd pushed through that hanging tarp without a care in the damn world? Little did he know that she was on the verge of potentially being disowned by her mother. Mr. Actual Hard Work didn't realize that *she* was going through her own personal hell, and that if he just made peace with her, he could take her morning from horrible to . . . well . . . slightly less horrible. But it would still be something. Simone's bottom lip trembled. Not only had she wrecked his project, but apparently, she'd also come off as an elitist asshole without realizing it. She didn't trust herself to say another word, and crying in front of him would only make things worse. Before she could break into tears, she turned on her heel and hurried back into the atrium. He didn't call after her, and she certainly didn't look back.

Her new boss, Frankie, was standing next to the ball pit, waiting for her.

"Having a look around?" he asked brightly. He was young for a CEO—twenty-eight, according to the *Globe and Mail* profile she'd read before her interview—with a slim build and a patchy beard and moustache that didn't quite connect at the sides of his mouth. In that same *Globe* article, she'd learned how Frankie had started the Rainbow Museum as a series of pop-up events where guests could learn about queer history, pose for photos on elaborate rainbow-colored sets, and shop retail items from queer-owned companies. Photos from the pop-ups had gone viral, which had led to visitors lining up around the block, which had led to Frankie raising twenty million dollars in venture capital to open a permanent brick-and-mortar location in the Village, with plans to open more locations nationwide. The *Globe* had called Frankie a "wunderkind"—and here was Simone, about to look like a total fool in front of him.

"I accidentally knocked over some pieces of the dragonfly sculpture," she confessed immediately. She didn't want to keep quiet and have Frankie learn about the incident from Mr. Actual Hard Work.

"Oh no, do we need to go pick them up?"

We need to not go anywhere near that man ever again, Simone thought. "The guy who was working in there—I didn't catch his name—he said he could handle it on his own."

"Ryan Foley," Frankie supplied. "Our head carpenter. He and the rest of our production team have been working their asses off to get the place done by the end of the month. They're almost there."

They were *almost there*, she amended in her head. She still would have felt guiltier if it hadn't been for his asshole comment at the end—his apparent assumption that she'd never struggled a day in her life. *Men*. They could be so self-centered. It was a good thing she didn't have to date them anymore if she didn't want to.

"You're sure he doesn't want our help?" Frankie asked.

"I tried," Simone said, balling her hands into fists in the pockets of her coat. "He wouldn't let me."

Frankie chuckled and shook his head. "Straight people are such a mystery to me," he said conspiratorially, as though he also assumed *Simone* found straight people to be a mystery. She felt a swelling in her chest, counteracting the pressure that had been there all morning. Then Frankie clapped his hands. "Anyway, welcome to the Rainbow Museum! Allow me to give you the grand tour."

CHAPTER 2

ONCE UPON A TIME, SIMONE HAD been a straight person.

In high school, she really and truly believed it about herself. Like all the other girls her age, she had genuine crushes on boys—crushes that made her knees shake, her palms sweat, and her chest ache with longing. What more was there to say? Back then, it didn't remotely occur to her that the intense, borderline-obsessive friendships she had with a couple of girls might fall into the same category as the feelings she had for guys.

But then, in university, something strange started to happen. Every now and then, when Simone was drinking at a bar or a house party, she'd find herself making out with other girls. Or switching her dating app settings so she could see women, too. She never went further than kissing, and she never swiped right on any of the women; one thing might lead to another, and suddenly, she'd be forced to come out to her mother, crushing Kathy's dreams of having a daughter who was just like her, only younger and full of promise.

And Simone wouldn't dream of disappointing her mother.

At the urging of George's parents—George, apparently, had opted to "stay out of it"—Kathy had reluctantly given up a budding career in law in favor of raising the couple's three children. Her youth was the next thing to go. Simone saw how these losses ate at her mother—saw it in her snide remarks about working moms; in her never-ending string of beauty appointments; in the lotions she kept in her medicine cabinet, promising to lift, firm, rejuvenate, boost, lighten, and other gravity-defying verbs. Kathy had given up so much for Simone and her two brothers. Simone knew she hadn't asked for it, but somehow, the guilt still stuck. The least she could do was try to be the daughter her mother wanted.

Which was why, the mornings after her forays into embracing her own queerness, she'd chalk up the previous night's escapades to being "blackout," even though she remembered everything.

And then, at her first job—working as a project manager at an educational technology start-up called Sharpe Solutions—she met Bree.

Bree Park was a software engineer who also happened to be an out lesbian. Simone and Bree were friendly around the office, although Simone sometimes found her eyes lingering for longer than she cared to admit on Bree's elbow-length raven hair, the delicate floral tattoos that climbed up her arm, and her plump Cupid's bow lips.

In August, Sharpe Solutions was acquired by a British company and proceeded to lay off its entire Toronto-based team. After they learned they'd lost their jobs in an all-hands Zoom call with the new owners, who hadn't even bothered to break the news to them in person, Simone and some colleagues—Bree included—staggered to the pub across the street to drink away their sorrows. It wasn't long before Simone found herself taking whiskey shots with Bree.

Then, when she was pleasantly buzzed, she found herself touching Bree's arm and playing with her hair. Bree asked Simone if she wanted to come outside for a cigarette, and even though Simone didn't smoke and wasn't planning on changing that, she said she was happy to keep Bree company. She followed Bree out to the empty back terrace, only to vaguely recall that smoking wasn't allowed on restaurant patios.

"I think it might be illegal to smoke back here," she said.

"I know," Bree replied.

And then Bree was kissing her with those Cupid's bow lips, which were as soft as they'd always looked, and Simone was kissing her back, a treasure trove of feelings set free at last. Bree cupped Simone's jaw with one hand and caressed her hip with the other. "I always had a good feeling about you," she whispered.

Simone was used to abruptly cutting off her trysts with women—to blaming it on the alcohol and sweeping it under the rug—but that night with Bree was different. Maybe it was the fact that she'd been low-key crushing on Bree for years, or maybe it was the YOLO mentality produced by the mass layoff. Whatever the case, Simone accepted an invitation back to Bree's apartment, where for the first time in her life she went below the waist with another woman. Bree gently led the way. They started by making out on the couch, picking up where they'd left off at the bar. While they kissed, Bree's hand traveled under Simone's skirt and between her legs, cupping Simone's most sensitive spot through the barrier of her black nylons.

"You're soaked," Bree said with a satisfied smirk.

"I am?" Simone asked.

"Mm-hmm." She took Simone's hand and put it where hers had just been.

"Oh," Simone gasped.

Bree tucked a fingertip into the waistband of Simone's tights. "Can I feel?"

"Yes," Simone breathed, her heart racing with fear and desire. The next time Bree kissed her, she slipped a finger inside Simone.

Simone had come right there on the couch, and it was good—*so* good that when Bree asked Simone to hang out in the light of day the following week, she nervously agreed. They went for brunch at a hole-in-the-wall Egyptian place, where they shared a gooey grilled cheese with dates and honey, and fried cauliflower drizzled with tahini, before heading back to Bree's, where Simone returned the favors from the other night.

The first couple of times they saw each other, Simone could still believe her own lies about what was going on between her and Bree. Sure, they snuggled and watched travel vlogs on YouTube after fucking each other senseless, and Simone would drift off with her head on Bree's chest, but it wasn't as though she wanted to *date* her former colleague. They were good friends who had sex sometimes. It was no big deal. But the more they hung out, the more they talked and kissed and fucked and cuddled and fantasized about road-tripping in Norway together, the harder it got for Simone to deny that she might have real feelings for this woman—the same kinds of feelings she'd had for men she'd dated in the past.

And that was a problem.

Picturing herself with a girlfriend was as impossible as picturing a color she'd never seen before. She couldn't even bring herself to hold Bree's hand or kiss her in public. Maybe she'd feel more urgency to come out if she were gay and depriving herself of all pleasure by sticking to heterosexual relationships. But Simone liked men, too. She had the option to go on pretending to be straight and still have a decent love life.

That was the path she decided to take on that fateful afternoon in early November, when she and Bree had been seeing each other—or rather, *hanging out*—for a couple of months. She had no idea how much she'd regret it.

Simone and Bree were lying in Bree's bed, playing a game they'd invented and called Good Girl: Every time one of them applied to a new job, the other would give her an orgasm using the vibrator or body part of her choosing. For all the shame she'd inherited when it came to sexual orientation, Simone had never been shy about sex itself—not since she'd discovered masturbation in her early teens and realized how good it felt. Sex was less scary because it generally happened in private. She was a thousand times more comfortable going down on Bree in bed than holding her hand as they walked down the street, or introducing her to any of her friends—let alone telling her friends the true nature of her and Bree's relationship. As far as Laney, Mira, and the rest of them knew, Bree was just another one of Simone's Sharpe Solutions buddies—a former colleague she'd gotten close to through the shared ordeal of losing their jobs.

After Simone gave Bree a Good Girl reward with her tongue, Bree looked down as she wriggled back into her shorts and said, curiously, "I just realized I've never asked you: What do you consider yourself? Gay, bi . . . ?"

Simone pushed herself up to her knees and crossed her arms protectively. "I don't know," she said with a shrug, only her shoulders didn't fully drop from her ears.

"Well, do you like guys?" Bree asked kindly.

Simone nodded truthfully.

"Okay, then it sounds like you're bi. Or pan, or fluid, maybe? Some people like those words better, but it's totally up to you."

Simone froze, knowing that if she admitted that she was bi—

or pan, or fluid, or anything that wasn't straight—she would lose control of the life she'd built. *That* chaos would be way worse than any conflict she could possibly have with Bree. Whatever their relationship was, it wasn't worth turning her world upside down when she could just as happily be with men. "Actually," Simone told Bree, "I think I'm straight."

Bree snorted with laughter.

"No—no, I'm serious," Simone stammered. She climbed off the mattress and backed into the dresser, putting as much space as she could between them. "We're having fun, but I'm not, like, *actually* into girls."

Bree jerked her head back as though the words had hit her in the face. "You seriously think you're straight . . ."

Simone felt heavy all over, like she was buried in sand up to her chin. She managed to nod.

". . . even though your mouth was on my clit about thirty seconds ago."

"It's just sex," Simone said, refusing to think about the way they'd fallen asleep last night: Bree cradling her from behind, her lips on the back of Simone's neck; their legs and fingers intertwined and their breathing synced as though they were one. Of course, now it was all Simone was picturing in her head.

"Just . . . sex?" Bree asked slowly, her voice laced with hurt.

Simone felt like the worst human being alive, or quite possibly in history. The kindest thing she could do was put an end to Bree's suffering. "Listen," she said, "I've been super stressed about not having a job, and this has been a good distraction, but I'm not looking for anything more than that. I'm really sorry if I led you on."

"*If* you led me on?" Bree snapped. "We've been seeing each other for like, two and a half months now. You sleep here half the time."

"Yeah, because we're friends," Simone said, as though it were obvious, and another wave of nausea crashed through her.

"THIS IS NOT WHAT FRIENDS DO." Bree waved her arms around at the den they'd created in her bedroom: the half-drunk mugs of tea on the bedside tables; the rumpled and twisted duvet; the sex toys and laptop chargers lying across the mattress.

Simone knew it was true, that what they'd had was romantic and sexy and *real*, but she kept her mouth shut. Clenched her jaw and pushed it all down, like her mother had taught her to do.

Bree dragged her fingers through her hair and released an exasperated sigh. "You know what? I refuse to be gaslit by someone who can't admit what the fuck they want." She huffed a laugh. "God, I was going to ask you to be my girlfriend."

My girlfriend. The words hung in the air like an apple, shiny for a second before it withered and died. "Sorry," Simone mumbled, turning her gaze to the floor.

"Oh, babe, I'm good," Bree replied icily, grabbing Simone's laptop and thrusting it at her. "You're the one who's gonna spend the rest of her life lying to herself."

In the excruciating minutes that followed, Simone silently gathered her belongings from the bedroom and the bathroom. Her bones were heavy, her movements sluggish. Her body didn't want to leave the nest they'd built together, but her brain said, *Hurry the hell up*. She opened the laundry hamper and fished out the crewneck sweater she'd stained with tomato sauce when they made pizza the other night. Unplugged her phone charger from behind the bedside table. She trudged to the foyer and slid her feet into her loafers, which had been lined up neatly next to Bree's.

She let herself out of the apartment.

Simone was so distraught over the following week that she

tanked her interviews for two jobs and applied to zero more. Her head wasn't in the game. It wasn't even in the same city as the arena. All she could think about were Bree's last words: *"You're the one who's gonna spend the rest of her life lying to herself."* Believing the lie had always seemed easy enough since she'd started kissing girls in university. Then she'd met Bree, and it hadn't seemed so easy anymore.

Had it *ever* really been easy? Drinking to make those kisses "okay"? Window-shopping on the apps for partners she'd never actually get to try on? All of it left her with a longing in her chest. Dating men hadn't been so easy, either. Not one, but *two* guys she'd really liked had broken things off with her because she seemed to have a wall up, they'd said. These thoughts kept her up at night, clouded her every waking moment, made themselves utterly impossible to ignore—until one morning, Simone broke down crying in the shower, exhausted from yet another horrendous night's sleep.

What if she'd never be able to find true love with *anyone* until she was honest about who she really was?

Her arms hugging her naked torso, she spoke two words that scared the shit out of her, but so softly that she herself couldn't hear them over the pounding of the water.

She hadn't died. Hmm.

With a deep breath, she said the words again, a little louder this time:

"I'm bi."

Her heart thudded against her rib cage with the force of a thousand suns, but still, she was alive. She stayed in the shower for a long time, repeating the words like a mantra, until the rivulets running down her cheeks were a mixture of hot water and her own tears. When she finally got out and dried off, she felt lighter than she had before the breakup with Bree. She quite possibly felt lighter than she had in her whole life.

Fuck, maybe she *did* need to come out. And not just to herself and her bath products.

Though Simone was generally a self-starter, she knew that with this goal, she'd need some kind of deadline to hold herself accountable. She also still needed a job, desperately. A girl could only eat so many boxes of mac and cheese before she perished of scurvy.

The solution to both problems materialized on a bright November morning, when the air was cool and smelled faintly of overripe leaves. Simone was sitting outside at a coffee shop, scrolling through LinkedIn, when she came across the listing for the Rainbow Museum job. Her heart was racing by the time she'd finished reading the description. She filled out the application, vowing that if she got the job, she'd come out as bisexual in time for her first day of work. She spent a full minute hovering over the "submit" button before she finally worked up the courage to press it.

There was a whooshing sound and a confirmation message.

Suddenly, Simone was scared. Maybe she wasn't ready to turn her life upside down. She prayed the Rainbow Museum was already inundated with applications, and that hers would end up in the slush pile. While she was at it, she prayed to be launched into the sun.

The week before Christmas, she got an offer.

She would start after New Year's.

"Exciting life update," she wrote in her Instagram caption, beneath a selfie she'd taken on the roof of her apartment building. "I'm thrilled to share that I've accepted a new job as marketing project manager @TheRainbowMuseum, a new destination dedicated to celebrating 2SLGBTQIA+ pride all year round! In the spirit of pride, I think it's time I finally tell the world . . . I'm bi!"

CHAPTER 3

AS HE LED HER AROUND THE ball pit, Frankie flashed Simone a knowing smirk. "I saw your Instagram post this morning. *Epic*."

"Oh—thanks," she stammered. That explained why he'd made the joke about straight people being a mystery; he'd already known she was bi. It felt strange to be perceived as queer by someone other than Bree, and the fact that it felt strange made her wonder if she'd made a mistake. What if she actually *was* straight? No, that was another absurd thought brought to her by her own crushing anxiety. Straight people didn't cry literal tears of relief after finally coming out to themselves in the shower.

"You must feel so free," Frankie said.

"And terrified," Simone admitted. Kathy's text message flashed through her mind. *"Call me."* With a period and everything.

"Fair," he said. "But the good news is, there's no need to be terrified here. Our team is the best."

Except for Mr. Actual Hard Work, Simone thought. She understood why he hadn't wanted her anywhere near the wreckage she'd caused, but he could have at least accepted her countless apologies instead of glaring at her with those eyes of his. Her morning had been just as tumultuous as his, if not *more* so.

"Guests will exit through the gift shop, which is gonna be through there." He nodded at the plastic tarp on their left. Sweeping aside another tarp, he led her into a long hallway painted with bright rainbow stripes, plaques lining the walls. Simone glanced at the first one on her right: "1918: Canada's (and North America's) first known queer publication—a literary magazine called *Les Mouches Fantastiques*—is founded in Montreal by poet Elsa Gidlow and journalist Roswell George Mills."

"It's a whole timeline of queer history in Canada," Frankie explained. Before Simone could move on to the next plaque, he steered her through a doorway to another photo-friendly space, this one circus-themed, with swings suspended from the ceiling. The next space looked like a psychedelic trip with giant neon mushrooms and butterflies. Then they took the elevator to the second floor, where there were even more themed rooms, including one with an underwater mermaid aesthetic, and another with a rainbow picket fence and artificial grass dotted with pink flamingos, garden gnomes, and pinwheels.

Finally they took the elevator up to the management floor. "Our conference rooms are named after queer icons," Frankie explained. "That's Ru Paul, Cher, Freddie Mercury, Lil Nas X, and Elsa."

"Elsa?" Simone asked.

"From *Frozen*," he replied.

Simone raised her eyebrows. "Elsa's queer?"

"I mean, not officially, but the vibes are there. Her parents force her to hide who she really is, she ends up isolated from the rest of society, she doesn't end up with a dude at the end . . ."

"Whoa." Simone had watched the movie multiple times with her niece and never once put that together. "My mind is blown."

Frankie grinned. "Right?"

What she didn't tell Frankie was that the revelation also stressed her out. Not because she was some diehard *Frozen* fan, but because now she was wondering how many other queer symbols she was oblivious to. What if Frankie secretly suspected she wasn't *really* bi? She had an absurd impulse to blurt out that she'd had sex with a woman before—many times, in fact! Simone bit her bottom lip to prevent herself from getting fired for sexual harassment on her first day. She needed to get a handle on her anxiety. She also needed to rewatch *Frozen* and probably every movie she'd ever seen.

Frankie took her around the office to meet the museum's twenty full-time employees, starting with the creative team, whose desks were scattered with mock-ups of the rooms she'd seen downstairs. Then came the operations team, the guest experience team, the finance team, and finally, the marketing team—Simone's people.

As she shook her new colleagues' hands and surveyed their workspaces, Simone was struck by just how *out* they all were. Nina Gómez, the communications director, was a fortysomething woman with a long, slicked-back ponytail and a handshake that almost crushed Simone's metacarpal bones. On her desk was a lesbian flag sticking out of a pencil cup with stripes in the same colors. Seth Li, who ran the company's social media accounts, was dressed in billowy pleated pants and an oversize neon windbreaker, and was sipping from one of those giant Stanley water bottles with the words GAY AND TIRED emblazoned on the side. She smiled and complimented it, while wondering if she looked queer enough to fit in here. How did one go about *looking* more bisexual, anyway? When they reached her barren new desk, Simone decided she'd need to peruse Etsy for some blue, purple, and pink bisexual decor.

Frankie left her to get settled, and she plopped down at her desk. Seth, who sat next to her, slid over in his rolling chair and offered to get Simone set up on the Rainbow Museum's Slack. "This is the main room, for company-wide stuff, and then we have separate rooms for specific departments," he explained as he clicked away on her laptop. His nails were painted purple, a similar shade to his windbreaker. "Okay, that's probably good, work-wise. Now let's do the main event: the *fun* rooms."

Simone watched as he proceeded to add her to a dozen more Slack rooms that had nothing to do with the Rainbow Museum. One room was simply called "queer animals," and was entirely devoted to sharing links about, well, queer animals. Most recently, Frankie had dropped in a link about a giant tortoise in Ecuador who'd been in a bisexual love triangle for seventy-five years. People had responded with messages like *SAME* and *ICON*. Seth returned her laptop with a warm smile, and Simone spent the next little while clicking from Slack channel to Slack channel. A few colleagues sent private messages welcoming her—again—to the Rainbow Museum. Her anxiety got the message to lay off her for a bit. Simone's new coworkers—minus Mr. Actual Hard Work—were friendlier and more welcoming than she ever could have imagined. A grin crept across her face as she sat there staring at her laptop, not just from the Slack memes, but from *relief*. For the first time in her life, she wasn't hiding. She was exposed—and still, she was safe.

Simone looked up when Frankie rapped his knuckles on the edge of her desk. "Have a second to chat? I have super exciting news."

Simone wasn't sure anything could be more exciting than having found her way to this queer oasis, but she was eager to hear what Frankie had to tell her. She followed him into a conference room—Ru Paul—where they sat down opposite each other on beanbag chairs. Frankie leaned forward, put his elbows on his knees, and steepled his fingers.

"So," he said, "how do you feel about Whistler?"

"As in, the ski mountain?"

"Correct."

"I've never been, but I've heard it's amazing, obviously." It was the most famous ski destination in Canada. Simone had been skiing since she was three or four, but mostly in Ontario and once in Quebec. She'd been dying to ski out west at some point, where the mountains were massive and the snow was powder-soft.

"How would you like to go?"

Simone raised her eyebrows as her jaw dropped open. "Seriously?"

"Have you heard of the Whistler Pride and Ski Festival?"

Simone shook her head, although the word *Pride* gave her a general idea of where this was going. Adrenaline coursed through her veins, made her hands shake. She clamped them between her thighs as Frankie continued talking.

"It's basically a week of skiing and snowboarding during the day and Pride parties at night," he explained. "I've been a bunch of times before, and it's epic. Seriously, some of the best weeks of my life.

"But anyway, this year, I made a deal with them that the Rainbow Museum would provide selfie stations at all their events in exchange for a week of amazing publicity." Based on the look he gave her, he clearly thought he'd gotten the better end of the deal. "We'll get someone local to build the sets, but I also want one of our team members to be there in person repping the brand and getting people pumped about visiting us the next time they're in Toronto. And the plan is to open a Vancouver location at some point, too. Nina, who you met earlier, was supposed to go, but she has a family wedding or something." He waved his hand dismissively. "I know it's not quite in your wheelhouse, but I did hire you to focus on marketing projects, specifically. And we're a fairly small team—more like a family, really—so I rely on people to wear different hats sometimes. Whaddaya think?"

She wasn't going to give her new boss the honest answer, which was that (a) as much as she already loved the Rainbow Museum, the thought of being an outspoken brand rep had her stomach in knots; and (b) the prospect of attending her first Pride festival while out was exciting, sure, but also made her long to be swallowed whole by the squishy beanbag chair. She'd spent *checks watch* approximately three hours as an out bisexual. That morning's Instagram post had been the first time she'd declared her sexuality outside of her own shower. Was she really ready to put herself out there at a Pride festival? Was she even *qualified*?

"Oh, and you'd be totally free to ski or snowboard or whatever during the day," Frankie added. "You'd only really be working in the evenings."

Simone forced a smile. The promise of having free time to ski felt irrelevant compared to the magnitude of everything else.

Frankie was looking at her expectantly. She needed to give him an answer.

Nervous as she was to agree to the assignment, Simone wasn't about to let her boss down on her first day of work.

She glanced over his shoulder, through the glass wall of the conference room, to the group of people who'd welcomed her so warmly this morning. Maybe she didn't want to let *herself* down, either. She'd develop new career skills—*lean in*, or whatever it was that women were supposed to do in the corporate world. And it would be her first Pride as an out bisexual! Sure, she was nervous to put herself out there in such a big way, but her first morning at the Rainbow Museum had emboldened her. She released her hands from between her legs and placed her palms on her knees.

"I'm in," Simone declared, and as soon as she said it, she felt light and fizzy, like her body was filled with champagne. "When is it?"

"The end of January."

"The end of *this* January? As in . . . the end of this month?"

"Is that gonna be okay, timing-wise? I'd go myself, but it's the week before our grand opening, and I know I'll have so much shit to do here."

"That's totally fine!" It was more than fine—it was ideal. Invigorating. A way to celebrate the massive step she'd taken by finally coming out.

"Okay, *phew*. You're a lifesaver." Frankie leapt to his feet and clapped her on the shoulder. "I'm so jealous you get to go! It's, like, the queerest place on earth. You're gonna love it."

~

SIMONE CATEGORIZED HER FRIENDS INTO TWO distinct groups: the childhood friends she'd grown up with; and the friends she'd made in university. She appreciated them all for different reasons, but there was no one she would have felt comfortable opening up to about her sexuality. The people she'd grown up with were all straight, many of them already married or soon to be married. In the past year, Laney and her husband had welcomed their first baby, and Mira and her fiancé had closed on a house in Pickering with a front lawn, a backyard, and a two-car garage. Their conversations had shifted to mortgages and day care prices—not much room for Simone's *am-I-queer* chaos. She still met up with them for brunch. She liked baby photos. But as time went on, she felt the disconnect more and more—even when they were together.

The relationships she'd forged in university were more surface-level and situational than they were deep. The kind where once you're no longer sharing a house in Guelph or seeing each other in class every day, you make brunch plans you never follow through on, send a few *We should totally catch up!* texts, and then mutually ghost each other until the group chat dies of natural causes. She knew part of that was on her. She'd always kept a piece of herself walled off, and it had left a quiet space between her and everyone else.

Needless to say, when Simone looked up from her laptop to find her new colleague Lucy LaFrance standing next to her desk asking her if she'd like to grab lunch with her, Simone was more than happy to oblige. Lucy, a blond woman who looked to be around forty, worked in the finance department and had helped Simone get set up in the payroll system that morning. She wore a fuzzy white turtleneck tucked into high-waisted orange pants, and a long wool coat with a button pinned to the lapel that said CHILDLESS CAT LADY.

"I love the button," Simone said as she zipped up her parka.

"Thanks!" Lucy beamed. "I got it at this cute place around the corner. I can show you sometime."

"Cool," Simone replied, knowing she'd have to work up the courage to wear something like that herself.

She and Lucy walked north to a cozy café that served soup and sandwiches. Lucy was bubbly and warm, and by the time they'd arrived, Simone knew all about her wife, Holly, and her three rescue cats: Cheddar, Gouda, and Blue. She'd spent fifteen years working soul-crushing corporate jobs, until one day she came across a finance job at the Rainbow Museum, back when they'd just leased the building in the Village. She'd jumped at the chance to work for a company that seemed more aligned with who she was.

After they placed their orders at the counter, Lucy fished around inside her tote bag. "This is my treat, by the way."

"Really?"

"It's your first day," Lucy insisted. "Also, I heard you came out on Instagram this morning." She extricated her wallet and looked inside. "Oh shoot. Now, what did I do with my credit card? That is the question. Oh!" She shoved her wallet back into her tote bag, pulled out a paperback fantasy novel, and opened it to the middle, where her credit card was nestled in lieu of a bookmark. "Don't judge me! I was reading in line at the coffee shop this morning and it just happened."

Simone smiled. She usually shied away from chaos, but Lucy's personal brand was endearing.

They carried their food to a table by the window. "So," Lucy asked as they ate, "what have people been saying about your post? I hope you're getting lots of nice messages."

Simone intentionally hadn't opened the app all morning, and she'd turned off every form of notification. She confessed all this to Lucy, then said, "I guess I should probably look, shouldn't I? I'm going to have to do it at some point."

"It's up to you, but if you wanna do it, I'm here for moral support."

With a deep breath, Simone reached into the pocket of her parka, dug out her phone, and braced herself. "Okay. I'm doing it."

She tapped the Instagram icon—and almost dropped her phone into her tomato basil soup. "Oh my God."

"What is it?"

"Four hundred and seventy-six people have liked my post." Simone gazed up at her colleague in disbelief. "That's like . . . more than double the number of followers I have."

"Hell yeah!"

Simone turned back to the app, where she discovered that Seth had re-shared her post from the Rainbow Museum account. Complete strangers had been liking the post and leaving comments, from thoughtful messages to strings of rainbow emojis. She scanned the comments with that strange mix of relief and terror she'd felt after sharing the post. Each "congratulations" was a weight off her shoulders, but it also made her news more permanent. She couldn't go back into the closet now, even if she'd wanted to.

"Cheers to you." Lucy raised her water bottle before taking a sip. "It sounds like things couldn't have gone better today."

Simone sighed and put her phone down. "Sadly, not quite." She proceeded to tell Lucy about her mother's ominous text: "*Call me.*" "I am *dreading* having to talk to her," she said with a groan. "It's gonna be awful."

Lucy sighed and squeezed Simone's hand. "You poor thing. I remember that feeling. I was so nervous to come out to my mom, I puked into my purse on the bus ride to her house."

"*Into* your purse?"

"It was better than on my lap!"

"How did it end up going?"

"I put the bag in the wash. She lived."

"I meant coming out to your mom." She chuckled.

"Oh! *That* was a total nightmare," Lucy replied.

Simone grimaced. "Is she super homophobic?"

"The opposite," Lucy said. "She's a *sex therapist*." Simone clapped a hand over her mouth. Lucy leaned across the table and lowered her voice to a whisper. "When I told her I was into women, she went down to her office in the basement, came back with her female anatomy model, and literally started lecturing me on how to find the G-spot."

Simone would have killed for a sex talk from Kathy instead of whatever verbal thrashing her mother had in store for her. (This was saying something, given that in their actual "birds and the bees" conversation, Kathy had lectured a thirteen-year-old Simone on the dangers of being branded a "certain kind of girl" that no man would ever want to marry.)

The last thing Simone did before she left the office that evening was pop into the all-gender washroom. There were messages of affirmation stuck to the mirrors above the communal sink, and she read them under her breath as she lathered her hands with soap.

"I am a true work of art."

"I am proud of who I am."

"I am fierce and strong."

She wanted desperately to believe these things, but the confidence she'd started to develop at work today was in shambles at the thought of calling her mother on the way home. She dried her hands, zipped up her parka, and swung her tote bag over her shoulder. Outside the Rainbow Museum, the sun had already gone down, and the air was even colder than it had been this morning. Nevertheless, after taking the subway to Queen, Simone skipped the streetcar again and set off east on foot so she could make the dreaded phone call in relative solitude.

Simone was almost as nervous now as she'd been before posting her announcement this morning. All she could feel was the thump of her heart slamming into her rib cage. Panic zipped through her veins, numbing her hands and making her eyes feel too small for their sockets. Summoning what little strength she had left, she pushed the call button.

The phone rang three times. She wanted and didn't want to hear her mother's voice. She'd be relieved to get this over with, but at the same time, she knew it was going to be awful. After another ring, Kathy picked up. Instead of hello, she just said: "Simone."

Simone's heart was about to burst through the front of her parka and flop onto the pavement. "Hey, Mom."

Silence.

"You, um . . . you wanted me to give you a call? I'm assuming, um, that I know what it's about . . ."

"Your . . . news," Kathy said slowly.

The way she was stretching this out was somehow even worse than if she'd immediately launched into a disapproving tirade. Simone felt as if she were tied to a chair while her mother wound up gradually for one big knockout punch.

"It's really not that big of a deal," Simone blurted out, even though it had obviously been one of the biggest pieces of news she'd ever shared in her life. "I mean, when you think about it, isn't everyone a little bit bi? There's that country singer who came out last week, and that football player. Also, people think Eleanor Roosevelt was bi." (She'd learned this by reading through the Rainbow Museum Slack channels today, but good lord, why was she dragging Eleanor Roosevelt into this?) "And, don't worry, this doesn't mean I'm never gonna date men again and only be with women for the rest of my life. Not that it's bad to be a lesbian, either! I just meant that this isn't going to be some big, dramatic change."

More silence. Simone racked her brain for what else she could say to soften the eventual blow. But then she heard something unexpected on the other end of the call.

"Mom?" she asked, concerned. "Are you . . . crying?"

Kathy's answer came in the form of a loud sniff. "Oh, honey," she choked out, "I just love you so much, and I don't want you to have a hard life."

Simone leapt into the role of comforting her mother. "Oh, Mom, it's okay, I started a new job where everyone's super queer—"

It had been the wrong thing to say. "You may not realize this in your little bubble, Simone, but there are hateful, homophobic people out there!" Kathy wailed.

"It's better in some places than others," Simone said gently, even as fear climbed up her chest. What if her mother had a point? "I probably won't be moving to Florida anytime soon, but Toronto's pretty accepting . . ."

Kathy let out a sob. "So now you're done with coming down to the condo?"

"No, no, that's not what I meant!" Simone's voice wavered; she was on the verge of crying herself. "I'll always come visit you and Dad."

"Your father's worried, too," Kathy said. "You know how hard he worked to give you and your brothers a good life."

"Oh, Mom, you *both* worked hard."

"I appreciate that, darling." Kathy sniffed. "Your father and I both—we never want to see you suffer."

Tears ran hot and fast down Simone's cheeks. Making her parents angry would have been awful, but disappointing them was downright unbearable. She didn't know what to say except, "I'm sorry, Mom." The more her mother cried, the more Simone did, too.

As Simone started over the bridge to Leslieville, where she lived, Kathy finally seemed to catch her breath. "Well, I suppose there's nothing we can do about it now, is there?"

"No, I guess not," Simone answered guiltily. She never should have come out. This had been the biggest mistake of her life.

Kathy sighed. "Simone, this'll take some time for us to get used to, that's for sure. You'll have to be patient with us."

Simone wiped her eyes. "I will. I promise."

Another sigh. "Well, I need to go clean myself up before we head out to dinner, so I'll let you go."

"Okay."

"Talk soon, darling."

Simone stopped walking and stuffed her phone into her pocket. She was halfway across the bridge, the towering trusses to her left and the Don River to her right. She approached the edge, gripped the railing, and peered down at the black water. The metal in her hands felt like ice, and the river would be even colder. It would swallow her whole and she wouldn't feel a thing.

No sooner had the thought crossed her mind than she let go of the railing, took a big step back, and folded her arms across her chest. She hurried across the rest of the bridge. The relief she'd enjoyed at the Rainbow Museum was gone; the weight returned to her shoulders. If coming out was supposed to have made her life easier, then maybe she'd done something terribly, horribly, wrong.

CHAPTER 4

ANOTHER VAT OF COLD BREW IN hand, Simone dragged her weary corpse past the rainbow ball pit the next morning and jabbed the button for the elevator. She should have been excited to go upstairs and plan her trip to Whistler, but instead, the thought of attending the Pride festival made her want to face-plant into the ball pit and never resurface.

Instead of letting her sleep last night, her brain had graciously played her conversation with Kathy on a loop for seven straight hours. By the time her alarm had gone off, she wasn't going to lie: She was tempted to quit her job, post on Instagram that she was actually straight after all ("whoops, jk!!!"), and spend the rest of her life lying to herself but making her parents happy. If only she didn't need an income in order to live.

Moments later, the doors opened with a ding to the last person she wanted to see. Ryan Foley, Mr. Actual Hard Work, was in the elevator, where he was busy straightening a pile of boxes and power tools that were balanced on a dolly. When he looked up and saw her, he frowned. And he'd already looked pretty miserable to begin with. *Perfect.*

Simone slapped on a smile. Given that she felt like a pile of rotting garbage today, she figured the least the universe could do for her was grant her a fresh start with Ryan. "Morning!" she said a bit too cheerfully, sweeping her arm as she made room for him to step out.

Instead of returning her greeting, he just glared at her. What the hell?

"Er, do you need any help with that?" She nodded at the dolly. Then she remembered that offering to help Ryan had historically not gone well for her.

This time was no different. "I'm not getting off," he said in that deep voice of his. She felt it reverberating inside her chest—or maybe that was just the tremendous amount of caffeine she'd already consumed this morning.

"Oh!" she yelped. He must have gotten on in the basement and been headed to an upper floor. Without thinking, she darted into the elevator. It wasn't until the door slid shut behind her that she realized how cramped it would be with the two of them and the dolly in here. Though she was able to extend an arm and press the button for the third level, she wasn't confident she could fully turn around without her bag bumping one of Ryan's boxes. Since that was a risk she was very much *not* willing to take, she opted instead for keeping her nose mere centimeters from Ryan's sternum.

He cleared his throat but didn't say anything.

With less than a foot between their bodies, she couldn't help but notice his clean, earthy scent, like pine needles on a forest floor. Ryan was dressed in worn leather boots, brown work pants that were snug around his quads, and a plain gray T-shirt. His bare arms were lightly freckled and had a natural heft to them, unlike the meticulously sculpted bis and tris she saw on the weightlifting fanatics at her gym. What a waste of resources that someone so physically attractive had such a foul personality.

She would try for that fresh start anyway. She damn well *deserved* it, after everything she'd been through. She peered up at him—more at his chin, really, given how close she was. It was a very nice chin. Prominent, with a shallow dimple.

She hadn't yet opened her mouth when Ryan looked down at her, unprompted, and their eyes met unexpectedly in the cramped space. Heat rushed to Simone's cheeks, and Ryan quickly averted his gaze to the dolly at their sides.

Awkward, but she pressed on. "Hey, Ryan? I'm Simone, by the way. About yesterday, I just wanted to say, again . . ."

Ryan closed his eyes and grabbed a fistful of the dark brown curls that spilled onto his forehead. With a pang of guilt, she noticed the bandage on his wrist. Why did it seem to be so unbearably painful for Ryan to be in her presence? Was he like this with everyone, or was there something about Simone, specifically, that pissed him off to the point of wanting to rip his hair out?

". . . I'm really and truly sorry," she finished.

When he opened his eyes, she caught a glimpse of softness before his steely glare made a comeback. "I really and truly couldn't care less."

Scratch feeling guilty about the bandage. It was official: Mr. Actual Hard Work was one of the biggest assholes she'd ever met. In fact, he was rivaling the guy who'd laid her off via Zoom for the title of asshole in chief. There were some sadistic people out there who were allergic to making peace—who thrived on conflict and chaos. Ryan must be one of those people. A twisted part of him probably *liked* that she'd broken his precious dragonfly wings.

Simone would simply have to avoid him going forward. She looked down, pretending he wasn't there, until the doors opened on the second floor. She hopped out of the elevator to let him pass, and he pushed the dolly past her without a word.

I hope you have a wonderful day, too, she thought bitterly. *Dick*.

His pine-needly scent lingered in the elevator after he was gone, which Simone found annoyingly pleasant. She was *not* in a pleasant mood. She trudged to her desk, flopped into her chair, opened her laptop, and checked her calendar. She, Frankie, and Phillip, the Rainbow Museum's creative director, were meeting in a few minutes to review Phillip's designs for the Whistler Pride selfie stations. How was she supposed to focus on plans for a Pride festival when she was second-guessing ever having come out?

Lucy arrived in the office a few minutes later. "Happy second day!" she trilled with a wave.

"Morning," Simone replied, trying her best to sound cheerful.

Lucy dropped her coat on the back of her chair and took a closer look at Simone's face. "Hey, are you okay?" She hurried over to Simone's desk.

Simone shook her head, knowing that if she tried to explain what was wrong, she'd burst into tears.

Lucy was perceptive. "You talked to your mom," she said—not as a question, but as a statement of fact.

Simone nodded.

"It could have gone better."

Simone nodded again, this time closing her eyes.

"Ah, so it was a total fucking shit show. Got it. Do you want to go somewhere and talk?"

She did, but she didn't have time. "I have a meeting with Frankie in a minute. Maybe after?"

"Of course." Lucy gave her shoulder a squeeze. "Come find me."

In the conference room—Elsa this time—Simone found Phillip, a slender fiftysomething guy with a pointy gray mustache and a pencil tucked perpetually behind his ear. He was busy laying out a dozen different mock-ups for the selfie stations on the table.

"Wow," Simone said, impressed by the sheer quantity of options.

"Not my best work, but it is what it is," Phillip muttered.

"Are you swamped?"

"Beyond."

"I'm sure these will be okay."

"They'll have to be, because I have about six billion other things to do before we open." Simone didn't envy Phillip, who had the massive job of *designing the whole Rainbow Museum*. She'd gathered from their introduction yesterday that he came up with all the creative concepts for the production crews to execute, which also meant he managed all the contractors: people like the painters, the lighting technicians, and Mr. Actual Hard Work. Another reason Simone didn't envy Phillip.

But the number one reason she wouldn't trade places with the creative director was what happened when Frankie came into the room and surveyed his designs. Nearly thirty years as Kathy Whitaker's daughter had trained Simone to recognize her boss's tight-lipped expression as he peered down at the mock-ups. After an agonizing minute of silence, Frankie looked up at Phillip. "They're all step-and-repeat banners?"

Phillip sounded cautious when he answered, "Yes."

"I see."

"I think they'll work great. I have a guy out there who can print them, they're easy to put together, they won't break the bank . . ." Phillip trailed off. There was a long pause from Frankie. Simone wondered if they even remembered she was there, and kind of hoped they didn't. The tension in the room was palpable.

"We're the Rainbow Museum," Frankie said at last. "We don't make decisions because they're easy or because they're cheap. We make decisions because they're great."

It was all very dramatic for a discussion about selfie stations, but Simone wasn't surprised that Frankie had an inner shark concealed beneath the laid-back vibes he'd greeted her with yesterday. How else could he have grown the Rainbow Museum from a pop-up to a multi-million-dollar company by the age of twenty-eight? She made a mental note not to get on Frankie's bad side.

Meanwhile, things were getting heated between Frankie and his creative director. "Look," Phillip argued, "I know you probably wanted something more elaborate, but I'm busy trying to give you that downstairs, okay? I'm not just phoning it in. We're still building out the gift shop, we're sourcing props for all the rooms, we have a lighting issue on the second—"

"Okay, okay, I don't need to hear your whole to-do list."

"If I had one more full-time designer on my team—"

"That's enough." Frankie pinched the bridge of his nose. "You can both leave. I need to take a beat and think about what to do."

Scowling, Phillip swept his mock-ups into a pile, while Simone slipped from the room without another word. She'd never been so relieved to be dismissed from a meeting. She went to find Lucy, who was lying in a hammock in Freddie Mercury, squinting at a spreadsheet on her laptop. When she saw Simone, she sat up, draping her legs off the side of the hammock. She patted the fabric, motioning for Simone to come join her.

Simone didn't sit so much as she collapsed. "That looks . . . fun," she said, nodding at the spreadsheet.

"Oh, you know, the joys of processing paychecks for a billion different vendors and contractors, all of whom do their invoices in slightly different ways. What's really fun is that some of them forget to invoice at all, and then they wonder where their money is, and by the time they *do* end up invoicing, our budget's in a totally different place! Great times all around."

"Hmm." Simone tapped her chin, momentarily distracted from the reason she'd sought out Lucy in the first place. "Have you thought about ways to streamline the invoicing process?"

Lucy shook her head. "Trust me, I'd love to, but lately it's been so much to manage that I haven't even been able to come up for air. If your project manager brain has any ideas, I am seriously all ears."

"I can definitely help you," Simone said.

"Oh my God, really? That would be amazing, if it's not too much trouble."

"It's no problem." There was nothing Simone was better at than making other people's lives easier.

"Anyway"—Lucy closed her laptop and shoved it into the corner of the hammock—"how are you?"

Simone sighed as she remembered how god-awful her day had been. "I want to crawl into the ball pit downstairs and never come out."

"Oh no, please don't do that. Once we open, it's gonna smell like feet in there." Simone could barely manage a smile. "Do you want to tell me what happened with your mom?" Lucy asked. "We can also just sit here and rock if that feels better."

After the showdown between Frankie and Phillip on top of

everything else, Simone was officially too exhausted to feel her own emotions. She ran through the conversation with Kathy, listing each line like it was an item on a grocery list. Lucy, who *could* still feel feelings, looked appalled.

"Gimme a break with the whole 'I'm worried about you having a hard life' argument. You know what else is hard?"

"What?"

"SPENDING THE REST OF YOUR LIFE CLOSETED."

"I don't think she'd want that, either," Simone reasoned.

"So what *does* she want?"

She could tell Lucy was leading her to an answer—an answer that made Simone's heart sink when she landed on it. "For me to be straight, I guess."

Lucy gave her a pointed look.

"My mom does love me," Simone countered. "She's just worried about homophobia."

"I have no doubt that she loves you."

"So isn't it fair that she's worried?"

Lucy sighed and looked at the ceiling. "Listen, Simone, I obviously don't know this woman, so you can take this with a grain of salt. But your mom saying she wishes you weren't queer because homophobia exists is actually, like . . . pretty homophobic."

Simone furrowed her brow. "But homophobia *does* exist."

"Trust me, I'm not arguing that. She's clearly uncomfortable with the fact that you're queer, but she knows she shouldn't admit that, so instead of saying it directly, she said, '*I'm* not homophobic, but *some people* are.' It's bullshit. The biggest thing your mom should actually be worried about is her daughter's happiness, and ideally, she would promise to do everything in her power to fight back against the very real problem of homophobia. Your mom's too scared to ask the world to change, so instead she wants *you* to change yourself."

Simone had barely heard the end of the sentence above the memories that were swirling in her mind. She thought of the cartilage-piercing fiasco, when Kathy had disguised her disapproval as "concern" about Simone's "natural beauty." The truth was that she didn't want her social circle judging her for having an "alternative" daughter, but instead of trying to broaden her friends' minds, she'd pressured Simone to conform to their standards. And it had worked—because that's what Simone did best. She was a better contortionist than those people in Cirque du Soleil. How much more would she hurt herself to make her mother more comfortable?

Simone remembered peering over the edge of the bridge. A chill went down her spine. "You're right," she whispered, shaking her head. "You're so, so right. Last night . . ." Simone was choked up now. ". . . last night, I felt guilty for even *existing*."

Lucy rubbed her back in circles. "Simone, please know that I want you to exist. Everyone who works here wants you to exist. The whole damn queer community wants you to exist. Your mom wants you to exist, too, even though she clearly isn't capable of supporting you the right way—which isn't your fault. You haven't done anything wrong. You hear me?"

"Okay." Simone managed a weak smile. "I might need you to remind me every so often."

Lucy posed angelically with her hands under her chin. "Oh, don't worry, I will." A moment later, her face lit up with an idea. "This is random, but are you free on Monday?"

"Um, I think so?"

"Cool, 'cause a bunch of us go to karaoke sometimes at this bar around the corner from here. You should totally come."

~

BY THE END OF HER FIRST week, Simone was pleased to have made progress with her desk decor. She and Lucy had popped into a craft store on their way back from lunch that day, where Simone had bought three bunches of fake hydrangeas in blue, purple, and pink; a large mason jar; and rainbow ribbon. She'd tied a bow around the jar, and was arranging the flowers when Frankie rapped his knuckles on her desk. He had his laptop tucked under his opposite arm. "Working hard or hardly working?"

"Sorry!" she yelped, releasing the plastic stems like they were on fire. Speaking of being on fire: Her cheeks burned red-hot, and must have looked it, too.

Frankie snorted a laugh. "Oh my God, your face! I was just fucking with you."

"Oh. Ha!" She forced a weak laugh through the panic that hadn't quite left her chest. She was still scarred from the layoff last fall, terrified of once again being deemed "redundant."

"Got a few minutes? I wanna chat about those selfie stations."

Oh God, not the selfie stations again. "Sure!" she chirped. "Here, or a conference room, or . . . ?"

"Downstairs." He jerked his head toward the elevator.

Weird, but okay. Simone got up and followed her boss past three empty conference rooms that apparently wouldn't suffice for the meeting he wanted to have. Maybe they were going to find Phillip. In the elevator, her boss pushed the bottom button.

"We're going to the basement?" she asked, wondering if Frankie was "fucking with her" again.

"Listen, Phillip made it *very* clear yesterday that he didn't have the bandwidth to give us what we need, so I need to explore other options."

Simone felt bad that Phillip seemed to be getting cut out of the project entirely, but she was way too new here to speak up for him, so she just nodded.

"Our head carpenter, Ryan, has a good design sense, and he's been great with sourcing materials and getting shit done. I wanna see what he thinks."

Dread pooled in her stomach. She'd successfully avoided her work nemesis since Tuesday, when they'd encountered each other in this very spot. When she'd tried—again—to apologize for what she'd done, and he'd responded like the biggest jerk in the world.

The doors opened, and Simone took her first steps into the basement, where the air was colder, the lighting was harsh, and the walls were made of depressing white cinder blocks. No shocker that it was miserable down here; they were entering Ryan's evil lair. Her arms wrapped tightly around her torso, she followed Frankie past a boiler room and an electrical closet, and into a spacious workshop that looked just like the one in the theater where she'd had dance recitals as a kid, only she had no desire to go into this one. Because *this one* contained an angry giant hunched over what Simone recognized as one of the dragonfly wings she'd accidentally smashed to pieces on her first day. She felt a pang of empathy. Then she remembered who she was dealing with.

"Knock, knock," Frankie said.

Ryan was wearing earbuds and hadn't seemed to hear them come in. He was concentrating on carefully regluing a delicate wooden vein, his bottom teeth worrying his top lip as he worked. She was impressed by how still he was, save for his hands and mouth.

Frankie grabbed a damp, dirty rag off the lip of a metal sink and chucked it at Ryan to get his attention.

Ryan jumped when the rag landed on his shoulder and clung to the side of his neck. Dropping the piece of wood he'd been working so hard to position, he reached for the rag, and when he saw what it was, hurled it across the table with a disgusted expression on his face, like when she'd tried to clean his cut with her cold-brew napkin. He took out his earbuds and turned to face them. He looked exhausted, with bloodshot eyes and dark shadows underneath. Still annoyingly hot, though.

He addressed Frankie directly, like Simone wasn't even there. *Rude*. "What's up?"

"I wanna see what you think about something." Frankie marched over to the table where Ryan was doing dragonfly surgery and slammed down his laptop like he owned the place. Which, technically, he did. But Simone noticed how Ryan still winced when Frankie pushed aside some delicate pieces of wood to make room for his phone, too. She smirked to herself as she followed her boss to the table. She found it strangely satisfying to watch Mr. Actual Hard Work get put in his place, even if throwing the wet rag had been kind of shitty on Frankie's part. "Remind me: You two have met, right?" Frankie asked.

Simone decided to show her boss what a positive attitude she had, compared to the vortex of negativity that was Ryan Foley. "Yep!" she chirped, and threw in a grin for good measure. "We've met a few times, actually."

"Mm-hmm." Ryan finally deigned to make eye contact with Simone. His glare was as cold as the depressing cinder block basement. Her pulse betrayed her with a sudden skip. Probably from all the unresolved resentment.

He really must have been a demon who thrived on conflict. Yes, she'd ruined an elaborate carpentry project that had taken him weeks to complete—and inadvertently caused him to injure his wrist, and drenched him in cold brew—but those things had all been accidents, and she'd sincerely apologized. Meanwhile, Ryan still had no idea how much he'd offended her with his pointed remark about "actual hard work." She was the one who'd publicly come out that very morning, who'd had to listen over the phone as her mother cried tears of homophobia, who'd peered over the railing of the bridge and thought fleetingly of letting the icy water swallow her. Simone put on a syrupy-sweet voice, hoping that it would piss Ryan off even more. "I accidentally knocked over these dragonfly wings on Monday morning and felt *terrible*. Luckily, it looks like it's been an easy enough fix!" She patted the frame of the wing that was on the table. Ryan's jaw clenched.

Serves him right, she thought.

Frankie explained to Ryan that the Rainbow Museum was sponsoring Whistler Pride by providing selfie stations at all the events. Then he opened his laptop and *really* got down to business. "So, I love Phillip. You love Phillip. We *all* love Phillip. But Phillip came up with some preliminary designs for the selfie stations that I do not love."

Ryan furrowed his brow. "Okay."

Frankie pulled up a recent email. "I asked Whistler Pride to send me these photos. They show the areas in the different venues where our selfie stations are gonna go." He aimed the screen at Ryan and clicked through the images. "You agree we could do something better than shitty step-and-repeat banners, right?"

Ryan rubbed the corners of his bloodshot eyes. "I wouldn't say step-and-repeat banners are *shitty*, necessarily—"

"But you could do something better, right? Sets with different levels, fancy backdrops, rainbow arches . . . ?"

Ryan's neck swiveled from the laptop to the dragonfly wing and back again, and he let out an aggrieved-sounding sigh. Another pang of empathy cut through the loathing in Simone's heart. She ignored it. Ryan was probably *pleased* to be saddled with even more work; it would give him something else to be miserable about.

"I could send you some design ideas," he answered Frankie in a deep monotone.

"By when?"

"How many sets do you need?"

"Five."

Ryan scratched the back of his neck. "I don't know. Wednesday, maybe? At the earliest?"

Frankie grimaced. "Not Monday?"

"I'll probably be in the shop all weekend," Ryan said, casting another one of his icy glares at Simone.

"Tuesday, then," Frankie said with an air of finality.

"Sure."

"Fab." Frankie shut his laptop and pocketed his phone. "When you have the designs, send them to me and Simone, and then, Simone, after I green-light them, you'll work with Ryan to find contractors out there and loop in the Whistler team to make it all happen. Sound good?"

Simone didn't even like being in Ryan's general vicinity. The prospect of *working* with him on a project she was managing? No, it did not sound good. But Simone was a team player, and she refused to let her new boss think otherwise. "Sounds *great*," she said brightly.

Ryan grunted and popped his earbuds back in.

CHAPTER 5

SIMONE HAD BEEN TO A HANDFUL of queer bars before, but always as a "straight" girl—and never to belt show tunes in front of an audience.

"Er, what do I do with this, exactly?" Simone chewed on the straw of her vodka soda and contemplated the iPad Lucy had just dropped into her lap. It was Monday night, and they were at Dorothy and Friends, the queer bar with karaoke that Lucy had invited her to.

"You search for songs, pick whatever you want to sing, and add it to the queue." Lucy quickly whirled back to the stage, where their colleague, Nina, had just belted out a high note in a song from the musical *Wicked*. "Yessss!!!" Lucy cheered, clapping her hands above her head. Simone could see why Nina worked in comms, and why she would have been the perfect Rainbow Museum spokesperson in Whistler. Her confidence in front of a crowd was palpable. Simone wished she could absorb it for herself by some kind of emotional osmosis, although she was pretty sure that wasn't how confidence worked.

Lucy turned back to Simone. "Did you pick something?"

Simone shook her head, her knuckles white as she gripped the iPad. "Lucy, I don't know if I can get up there."

"Why not?"

"I'm a terrible singer."

"So's everyone! Well, except Nina. You just have to be confident."

"I also have the worst stage fright ever." She'd had panic attacks before every one of those cursed dance recitals as a kid, her legs shaking in her tights as she waited backstage for her entrance. She didn't want to disappoint her colleagues, but there was no way she was brave enough to go up there and perform.

Seth plopped down next to her on the banquette. The rose-gold highlighter on his cheekbones shimmered in the dim light of the bar. "What if we do it together?"

Lucy nodded along encouragingly.

Simone was still anxious. "What if I don't know any of the songs well enough to sing them start to finish?"

"Simone, I'm about to do 'Mamma Mia.' There is no way in *hell* you don't know 'Mamma Mia.'"

He was right, but she was afraid to admit it.

"You don't even have to sing if you don't want to," he added. "All you have to do is come up there with me."

Before Simone could voice another objection, Seth had eased her drink from her grip and set it on the table. Then he and Lucy each grabbed one of her hands and pulled her off the couch. Her cheeks were a thousand degrees, and she knew her neck must be covered in hives, but she also had to admit how nice it was to be part of this little community. *This enormous community*, she realized as she climbed up onstage, where Nina was taking a final bow. The space had filled out since they'd arrived. Didn't these people have anything better to do with their Monday nights? Why were they here, with their eyes on the stage, instead of literally anywhere else?

"GO, SIMONE!" screamed a chorus of voices over at the bar. Lucy, that scoundrel, had rallied a group of strangers to cheer Simone's name while she waited for another drink. Nobody would be cheering when Simone anxiety-puked all over the stage. She decided to keep her eyes on the microphone that Seth thrust into her hands.

The bouncy intro music started to play, and the crowd cheered some more. Simone's knees trembled the way they had when she was little. Then Seth started singing—and Simone looked up in sheer disbelief. His singing was awful. Atrocious. An honest-to-God crime. And then there was his dancing: a frankly appalling combination of limb-flailing and hip-gyrating. But the guy was enthusiastic. By the first chorus, Simone didn't feel so afraid any-more. Seth waved for her to mirror his movements. Laughing nervously, she started to dance alongside him. The crowd went wild; the strangers by the bar were chanting her name. Then, right in time for the second chorus, Simone raised the microphone to her lips and sang the lyrics.

When the song was over, Simone looped her arm through Seth's and stumbled giddily off the stage, her limbs vibrating with an electricity she never thought she'd experience from performing in front of a crowd. Lucy was waiting nearby with open arms. She folded Simone in a hug, and Seth hugged Simone from behind, and Simone was pretty sure she could still hear strangers cheering for her. Never in her whole life had she felt so safe—so loved. And she'd only known these people for a week. Simone started to laugh, and then she started to cry, and then she was laughing at the fact that she was crying and crying at the fact that she was laughing. Lucy and Seth held her and let it all happen, despite the not-unlikely chance that Simone was getting tears and mascara all over Lucy's blouse.

"My sweet, sweet baby gay," Seth cooed.

"Baby *bi*," Lucy corrected him.

Simone gently extricated herself from their embrace and wiped her eyes. "Oh my God, why am I like this?"

"Relief," Lucy said. "You can just be yourself, do whatever you wanna do, without having to worry. Especially in a place like this." She gestured at the bar around them.

Simone let her gaze rove freely across the sea of people. She was used to keeping her eyes down in crowded bars and parties, lest they land on a woman she found attractive. She didn't have to worry about potentially confronting her queerness anymore. She was out. This freedom, Simone realized, was a little like lucid dreaming. It was liberating and terrifying all at once. She could finally do whatever her heart desired, but also, *oh God, she finally could do whatever her heart desired*. She could kiss a woman, or sleep with a woman, or—possibly the most intimidating option of all, because it was visible to the rest of the world—even *date* a woman.

But first, she needed to *not* be covered in splotches of tears and eye makeup. Simone waved a hand in front of her face. "I'm gonna go clean all this up," she told her colleagues, before scurrying to the washroom.

She was standing at the mirror, dabbing her cheeks with a damp paper towel, when a stall door swung open behind her with so much force that it banged into the wall. Simone gasped.

"Whoa! Sorry about that," exclaimed the woman who stumbled out in a pair of high-heeled boots. Suddenly, her face lit up, and she cried, "SIMONE!"

Simone felt the surge of dread she always got when she blanked on someone's name, although in this case, she couldn't even recall having *seen* the woman before. She felt like she would have remembered her if she had. She was striking in a queer goth sort of way, with bleach-blond hair, alabaster skin, and long, willowy limbs clad in an all-black outfit. Wincing, Simone opened her mouth to apologize for the faux pas, when the woman cut her off.

"You don't know me! I'm Kenzie. Your coworker told me to cheer for you when you were up there doing karaoke." Her voice was loud and raspy, the latter quite possibly due to the former.

Simone let out a sigh of relief and smiled. "That was you?"

"And a bunch of my friends," Kenzie boomed. "You were *sensational.*"

"Seriously?"

"Okay, actually, I don't really remember, because my one friend keeps buying us all shots. But I *feel like* you were sensational. I can just tell. By your vibe."

Simone laughed nervously. She'd exchanged countless gushing compliments with tipsy women in bar bathrooms, but never before in a *queer* bar bathroom. Was Kenzie just being friendly, like Simone was used to, or was she hoping for something more? And how was Simone supposed to tell?

Kenzie washed her hands and dried them on her jeans. "I'll see you out there," she said with a waggle of her fingers. "And don't worry, your eye makeup looks hot as fuck."

Heat rushed to Simone's cheeks. "Oh—um, thanks," she stammered, but the woman was already gone. Simone didn't know what to make of the encounter. Shaking it off, she tossed the paper towel in the garbage and went back out to rejoin her friends.

Over the next two hours, Simone got onstage three more times—

willingly. She also drank one and a half more happy-hour vodka sodas, but she was pretty sure the karaoke and overall camaraderie had loosened her up even more than the alcohol had. She was having the time of her life, and at a Monday-night work outing, of all places. She couldn't believe that in a few short weeks, she'd be partying at Whistler Pride.

Simone was making her way from the washroom back to her colleagues when a hand caught her by the shoulder. She spun around. It was Kenzie, of possible-flirting-in-the-washroom fame.

"Hey!" Kenzie yelled in her raspy voice. She nodded toward the stage. "I actually heard you the last time you sang, and I was right."

Simone made a polite-but-confused expression. "You were right? About what?"

"You *are* sensational."

That seemed like a stretch, seeing as she'd mostly swayed in the background while Seth performed a rousing rendition of "Lucky" by Britney Spears, but whatever. She'd take the compliment. She knew, this time, that they weren't having a tipsy platonic bonding sesh. Okay: Maybe they *were* both tipsy, but Kenzie was definitely flirting with her. She could tell by the mischievous smirk that played across her lips, the way her eyes lingered on Simone's mouth. Suddenly, Simone's heart was at risk of exploding through her rib cage. She knew she should say something in response to Kenzie's compliment, but she quite frankly had forgotten how words worked.

She was saved by Taylor Swift. "Oh my God," Kenzie gushed as the karaoke machine blared the opening bars of "Love Story." "I fucking love this song."

Simone loved this song, too. The next thing she knew, she and Kenzie were scream-singing the words and acting out the lyrics by way of dancing. When they got to the final chorus—to the part about Romeo proposing to Juliet—Kenzie knelt down on what had to be a very sticky floor and mimed pulling out a ring. Simone grabbed her by the hands and pulled her up so they could belt out the rest of the song together, but Kenzie stumbled in her high-heeled boots, stumbled closer to Simone, so close that Simone could smell the traces of tequila on her breath . . .

. . . and then they were making out.

Kenzie's kiss was the sexual equivalent of how she'd burst from the stall in the washroom. It was vigorous and kind of chaotic, her jaw and tongue both moving faster than Simone was expecting. She couldn't find the rhythm—that is, if there was even a rhythm to find.

And still, despite the fact that she was at risk of developing TMJ from excessive jaw strain, Simone felt light as air. She was making out with a cute woman in the middle of a bar, and she didn't have to worry about what it meant, or figure out how she'd sweep it under the rug tomorrow. It was arguably one of the worst kisses of her life—on par with that from the guy in high school who'd licked the whole area around her lips—and she would definitely not be following up with Kenzie after tonight, but Simone still had a feeling she'd cherish this moment forever.

~

SIMONE WOKE UP THE NEXT MORNING with a sore jaw and a full heart. She felt like nothing could bring her down as she swung by her usual coffee shop across from the Rainbow Museum. Today, she would not require an Olympic swimming pool's worth of cold brew. She would treat herself to something fun and festive, like a maple spice latte.

She got in line behind a tall person in an olive-green toque and a brown Carhartt jacket. Everyone and their mother wore Carhartt these days, so she didn't think twice about the customer in front of her until she picked up on a familiar evergreen scent.

Oh no.

Her traitorous nose inhaled the clean aroma, her chest expanding to make space for it in her lungs.

Will you stop? she silently hissed at her own respiratory system. *We are not supposed to like anything about Mr. Actual Hard Work.*

Simone's first instinct was to turn on her heel and get the hell out of there to preserve the peace of her morning, but she stopped herself. For one thing, Joe the barista, with whom she was now on a friendly basis, had already spotted her and waved hello; for another thing, she really liked the coffee from this place, and her brain would shut down without it. Also: Why should she care about preserving the peace anymore? She'd apologized to Ryan Foley about a billion times, and he still insisted on being a moody asshole in her presence. She'd generally been trying to avoid him, but today she felt the urge to do something different: to stand up for herself. To be so kind that it killed him. Last night had emboldened her. And besides, she couldn't keep avoiding him this week, anyway; they'd have to communicate about his designs for Whistler Pride.

Ryan was at the register now, placing his order. He still didn't know she was there. When Barista Joe rotated the credit card machine so Ryan could pay, Simone 2.0 darted forward, leaping into action. "Hey, Joe!" she said cheerfully. "I'm gonna get this guy's coffee today." She clapped a hand onto Ryan's shoulder for good measure, and—jeez, was he ever solid under there. The man was sturdy as an oak tree.

Ryan peered down at her like she was a dog who'd decided to piss on said oak tree. His eyes looked even more exhausted than last week. She remembered him saying he'd be in the shop all weekend—and then he'd had to make the designs for Frankie, on top of whatever else he still had to get done ahead of the Rainbow Museum's grand opening. But whatever compassion she might have felt was squashed by the way Ryan proceeded to snap at her. "I don't need anyone paying for me."

"I know you don't, but I insist, seeing as I'm the one with the *fancy desk job*." She'd stunned him into silence with that one. With a triumphant smile, Simone turned to Joe. "I'll do a small maple spice latte with oat milk and a morning glory muffin, please. Ryan, did you want anything to eat, or . . . ?"

"No." His voice was dangerously low, and if she thought he'd glowered at her before, well, he looked even angrier now.

Good, she thought as she whipped out her Apple Pay. Never in her life had she reveled in someone being this upset with her. Never in her life had she reveled in someone being upset with her, period. Ryan was bringing out a whole new side to her, and she liked it.

Without saying thank you—not that she'd expected him to—he stalked over to the window to wait for whatever he'd ordered. Simone bounced to his side, grinning like a ray of sunshine. Ryan crossed his arms. "What are you doing?"

"What do you mean?" Simone asked sweetly. "I'm treating my esteemed colleague to coffee."

"I mean, what are you *doing*?"

"I just told you—"

"Why are you *like* this?" he asked, waving a hand in exasperation.

Simone cocked her head politely. "So friendly and generous?"

"So irritatingly chipper."

Uncomfortable as she was, she would not let him pierce her cool exterior. "Why does my positivity annoy you so much, Ryan?"

He spoke slowly, like he was saying the words as he etched them into stone. "Because it borders on obliviousness."

Old Simone would have been well into her apology tour by now—anything to make the altercation end—but Simone 2.0 would stand her ground. She took a step closer and locked eyes with Ryan. His olive-green toque made the matching bursts of color at the center of his irises that much more remarkable, but Simone refused to be flustered. *Certainly* not by his handsomeness. "You know what?" she fired back. "I think you kind of like it."

"Like what?"

"When I ruin your day with my *oh-so-irritating chipperness*."

"Why would I enjoy that?"

"I don't know. Maybe you're one of those people who secretly love to suffer."

He grabbed her shoulder. For a split second, she thought he was going to shove her aside. But then he said, "Watch out," and guided her out of the way of a delivery person carrying a crate full of almond milk. "Guy almost walked straight into you," he muttered as he dropped his hand to his side.

Simone was still processing Ryan's surprise burst of courteousness when Barista Joe called out from behind the counter: "I have two maple spice lattes for Simone, one with whole milk and one with oat!"

Simone's lips quirked into a satisfied smirk. Mr. Actual Hard Work—Mr. I-Primarily-Communicate-in-Grunts-and-Frowns—had ordered the same fun and festive winter beverage as she had. Her plan to kill him with kindness was going even better than she could have imagined. "See?" she said with her brightest, most upbeat voice. "We were destined to be friends."

Ryan let out a sarcastic, disbelieving laugh. Then he sidestepped Simone, swiped his coffee off the counter, and made for the door.

"Can't wait to see those designs today!" she trilled after him.

Ryan didn't turn before barreling out of the shop. Simone watched him go, the satisfied smirk still playing on her lips. She hadn't shied away from conflict like she usually did. She'd sprinted at it, full tilt. She felt powerful.

When she went to collect her own latte, she saw that Joe was still watching Ryan through the window as he charged across the street. "He's in quite the mood, eh?"

"I think that's just his personality," she replied.

"Really? He's usually pretty chill."

Simone frowned. Lucy had said more or less the same thing when she'd mentioned her squabbles with Ryan the other day.

"Seems like it's just been a recent thing," Joe added.

Or it's just a me *thing*, Simone thought bitterly as the barista waved goodbye and went to take the next order.

Ryan's designs landed in Simone's and Frankie's inboxes later that day. With everything else he was working on, Ryan had somehow found time to make three-dimensional renderings of five different sets, each one fun, bright, and inviting. The opposite of Ryan's personality.

"LOVE," Frankie wrote back in all caps. "Now, let's make it happen."

"Will do," Simone wrote back on the thread. "Ryan, you and I can message separately about contractors." Before she sent it off, she added one more line. She couldn't help herself. "By the way, these designs are delightfully chipper!" She pressed send and took a satisfied sip of her licorice tea as she imagined Ryan glowering at the message.

She'd just started drafting an email to Whistler Pride when a new message whooshed into her inbox. It was a reply on the other thread—from Ryan. "Glad to hear you both like them. Simone, see below for the names of three potential contractors. If they want to talk to me directly, let me know. Happy to suffer through as many calls as need be."

Simone stared at his message. *Happy to suffer*. Heat bloomed in parts of her body that didn't typically get hot from reading work emails, and she toggled back to her draft before Ryan could distract her any further.

She spent the next hour shooting off messages to the contractors Ryan had named, asking if they were available at the end of the month to build a handful of selfie station sets.

By the following afternoon, they'd all regretfully declined the offer, citing larger-scale projects they had to prioritize. When Frankie Slacked her asking for an update, she nervously told him the truth.

There was a harrowing hour of radio silence in which Simone became increasingly convinced that her boss was planning to fire her less than two weeks into her job. Here was the first big project he'd trusted her to manage, and she hadn't even gotten it off the ground. In her defense, he could have just gone with Phillip's original step-and-repeat banners, but still, she was at Frankie's mercy, and his behavior had turned out to be somewhat unpredictable.

At five o'clock, Simone got a Slack message from Frankie asking her to come by his office whenever she had a chance. As soon as she read it, a pit formed in her stomach. The layoffs at her last job had been announced at the end of the day.

She pushed herself to standing and dragged her feet to Frankie's glass-walled office. When she got there, he was sitting at his desk and staring at his phone, nodding his head to an intense beat she couldn't hear. With a jittery hand, she rapped on the soundproof glass. Frankie blinked in surprise, his forehead still creased with concentration, and waved for her to come in. Techno music was blaring from his speakers. He might as well have been working at a day club in Ibiza.

He cranked down the volume. "It's my music for getting shit done," he explained matter-of-factly, like a doctor explaining a surgical procedure to a patient. Simone prayed the "shit" he'd been getting done this afternoon was something other than her termination paperwork. She had a bad feeling about this meeting. "Sit down," her boss said, and she shuffled into the room, grabbing one of the chairs in front of his desk.

"Well," he said, "this is a huge fucking disappointment."

A cannonball hit Simone in the gut. She didn't know how she could have done a better job convincing the contractors to drop everything to build a few selfie station sets, but she'd take the blame anyway. "It's my fault. I—"

"What are you talking about?" Frankie asked, cutting her off.

She blinked. "You just said you were disappointed."

"Not in *you*. In these asswipes who turned us down!"

"Oh!" Simone let out the breath she'd been holding and leaned back in the chair. She did feel bad that Frankie had called the perfectly nice contractors "asswipes"—a word she hadn't heard since her older brothers would play video games in the basement—but at least she wasn't about to be fired. "What do you think we should do about the selfie stations?" she asked Frankie. Maybe they would go with the step-and-repeat banners after all.

"I don't think. I know. And it's all gonna be fine."

"Oh—awesome!"

"I'm sending Ryan to Whistler with you."

Another cannonball slammed into her gut, bigger and heavier than before.

"If you want something done right, do it yourself, you know? And honestly, I trust Ryan to get the job done more than I trust these randos. I assume that's okay with you?" He cocked an eyebrow in a way that implied it had *better* be okay with her.

Oh yeah, it's totally okay, she thought, *except for the fact that he hates everything, including—no,* especially*—me.*

Simone hadn't seen Ryan since their face-off in the coffee shop yesterday morning, when she'd been riding the high of karaoke night and feeling unusually bold. She'd been able to stand her ground for the time it took Barista Joe to make their maple spice lattes, but a *whole work trip* with Ryan? That was a different matter entirely—one she might not survive. She'd get pulled into his whirlpool of misery and drown.

Nevertheless, she had to admit that Frankie was right: Ryan *would* get the job done better than anyone else, judging by what she'd seen of his work at the Rainbow Museum. Also, she'd vowed not to get on her boss's bad side. She swallowed hard and forced a close-lipped smile. "Of course it's okay," she told Frankie in a voice that was several octaves higher than normal. "The more the merrier."

"Great. I just texted him, and he's in. He's going to fly out early next week and take care of all the sets, get 'em ready for when the festival starts. When you fly out next Friday, he'll drive down to Vancouver to pick you up and bring you back to Whistler, and he'll stay on through the festival to make sure they all get set up properly at the different venues."

"That sounds great," she said in the same weird voice as before. "It'll be great for the Rainbow Museum to have him there." Maybe if she said the word *great* twelve hundred more times, Ryan's personality would magically improve in time for the trip.

She felt like a giant slab of concrete as she dragged herself back to her desk. When she got there, she looked at the little bisexual Pride flag she'd bought at the bookshop where Lucy had found her CHILDLESS CAT LADY button. She'd stuck the flag in the mason jar along with the hydrangeas. Was she really going to let some brooding carpenter ruin her first Pride celebration as an out and proud bisexual? No, she was not. She deserved better than that. As she looked around the office at the rainbow walls and the rainbow flags and all her new friends, Simone resolved to focus on what really mattered in Whistler, besides marketing the Rainbow Museum, obviously:

Pride.

Maybe she'd have another sapphic hookup—something more than a drunken dance-floor make-out. She imagined sex with a woman was significantly more enjoyable when you weren't pretending to be straight the whole time.

She wasn't going to waste her energy worrying about Ryan. She was going to spend it on making the Whistler Pride and Ski Festival the queerest week of her life.

CHAPTER 6

ALTHOUGH SHE'D NEVER BEEN TO VANCOUVER before, Simone felt at home as she waited for her suitcases at baggage claim. She could tell just by looking around that she wasn't the only traveler headed to the festivities in Whistler. There were people with Pride flags, people with rainbow-colored hats and mittens, and even one person who'd decided to blast Chappell Roan from a Bluetooth speaker while they hung out by the carousel. Simone bopped her head and mouthed the lyrics she knew, letting the music fill her up before her two-hour car ride with Ryan sapped her of all her energy.

She collected her two suitcases—the smaller one filled with her own belongings, the larger one with Rainbow Museum merch to hand out at parties—and wheeled them to the passenger pickup zone. Her plane had arrived ahead of schedule—how on-brand for her—so she was surprised when she got a text from Ryan that he was already there to pick her up.

Well, actually, he'd just written: "Here."

The blue SUV was easy to spot along the curb to her left. When he saw her coming down the walkway, Ryan popped the trunk and climbed out of the car, dressed in his brown leather work boots, a pair of jeans, and a gray crewneck sweatshirt. The mild breeze rustled his brown hair. He nodded by way of greeting, his eyes meeting hers for mere milliseconds before he looked away.

Do not let this straight man ruin your trip, she reminded herself. She would be a bubble of queer joy for as long as she possibly could—and as a bonus, her cheerfulness would piss Ryan off. "Hey, you!" She gave him a big, friendly wave. "Thank you so much for coming to get me. How was the drive?"

"Fine," he replied flatly. Simone was surprised he'd even gotten out of the car to greet her. "Here," he said, and walked right up to her.

"Huh?" She was startled by their sudden closeness, by their fingers touching on the handles of her luggage.

"Lemme take these." Ryan grabbed the suitcases and carried them around to the back of the car. He made them look like they weighed nothing, even though Simone knew for a fact that they did not. She'd stuffed them both to the brim.

"Oh wow—thank you." Had she touched down in Vancouver, or the twilight zone? Why was he being courteous all of a sudden?

"Just trying to get on the road as soon as possible," he clipped out without looking up, and loaded them into the back. *Aww*, that was the Ryan she knew: doing everything in his power to shorten the amount of time they had to spend in each other's presence.

As he reached up to grab the door, the hem of his sweatshirt rose just enough to reveal a sliver of taut skin and a trail of hair coming up from the waistband of his jeans. Simone blinked and looked away when she realized she'd been staring. "Nice . . . car," she said. "Very . . ." Simone's car knowledge was limited to the old Volvo she'd inherited from her brother Jason, which she only used on the rare occasions she couldn't rely on Toronto's public transportation options. ". . . blue," she finished.

"Yes." Ryan sighed impatiently and slammed the trunk shut. "Now, let's go. Watch your step getting in."

She wished she could sit in the back to be as far from him as possible, but then she'd be treating him like her driver, and that would be weird. She climbed into the passenger seat next to Ryan, who pulled a small bottle of hand sanitizer from his pocket and squeezed a dollop into his palm. He held the bottle out to her, too, and she let him give her a few drops.

"Was touching me *that* repulsive?" she teased as they both rubbed their hands.

He stilled, and for a second, she thought he might actually answer her—but instead, he ignored her as he pulled up the route on his phone's GPS. Was his plan to conduct the entire ride in silence?

She took another swing, just to rile him up. "You know, for a carpenter, you sure don't like to get your hands dirty."

"Will you please put your seat belt on?" he muttered as he started the car, and they drove out of the airport in tense silence.

The next two hours were about to feel like two years. Thankfully, Simone had assumed this would be the case, and had planned exactly what she was going to do to pass the time in the car. "You mind if I make a phone call?" she asked as they drove through South Vancouver.

Her oldest brother, Matt, had sent her a very un-Matt-like text, checking in to see how she was doing, and asking if she wanted to catch up on the phone. Not that Matt wasn't friendly, but Simone and her brothers just didn't have that kind of relationship. There were six years between her and Matt, and four between her and

Jason—big divides, when you're kids. She'd never overlapped with either of them at school, never had mutual friends, and *certainly* never talked about anything deep with them. She'd been touched, and also a little embarrassed, when they'd both sent supportive texts in response to her coming-out post.

"Sure," Ryan grunted, eyes locked on the road.

She rolled her eyes and called her brother.

"Hullo?"

"Hey, Matty. How's it going?"

"Just at work, doing stuff."

"Cool."

"Yeah. Uh, what about you?"

Even though they weren't used to talking on the phone, there was something warm and relaxing about hearing her brother's familiar voice. She rested her head against the window. "I'm actually in Vancouver, on my way to Whistler. For a work trip."

"Whoa. What's the trip for?"

"My company's helping sponsor Whistler Pride." Her heart thudded.

"Cool," Matt replied.

"Yeah. It'll be fun."

"The new job's going well, then?"

"It's great." *Except for the jerk sitting next to me*. "The place looks amazing. We're officially opening next month."

"Megan and I were just saying we should bring the girls one weekend."

She grinned, her right cheek pressing into the cool glass. "That would be awesome. Cici would love the ball pit." Cici—Cecilia—was Matt and Megan's three-and-a-half-year-old daughter. "It has these awesome rainbow slides going into it."

"Why do I feel like Jason would love that, too?"

Simone chuckled at the thought of her floppy-haired middle brother catapulting into the ball pit. She could see it, too. "You're all welcome anytime. I dare you to bring Mom and Dad, while you're at it."

Matt's laugh turned into a sigh. "Yeah, well, that's part of the reason I wanted to check in. Megan and I were on the phone with Mom the other day, and she told us she called you crying about your Instagram post, and it sounded kinda extreme. After, Megan was like, 'Yo, you might wanna check on your sister.'"

Her chest swelled with affection for her brother and his wife. "Matty, you have no idea—that call—it was the worst thing ever."

"Oh God, what'd she say? I'm sure she didn't give us the full story."

As Simone went into detail—starting with Kathy's "*Call me*" text—it hit her: Ryan was her captive audience. Sitting next to her in the otherwise silent car, he had no choice but to listen to what she'd been through. *Oblivious, my ass*, Simone thought with triumph as she continued telling Matt the story.

"Shit, Simone," her brother said when she was finished. "I'm so sorry."

"It's not your fault. This is how she's always been with me—trying to like, mold me into this perfect daughter who makes her look good. And I have to stop letting her."

"Hmm." Simone worried that Matt would say she was selfish. Instead, he replied, "Megan has a theory, and I think I agree with it, that Mom's always resented Dad for letting Grandma and Grandpa bully her into giving up her law job. Maybe she feels like having a 'perfect daughter' would validate this big sacrifice she made."

"Whoa."

"What?"

"That was . . . really insightful, Matty."

"Oh—thanks."

There was a beat of silence. Simone pictured her relationships with her siblings like a blank canvas, full of possibility.

"Anyway," Matt went on, "I'm sorry you've been dealing with all this."

"It was rough for a while, but everyone at work has been super supportive." *Everyone except for the man sitting next to me, who'd better be feeling like a dick right now.* "I've been doing a lot better lately."

"You sure?"

"I promise. I'm super excited to spend the week at a Pride festival."

"Okay, good. And, uh, if there's anything you ever wanna talk about, I'm, uh—I'm here. Megan, too. And the girls. They don't know what's going on, but they're cute." She chuckled again. Who knew that talking to her brother about feelings could actually be sort of . . . nice? "Shit, my boss Slacked me ten minutes ago and I didn't see it till now. I gotta get back to him."

"Go, go, go," she said.

"Have fun on your trip."

"Thanks. And Matty?"

"Yeah?"

"Thanks for checking in. Seriously."

"No problem."

"Talk to you later."

"See ya."

She hung up with tears in her eyes. She loved Matt a lot, although she'd never said it out loud. That would be weird.

Speaking of weird . . .

She'd been off the phone for a few seconds, and Ryan still hadn't said anything: no "Sorry I assumed you were a careless ditz who thinks everything is sunshine and roses"; not even a "Sorry to hear that happened to you." And when she stole another quick glance sideways, she found a tight frown on his face, as though he couldn't tolerate hearing one more word out of her mouth. *Dick*.

"Thanks for your patience with that!" she chirped. "Don't worry, I'll shut up now."

Simone looked out the passenger-side window and rolled her eyes in private. She was getting tired of his moodiness, and they were only thirty-three minutes into the two-hour drive—barely a quarter of the way there. If she didn't put on some music, she would perish.

She could see on the screen that Ryan's phone was connected to the car's audio system. She wondered what kind of music he liked. German death metal? Medieval funeral dirges? Without asking for his permission, she tapped the button to resume whatever he'd been listening to on his way to pick her up from the airport.

It wasn't German screaming. Or Latin chanting.

It was the rich, soulful voice of Adele, belting "Someone Like You."

"What the—" Ryan took one of his hands off the wheel and jabbed frantically at the screen, like he was trying to shut off the music, but he only succeeded in jumping to the next song: Sinead O'Connor's "Nothing Compares 2 U." "Goddammit," he growled when it happened again, and now they were listening to Ariana Grande's "Thank U, Next." "I'm not used to this fucking car. Can you turn this off? Immediately?"

There was a vulnerable note in his voice Simone had never heard before. Suddenly she felt as if she'd accidentally walked in on him naked in the bathroom. This playlist was clearly personal to Ryan—and it was full of breakup songs. She pressed the stop button immediately.

"I'm so sorry," Simone said—not just to keep the peace between them, but genuinely, from the bottom of her heart. "I shouldn't have turned on your playlist without asking."

"Please disconnect my phone." His knuckles were white on the steering wheel. *"Now."*

Simone did as she was told.

The silence in the car was deafening, the tension thick and charged. She felt bad for having exposed him like that, but now she was also desperately curious to know more. Did that playlist have something to do with the reason he was being such a dick to Simone? She remembered what Barista Joe had said: that Ryan was "usually pretty chill," and that his atrocious demeanor had seemed like more of a mood than a permanent personality trait. *Hmmm.* Simone turned and looked at Ryan—*really* looked at him, in the midday sun shining through the window. He steered with his right hand only, his left elbow resting on the door, but his relaxed (and admittedly, hot) driving posture couldn't belie what she noticed in his face. His jaw muscles were clenched, and his gray-green eyes were locked on the horizon. He was trying to put up a steely facade, but Simone caught glimpses of pain and exhaustion in the creases of his brow, the fine lines around his mouth. *Hmmm* indeed.

"You know," Simone began tentatively, "I went through a shitty breakup last year, and listened to a ton of songs like that."

Silence.

"It sucked when I was going through it, but thankfully, I'm doing a lot better now. It sounds cheesy, but the whole 'when one door closes' thing is true. If I hadn't screwed up that relationship,

I probably never would have come out as bi, and I wouldn't have ended up here, ready to have the queerest holiday ever!" She'd tried to inject as much hope into her voice as she could. The jazz hands on "queerest holiday ever" might have been a little over-the-top, but whatever. She was trying to help.

She thought that coming out to him and sharing her personal relationship history might do *something* to get through to him, but still, Ryan said nothing. That is, until he asked: "Why don't you put on some of your own music?" There was barely any inflection at the end of his sentence.

"Yes, sir," she muttered in response, her voice dripping with sarcasm. When she rolled her eyes this time, she didn't care if he saw. She'd genuinely apologized for putting on his breakup playlist, just like she'd genuinely apologized for breaking the dragonfly wings. What more did he want from her? He was impossible.

Do not let this straight man ruin your trip, she reminded herself yet again. Then she connected her phone to the audio system and put on the Pride playlist Seth had shared with her before she left.

At least the views were spectacular. No other word would do justice for the mountain highway that ran along the Howe Sound, with evergreens and rock faces to either side and enormous snow-capped peaks up ahead in the distance. Eventually, they started to pass turnoffs for other hotels, which meant they were getting close—thank God. There were only so many more minutes of this tense car ride Simone could endure.

At last, they reached a green sign with an arrow pointing them toward their final destination. They veered off the highway onto Village Gate Boulevard, where an iron sign welcomed them to WHISTLER VILLAGE: HOST MOUNTAIN RESORT FOR THE 2010 OLYMPIC AND PARALYMPIC WINTER GAMES. Canadian flags hung from the lampposts, with rainbow stripes instead of the usual red. Her body buzzing with adrenaline, Simone leaned forward, peered out the window, and tried to take it all in.

"We're here!" Simone exclaimed.

"Finally," Ryan muttered.

When they got to their hotel, they parted ways—*finally, indeed*—so Simone could get settled and Ryan could transfer his selfie station set from the rented workshop to the venue for tonight's welcome party.

Simone showered off the plane slime and changed into wide-leg silver pants and a long-sleeve purple crop top. She'd bought the new items on an after-work shopping trip to one of Lucy's favorite thrift stores: a sprawling basement establishment that required a tremendous amount of patience and strategy to sift through, but that Lucy *swore* was full of hidden gems. She'd been right. While Simone explored the racks, it had dawned on her that ninety percent of her clothes had been Christmas and birthday gifts from her mother: cardigans, blouses, skirts, and dresses in floral, gingham, paisley, and houndstooth. Clothes that fit her perfectly well on the outside, but made her feel, on the inside, like she was a straight woman at a country club. She didn't need to perform that role anymore.

At five o'clock, she zipped up her parka, grabbed the suitcase full of merch, and headed into Whistler Village on foot. The sun had sunk behind the mountains, giving way to twinkling stars. Streetlamps illuminated the stone walkways and the snow-dusted awnings. She walked past pubs and restaurants, candy stores selling chocolate and fudge, gift shops, sporting goods stores, and tour companies where you could book heli-skiing and snowmobile excursions. Warm lights glowed from every window, beckoning Simone inside, but she had a welcome party to get to.

When she walked into the spacious lobby of the art museum, Ryan was standing across the room in a flannel shirt with the sleeves rolled up to his elbows. Dread bloomed in her stomach at the prospect of spending more time together.

Then she saw his first design in real life, and her jaw dropped.

Tonight's set consisted of a wide wooden staircase, each step a different color of the rainbow. Guests could stand, sit, or even drape themselves across the different levels. Behind the staircase were billowing clouds of white and silver balloons. Simone knew from the Rainbow Museum that Ryan worked with other materials besides wood, but *balloon sculpture* really seemed to go above and beyond the bounds of carpentry.

"Oh . . . my . . . God," she said as she walked over to him, temporarily forgetting that this man was her nemesis.

"What?" he asked.

She grabbed his forearm, which happened to be wonderfully warm against her chilly hand. *Jeez*, she thought, *his forearm is as thick as a tree branch*. "It's amazing."

Ryan's gaze went straight to Simone's hand, then traveled slowly up her arm. When he reached her face, he squinted at her suspiciously.

She let go of him and crossed her arms. "What, you think I'm lying?"

"I never know with you."

Simone jerked her head back. "What's that supposed to mean?"

He narrowed his eyes even more. "I mean I don't think you've ever been real with me."

A shiver went down her spine, like he'd undressed her with his words. Feeling exposed, she hugged herself tighter. He looked like he might say something else, but she cut him off. "That's absurd," she countered, but her voice wavered. Technically, she *did* have a history of drowning him in fake kindness. Then again, that was only because Ryan had been a dick to her to begin with! If he was frustrated with Simone, he had no one to blame but himself. Period. When Simone spoke again, it was with newfound conviction. She would make him regret being such a jerk. "I really *do* think the set looks amazing, Ryan. I think the whole entire Rainbow Museum looks amazing. You're a really good carpenter and you're allegedly a good person, too"—*according to Barista Joe*—"but for some reason, you hate me, and I'm tired of trying to change that, so I give up." Simone was breathless, like she'd just sprinted around a track. Never in her life had she unleashed on someone like this, but somehow Ryan had brought it out of her. "In the future, I'll keep the compliments to myself," she finished, then turned on her heel and went to set up the merch table. She didn't care if he'd had his heart broken recently. Simone was officially done being nice to Ryan Foley.

At six, guests started trickling in through the doors, and it wasn't long before a crowd had materialized beneath the slatted wood ceiling. Everyone was talking and laughing and clinking glasses and throwing their arms around each other, all of them palpably excited for the weeklong festivities that were only just beginning. Everyone except for Ryan, that is, who was brooding next to the selfie station like an astonishingly good-looking gargoyle. Remembering his breakup playlist, she wondered if she'd gone too hard on him.

No.

She'd been through some serious stuff, too, and she wasn't over here dragging people into a whirlpool of misery. She was a radiant ball of sunshine, in fact. And she would use that light to attract as many women as she possibly could. She would not let Ryan occupy one more iota of space in her brain. She shot a quick text to Lucy saying hi and asking how she was doing. She could use a dose of Lucy's warmth right now.

"SIMONE!!!" she wrote back. "I'm at karaoke at Dorothy and Friends! Everyone says hi and they miss u!!!"

"Awww, tell everyone I miss them!" Simone was beaming as she typed.

"Also, I finished work two hours earlier than usual again, thanks to u. My invoice-streamlining queen!!!"

"Happy to be of service."

"How are things going with Ryan???" Lucy asked.

Simone sent back a string of skull-and-crossbones emojis.

"Ooooof," Lucy replied. "Well, how are the other people? Does anyone seem interesting???"

Simone knew her friend was asking about women. She thought about the people she'd met at the welcome party so far. "There was an Australian ski instructor who seemed cool," she typed back to Lucy, remembering the woman—Margot—with freckles, dirty-blond braids, and an accent that had made her knees weak. Margot had complimented Simone's silver pants, and Simone's heart had pounded as she'd stammered her thanks, and then they'd talked about what had brought each of them to Whistler Pride: Simone to represent the Rainbow Museum, Margot to lead a guide group. Whistler Pride offered free daily guide groups for different levels of skiers, ranging from novices who were most comfortable on green circles to experts who could handle black diamonds and beyond. The guide groups would go off on the mountain for a few hours, then reconvene for lunch, followed by an après-ski party in town.

"Oh yes???" Lucy wrote back. "Tell me more!"

Simone felt herself blushing as she typed a response. "She said I'm welcome to join her guide group if I want. Which would mean skiing together for the rest of the WEEK."

"Well then," Lucy replied, and Simone could just *see* the impish smirk on her face, "I think we both know what you're doing tomorrow." She quickly followed it up with: "Gotta go—Seth's making us do 'Shallow.'"

Simone laughed. "Break a leg!"

"You break a leg tomorrow!!! In the wooing-a-sexy-Australian way. Not the literal skiing way."

CHAPTER 7

AFTER HITTING UP THE RENTAL SHOP first thing in the morning, Simone rode the gondola to the Roundhouse Lodge, where she'd be meeting up with her guide group at nine forty-five. The temperature was a few degrees above freezing, and the sun was shining in a cloudless sky, bathing the mountains in light.

"It's gonna be a spectacular day," said an older man with a bushy white mustache who was riding the gondola alone and gazing out at the view.

"I hope so," Simone said back to him, thinking of Margot.

She got off the gondola and put on her skis. From there, it didn't take long for her to spot Margot, who'd told Simone she'd be wearing a neon-orange ski suit. She was standing next to her skis and her poles, which were planted vertically in the snow. When Margot spotted Simone skiing over to her, she jumped up and down in her ski boots. "Oh, yay, you both came!"

Both? For a terrifying second, Simone wondered if Ryan had followed her up here to intentionally ruin her day. Then she looked to her left and saw that the friendly older man from the gondola was also making his way toward Margot. Phew.

Simone's heart skipped a beat, then several more when Margot jogged over as gracefully as her ski boots made possible and wrapped her in a hug. "It's great to see you again."

"You, too," Simone said, suddenly very nervous. Her heart had jumped into her throat, and it had taken some effort to squeeze her words out.

Margot released Simone and gave Gondola Man a clap on the shoulder. "C'mon, lemme introduce you to the rest of the group."

As she turned and led them to the four other skiers who had already gathered, Simone made a mental note that Gondola Man hadn't received a hug. Maybe she was reading too much into it—maybe he just hadn't talked to her for as long as Simone had last night.

Her spine crackled with electricity all the same.

Gondola Man turned out to be Glen, a guy in his sixties from Toronto who gave her a high five that nearly knocked her over when she said she was from there, too. Then there was Phoenix, a gangly twentysomething from Montreal who had a trans flag tucked behind the strap of their goggles like a feather in their cap; and Luis and Roberto, a middle-aged couple who'd traveled all the way from Ecuador.

Finally, Margot put her mitten on the shoulder of a woman with long black curls. "And this lovely sheila is Thea," she said, "my girlfriend."

"Oh!" Simone said brightly. "It's great to meet you!" Meanwhile, her chest deflated like a balloon. She stealthily pulled out her phone and texted Lucy: "Update: Margot has a gf. Womp womp."

As Margot put on her skis, Simone mentally replayed their interaction from last night. Margot *had* seemed into her. She'd said she liked her silver pants! Then again, when she'd walked out of the thrift store changing room and shown Lucy the silver pants, Lucy had thrown an arm over her forehead and pretended to faint from how good they looked. Women gave each other pants-related compliments all the time, which on the one hand was really nice, but on the other hand made it feel like you needed the goddamn quadratic equation to know whether someone was flirting with you or not. Putting herself out there was going to take practice.

Lucy texted her back: "Maybe they're in an open relationship."

Simone chuckled under her breath and replied: "Friendly reminder that I've been out for less than a month? I'm pretty sure this is not the right time to introduce polyamory."

Margot led them to a green circle for their first run of the day. "We'll meet at the bottom of that lift," she said, pointing to their destination with her ski pole.

Adrenaline zipped through Simone's body as she propelled herself over the edge. She hadn't been on the slopes since last spring, and it would take time for her to "get her ski legs," as an instructor had once referred to that shaky first run of the year. It helped that the snow here was buttery soft compared to the icy conditions she was used to back east. Simone felt like she was frosting a cake with her skis.

Margot and Thea crisscrossed the run in wide, graceful arcs, with Margot slightly ahead of her girlfriend. Simone noticed how every few turns, Margot slowed her pace and glanced over her shoulder. At first, Simone figured she was taking in the view, but then, when she saw her head swivel back and forth before landing in Thea's direction, she realized she was checking to make sure her partner was okay. It was so romantic, Simone could have melted. She wanted a woman to love her the way Margot clearly loved Thea. And Simone wanted to love a woman the same way.

The group circled up at the bottom of a three-person chairlift, where Simone grabbed a seat with Glen and Phoenix. Even though the Margot situation hadn't gone the way she'd hoped, she was happy to be on the mountain, enjoying this perfect day with her soon-to-be new friends.

She chatted with Glen and Phoenix about how long they'd all been skiing. She told them how growing up, she'd begged her parents to let her play soccer and baseball like her brothers, but Kathy had signed her up for dance instead. Eventually, skiing had been the one sport her parents had caved for. They were Canadian, after all.

"I hated dance when I was little," Phoenix said. "I'd literally sob on the way to ballet class. Turns out I actually like dancing, though. I just didn't want to wear the fucking tutus!"

They all laughed. Then they chatted about their favorite skiing destinations in Ontario and Quebec, with Simone and Glen discovering that they'd both spent a great deal of time at Earl Bales, the ski hill in the city of Toronto, and both shared a nostalgic love for the hot chocolate they served there—which, they controversially agreed, came close to rivaling Tim Hortons', if not surpassing it.

Even in the cold mountain air, Simone felt snuggly and warm. Talking with Glen and Phoenix felt like tucking into a warm bowl of stew on a winter day. She wondered what Ryan was up to—not that she really cared. He was probably wallowing in his own misery by aggressively hammering nails into a two-by-four, or maybe sitting in his hotel room and staring at the wall. With the lights off. Like the masochistic weirdo he was.

~

THAT NIGHT, SIMONE LIFTED HER CHIN and rolled her shoulders back before she strode through the doors of the nightclub. That night's event was a retro-themed dance party, and underneath her parka she wore a colorful disco-themed jumpsuit she'd ordered online. She felt hot. Powerful. Ready to ignore the hell out of Ryan Foley.

For tonight's set, Ryan had taken the staircase he'd built for the welcome party and placed it in front of a wooden arch with a giant disco ball dangling from the center. She pictured him walking out of the nearest party store with the glittering ball in his arms and a scowl on his face. *Masochistic weirdo*. True to form, he'd blatantly ignored the party's theme and was dressed in another flannel shirt and jeans.

He turned around when he heard her wheeling the suitcase full of Rainbow Museum merch across the dance floor. "Simone. Hey."

Go fuck yourself, she thought as she stalked past him without a word and went to set up the merch table.

She was trying to be engrossed with fanning out the tote bags when Ryan wandered over and interrupted her state of calm. "Do you have a minute?"

She looked up. Simone was used to his icy glare, but this was something different. Something softer. This had to be a trap, because Ryan Foley didn't have a soft cell in his body. Also, he seemed to be unable to meet her eyes.

"Not particularly," she snapped, turning back to the tote bags.

"Listen, Simone, I think we should talk."

He really needed to stop using her name, because the more she heard it in his deep voice, the more it turned her insides to liquid and weakened her steely defenses. "Why would you want to talk to me? You think I'm oblivious and fake—"

"I was wrong," he blurted out. Simone looked up again. Ryan jammed his hands in the pockets of his jeans, but his shoulders stayed up by his ears. His eyes were fixed on a random spot on the merch table. He looked so uncomfortable, like whatever else he was going to say was costing him every ounce of energy he had left. "And I wanted to say I'm sorry. For the way things have been between us."

Ryan's apology, however stiff, had short-circuited her brain. Smoke was probably hissing out of her ears. She was trying to make sense of the words he'd just uttered, but all she could manage to do was blink at him.

"I've been going through some shit lately," he said. "Stuff you don't know about."

When people apologized to Simone, she usually bent over backward to assure them that everything was fine. That they didn't have to worry one bit—that she barely had feelings anyway, even though she did. She wanted to make people happy, no matter what it cost her. Ryan was maybe the only person on the planet she didn't feel the need to make comfortable. "That's not an excuse," she hurled back, her voice gaining volume and momentum. "You don't think I've been through my own shit lately?"

He hung his head. "I shouldn't have started with that."

But Simone was too fired up to stop now. "I went through a breakup. I had a whole goddamn existential crisis and came out as bi, which my parents absolutely *hated*, but am I a miserable gargoyle like you? *No*. I'm a delightful fucking SUNFLOWER." Except for right now. With Ryan, she wasn't a sunflower. She was a five-foot-eight man-eating Venus flytrap. "Do you know why I accidentally knocked your stuff over on my first day of work? I wasn't just some naive little girl skipping through a fantasyland. I was freaking out because my mom had just seen my coming-out post, and I was trying to find a quiet place to call her and get disowned, and yeah, I went for the room behind the tarp." Wow, this whole honesty thing was liberating. So was the look on Ryan's face: like she'd doused him with another vat of cold brew. Take *that*, Mr. Actual Hard Work.

"Can I say something?" Ryan asked.

"As long as it's not another excuse." Simone crossed her arms.

"I feel like the world's biggest asshole for the way I've acted. I know you've been through your own shit. I listened to your call in the car the other day—"

"Oh, *did* you?"

He furrowed his brow. "You were talking out loud."

"Jesus, Ryan, I don't care that you listened," she fired back. "I care that you apparently felt sooo bad, but didn't feel the need to apologize until now. Frankly, I hate that I had to sink to your level and lose my shit for you to finally consider saying you were sorry."

"I was *going* to apologize in the car," Ryan insisted. "I was sitting there, trying to figure out how to put it all into words . . . and then you turned on the music."

Now Simone felt like *she'd* been doused in cold brew. When she'd hung up with Matt in the car that day, she'd taken Ryan's moody silence as a sign that he was annoyed with her—not that he was quietly toiling away on an apology.

"Last night," he said, "I tried to bring it up again . . ."

She huffed out a sarcastic laugh. "When you accused me of being fake?"

"I know my delivery wasn't great, but I was *trying* to say that you don't always have to put up a positive front around me."

Simone uncrossed her arms and transferred her hands to her hips. "Your delivery was abysmal, Ryan."

"Look, I'm not all, I don't know, *sunflowery* like you. You're right about me: I'm fucking miserable and I don't know how to get out of it." At last, he made eye contact with Simone, and Simone knew with certainty that this wasn't some kind of trap. This was a vulnerable man who needed help.

Not that it was on *her* to fix his problems. He was a grown-ass adult, and Simone had her own life to worry about. But after speaking her mind so openly, she noticed she had a rush like a runner's high. Was this how it felt when you stopped trying to make everyone happy? When you prioritized your *own* comfort? She wouldn't have had the courage to test this new theory on someone she actually liked, but she had no qualms being honest with Ryan. Her nemesis. Maybe they both had the potential to help each other.

There was also the fact that they still had to work together for the rest of the week, and getting along would certainly be easier than, well, whatever the hell they'd been doing until now.

What Simone was about to say was against her better judgment. She sighed, rested her palms on the table, leaned forward so she was closer to Ryan. God, how did anyone keep their scent so deliciously clean and woodsy after setting up a selfie station in a club that reeked of stale beer and sweat?

"I have a thought," she said.

Ryan raised his eyebrows in another expression she'd never seen on him before. It looked a little like hope.

"D'you ski?"

"Yeah."

"What level?"

"I've been doing it since I was a kid."

Well then. It was the first thing they'd ever had in common besides working at the Rainbow Museum. Simone hoped that was a good sign, and that she wouldn't come to regret this. She took a deep breath.

"Any interest in joining my guide group tomorrow?"

CHAPTER 8

"**I HOPE YOU DIDN'T LURE ME HERE** to murder me." Ryan was peering over the tips of his skis as he and Simone rode a chairlift over an icy chasm that looked more than happy to swallow them whole.

"Be nice to me, or I'll consider it," Simone fired back.

Ryan let out a nervous-sounding "Hah," as though he wasn't a hundred percent sure she was joking. *Good*, Simone thought. *Let him fear me.* She felt intoxicatingly powerful.

Ryan cleared his throat. "So . . . uh . . . you mentioned that you just came out?"

As powerful as she felt in this moment, she would still need some time to get used to Ryan making non-hostile conversation. It was weird. "I did," she replied.

"Congrats. That's awesome."

"Thank you, Ryan. That's very kind of you to say." Her tone was coming off sort of patronizing, but she didn't mind it. After the way he'd treated her, it felt good to put *him* in his place.

"In the car the other day, you said something about wanting to have the queerest holiday ever?"

"Yes, I did."

"What does that mean, exactly—to have the queerest holiday ever?"

She dropped the patronizing tone. "That's a good question, actually." Simone considered it for a moment. She was so new to being out that she didn't even know the full extent of what was possible. What she *did* know was that she craved that electrifying feeling she'd had at karaoke night back in Toronto. "Anything that makes me feel excited to be out?" she ventured. She thought of making out with Kenzie on the dance floor that night. "And maybe meeting women," she added.

"If you're bi, that means you're also into men, right?"

"Well, yeah, but using my first Pride to meet dudes feels like . . ."

". . . a waste?"

"Exactly."

"Makes sense."

They lapsed into an oddly peaceful silence as the chairlift glided over a peak that gave way to a valley thick with trees. The snow sparkled in the late-morning sun like it was made of crushed diamonds.

"This is really nice," he said.

She nodded. "I can't believe the view from up here."

"I meant . . . this." He gestured between himself and Simone.

For the love of God. "Okay, now I really am going to push you off this chairlift," Simone warned him only half jokingly.

"What did I do?"

"You're only *just now* realizing how nice it is to have a non–

openly hostile conversation now and then?" She rolled her eyes, then remembered she was wearing reflective goggles. "Just so you know, I'm rolling my eyes right now."

"Thank you for the clarification."

"Seriously, though, look at how nice and easy it is to not be a giant dick." She stopped herself from adding, "No offense," because he *had* been a giant dick, and she wasn't afraid to say so. "I don't get why this was so hard for you."

Now it was Ryan's turn to mull things over. "Lately, whenever I'm around people like you—"

"People like me?" She arched an eyebrow behind her goggles.

"People who are upbeat," he clarified. "Whenever I'm around that energy, it just reminds me how shitty I feel, and I end up acting like . . . like a giant dick, as you say. My buddy Dom has been calling me out on it, too."

Simone wondered what had put him in such a funk, but she didn't want to give him the satisfaction of asking about it. If he wanted to share it with her, he could work up the courage to do it himself. "I'm shocked to hear you have a friend," she said instead, which, to her credit, was also true.

"Well, I'm usually a lot less of a miserable gargoyle." For the first time ever, Simone detected a trace of playfulness in his voice. "Sometimes I'm actually fun."

"Oh yeah?" Simone huffed out a laugh. "I'll believe it when I see it."

The chairlift deposited them far above the tree line at Little Whistler Peak, where they circled up with Simone's guide group at the top of a blue square. It ran along a serpentine mountain ridge, which looked to Simone like the back of a sleeping, snow-white dragon—a dragon so massive that the skiers and snowboarders looked like dots in the distance. She was as awestruck as if she really *had* stumbled upon a mythical creature.

Ryan took off slightly ahead of her. If there was one thing about him she didn't have to question, it was his assertion that he'd been skiing his whole life. He flew along the mountain ridge like his body was made to do it, his torso still while his legs swung left and right, his skis perfectly parallel. As Simone carved her own path through the snow, she tried to take in the sprawling views, but her eyes kept darting away, kept scanning the run for Ryan's white helmet and charcoal-gray jacket.

Why was she so obsessed with keeping him in her sights? He was perfectly capable—obviously. And Margot had given them clear directions to where they were going to circle up next. It wasn't like she was picturing his abs, quads, and glutes working underneath all that outerwear. She was simply a lifelong skier impressed with a fellow athlete's impeccable form.

That was all.

That night, Simone cupped her hands around her mouth and whooped as a drag queen in a blond wig and a pink minidress marched across the stage and grabbed the mic.

"Hell-ooooooooo, Whistler Pride! I'm Vajeena George, and I'll be your host for drag bingo tonight! It's cold outside, but damn, everyone is hot as hell in here!"

As the audience cheered, Simone looked over at Ryan. Because for some reason, her eyeballs were still magnetically drawn to him, even though they weren't on the mountain anymore. His latest selfie station had three giant wooden blocks shaped like Tetris pieces, and he was busy nudging them this way and that in search of the perfect composition. She didn't know what was hotter: the way his forearms flexed when he moved the blocks, or how he furrowed his brow and stuck out the tip of tongue when he stepped back to survey his work.

The correct answer is neither, because Ryan is not hot, she reminded herself. Although she had to admit she didn't regret asking him to ski with her today. They hadn't squabbled once—except for at lunch, when Ryan bought them a plate of poutine to share, and they disagreed on the ideal way poutine should be eaten, Ryan suggesting the gravy should be on the side so that the fries didn't get soggy, Simone adamant that the gravy should be on top so that the cheese got sufficiently melty. In the end, Simone had won. Obviously.

Fine, then. Simone could admit that she and Ryan were on their way to not exactly hating each other's company. She could also admit that Ryan possessed certain attractive qualities, from a purely physical and scent-related standpoint. But she would not bestow upon him the sacred label of "hot." There was no way in hell.

She turned back to the stage.

"Our first round is the warm-up round, where you'll be competing to win"—Vajeena George yanked a metal cloche off one of the hidden prizes—"a deluxe body glitter kit! Whoever wins this one is going to look fabulous at the parade and can enjoy picking glitter out of their orifices for the next five years or so." Then she made her way to a cage of neon bingo balls and kicked off the game.

The rounds moved quickly and the prizes varied dramatically, from a set of Pride-themed temporary tattoos to a brand-new Apple Watch. Simone wasn't playing with a card of her own—it would be weird if the sponsors of Whistler Pride took home prizes over the paying guests—but Glen and Phoenix were sitting nearby, and she was having plenty of fun rooting for her friends. She didn't care that she couldn't win anything; the best prize of all was simply being at drag bingo as an out queer woman.

It was late in the evening when Vajeena George announced that the next prize would be the grand finale, and the biggest one yet.

"The winner of the next round will get . . . a four-night, all-expenses paid vacation for two to beautiful Vancouver Island, courtesy of our friends at Destination British Columbia! You'll stay in a stunning wilderness lodge, where you'll enjoy activities like ocean kayaking, hiking, and whale watching."

There were whispers of excitement around the room. At Simone's friends' table, Glen rubbed his palms together feverishly. Phoenix scooped up a handful of plastic chips and blew on them for good luck. Vajeena George picked up the first bingo ball of the round.

"B7!"

Glen and Phoenix both pumped their fists and reached for plastic chips. Next came O63, G51, I23, and B4. Both of her friends were making progress, but Glen seemed to be surging ahead. His hands were moving quickly, his brow furrowed with concentration behind his whimsical round glasses. "Would you look at that," he said. "I almost have—"

"N33!"

"BINGO!" Glen jutted his hand in the air.

Simone squealed with glee. She adored all her guide group friends, but Glen held an extra-special spot in her heart. He was the oldest and wisest member of the group, *and* he had total cool-grandpa vibes. Plus, the poor guy deserved a win. He'd taken a nasty fall on some moguls this morning and hurt his hip—badly enough that he'd had to pack it in for the day. She raced to Glen's chair and was about to pat him on the shoulder when Vajeena George made an announcement: "It looks like we have not one, but two bingos!"

"What?" Simone cried.

She looked out at the sea of people and her heart sank. Across the room, a jacked guy in a tiny tank top was also on his feet with his hand in the air.

"Let's have each of you read off your numbers," the drag queen said.

Glen and Tiny Tank Top each did as they were asked. Vajeena George confirmed they both had bingo.

"You know what that means," she announced. Her voice had a mischievous edge to it. "There's only one fair way to break this tie, and that's a dance-off."

The crowd went wild. Not Glen, though. "Oh, dang it. There's no way I'm dancing with this hip."

"Can someone go up there for you?" asked Phoenix, whose squeamish expression suggested they weren't exactly wild about volunteering.

Simone swallowed hard. She wanted to dance for Glen, she really did, but this would be different than singing karaoke in a tiny dive bar. There were at least two hundred people in the audience here. *Okay, Simone. You got this. Imagine Seth is up there with you, doing his ridiculous Seth dance moves*. With a deep breath, she opened her mouth to volunteer, but someone else beat her to it.

"I'll go."

It was Ryan.

She blinked at him in disbelief. When she tried to imagine him dancing onstage at drag bingo, her brain spat back a 404 error. Page not found.

Vajeena George gestured to the stairs leading up to the stage. "Will our two fabulous winners please come on up and join me?"

Ryan was off without another word. He couldn't have looked more out of place as he climbed onstage in a Carhartt hoodie and jeans, but he walked right over to the drag queen and whispered something in her ear, pointing between himself and Glen. Vajeena George nodded and gave a thumbs-up.

"Now let's meet our competitors, one of whom is kindly dancing on behalf of an injured winner. Everyone, please send healing vibes to Glen!"

Then she turned to Tiny Tank Top, who was bouncing on the balls of his feet and shaking out his arms like a boxer before a fight.

"Tell us your name, and a fun fact about you!"

"I'm Hank, and my fun fact is that I have a tattoo of a tiger on my abs."

The audience roared.

"You'll have to show me that later," Vajeena George replied with a theatrical wink. She turned to Ryan. "And what about you, our stand-in dancer? Tell us your name and a fun fact."

"I'm Ryan," he said, sounding oh-so-very moody and *Ryan*, "and my fun fact is that contrary to popular belief, I *am* actually fun sometimes." With that, he peered out into the audience until his eyes found Simone's. *I'll believe it when I see it*, she'd told him earlier. Evidently, he was determined to prove himself to her, even if it meant humiliating himself in front of an audience. She cracked a smile. How could she not?

"Well, you'd better show us just how fun you can be!" the drag queen proclaimed. "Okay, now, you'll both have one minute to dance your hearts out—Hank, you'll be on that side, and Ryan, you'll be over there—and at the end, we'll all vote for an ultimate champion. Sound good?"

Hank and Ryan both nodded. From far away, Simone could see that Ryan's jaw was clenched hard.

"Let's play that music!"

On the drag queen's command, an R & B song blared from the speakers. It was that song from *Magic Mike*: "Pony"—aka the striptease song to end all striptease songs.

Simone couldn't watch. It had been weird enough making nonhostile conversation with Ryan today; her brain might implode if she witnessed whatever kind of dancing he was about to attempt. She looked at Hank instead, who apparently had no emotional attachment to his tiny tank top. He grabbed it in the center of his chest, flexed his enormous biceps, and ripped it off his body in one fell swoop, showing off the tiger tattoo that did, in fact, take up a sizable chunk of his torso. People crowded the front of the stage, screaming for Hank.

Phoenix twisted around in their chair, turning to Simone and Glen. "Okay, but can we talk about how Ryan has *moves*?"

Simone dragged her eyes off Hank, forcing them to the other side of the stage, where—oh. Oh wow.

Ryan was thrusting his hips with a natural rhythm.

The natural rhythm of a person who was very, very good at sex.

Biting her bottom lip, she looked away again. Back to Hank, who was miming riding a pony, with one hand on the imaginary reins and the other swinging a piece of his shirt above his head like a lasso. Even though Hank had the ostentatious overconfidence of someone who was very, very *bad* at sex, watching him did nothing to quell the buildup of heat she'd experienced from watching Ryan.

Maybe it was just hot in the bar. It was, wasn't it? She reached for the glass of ice water she'd been sipping and took a giant swig.

"Fifteen seconds left!" Vajeena George announced. People were still going wild for Hank.

Phoenix gasped. "LOOK AT RYAN."

Simone looked back. Somehow, Ryan had launched himself into a handstand, leather work boots in the air, and now was gracefully lowering his body onto the floor. Simone's breath caught in her throat. Now he was horizontal, thrusting his hips into the stage like he was giving it the best lay of its life. Scratch what she'd thought to herself on the ridge today; *this* was what Ryan's body was made to do.

Logically, she should have known he could move like that. He *was* Mr. Actual Hard Work, brimming with physical strength. He was an all-star skier. But it was one thing to know this and another thing to *see* it. To look at her nemesis up onstage and imagine what it might be like to fuck him and be fucked by him.

At last, the music cut out.

"Make some noise if you think Ryan should win!"

Glen and Phoenix screamed at the top of their lungs until their voices cracked. There was a polite smattering of applause from the rest of the room. Simone was too busy chugging the rest of her ice water to do anything in the way of cheering.

"Now make some noise if you think Hank should win!"

The response was booming—a sheer tsunami of sound that crashed through the bar.

"I think we have a winner, folks. Let's give it up for Hank!" Vajeena George rushed over to give him a hug. "After you go whale watching, you'll need a humpback tattoo to go with your tiger."

Ryan shook hands with Hank and thanked Vajeena George.

Then he jogged down the stairs and made his way back to the group. "Sorry I didn't win," he said to Glen.

Glen waved a hand in the air. "Are you kidding? I got to see you do that handstand move. That was just as good as winning."

"He should have won though," Phoenix chimed in. "Hank couldn't dance; he just had a dumb tattoo and a cheap shirt. You were totally robbed, Ryan."

Ryan smirked. "Appreciate the support."

While Phoenix continued lamenting the injustice of it all to Glen, Ryan sidled over to Simone, his hands in the pocket of his hoodie. He was still smirking.

"Well?"

She hoped he couldn't tell she was sweating. "Well what?"

"Do you believe it now?"

"Believe what?"

"That I can actually be fun."

"Hmmm." She stroked her chin. "I'd say you're maybe five percent less gargoyle-y than I previously thought."

"Only five percent?"

"You like your poutine with gravy on the side, Ryan."

"Still, I think five percent is—"

"Don't push it," she snapped playfully, "or I'll knock you down to three."

Ryan held up his hands in mock surrender. "Consider it not pushed."

"That's more like it," she said. God, why was she still sweating? She needed more water, so she excused herself to go to the bar. When she returned, Glen was explaining that he was taking the day off skiing tomorrow, but that he'd give Phoenix money to buy lunch for Ryan on the mountain: a thank-you gift for dancing on his behalf. That meant Ryan was going to ski with them again tomorrow.

Simone took another big gulp of ice water.

~

GLEN GAZED ADORINGLY AT RYAN AS he raised his mulled wine in the air. "To our dancing queen!"

It was the following afternoon, and they were sitting around a bonfire at the après-ski. The back terrace of the Whistler Village bar was crowded with skiers and snowboarders who were fresh off the mountain, their cheeks red and their hair mussed from their helmets. Glen, who'd taken the day off to rest his hip, had come out to join them for a drink.

"TO OUR DANCING QUEEN!" cried the rest of the guide group, including Simone, who held up her own mulled wine. The bartender had ladled the drinks from a cauldron suspended over a fire, like something out of a wintry medieval village.

Ryan had wrinkled his nose at the questionable cleanliness of the cauldron's interior, which Simone was simply trying not to think about as she raised the paper cup to her lips. A plume of steam danced from the top, and she breathed in the aroma of warm spices, like gingerbread cookies fresh from the oven. She took a sip. The ginger, cinnamon, cloves, and other spices were perfectly balanced out by the sweetness of the red wine and the stewed apples and oranges.

Simone watched the bob of Ryan's Adam's apple as he swallowed a sip of his IPA, which he'd poured neatly from the can into a plastic cup. A few times since coming out, Simone had "tested" her attraction to men by looking at cute guys on the street or at the gym. Given how intensely she'd repressed her attraction to women, she'd wondered if there was a world where she was a lesbian, and not *actually* interested in guys at all. Now, as she gazed at the ruggedly handsome man in the chair next to hers, Simone confirmed to herself, once again, that she was genuinely into men, too.

But after another day of skiing with Ryan, in which he'd continued to emerge from his whirlpool of misery, Simone couldn't deny that there was also something specifically about *Ryan* that drew her in. Maybe it was the fact that he had the head of a North Face model and the body of an oak tree, or the fact that he shared her love of the outdoors. Maybe it had something to do with how free she felt to express herself around him, not to mention how hard he'd been trying to be nice. Maybe it was all of the above.

Simone tucked her knees up against her chest, which was difficult to do in snow pants and while holding a hot beverage. She managed it anyway. Not only was it weird to be crushing on Ryan, her former nemesis, but more importantly, she was on a mission to meet women, and she wasn't about to lose focus.

"I didn't think I'd feel like this again," Ryan said to Simone as they both gazed into the flames. The rest of their friends were engulfed in their own conversations.

"Feel like what?" she asked.

"Like my life might not be a pile of shit forever."

"Ah." She was still curious to know what he'd been through, but she was scared to ask him outright. Not because it might make him uncomfortable—she kind of *liked* making him uncomfortable, to be honest—but because she didn't want to bond with him any deeper. "So," she began instead, "how did a straight, IPA-drinking guy like you end up so comfortable in queer spaces like this?"

"By having two moms."

Simone raised her eyebrows in surprise. "No way!" she said

brightly, and maybe a little enviously, too. Growing up, she'd had exactly zero exposure to what a happy life as an out queer woman could look like. "That's so cool. And it makes sense now why you're so comfortable—you've been around queer people your whole life."

"It's all normal for me. Honestly, I was scared to tell my parents I was *straight*."

She snorted. "Must be nice."

"When I was a kid, and they'd ask me about my crushes, or if I was taking anyone to a dance, they'd always be super inclusive about it: like, 'So, Ry, is there a special girl or guy or any other person you're thinking about asking to semiformal?'"

"They call you 'Ry'?" she interjected.

"Uh-huh. If I ever hear 'Ryan,' I know I'm in deep shit."

"It's the same when my parents use my first name and my middle name together."

Ryan smiled. "What's your middle name?"

Simone wrinkled her nose. "It's awful."

"C'mon."

"It's the preppiest name in the history of the world."

"Now I *need* to know."

She grimaced. *"Tinsley."*

His smile became a grin.

"It's not funny!" she protested.

"I'm not laughing," he replied. "I think it's cute. Simone Tinsley."

She waved him off, trying to ignore the way her heart had swelled when he'd used her full name. "I interrupted you. You were saying how your parents would always be super inclusive . . ."

With another sip of beer, he picked up his story. "I always knew I was free to be with whoever, which was great, but I also knew pretty early on that I was straight. So, this one summer in high school, we were at Pride, and this guy was handing out buttons with different labels on them. I took one that said 'ally,' and my parents were like, 'Oh, honey, we're so proud of you for living your truth!'"

"Oh my *God*."

"I know. I came out as straight to my lesbian moms at Pride."

"That's hilarious," she said, and she wanted to laugh, but there was a tinge of envy getting in her way. If she'd grown up the way Ryan had, she would have always known she was bi, and she never would have been ashamed of it. She probably would have had all *kinds* of sexual and romantic experiences by now. Instead, she was a twenty-nine-year-old who couldn't even tell when women were flirting with her.

"For the record, I'm aware of how privileged I am that I got to 'come out' to my parents as a straight man. I do think they were a little disappointed," he added as an aside, "but in no way am I comparing my situation to yours."

She sighed.

"You okay?" he asked, leaning forward and resting his elbows on his knees.

Simone hadn't wanted to get all deep with him, and yet, there was something about the way he gazed at her that made her want to do just that. She explained what her parents were like, how she'd had almost no exposure to queerness growing up, and why it therefore took her so long to realize she was bi, and even longer to embrace it.

Ryan listened intently until Simone was finished. "I'm sorry you had to deal with that. And I'm happy you ended up finding the Rainbow Museum."

"Me, too." She drained the rest of her drink and gazed into the bonfire, grateful their conversation had reached a natural end point. She'd been getting way too comfortable opening up to Ryan. "Now I just need to meet more women."

Pleasantly lightheaded from the mulled wine, she leaned back and stretched out her legs. She was that perfect level of buzzed where she could feel herself loosening, like warm honey was oozing through her limbs. And then an idea popped into her head. Something brilliant. Something devastatingly platonic.

"Ryan," she said, turning to face him head-on, "you should totally be my wingman."

He blinked at her. "Me?"

"C'mon, it'll be fun. You are, famously, fun sometimes."

He swirled what was left of his beer and raised it to his lips, but he kept his eyes on her face—which was *definitely* only warm because of the bonfire, and not because of anything to do with Ryan. "All right," he said slowly.

She beamed at him. Thank God he'd agreed. "Cheers!" she exclaimed, raising her empty cup. "To my new wingman."

"Cheers." Ryan wasn't smiling the way Simone was—but then again, was he ever?

CHAPTER 9

"**HEY THERE! ANY CHANCE I CAN** interest you in a free tote bag?"

Simone had just wandered over to a cluster of people at the selfie station who were waiting for their pictures to print. She was particularly interested in the purple-haired woman on the edge of the group, whose possibly homemade fairy wings had caught Simone's eye from the moment she'd joined the line.

The woman didn't seem to have heard her. Simone took a deep breath, rolled back her shoulders, and said at double the volume: "Hey there! Want a free tote bag?"

Visibly startled, the woman turned to Simone with raised eyebrows. Great: Simone had just scared the shit out of her. *Way to make a winning first impression*. She was almost as bad as Ryan. "Sorry, what did you say?" the woman yelled, straining to make herself heard over the thumping music.

"I was asking if you wanted a tote bag from the Rainbow Museum. We're an immersive experience in Toronto dedicated to celebrating, amplifying, and giving back to the 2SLGBTQIA+ community. We're one of the sponsors of Whistler Pride."

"Oh! Cool!"

It was unclear whether she'd heard anything Simone had actually said. Simone thrust a tote bag at the woman's chest. She accepted it reluctantly.

"You should come check us out the next time you're in Toronto," Simone yelled.

"Totally!" The woman flashed her a pinched smile before turning back to her friends, and Simone backed away, her cheeks blazing. Why had she thought her Rainbow Museum marketing spiel would be the best way to win over a cute stranger? As she watched the woman and her pretty purple hair disappear onto the dance floor without so much as a glance in her direction, Simone was forced to confront a painful truth: Now that she was out, she had absolutely no idea how to flirt with women.

Flirting with men, as a woman, came easy to Simone. A lot of the time, you just had to exist in their general vicinity. But if that was how women tried to flirt with each other, they'd be standing around like bowling pins, waiting to be knocked over by a ball that would never come. Simone figured she'd have to take *some* sort of action if she wanted to flirt with women, but she didn't want to come off like the men who sent her winky faces on dating apps or eye-fucked her in bars—the men who made her feel like a juicy slab of meat in front of a hungry dog. That said, she couldn't keep things too PG, either, because then she'd end up repeating what she'd done with the tote-bag girl. She closed her eyes and pressed her fingertips into her temples, wishing there had been more queer love stories for her to study in the movies and TV shows she'd watched growing up. She felt so stupid, so awkward, like at the party in high school when she French-kissed someone for the first time, and the hot South African exchange student pulled back and said, "Simone, you're making out with my nose."

"Are you okay?" It was Ryan. When Simone opened her eyes, she found him peering at her with concern.

"I'm terrible at flirting with women," she groaned.

"Everyone sucks at first," he replied. "You just have to practice with more people." He turned to the writhing mass of bodies on the dance floor.

Simone could still feel the sting of the woman's tight smile after she'd pitched her on the Rainbow Museum. "I don't know if I can talk to anyone else tonight. It's too stressful. *Uggghhh*." She felt so behind, being twenty-nine years old and having no clue what she was doing. She was a tragic Victorian spinster. She suddenly felt the urge to cry, and pinched the bridge of her nose to stem the tears.

"Hey, it's okay. This stuff takes time."

"I don't want to be in my thirties and still figuring out how to flirt," Simone said, distressed.

"Okay, well, what if you practiced on me?"

"What do you mean?"

"Pretend I'm a woman you're flirting with."

"Seriously?" she asked.

"Only if you want to."

She didn't. Not with him. But she also desperately wanted to get better at this. "All right," she said tentatively.

"Okay, then go for it."

"You're the best wingman ever," she said, reinforcing their strictly platonic relationship.

"I'm not your wingman. I'm a cute girl at the bar." Ryan waved his hand over his face, miming a transformation.

Simone snorted. This was totally ridiculous, but she *did* need the help, and it was definitely more fun to be laughing with Ryan than spiraling about her lack of romantic skills. "Hi," she said sweetly. Then she winced. "Oh God, I don't even know how to start besides saying hello."

"Maybe you could compliment her—I mean, me," Ryan stammered, which made both of them laugh. She liked the way his sounded: deep and rich, like dark chocolate.

"Okay." Simone shook out her shoulders and slipped back into character. "Hi! I really like your . . . flannel?"

They both stifled another laugh at how absurd they were being. Ryan didn't bother trying to alter his voice when he replied to Simone. "You're into it? I know it's a little out of place at a club, but I tried to pack light."

"The green and gray match your eyes."

Ryan broke character as a genuine grin appeared on his face. "Whoa, Simone, that was actually a good line."

"Was it, though?" She remembered the way she'd misread Margot's signals the other night. "I feel like some women would say the same thing to their friends."

Ryan stroked his chin. "Hmmm. Maybe it's *how* you say it."

Simone dropped into a deep, sultry voice. "The green and gray match your eyes."

They both erupted in laughter again. Ryan fought to regain his composure. "Right, so you totally could do whatever *that* was . . ."

"I'll be sure to only talk in that voice from now on."

". . . or," he went on, "you could say the same thing, but make it a little more intimate—like, with your eyes." He angled himself so he was facing her head-on and fixed her with a determined gaze. It cracked her open and sent the air whooshing from her chest.

She tried not to let her reaction show on her face. They were just joking around.

"Then," he said, "you could touch her arm, like this." If not for the calluses on his fingers, she might not have felt his hand at all; that was how gently he grazed her elbow. Shivers traveled up and down Simone's arm. He kept his eyes on hers as he repeated her initial line back to her. "I really like your flannel."

Simone was fairly certain that never in the history of humankind had anyone made flannel sound so goddamn sexy. It was somehow even sexier that he hadn't actually been trying to seduce her, as far as she knew, but rather to genuinely help her embrace this new side of herself. Ryan was just that hot *naturally*.

"Thank you," she breathed, forgetting who was playing which role at this point.

She felt heat and pressure building up inside of her, the same as she had while she'd watched him onstage at drag bingo. A wild thought crossed her mind that she could just give in to the tugging in her core, could let herself close the gap and kiss him in that flannel shirt that really did match the colors of his eyes.

"Do you want to try?" Ryan asked.

Her heart skipped several beats before she realized what he'd actually meant: that she should try delivering a compliment again. Right. *Stay on task, Whitaker*. She shook out her shoulders and regained her focus—only to have it slip away again the moment she touched his arm. "I really like your flannel." She didn't have the slightest urge to laugh as they replayed their previous exchange.

"You're into it? I know it's a little out of place at a club."

"The colors bring out your eyes."

He fixed her with that determined gaze again—then blinked. "Sorry."

"What is it?"

"*Your* eyes. They're stunning."

Was he saying that to keep the scene going, or did he really mean it? "They're just plain brown," she said.

"Plain?" He raised his eyebrows. "No. They're like walnut. Chocolate brown with the tiniest hint of purple."

"Purple?"

"Yes."

"No one's ever said that before."

"Then no one's looked closely enough."

A stranger's voice sliced through the silence that followed. "Excuse me? Is there a way to get more copies of our photos?"

A guest was calling to them from the printer, while their friend inspected the buttons on the side of the machine.

Simone and Ryan blinked at each other as though they were both coming out of a trance. Ryan was the first to pull himself together, striding to the pair of guests and helping them print more copies. Simone shook her head to clear it of the ridiculous idea she'd had a few seconds ago. The idea that she should kiss Ryan Foley, when one of her goals in coming to Whistler was to kiss more *women*.

Ryan slowly wandered back to Simone. He jerked his thumb over his shoulder. "Got that sorted."

"Thanks," she said, trying not to look at his eyes, his lips. It was all too dangerously tempting.

He paused. "Did you want to keep practicing?"

She didn't want to make things awkward with a vehement no, but she needed to turn her attention back to the women in the room. "I super appreciate it, but I'm not sure I'll actually get better at flirting with women unless I do it for real, you know?"

"Yeah, totally."

She thought she detected a hollowness in his voice, but then again, he was Ryan: notoriously moody.

With that, Simone crossed her arms and scanned the room for someone else who made her heart skip a beat.

CHAPTER 10

SIMONE WAS LYING ON HER STOMACH on a mattress that felt like a cloud. Sunlight streamed through the window, warming her smooth, bare skin.

Buzzzzzzzzzzz.

Her lips curled into a smile at the sound of the vibrator. She parted her legs.

Buzzzzzzzzzzz.

Simone shivered as the wand grazed the inside of her knee before tracing its way up her thigh at a teasingly unhurried pace.

The higher it wandered up her thigh, the more the pressure mounted between her legs. She ground her pelvis into the mattress, aching to relieve it, but the mattress was too soft, and she moaned, wanting more. She arched her back, lifting her ass in the air—anything to get the wand where she wanted it.

Buzzzzzzzzzzz.

The vibrator was close enough to her core that its rumbling radiated to her clit, like ripples in the surface of a pool. But she needed more than gentle lapping; she needed a tidal wave of pleasure to crash into her and sweep her away. Again, she arched her back, desperate for more contact . . .

"Please," she murmured.

"You're so stunning," a low voice said back.

Buzzzzzzzzzzz.

"Please," she moaned again.

"Not yet. Let me look at you first."

"Ryan, please . . ."

Buzzzzzzzzzzz.

Wait. That buzzing wasn't a vibrator. It was the morning alarm Simone had set on her phone, which was vibrating on the bedside table in her Whistler hotel room. Her body slick with sweat, Simone extracted herself from the damp tangle of bedsheets and scrambled to shut it off. Before she went to meet Ryan at the gondola, she needed to get in the shower. She was soaked—and not just with sweat. She'd been *this* close to having an actual orgasm in her sleep . . . and with Ryan's name on her lips.

Fuck, she thought.

She'd spent so many years resisting her heart's truest desires before she'd finally summoned the courage to come out. At long last, she was ready and excited to be with women—which was why it felt like a cruel and unusual punishment that the person she seemed to desire more than anyone else was Ryan. Ryan, who happened to be a straight, male, flannel-wearing carpenter.

Being into him felt like a waste of an opportunity.

Simone cranked the faucet to the coldest setting. She gritted her teeth as she stepped into the shower and the icy water bit her skin. She remembered an Instagram Reel she'd seen about sleep orgasms, and how you had a higher chance of having one if you were lying on your stomach, with your most sensitive parts pressed against the mattress.

Simone would be sleeping on her back for the rest of the trip.

~

SHE SQUINTED UP AT THE SKY through the window of the gondola. "It's not as a sunny today, eh?"

"Yeah," Ryan said. "It's windier, too."

"D'you think it'll snow?"

"Maybe."

Simone was fully aware that she was asking the dullest questions imaginable, but between the flirting practice and the sex dream, there was a fire in her belly for Ryan that she was eager to stamp out. Soon, she'd be back in Toronto, where she wouldn't have to see him all the time, and it would be easier to focus on meeting women. Until then, she'd work hard to keep things strictly platonic between the two of them.

How ironic, Simone thought wryly. *This trip would have been easier if he were still my nemesis.*

They rode the first few chairlifts of the day with other members of their guide group. They talked with Margot and Thea about what it was like spending their summers in Australia and their winters in Canada so they could ski all year long; with Glen about how he'd founded a nonprofit called Loving Minds that provided mental health care to the queer community in Toronto; with Phoenix about their experience coming out as nonbinary just a month before Simone had come out as bi; and with Roberto and Luis about the differences between skiing in the Rockies and the

Andes. Simone thoroughly enjoyed these conversations, not just because she was deepening her connections with her new friends, but also because they pulled her away from Ryan.

Noon was already approaching when Simone and Ryan ended up alone on a chairlift together for the first time all morning. It was a three-seater, and Simone made sure to leave a healthy gap between their bodies.

As they rose into the air, Ryan lowered the safety bar. It landed with a thunk, made even louder by the silence between them.

"Hey," Ryan said. There was a tentative note in his voice that made Simone nervous and even a little embarrassed, like there was a chance Ryan knew about the sex dream, even though that was impossible.

"What's up?" she asked.

He pulled his goggles up onto his helmet so he could look at her directly. "I just wanted to make sure that you were okay."

"Why wouldn't I be okay? I'm totally fine! Look where we are!" She gestured at the mountains, trying to come off as easy and breezy as possible.

"You don't seem fine," he said matter-of-factly, "and I wanted to make sure I didn't cross a line with any of the flirting stuff last night."

Simone dropped the easy-and-breezy act. "Oh my God, Ryan, *no*." She generally enjoyed putting Ryan in his place, but she couldn't let him think he'd done something wrong when in reality he'd been trying to help her embrace her queerness. The only thing he'd done "wrong" last night was cast a spell on Simone that made her think about kissing him. She couldn't tell him that, though. "You didn't cross a line at all."

"You sure?"

"Ryan, I promise." Sighing, she racked her brain, knowing she still needed an explanation for why she'd been awkward all morning. Eventually, an idea came to her. "Pretending to flirt made me think about my ex," she said. "It put me in bit of a funk, I guess."

She could see the relief in Ryan's posture, but his voice still had traces of concern. Concern for *her*. "The person you said you broke up with last year?"

"Yeah. Bree. We were never official, so I don't know if I can *really* call her my ex, but I liked her a lot, and the breakup, or whatever you wanna call it, was really bad."

"What happened?" he asked.

Her relationship with Bree was still a sore spot for Simone. Somewhere deep down, she was pretty sure she still had feelings for her former coworker, but they were vastly outweighed by shame over the way she'd acted. She wished she could carve out the memory of their fight the way you sliced the bruise off a banana. Simone turned to Ryan with a grimace on her face. "Let's just say I was still insisting I was straight the entire time we were together."

"Ah."

"Yeah. Not ideal."

"But then you came out."

She nodded. "A few months after we ended things. She said I'd never be happy if I kept lying to myself, and eventually, I realized she was right."

"Does she know?"

"That I came out? I don't think so." They hadn't spoken since the fight, and Bree had unfollowed Simone on Instagram. Simone had considered getting in touch—maybe sending Bree a link to her coming-out post—but she was still so ashamed of her behavior that she'd chickened out every time.

But now that Simone was thinking about it again, she realized there *was* a chance that Bree had seen her post. They still had a bunch of mutuals from their old job, and didn't the algorithm sometimes show you popular posts from friends of friends? Maybe Bree *had* seen the post. Maybe she'd even liked it, and Simone had missed her name among the hundreds of notifications.

"You know what? I should actually check to make sure."

Simone plunged her mitten into the pocket of her parka, grabbed her phone, and pulled it out as fast as she could. She didn't consider how risky it was to take your phone out on a chairlift, or that it was even *riskier* to do while wearing thick mittens that made it hard to grip objects.

At least, she didn't consider these things until the phone slipped from her grasp and bounced off her snow pants. She and Ryan gasped in unison as it plummeted through the air, then watched helplessly as it disappeared into a thicket of trees at least fifty feet below them.

"Oh no!" Simone cried. She twisted around in the chair, trying to memorize where her phone had fallen. With a flicker of hope, she noticed the trees that had swallowed it were next to a run. The drop hadn't been *that* far, and if it had landed in the plants or a pile of snow or something, there was a chance it had survived the fall.

When they reconvened with their guide group at the top of the chairlift, Simone explained to Margot what had just happened. "It's in the trees at the side of the run we just crossed over on the lift," she said. "Can we ski down there so I can look for it?"

Margot gazed toward the run and bit her bottom lip. "My concern is that it's a double black, and it's gnarly. A mate of mine tore his ACL there a couple of years ago."

"Oooh, I remember that," Thea added with a wince.

"If you wanna ski down there on your own, you're more than welcome to try it out, but I don't think I can risk taking the group there," Margot said with a quick glance at Glen, who was back on the mountain but trying to take it easy after his fall. "I'm so sorry."

Simone considered her options. She'd skied a few double blacks before, and she'd like to at least *try* to get her phone back. "I think I'm gonna go down there and have a look," she decided aloud.

"You want me to come with?" Ryan asked immediately.

"It's super dangerous."

"Although it is a good idea to ski with a buddy," Margot chimed in. *Thanks, Margot.*

"I'll be all right," Ryan said. "I've been skiing a long time."

Simone gazed toward the run. She wasn't exactly eager to spend alone time with Ryan in the woods. What if he decided to be irresistibly attractive again? But she really *did* need all the assistance she could get. She turned back to Ryan. "You sure?"

"Let me help you, Simone."

The sound of her name in his voice was enough to make her cheeks burn, even in the cold. She held up her hands. "Okay, but I cannot be held responsible for any injuries that might occur."

He was already pushing off toward the run.

Even though Simone had skied a handful of double blacks before, her stomach still plummeted faster than her phone had from the chairlift as they approached the top of the run. The slope was so steep that from a few meters away, they still couldn't see past the lip. This was less of a hill and more of a cliff. There were only two other skiers on the slope ahead of them, both of them apparently experts, judging by the GoPros on their helmets—and even *they* had to stop a few times to strategize their next moves.

"Well, shit," Ryan said.

"You can still turn back if you want."

"I'm not letting you do this alone."

"Are you sure?"

"I'm sure."

"Okay." Simone surveyed the path of the chairlift. "My phone must have fallen somewhere over there."

Simone needed maximum visibility if she was going to make it down this run alive, and she didn't appreciate the way the wind was lifting the powder off the ground and blowing it into her goggles. "Argh!" She shook the snow out of her eyes. Her pulse pounding, she inched her skis farther and farther over the edge, until her weight shifted and she tipped onto the slope.

The next thing she knew, she was skidding down the hill sideways.

She let out a string of curses under her breath. Her form was terrible, but she didn't want to attempt a single turn, scared of what would happen if her skis faced downhill for even a fraction of a second. She transferred as much of her weight as she could onto her uphill ski, and finally came to a stop about a quarter of the way down. Her heart was jackhammering and she was out of breath, even though the whole thing had lasted about five seconds.

She glanced up the slope at Ryan, who was tackling the hill . . . not as gracefully as usual, but with considerably more control than she'd been able to muster.

"You should have led the way," she said when he reached her.

He planted his poles in the ground. "I wanted to be able to see you."

Refusing to let his words remind her of the sex dream, she skidded and sidestepped the rest of the way to the trees where her phone had fallen. Ryan followed, keeping watch over her. Once they were both there, they took off their skis and leaned them against some sturdy-looking trees. What a relief it was to dig her boots firmly into the snow. Ryan took off his helmet and shook out his hair. After two days of skiing, there was color on the tops of his cheeks and the tip of his nose.

Simone led the way into the trees.

"Peaceful," Ryan mused.

It was. They'd stepped off the mountain and into a winter wonderland, population: two. The branches overhead provided shade and shelter from the wind, and the snow was untouched, save for the footprints they were now making. They looked up as they trekked through the snow, trying to determine exactly where the phone would have fallen. They stopped when they were underneath the chairlift.

"I guess this is where we should look," she said.

Scanning the area, Simone already felt hopeless. Her phone could have tumbled into any of a hundred snowbanks or tree wells. Ryan tried calling her number, but Simone was pretty sure her phone had been on vibrate, so even if it *was* still functioning, they wouldn't be able to hear it.

"Oh!" she suddenly exclaimed.

"Did you hear it?"

"No, but I just had a thought. Can I log into the Find My Device thing on your phone?"

"I don't know. I'm pretty basic when it comes to tech." He passed her his phone. "Wanna try?"

"It's worth a shot." When she glanced at his screen, she grinned. "Of *course* your wallpaper is mahogany in high-def."

"It's maple, actually."

"Is that your favorite?"

"It's hard to pick a favorite. I like different woods for different projects. But visually, I like that one a lot." He nodded at the wallpaper. "See how it's all wavy? Like flames, almost? It's called curly maple. Happens when the tree has some kind of weird growth pattern that compresses the wood fibers. It's cool, 'cause what started as a problem turns out to be something really beautiful."

Kind of like us, she thought.

She was getting way too distracted. "That *is* cool," she said quickly, pulling up the search bar. She found the app, plugged in her credentials, and let out a gleeful yelp. "It worked!"

"What now?"

"Let me see. Looks like I can press this 'play sound' button, and my phone will ring, even if it's on silent." She pressed the button, and they listened intently. Nothing. "That's assuming my phone isn't totally broken," she added, already deflating.

"Maybe we're just not close enough to hear it. C'mon."

"We should try to be quiet," she whispered.

"Good thing we're wearing ski boots."

She snorted. There was no clunkier footwear on earth. She followed him deeper into the woods, stepping directly into his deep footprints to minimize the crunching of snow.

After twenty minutes, they still hadn't heard anything. Ryan stopped walking, so Simone did the same. She planted her hands on her hips and sighed. "I feel like we're doomed. I should prob—" She was about to suggest she look into buying a new phone in town, when Ryan held up a gloved hand, cutting her off. "What is it?"

"Do you hear that?"

Perking up again, she strained her ears. All she could hear was the wind and the groaning of branches.

"Listen," Ryan whispered.

"I still don't hear it," she whispered back. She should probably get her ears checked.

Without warning, Ryan took off through the trees, boots crunching through the snow. Then, like a snow leopard who'd been stalking his prey, he dove to the ground, dug around, and raised his fist in the air. Simone gasped. Clutched in his glove was . . .

"MY PHONE!"

She turned off the tracking alarm and raced toward him through the ungroomed woods. Running on uneven ground was hard enough, but it was even harder when you were in ski boots. She was an arm's length from Ryan when she tripped and fell into his chest, sending them both tumbling down into the snowy hollow beneath a spruce tree.

For a split second, there was silence.

Was he hurt?

"Oh my God, Ryan, I'm so sorry—"

Ryan cut her off with a snort of laughter—a low rumble that made her insides turn warm and liquid. "What's so funny?!" she demanded.

"You looked"—he was straight-up gasping for air—"like a flying squirrel."

The next thing Simone knew, she was cackling, her other worries temporarily forgotten. "I was excited, okay? You can't judge me."

"Oh, I'm not. It was one of the greatest things I've ever seen."

She wanted to swat him on the arm, except her own arm was somehow pinned behind his back. That was when it dawned on her, fully, that she was tangled up beneath a spruce tree with the man she'd thought about kissing last night. Her nose was inches from Ryan's neck, which smelled musky and warm, the aroma mixing with the evergreen scent of the spruce tree to create something masculine and soft at the same time.

"We should probably find a way to get out of here," she said.

Ryan climbed out of the tree well first, then turned around and offered her a hand, which she had no choice but to take, given the challenge of escaping otherwise.

When they were both on their feet again, they passed each other their phones. Simone's screen was shattered so badly, it looked like three centuries of cobwebs had accumulated on it, but when she tapped the ruined glass, the phone still lit up behind it. "Oh my God." An incredulous laugh bubbled up from her chest. "I can't see a single thing, but it works!" She would have to leave a five-star review for her rainbow protective case. "I'll have to see if there's a tech place nearby that can fix my screen. Shoot, I just realized I can't even look it up."

Ryan led her back toward the slope. "C'mon. Let's get down this hill, and then I'll take you wherever you need to go."

CHAPTER 11

THERE WAS GOOD NEWS AND BAD news when it came to Simone's phone. The good news: Whistler Village had a tech shop, and the guy there could fix her shattered screen, no problem. The bad news: It would cost her a sizable chunk of change. The worst news of all, of course, was that Simone had to spend even more time with Ryan Foley today than she'd planned for. With a sigh, she handed over her credit card. The guy behind the counter told her to give him a few minutes, gesturing to a chair against the wall.

Simone trudged over, followed by Ryan, and slumped into the seat. "You don't have to stay here," she said, looking up at him. Their hotel was within walking distance of the store.

"You want something to eat?" he asked, ignoring her suggestion.

At the mention of food, Simone felt the emptiness in her stomach. They'd missed today's lunch with their guide group. She took out her wallet to give him some cash, but he waved her off. "It's on me."

Why did he have to be so hot and *courteous?*

"Thank you," she said, and Ryan ducked out of the store.

When her phone was ready, Simone went outside and found

Ryan waiting for her on the sidewalk. He held up a flat cardboard box with a cartoon beaver on the lid. She felt a grin creep across her face. "Wait, is that . . . ?"

He cracked the lid of the box, releasing a plume of steam that smelled like sugar and maple and fried dough. It *was*.

"How did you know I love beaver tails?"

"You mentioned that you used to get them at Mount St. Louis as a kid," he replied matter-of-factly.

"I can't believe you remembered that." It had been one of about three billion random things she'd said to him over the past few days.

"Should we eat this thing before it gets cold?"

At the end of the street, they came across a crackling bonfire in front of a tourist information center housed in a cozy log cabin.

"We're tourists, sort of," Ryan said with a shrug.

"And we *love* information," Simone added.

They claimed the two empty Muskoka chairs next to the fire. After a cloudier morning, the sun had finally come out, giving them a stunning view of the mountains: white and gray against a cornflower-blue sky.

Ryan placed the box on the armrests between them. When he opened the lid, they both leaned in, breathing in the warm scent of fried pastry topped with a drizzle of sweet maple cream. It was the smell of Canadian winter. For the second time in twenty-four hours, Simone realized that if she leaned in a few more inches, she could kiss him.

She straightened back up in her chair. "So, how should we eat this?"

"Shit, I forgot forks."

"I'm okay with hands as long as you are."

He paused. "I'm good with my hands."

She remembered the sex dream again, and suddenly she was crossing her legs to relieve the ache that had sprung up. It took a second for Ryan to realize how he'd phrased his last statement, but when it hit him, a flush crept up his neck. "I mean I'm good with *using* my hands—on this. Uh, here. Do you mind?" He pulled out his travel-size hand sanitizer, and they passed it back and forth.

They ripped off pieces of the beaver tail and placed them in their mouths. *"Mmmm."* Simone couldn't help but moan as the sugar touched her tongue. Oh God, she sounded like she had in her dream this morning. She covered her mouth and fell silent, but not before Ryan's neck had turned an even deeper shade of pink. Why did everything seem so sexual?

Ryan looked at her and smirked. "Simone."

"What?"

"You have maple cream on your nose."

"I do?" she asked, mortified. She instantly tried to wipe it off. "Did I get it all?"

"There's a bit more . . ."

"Where?"

"Here, let me help you." Ryan reached forward and took her hand, steering it to where the remaining maple cream was. Somewhere between the bridge of her nose and the corner of her eye, which, how? Whatever. She couldn't think straight: Her head felt fizzy at Ryan's touch. "There you go. You got it."

Simone instinctively put her finger to her lips and licked off the sugary residue.

Why was Ryan looking at her mouth? And why was it making her stomach clench to be watched like that?

"Are you horrified?" she teased.

His eyes darted back up to hers. "What?"

"That I just ate icing off my own face. Seems . . . I don't know. Germy."

"It wasn't the worst thing I've ever seen."

The fluttering in her chest made her cast around for something not remotely sexy to talk about. Maybe now was the right time to ask the question she'd been curious about for the past few days—even if it meant deepening the conversation. She'd do anything right now to ease the ache in her core. "So, random question . . ."

Ryan arched an eyebrow.

". . . you know this 'funk' you've been in?"

His eyebrow dropped. "What about it?"

"Did something . . . cause it?"

Frowning, he turned to the flames dancing just beyond their feet. "You really want the whole story?"

Yes. No. Maybe. "Only if you want to share it," she said.

Ryan let out a long sigh. "My ex, Victoria—the person I thought I was gonna marry—she cheated on me. I found out at the beginning of December, but it was happening for at least a year."

That explained the Adele in the car. "Oh, Ryan, that's horrible."

"Yeah. The guy was a Bay Street finance bro. A total piece of shit, but he's loaded. When I found out and confronted her, she basically said it was *my* fault she'd wanted to be with this guy, because I just started my own business and it'll be a while before I'm making a halfway decent salary."

"What?" Simone objected, jerking her head back. "Starting your own business is really impressive."

He gave a humorless smile. "She never liked what I did for work anyway. There's good money in carpentry, but it's still blue-collar."

Simone was feeling defensive of Ryan all of a sudden. "What does *she* do, cure cancer?"

"She's actually training to be a brain surgeon."

"Oh." Simone sat back in her chair, defeated.

"And I guess she wanted an equally impressive partner to show off to all her friends."

She thought of her phone call with Kathy the day she'd come out. She knew how shitty it felt to disappoint someone you loved. And in that moment, she didn't care that it was intimate: She reached out and touched Ryan's wrist. "I happen to think you're very impressive," she said. "Every time I've complimented your work, I've meant it from the bottom of my heart. You're talented, Ryan."

He shrugged.

"Also, can we talk about how hard you've been working at the Rainbow Museum?" She remembered his shadowy, bloodshot eyes. "You were so close to being done, and then I come along and smash this thing that took you weeks, and Frankie's demanding you design a bunch of selfie stations, and still, you get it all done. Like, hello? That's also very impressive."

"I'm just a perfectionist."

"Not when it comes to accepting praise, apparently."

A smirk crept onto his face. "Apparently not."

She was enjoying teasing him again. "We'll have to work on that."

"Will we?"

"Say, 'Thank you.'"

"Thank you."

For what felt like a long time but might have only been a few seconds, they looked each other in the eyes. Was she imagining it, or had his pupils dilated? Black inside green inside gray. She would gladly have fallen into them headfirst. Warmth swirled in her belly, growing until it spread across her chest, into her cheeks, down to the tips of her fingers and toes. When she realized she was still holding on to his wrist, she abruptly let go. "You want the last little piece?" she asked, nudging the beaver tail box in his direction.

Ryan blinked at it, like he'd forgotten it was there. "You don't want it?"

"Nah, I'm full," Simone answered. The truth was that the tidal wave of heat had been followed by a thunderclap of anxiety, and now the thought of stomaching food made her queasy.

He picked up the last morsel of sweet fried dough and placed it in his mouth, closing his eyes and chewing slowly to savor it. "God, that's good."

Great, now I'll probably dream about him uttering those words with his eyes closed. "Well, anyway, I appreciate you sharing all that with me."

"Thanks for listening."

"Now I get why you were in such a bad mood when we met—you know, besides the fact that I destroyed your work."

"I still shouldn't have been such a dick."

She waved her hand in the air dismissively. All their animosity felt like water under the bridge now. "Hey, I was pretty annoying, too. When you refused to accept my apologies, I made it my personal mission to kill you with kindness, which I guess made you even more miserable."

Ryan shook his head with a wry smile. "Yeah, you were annoying. It was . . . effective."

She teased him back, hoping it didn't sound flirty. "Super toxic pairing right here." She gestured between the two of them. "There should be caution tape or something."

Ryan chuckled. But as he walked her back to the store to pick up her phone, guiding her around a puddle on the way, Simone couldn't help but think they might not be so toxic for each other after all.

~

AFTER EVERYTHING SIMONE HAD DONE TO rescue her phone, it turned out Bree still hadn't liked her coming-out post. So much for having *that* to distract herself from the dreamy straight guy riding the gondola with her the next morning.

As they carried their equipment to a clear spot on the snow, Margot hiked over to them in her ski boots. She had a six-foot-tall Pride flag strapped to her backpack. "Can I talk to you two for a sec?" she asked. There was a note of urgency in her voice.

"Is everything okay?" Simone asked, scanning the crowd outside the Roundhouse Lodge. She wondered if someone had gotten hurt again—until she spotted the rest of their guide group putting on their skis. Everyone seemed to be intact.

Margot stepped closer to them and lowered her voice. "Please don't say anything to Thea, but I wanted to let you guys know in advance . . . I'm going to propose today."

Simone's eyes went wide behind her goggles. "No way!"

"Congrats, Margot," Ryan added.

"Shhh," Margot said, but she was beaming. "I wanted to do it today 'cause it's our eight-year dating anniversary. The rest of the group knows, too, except for Thea. I was hoping you all could take pictures, if it's not too much trouble."

"We'd be honored to," Simone said, grinning. She'd never been involved in a proposal before, and it was extra exciting that she'd get to watch two *women* get engaged.

Ryan nodded to let Margot know he was down to take photos, too. Margot quickly explained the plan. "I told Thea I was running to the loo just now, so lemme go do that, and I'll meet you back with the others."

"You got it," Ryan said conspiratorially. When it was just him and Simone making their way over to the group, he whispered, "This is going to be amazing."

"Amazing" was far from how Simone was feeling at the moment. The knowledge that these two women were about to pledge their lives to each other had shaken her out of the spell she'd been under since they'd shared the beaver tail yesterday. What if *she* could love another woman like that? What if she never experienced sapphic love because she was hung up on a straight dude?

All she had to do was resist Ryan's appeal for one more day. Then they'd be back in Toronto, not spending every waking minute together, and Simone could focus on meeting the kinds of partners she'd denied herself for so long.

When Margot returned to the group, she led them over to the Peak Express chairlift, a four-seater that carried riders to the summit of Whistler Mountain. Simone and Ryan rode the lift with Glen and Phoenix, and she was grateful that it wasn't the two of them, alone.

"What a place to get engaged," Phoenix said in awe, as they neared the top of the lift.

"No kidding," Glen agreed.

Known to the locals as "the Top of the World," the summit was all snow and rock, with no trees to obscure the spectacular view. The snow-covered mountains surrounded them like white-capped waves in an ocean.

Ryan pushed up the safety bar, and the four of them glided

down the ramp. Margot and Thea arrived a few seconds later, at which point Margot suggested they stop for photos before taking off on a run. She led them to a lookout point, where she planted her rainbow flag in the snow. She waved for Thea to come join her. "Babe, c'mere. We have to take an anniversary pic."

Simone's heart thudded with anticipation as Thea skied over to Margot. She had no doubt Thea would say yes. What worried her more was that she'd been sucked back into the same internal conflict as before: She wanted to pursue women, but Ryan Foley was disconcertingly attractive.

One more day until I'm back in Toronto, she reminded herself as she took out her phone and opened the camera app.

Margot got down on one knee and plucked a jewelry box from her pocket. Thea squealed with joy. Margot eased off her mitten and slid the ring onto her finger. She got to her feet and wrapped Thea in a bear hug. Simone's goggles fogged up; she was crying for them. She was so incredibly happy for Margot and Thea—for the beautiful queer love story that was playing out before her eyes. Maybe she was crying for herself, too—for all the beautiful love stories that might be awaiting her, if she only seized the chance to explore them.

~

AT THREE O'CLOCK THE FOLLOWING AFTERNOON, Simone and her guide group joined the hundreds of skiers and snowboarders who'd gathered on the mountain with Pride flags in hand. Glen patted Simone on the back. "I'm assuming this is your first Pride march since coming out?"

She nodded. Her goggles were already fogging up again.

"Me, too! Well, sort of." On her other side, Phoenix put an

arm around her shoulders and lovingly tapped their helmet against Simone's. "It's my first enby Pride."

"Look at us go." Simone put her arm around Phoenix, too.

"Proud of us," they said.

"Stop, you're going to make me cry."

"Go ahead and cry," Glen chimed in. "This kind of thing didn't happen when I was growing up. Makes *me* emotional, too, if I'm being honest." He gestured at all the people getting ready to bear their flags down the mountain. "Just look at how unbelievably beautiful this is."

On the word *beautiful*, Simone's eyes flitted to Ryan of their own accord. He was helping a stranger attach a Pride flag to the back of their helmet. Her heart swelled as much for him as it did for the rainbow brigade assembled on the mountainside.

I'll be home tomorrow, she thought, *and then I can focus*.

Meanwhile, two skiers were unfurling the biggest Pride flag Simone had ever seen—possibly the biggest flag she'd ever seen, period. It was the size of her parents' swimming pool. An organizer with a megaphone explained what would happen next: that they would ski and snowboard as a group to the base of the mountain, and then the march would continue through Whistler Village. With a round of cheers, they were off, streaming down the mountain like a rainbow avalanche, their flags billowing proudly in the air. Bearing a flag of her own as she glided down the slope with Glen, Phoenix, and her other new friends at her side, Simone forgot about speeding up time—at least for a little while.

CHAPTER 12

TEN MORE HOURS.

Simone was sipping a coffee and eating a bagel from the hotel's breakfast buffet while she waited for Ryan to come downstairs with his luggage. Matilda and Thea's engagement had had a profound effect on her, as had yesterday's Pride parade. The night had culminated in a party called the Snow Ball, where Simone had been empowered to strike up conversation with more women than she had all week. She'd even managed to get a few people's Instagram handles. Unfortunately, she hadn't managed to get Ryan out of her head, but that problem would be solved soon enough.

While she ate breakfast, she checked the news on her phone.

That's when she read about the blizzard.

According to CP24, a storm was about to dump an ungodly amount of snow on the greater Toronto area. She swore under her breath and checked her flight status. It was still showing up as "on time," although a lot could change between now and when they were scheduled to take off. Then again, planes could still fly in weather, couldn't they? This was a Canadian airline. They *had* to be accustomed to operating in snow. Simone decided she wouldn't worry until she actually had a reason to.

Ryan came downstairs in the same gray crewneck he'd worn to pick her up from the airport. It was the cozy kind of sweatshirt that made you want to cuddle with the person wearing it. She wished he'd worn something else. Chain mail, perhaps.

"How's it going?" he asked with a smile, but it didn't reach his eyes. She had no doubt Ryan had sensed her pulling away in the past day.

"Hoping our flight's still on time. Did you see there's a blizzard hitting Toronto?"

He blinked. "Shit, really?"

"Yeah. It sounds pretty bad."

In the car, Simone's veins buzzed from the surprisingly strong hotel coffee, but she leaned her head against the window and closed her eyes, claiming to be tired from their late night at the Snow Ball.

"You mind if I put on some music?" Ryan asked.

"Go ahead," she murmured, fake-sleepily.

"Any requests?"

"Whatever you feel like."

"Maybe something depressing by Adele, for old times' sake?"

Biting her tongue to keep from laughing at his joke, Simone kept her eyes shut.

She stayed like that, pretending to sleep, for the next two hours, missing the scenery she'd enjoyed so much on the trip up. Oh well—at least she'd seen it once. Better to keep her eyes shut than to spend the drive talking to Ryan, who was liable to say any number of things that were inconveniently endearing. An hour into the drive, her neck was screaming from the angle at which she was leaning against the window. The chiropractor from the viral back-cracking videos she sometimes watched before bed would probably have a field day with her. *Oh well*, Simone thought again. She'd picked up some good stretches in Pilates that she could try.

When the car stopped, she felt his hand on her arm, as gentle as a leaf landing on the surface of a stream. "Simone?" he whispered. "We're here."

"Oh!" She fluttered open her eyes and sat upright, shrugging his hand off and her parka on.

"You were out the whole time?"

She nodded. "I think this week's finally catching up with me."

As Ryan settled into a chair at the airport gate, Simone announced that she wanted to get some steps in between the two-hour drive and the five-hour flight. She took her time buying water, snacks, and the latest issues of *Women's* and *Men's Health*, then wandered aimlessly around a bookstore, a tacky souvenir place, and a duty-free shop. When she couldn't smell another perfume sample without gagging, she finally made her way back to the gate.

While most passengers were hunched in their chairs looking at their phones, Ryan was sitting by the window, gazing out at the airplanes. She walked over to him, trying to ignore how good he looked in that goddamn sweatshirt.

Not long after she'd sat down, they both got text message notifications from the airline. Simone swore. Their flight was delayed by an hour.

"It's never a good sign when they're delaying it this far in advance," Ryan said.

"Maybe it means they're super on top of it," Simone said, her voice laden with false hope.

As they waited at the gate, they tracked flights to and from Toronto to see if any were having luck. Simone had to admit the prognosis was looking grim, but on the bright side, they now had a way to pass the time that didn't involve any more flirting.

The hours went by. Their flight was delayed three more times. They took turns watching each other's stuff as they went to the washroom and bought more snacks—all of which they ended up sharing on the duffel bag they'd converted into a makeshift picnic table. Ryan was trying to split a granola bar in half without it crumbling into dust when they both received the message Simone had been dreading. Their flight was canceled.

"Oh no!" Simone cried.

"I had a feeling," Ryan said.

"It says I'm rebooked on a flight that leaves tomorrow."

"Me, too."

Simone tipped her head back and groaned at the ceiling. "Ugh. This is so inconvenient."

"No kidding." He stretched his arms above his head and his legs out as far as they would go. The tip of his boot touched hers, and a bolt of lightning traveled up her leg to her heart. With a sigh, he reached for the granola bar again and held out half. "You want some?" he asked.

"Thanks." Their fingers brushed when she grabbed it. "Well, I guess I'm gonna call around to see if any hotels have rooms available."

"Same here," Ryan said.

Simone put on her headphones. Nibbling her granola bar, she started reaching out to the nearest hotels. A few had last-minute rooms available, but the prices were exorbitant. Although she knew the Rainbow Museum had money, and that Frankie would reimburse her, she didn't want to accidentally overstep a boundary, and five hundred dollars for a single night in Vancouver seemed like a lot. Her boss would appreciate her keeping spending to a minimum, especially with what he'd already invested in this trip. Another hour went by. It was late afternoon, and the sky outside the airport was already darkening. She was supposed to be halfway to Toronto by now.

Finally, she spotted something: a deal on a halfway-decent hotel chain offered through her credit card company. She wanted to smash the button to book it, but there was a problem: Apparently, there was only one room left at that price, and she felt bad leaving Ryan out in the cold.

She took off her headphones. Ryan saw and did the same.

"Any luck?" she asked him.

"Everything's so expensive," he said, frowning. "I might have to camp out here."

"Really?" Her chest twinged at the thought of Ryan sleeping on the airport floor. Who knew how much hair, dead skin, and potato chip dust was embedded in the grimy gray carpet?

"It's just one night." His gaze lingered on the used Band-Aid dangling from the seat cushion a few chairs down from Simone.

She tried not to picture him here as the moon rose in the sky. Who would watch his bags when he needed to use the washroom? Would he be able to sleep with the fluorescent lights overhead? The next thing Simone knew, the words were tumbling out of her mouth.

"I found an affordable room, but there's only one left at this price," she said. "Do you want to share it with me?"

~

SIMONE CHEWED HER BOTTOM LIP AND tapped her driver's license on the surface of the check-in counter. She tapped it three times, twirled it between her thumb and middle finger, then tapped it three times again. The receptionist probably thought she was a married woman who was nervous to be there with her side piece. *Nope, just a bisexual woman nervous to be here with an incredibly sexy straight guy*.

The receptionist punched some data into his computer. "So, Ms. Whitaker, we have you in a basic room with one queen bed. Is that correct?"

"Wait—there's just one bed?"

"Is that not what you booked?"

She'd been so eager to snag the room that she'd missed the detail about the bed. "I'm curious, do you have any rooms with two beds instead of one?"

"Let me see . . ." He clicked around on his computer. "Aha. It looks like I could put you in our deluxe Captain's Suite, but it would be an extra seven hundred dollars for the night."

Simone balked at the price, and Ryan waved his hand. "It's okay, I'll just sleep on a cot. We can do a cot, right?"

The receptionist winced apologetically. "Unfortunately, our basic rooms aren't large enough to accommodate a cot."

"Ah," Ryan replied. There was nary a drop of blood left in Simone's face.

"Would you like to stick with the basic room?"

"Do you have any other basic rooms available? Like, if I wanted to book my own?" Ryan ventured.

Another apologetic wince. "Not at the basic level, I'm afraid."

Ryan looked at Simone. "I'll go back to the airport."

"Are you kidding? I offered to share my room; you're not—"

"I don't mind. Seriously."

"The dangling Band-Aid," she said under her breath. Simone turned to the receptionist.

"We'll take the basic room," she announced. She turned back to Ryan and, in a lower voice, said, "We'll figure something out."

What that "something" would be, Simone had no idea.

"Fabulous." The receptionist slid two plastic cards and two small slips of paper across the table. "Here are your room keys," he said, "along with vouchers for twenty dollars off your order at Bar Burrard, since you booked through Capital One. You'll find it just behind you."

"Thanks," Simone mumbled, before scooping up the keys and vouchers and leading the way to the elevators, all while making as little eye contact with Ryan as humanly possible. She pressed the button for the fourth floor. The elevator felt impossibly small for the two of them and their bags; she could feel the heat of his body and smell the piney scent of whatever deodorant or body wash he'd used that day. The walls were mirrored, so everywhere she looked, she saw Ryan from a new angle. There was his brown hair curling deliciously around his ear . . . There was the dark stubble on his jaw . . . There were his hands, which she'd imagined working their way around her body . . .

She tapped the key card against the door, held her breath, and turned the handle. The door opened with a long, ominous creak. She wheeled her suitcase past the bathroom and laid her eyes on the singular bed that occupied the vast majority of the room.

Was it just her, or was this the smallest hotel room on planet Earth?

Ryan followed closely behind her. "You know, I'd honestly be happy to—"

"You're not going back to the airport!" she interjected, although a part of her wished he just would.

"Actually, I was going to offer to sleep upside down in the closet like a bat."

A laugh bubbled up inside her and forced its way out, dissolving some of the tension in the too-small hotel room. She turned around and managed to look him in the eye. "That would be great, actually. Thank you." The knot in her chest loosened. She couldn't do anything about the fact that she and Ryan were sharing a room, but she found it was easier to at least acknowledge the weirdness than try to dance around it. "What do you think is more awkward," Simone asked, "the two of us sharing this very tiny room, or you losing a dance-off to a guy with a giant tiger tattoo?"

"Oh, that's obvious," he said. "Me losing a dance-off to a guy with a giant tiger tattoo."

They laughed together, and the tension melted even more.

Ryan laid a hand on his stomach. "I don't know about you, but I'm starving."

Simone was hungry, too. She'd eaten the bagel in the hotel lobby and snacks at the airport all day, but nothing that had amounted to a complete meal. She held up the slip of paper the receptionist had given her. "Shall we redeem our vouchers at the fine establishment downstairs?"

Bar Burrard looked like a cross between a conference center and an Outback Steakhouse, and speakers pumped out synth-heavy eighties music. A few bleary-eyed solo travelers sagged on the bar stools, while the tables were occupied by a group of businesspeople hunched over laptops; a rowdy bunch of Brits who were playing a drinking game; and a family that appeared to include six children under the age of six.

"Super confusing vibe in here," Ryan said as they waited to be seated.

"I kind of love it," Simone replied, because at least it wasn't romantic.

The host showed them to a corner booth and dropped a stack of laminated menus on the table. "Nellie will be over in a sec to take your drink orders," she told them.

They slid in from opposite sides, with Simone making sure to leave plenty of space between them. Ryan reached for one of the menus, wrinkling his nose when he had to peel it off the sticky surface of the table. "I could definitely use a drink," he said.

"Do they have an IPA?"

"I might need something stronger, after the day we've had."

And the night we're about to have, Simone thought. "All right," she said, reaching for the other menu, "I'm going whiskey."

"I'll join you," Ryan said.

They both polished off their first glasses quickly, so they ordered another round, along with two grilled chicken sandwiches and a side of fries to share.

When their food came, they dug in like two people who'd just spent a long day in the airport and then consumed exactly one and a half alcoholic beverages each. They reminisced about their time in Whistler, laughed about the funniest moments with their guide group. Since they'd sat down at their booth, Simone was finally feeling relaxed. The matter of sharing a bed with Ryan was still on the horizon, but she'd cross that bridge later; for now, she was having fun drinking whiskey with him in this hilariously absurd hotel bar.

She held up a French fry. "Let's play Fuck, Marry, Kill," she said. "Regular fries, sweet potato fries, and truffle fries."

"You're going to make me kill *any* kind of French fry? That's rude," Ryan answered.

"Okay, okay, I'll go first. I feel like I have to marry the truffle, right?"

"Why's that?"

"It's the most premium option."

He arched an eyebrow. "Oh, so you want to marry rich?"

"NO!" She swatted him in the arm. "I genuinely *like* truffle fries, okay?"

He smirked. "I'm just teasing. You and truffle fries would make a beautiful couple."

Simone's chest fluttered at his use of the words *you* and *beautiful* in the same sentence. Why had she suggested they play such a flirty game in the first place? She blamed the whiskey. "I think I'd kill the sweet potato fry," she said, "because they're trying to be all 'healthy' and that's not something I'm looking for in a fry."

"Wow, *great* point. So you're fucking the regular fry?"

"I suppose I'm fucking the regular fry."

"Anything you're looking forward to about the experience?"

"Hmm." She grabbed a fry, dipped it in chipotle aioli, and took a bite. "Regular fries are super versatile. They pair well with a lot of different things." She dipped the opposite end of the fry in ketchup.

"Are you saying regular fries are bi?"

Simone nearly spit out her last bite. "YES," she said, after she'd managed to swallow. "And I think truffle fries are gay, and sweet potato fries are straight."

Ryan slapped a hand to his chest. "Of *course* you killed the straight fry."

"That doesn't mean I wanna kill you!" She grabbed the hand that was over his heart and pulled it away.

She hadn't meant for them to end up holding hands. It had just . . . sort of . . . happened. Now Simone stared at their intertwined fingers on the tabletop, wondering if she should say something. It felt as though the waiter had brought her a slice of cake she hadn't ordered, but it looked delicious, and she didn't want to send it back, even though she knew it was the right thing to do. Simone risked a glance at Ryan's face. He was looking into her eyes.

"Hi," he said.

"Hi," she said back.

His gaze flickered to their hands. He swallowed. "Is this . . . okay?"

Simone nodded. She was fizzy and warm and having a good time, and she wasn't in the mood to keep fighting her attraction to him.

"Can I ask you something?" Ryan ventured.

"Sure," she said as calmly as she could.

His voice was slow, tentative. "The other day, you said that being with a guy this soon after coming out would feel like a 'waste.' Is that"—his eyes wandered to their intertwined hands—"still the case? I guess I'm a little . . . confused."

Simone's shoulders tensed, but he was asking a perfectly valid question. It wasn't fair of her to be this forward with him if she was just going to back down. She wanted to be honest, but the problem was, she didn't know the answer to his question. Maybe the fairest thing she could do was give him the complicated truth.

"I'm confused, too," she admitted. "Now that I'm out, I feel like I *should* be trying to date women, but I'd also be lying if I said

I didn't find you, well"—her heart was thudding hard enough that Ryan could probably feel it through her palm—"extremely attractive."

Her words had an instant effect on him; she could see it in the way his pupils widened—feel it in the way he strengthened his hold on her hand. Whether the effect was good or bad, she couldn't say for certain, and that made her nervous, which explained why she started to ramble.

"And yeah, it's sort of weird to say that, given that we hated each other a week ago, but it's true."

"I also think you're . . . extremely . . . attractive." He delivered the words with slow intention, like he was testing out the weight of each one. "I always have."

"Even when I was annoying the hell out of you?"

"Even then. Honestly, the fact that I was so fucking attracted to you was part of the reason I got so annoyed."

Her heart thudded harder, faster. "What do you mean?"

"I didn't want to have feelings for anyone so soon after . . . everything. But then *you* showed up with your perfect walnut eyes and your nose all pink from the cold, and my plan went out the window."

She toyed with one of her ginger curls. "The first thing most people notice is my hair."

"And it's beautiful, don't get me wrong—but for me, it was your eyes."

"I noticed yours, too," Simone admitted. "Gray with a burst of green."

Ryan arched an eyebrow. "So, when I was being an asshole, you also—"

"Thought you were hot? Yes. Trust me, it was incredibly frustrating."

"I don't know if I should apologize or say thank you."

"You've already apologized. Now you can just thank me."

He smiled. "Well, thank you." She nodded, and Ryan took a breath. "So, yeah. I've always thought you were attractive. But once we got on the same page, I realized you were also really smart and sweet and . . . just awesome to be around. But I didn't want to be too forward, because I knew you'd just come out, and you had a whole plan in place."

"A plan that you totally derailed," she said teasingly, even though it was also true.

With a crease between his eyebrows, Ryan bit his upper lip, sending shock waves through her core as though he'd also bitten hers. It was the look he seemed to get when he was focusing hard on something. Something he wanted to get right. "Can I say something?"

"Of course."

"I really want to kiss you, Simone."

"I want to kiss you, too," she whispered. She felt like she was falling—like her seat had disappeared from underneath her. When she shifted her body to get a grip on reality, she could feel how wet she was already. "But, Ryan—"

"What?"

"I think we should say that whatever happens, it's just for tonight."

Ryan hesitated before responding. "Just for tonight," he repeated.

She nodded. "The last thing I want to do is hurt you because I still don't know exactly what I want."

His thumb caressed her hand, sending shivers down her spine.

"No, that's probably what's best for me, too. I'm not sure I'm ready for something new yet."

Simone squeezed his hand, liking the way this was going. She could have the best of both worlds: getting to hook up with Ryan, but still having the freedom to date whomever she wanted when she got back to Toronto. She stared into Ryan's gray-green eyes and smirked. "Should we grab the check?"

CHAPTER 13

SIMONE'S PULSE THUMPED LIKE A BASS drum as they stepped into the small elevator. The doors were sliding closed, about to seal them in privacy for the first time since they'd admitted their feelings to each other, when a man jammed his beefy forearm into the gap between the doors.

"Oof—sorry 'bout that!"

Two of the Brits from the bar crammed themselves into the already-tight space. Simone and Ryan pressed their backs into opposite walls to make room for the new arrivals.

"It's bloody sardines in here," the second man said.

"S'pose we could wait for the next one," the first man replied, despite clearly having no intention of doing so. He pressed the button for the fifth floor.

Simone and Ryan made eye contact in the mirrored walls. She wanted him so badly, and not being able to touch him yet only made her crave him even more. Ryan raked a hand through his hair, his eyes boring into the screen that announced the floors. The ripple in his jaw told Simone he was clenching his muscles, that he was just as impatient to get the hell out of here. There was an ache in her core that spread across her chest and down to the space between her legs—an ache that she couldn't relieve just by pressing her legs together, which was what she was doing now, to no avail. Was this the slowest elevator in Vancouver, or in the world? It felt like the slowest elevator in all of history.

At last, with a cheerful ding, they arrived on the fourth floor. She didn't even wait for the Brits to step out and make room. Instead, she launched herself into the hallway, then whirled around, breathless, as Ryan squeezed out behind her.

The elevator doors slid shut.

As soon as they were alone in the dimly lit corridor, she rushed to close the distance between them with weeks' worth of pent-up energy. When he opened his arms, something came over her—a wordless message passed between them—and she jumped. He caught her with strong hands that cupped her ass and pulled her in close as she wrapped her legs around his waist. Now that she was in his arms, there was only one thing left to do. With her arms around his neck, she leaned in and kissed him.

She could taste the woodsmoke from the whiskey on his lips, which were soft and full and slightly parted, beckoning her inside. When their tongues met, the smoke became a fire, its flames unfurling in every inch of her body. Ryan moaned, and the sound vibrated in Simone's core. He dug his fingers deeper into the denim stretched across her ass. What was she doing wearing pants at a time like this?

Simone drew her head back. Ryan's cheeks were as flushed as they'd been on the cold mountaintop. "Maybe we should go to the room," she murmured.

"Good call." He peered over her shoulder without relaxing his grip. "Which way are we again?"

"Uh . . ." Simone had temporarily lost her bearings, too. "W-we're the first door that way." She pointed, and he carried her. "You know you can put me down if you need to," she told him.

"I don't," he said simply. Simone was impressed. Hooking up with someone who hauled wood and operated power tools for a living had its perks. "I think I put the key card in my back left pocket, if you can reach it."

They laughed breathlessly as they contorted themselves so that Simone could reach the card without Ryan putting her down. When she slipped her hand into his pocket, she felt his firm glutes, and again, she cursed the existence of denim. "Got it," she said, and pulled out the card. Ryan rotated their bodies so she could tap it on the door, turn the handle, and let them in. He didn't put her down until he'd carried her all the way to the bed, where he bent his knees and eased her onto the duvet. She kicked off her shoes.

They'd left the bedside lamp on before they'd gone down to the bar, and now it cast a warm, golden glow over their bodies. It was funny how the room had seemed tiny when they'd first checked in; now, it seemed intimate.

Simone lay on her back with her legs bent. He stood at the edge of the bed, his palms resting on her knees, and gazed down at her, his eyes traveling slowly from her waist up, like he wanted to absorb every inch of her. She felt powerful, being looked at like that. She thought back to the satisfaction she'd gotten from putting him in his place.

She propped herself up on her elbows. "You look really fucking good in that crewneck."

"Oh yeah?"

"Too good. Take it off."

She didn't just hear Ryan's breath hitch; she saw it, too, in the way his Adam's apple bobbed and a shudder passed through his body. With a spasm of panic, she wondered if she'd freaked him out. But then, obediently, he grabbed the hem of his sweatshirt and started to pull. *Well then. Ryan likes being told what to do*. Simone would keep that in mind, or she would try to. Her brain was addled by the sight of him towering over her shirtless. He was muscular—sturdy, rather than lean—with a dusting of freckles across his broad, hairless pecs and shoulders.

"Fuck, Ryan." Her voice was raspy. His fingers moved to his belt, but she said, "No. Not yet." The whiskey was making her confident, and she wasn't done appreciating what he'd just revealed to her. Instead of lying back down, she pushed herself all the way up. She scooted to the edge of the bed, so that her eyes were in line with his sternum. She lifted her chin. She would make him stoop. "Kiss me." Ryan bent down, cupped her jaw, and kissed her more deeply than before. He kissed her like he had something to prove, and Simone wanted nothing more than to be his proving ground.

Her hands explored the solid mass of his torso, felt his heart beating under skin that was hot to the touch. She was hot, too. She was on fire. She tugged her chunky sweater over her head, remembering at the last minute that she was wearing a basic gray sports bra underneath: something that would have been comfy on the plane, but wasn't exactly *sexy* by most people's definitions.

It was by Ryan's definition, apparently. With his hands resting lightly on Simone's shoulders, he took a small step back to survey the new parts of her that he could see. "Wow," he murmured as his fingertips traveled south, lightly tracing the edges of her bra straps. Simone felt a surge of heat between her legs when he reached the outer curves of her breasts, when his featherlight touch teased her through the fabric. *Off*. She needed it off. But she didn't want Ryan to stop touching her. Instead of taking it off, she simply pulled down the fabric in front so that it was under her naked breasts, lifting them in a way that was somehow even hotter than what fancy lingerie could do.

Her breasts had an instant effect on Ryan, who dropped to his knees in reverence. He gripped her waist, and she liked the feel of his callused palms, the way it contrasted with the unbearably soft kisses he was planting around the edge of her left breast. Then around the edge of her right. He went back to the left, his lips and tongue moving closer and closer to her hard nipple, until at last he took it in his mouth and sucked.

"Fuck, Ryan," she said again, her voice even raspier than the first time. She hadn't felt this good in months. Running a hand through his unruly curls, Simone purred, "You're doing *such* a good job at that."

Ryan moaned around her nipple and sucked harder. The vibration of his moan coupled with the increased pressure felt so good that Simone had to throw her head back, arching into him. The shift resulted in her already-swollen clit rubbing against her jeans, and she wondered again what she was doing wearing pants at a time like this. While Ryan continued worshipping her breasts, Simone scrambled to unbutton her jeans. Then she felt her cotton underwear.

"Give me your hand," she said. Ryan had just moved his mouth to her right nipple. Without releasing it from his mouth, he did as he was told, and Simone guided his hand to the drenched fabric between her legs. "Do you feel that?"

He nodded as he sucked. Simone was lightheaded, dizzy on the power dynamics she'd never explored with anyone until she'd met Ryan.

"You got me soaking wet," she said. "Now what are you going to do about it?"

Ryan released her breast from his mouth. Still kneeling between her legs, he looked up at her. "I'm going to make you come."

Simone could probably have come just from hearing him *say* that. Her sports bra still on, she lay on her back. Ryan stood up and helped her shimmy the rest of the way out of her jeans. Then he eased her underwear over her hips and all the way down her legs, until they were off and she was lying there, glistening for him.

"Do you mind if I—" His hands went to his belt again. "Not to—just because it's easier to kneel when I'm out of my jeans."

"Of course." She watched as he undid the buckle and took off his pants.

"Don't mind me," he said, and it was clear he was referring to the giant bulge straining against his black briefs. He got back down on his knees and slid his muscular arms under her thighs. Simone let out a soft gasp as he tugged her to the very edge of the bed as easily as if he were moving a pillow.

Now his eyes were in line with her vulva, his mouth less than an inch from her. She could feel his every exhale on all her most sensitive parts, and then she heard his voice.

"Can I finger you while I lick your clit?"

"Yes," she breathed. *Please.*

He started just with his tongue, hot and wet and—fuck, she might actually be melting. Her whole body was liquid. Then she felt his hand—felt one of his thick fingers sliding into her, opening and filling her up—and just like that, she was vapor. She'd floated up to the stratosphere.

"Does that feel good?" Ryan murmured, his lips still grazing her skin, his finger still curling against the front wall of her vagina.

"Yes," she replied. "So good—it's so, so good, Ryan."

"Good." And then he buried his face in her again.

She wanted this to go on forever, but she was already so turned on that her climax was inevitable. "I'm right there," she said, her voice ragged, and then— "Fuck, Ryan, I'm coming."

With his finger still inside her, he licked her over the edge. Then, when her throbbing clit was too sensitive for direct contact, he massaged her G-spot the rest of the way through her orgasm.

When he'd finally drawn the last of it out of her, Simone was spent in the best way possible. Breathing heavily, she lay there on her back, noticing the cracks in the ceiling for the first time. For a while there, he'd had her on another plane of existence.

"Simone."

The urgent note in Ryan's voice shook her from her post-orgasm haze. "Are you okay?" she asked, pushing herself up to a seated position. She looked down at Ryan to see what the matter was.

He tugged down his briefs and freed his hard cock, even larger now than the bulge she'd seen earlier.

"Wow," she said, genuinely impressed. It was the nicest dick she'd ever seen, and Simone had seen a fair number of dicks in almost thirty years of exclusively dating men.

"I got so hard from eating you out," he whispered, wrapping a hand around the base of his shaft, but he didn't stroke. "I'm already so close."

If she'd been delirious with power before, it was nothing compared to how she suddenly felt knowing she'd brought him to the brink of orgasm without so much as touching him. He was getting off on making *her* feel good. And he'd performed admirably. He deserved a reward.

"I want you to make yourself come," she coaxed him from

above. "Make yourself come for me." If only the Simone of four weeks ago who'd been terrified of Ryan's wrath could see her now.

As Ryan started to pump his cock, Simone inched forward, slid a hand into his curls, and caressed the side of his head. Taking deep, measured breaths, he gazed up at her, but it wasn't long before his breaths had shortened to gasps. "Fuck, Simone." He closed his eyes, and she saw his abs clench as he worked to keep himself under control. She wanted to see him unravel.

"Be good and make yourself come for me," she purred.

She was whispering words of praise in his ear when he finished all over himself, still kneeling between her legs.

It was the single hottest thing Simone had ever witnessed.

Ryan sighed with pleasure, softly kissed her inner thigh, and collapsed with his head in her lap. She cradled him there, stroking his hair.

"Holy shit," he said, with a faint laugh. "That was . . ."

"Incredible," Simone whispered.

Ryan nodded. He picked up his head and kissed her between her legs. She moaned. "You're wet again."

"From watching you."

And the next thing Simone knew, Ryan was making her come again with his hands and mouth, before he'd even had the chance to clean himself up. It was electrifying, how badly he craved *her* pleasure. She'd spent so much of her life trying to please everyone else. But somehow, Ryan—stubborn, infuriating Ryan—had helped her realize she deserved to be pleased too. A silver lining to their rocky beginning.

When Simone recovered from her second climax of the evening, she propped herself up on her elbows. "You really like to be of service, huh?"

"I do," he said, unashamed.

"Noted."

As Ryan stood up and went to the bathroom to wash off, Simone bit her bottom lip, realizing she shouldn't have said that. Why would she need to make a note about something that wasn't going to happen again?

CHAPTER 14

THE WOMAN ON THE SCREEN WAS take-your-breath-away beautiful. A toothpaste-commercial smile; giant, round eyes that glowed as much as her dewy skin; thick hair that cascaded in gorgeous waves down her back. According to her profile, she was a physiotherapist; she loved hiking in the summer and skiing in the winter; she had an adorable dachshund-Chihuahua mix with ears like a bat's; her ideal Friday night was screw-top wine and takeout Thai; and she lived downtown, not far from Simone. She was easily the most promising woman Simone had encountered since downloading this dating app for queer women.

She held her breath as she hovered her thumb over the heart button. Then, with a sigh like air whooshing out of a slashed tire, she put her phone face down on the toilet paper dispenser and finished what she was doing in the washroom.

Simone stuffed her phone deep into the back pocket of her jeans before she washed her hands and went back out into the office. She'd had just about enough of torturing herself for the day.

Now that she was back from Whistler, work was stressful enough on its own. The air was getting thicker with nervous excitement the closer they got to next Friday night's launch party. Frankie had made it clear that the launch party was just as important as when they opened their doors to the general public the following week, if not more important. On Friday of next week, they'd be hosting a respected group of journalists and influencers whose early reviews of the Rainbow Museum could make or break the company's success, as well as a bunch of powerful investors who'd want to see their financial contributions had been put to good use.

Simone trudged back to where she'd been working at the office kitchen counter, which Nina was also using as a standing desk. The communications director was guzzling a glass of cold brew and cursing the members of the press who still hadn't RSVP'd to the event. "It's fucking homophobic," she declared. Nina tended to say this in regard to *most* inconveniences, no matter how trivial: the time they ran out of oat milk in the office fridge; the time the Wi-Fi went out for a few minutes; the week the streetcars were running on an alternate route due to construction. Simone adored Nina, but it could be hard to tell when she was kidding and when she was serious. Simone plopped back onto her stool and returned to the emails she'd been exchanging about marketing assets with their freelance graphic designer.

A few minutes later, Seth wandered over to refill his Stanley. He eyed Simone, who was hunched over her laptop like a jumbo shrimp, and Nina, who was glaring at her screen like she wanted to set it on fire.

"Either of you know if we're allowed to bring plus-ones to the party?" he asked.

"We are," Nina answered bluntly.

"Okay, sick, because I already invited Claude." Claude was

Seth's new boyfriend, and they were still very much in the honeymoon phase. Case in point: "He says he wants me to teach him some of my makeup looks, and that he'd be down to try them out for the party. Couldn't you just *die*?"

"Cute," Nina said without looking up from her laptop.

Frankly, Simone *could* just die, although Claude learning to apply shimmery highlighter would not be the cause. The cause would be Simone ripping her own brain out, because every time she thought about the prospect of dating new people, her mind inevitably went back to that Vancouver hotel room.

To Ryan.

The sturdy, six-foot-two straight man who got off on making her come over and over again.

Whenever she saw him around the office now, she made sure to keep their interactions strictly platonic. They were just friends. Friends who'd had a singular night of mind-blowing sex, never to be repeated again. She'd told him that her gym got a SkiErg and joked that it was almost as fun as actual skiing (not); he'd shown her a photo of the chili he'd made, using the recipe he'd gotten from the Roundhouse Lodge.

But if their interactions were family friendly, the memories running on a loop in Simone's head were very much rated X. She'd been riding the stationary bike at the gym last night, when bam!—she was thinking of his face between her thighs, his magical tongue and hands, the way he'd catapulted her into another plane of existence. She'd had to get off the bike and end her ride early to avoid orgasming in public. At home, she'd stripped off her workout clothes, pulled out her vibrator, and cued up something sexy to watch. Something with women only, so she was less likely to think about *him*.

When she climaxed, she wasn't watching the screen.

In fact, her eyes were closed. She was picturing Ryan kneeling on the floor and freeing his rock-hard erection from his boxer briefs.

After, she tried telling herself the *video* had been the problem: that the music had been distracting and the script had been cheesy. But deep down, Simone knew those weren't the *real* reasons she'd come thinking of Ryan. The truth was, she wanted him desperately, for more than just one night. She also knew that was a terrible idea, for the same reasons they'd listed when they'd agreed to hook up in the first place. Simone deserved to live her best bisexual life, and Ryan deserved a partner who knew exactly what she wanted.

"Simone, what about you?" Seth asked.

She snapped back to the present moment. "Hmm?"

"Are you bringing a date to the launch party?"

"Oh. Um . . ." She paused to consider the question. She didn't want to bring a date to the party—didn't want to date anyone else, period—but maybe she needed to force herself out of her comfort zone. It wasn't like she was ever going to date Ryan, so what was the point in avoiding every other potential partner? "Maybe," she told Seth.

When no one was looking, she pulled her phone from her back pocket and opened the dating app again. The gorgeous physiotherapist—Erica—was still smiling at her. Simone held her breath and tapped the heart button.

Well then.

It would seem they were a match.

~

AFTER A FEW DAYS OF MESSAGING, Erica wanted to know if Simone was free for a drink on Tuesday. Simone said yes, she was, and she would love to meet up.

Only now it was Tuesday, the date just an hour away, and Simone's insides were churning as she packed up her things. She told herself it was butterflies, but if she was being honest, it felt a lot more like a stomachful of eels.

That was to be expected when you were meeting a total stranger, wasn't it? She'd have normal butterflies on the next date, when she'd confirmed that Erica wasn't a catfish or a secret axe murderer or something. Or maybe she was anxious because she'd dreamed of doing this for so long—going on an actual date with a woman—and now it was finally happening. Her life was about to take on a whole new dimension.

She took the elevator downstairs to the atrium, and was heading to the employees' exit when something across the ball pit caught her eye. Something beyond the archway that had been covered by a tarp on her first day. A sliver of woodwork that seemed impossibly intricate.

Simone checked the time and saw she could spare a few minutes before she left for the wine bar. Besides, she just wanted a quick peek. She hurried past the ball pit and through the archway into the room with moss and flowers covering the walls and took in the finished wooden dragonfly in all its glory. She thought back to Whistler, to Ryan explaining that his ex had looked down on his work. The idea that Ryan had ever questioned his own talent was so absurd, it made her angry. "Don't you see how talented you are?" she whispered to the empty room.

"I'm working on it," came a deep voice from behind her. She spun around, and there was Ryan, standing in the archway. *Really? I'm about to go on my first date with a woman and I run into the one guy I'm trying to forget?*

"Oh—hi!" she stammered. Taking a shot of Ryan Foley wasn't

exactly how she'd planned to kick off her date night. "Um, I was just on my way out, and I happened to glance over here, and I saw that the dragonfly was finished, and I thought, 'I should go take a look at that thing I destroyed on my first day!'" Not only was she rambling, but she sounded like she'd inhaled helium. *Good going, Simone.* This wasn't awkward at all.

"I'm glad you like how it turned out," he said, crossing his arms. *Arms that had carried her down the hall to their hotel room—that had gently lowered her onto the bed . . .*

The blood in Simone's head had rushed to her navel when Ryan appeared, so that all of a sudden, she was both very lightheaded and very turned on. Why did her body insist on reacting this way to him—the man she'd vowed never to sleep with again?

"It's a good thing I ran into you," Ryan said.

"It is?" Simone's traitorous heart skipped a beat. *We're supposed to be excited about our upcoming date with the gorgeous physiotherapist!*

He nodded at the dragonfly. "That was the last thing I had to finish. I'm done here, as of today."

She blinked at him. "Done, like . . . forever?"

"For a while. Until whenever Frankie decides he wants to switch up the designs—and that's assuming he'd want to hire me again."

"Of course he'd want to hire you again," she insisted, needing it to be true.

The news that Ryan wouldn't be around as much had hit her like an icy shower. *This is good news,* she tried to remind herself. It didn't feel like good news, though. Truthfully, she'd enjoyed coming to work knowing there was always a chance of seeing Ryan, awkward as their run-ins might be.

"Will you be at the launch party?" she asked.

He shook his head. "It's one of my moms' birthdays on Friday, so I'm driving up to Barrie for the weekend."

Simone remembered him saying his moms had retired an hour and a half north of Toronto so they could spend more time in nature. She tilted her head and forced a smile. "Aww, that's nice!"

"Yeah, should be good."

A beat of awkward silence passed between them.

"Anyway," he said, "I guess this is goodbye—at least for a bit."

"Right." She swallowed hard. "Well, congrats on being done! And good luck with whatever you end up working on next. I know it'll be amazing." She paused again. "*Everything* you do is amazing."

"Thank you."

"I really mean it."

He looked her deep in the eyes. "I know you do. And I appreciate it."

A sad smile crept across her face. "I know you do, too."

They hugged. He smelled musky and warm, like always. She wanted to stay there, with her cheek to Ryan's chest, but she knew she had to leave. For everyone's sake. She let go and crossed her arms. "Well, see you . . . at some point."

"See you at some point," he said, stepping aside to let her pass through the archway.

~

SHE WAS MEETING ERICA IN THE Village, at a cozy, quiet wine bar housed in a redbrick Victorian manor. The first thing Simone thought after walking through the door was that Ryan would have appreciated the wooden balustrade on the staircase. The second thing she thought was that she shouldn't be thinking about Ryan—she *couldn't* be thinking about Ryan—on her first date with a woman since coming out. She owed it to herself. Owed it to the old, closeted Simone who'd tried so hard to believe that she was only sexually—not romantically—attracted to women, even as she smoldered with envy at the sight of two women holding hands in the light of day. Never again would she have to mourn the queer life she'd never get to have, because now she was living it. She would be present, and grateful, and focused, and all the other words her Pilates instructor was always throwing out at them.

She turned away from the staircase and approached the host stand, forcing a smile. "Hi! I'm meeting someone here at six thirty? The reservation's under Erica, I think?"

The host smiled back at Simone. "You can follow me right this way. The other member of your party just arrived."

"Great!"

The host led Simone through an archway into a pretty candlelit room, where Simone tried not to think of Ryan again when she noticed the wood paneling on the walls. *Note to self: Plan future dates away from impressive works of carpentry.* She followed the host to the back corner of the room, where Erica stood up from the table, flashing that toothpaste-commercial smile. Simone was taken aback; she was even more gorgeous in person than she was in her pictures, her big, round eyes sparkling underneath the voluminous dark brown waves that were tossed to one side of her head.

"Hi!" Erica hugged her like they were old friends, enveloping Simone's face in her mountain of hair. It smelled like rose petals, feminine and sweet. They sat down on opposite sides of the table.

"Your curls are *amazing*," Erica gushed.

"Aww, thank you," Simone replied. Her hair was the first thing everyone noticed when they met her. *Everyone except for Ryan.*

"How do you get them to be so springy? Mine never corkscrew like that."

Simone told her about the life-changing curl cream she'd found after tumbling down a Reddit rabbit hole. "You put it on in the shower, when your hair's still wet, and then you wrap your hair in a microfiber hair towel."

"Whoa. You're talking about things I didn't even know existed."

Simone chuckled. "Then, when my hair's dry, I'll run a few drops of oil through it to prevent any frizz."

Erica clasped her hands in front of her chest. "Oh my God, I need all your tips. I've been straightening my hair forever, and I'm just now embracing my curls. It's been a journey."

"Well, I'm just now embracing that I'm into women, so sounds like we can both support each other," Simone joked.

Erica grinned. With Lucy and Seth's guidance, Simone had put it right there in her profile that she was new to dating women. She might get fewer matches, since not everyone had the patience or desire to be someone's "first," but the people she *did* match with would presumably be open to it. ("Quality over quantity," Seth had explained.)

"Oh my God, I just realized," Erica gasped, "I'm new to curls, you're new to girls." She giggled. "I think we're going to make a good team, Simone."

"I think so, too," she agreed. But when the server came to take their orders, and they both ordered a glass of the same prosecco, Simone had the strange urge to cry, but not in a happy way. Like after everything she'd done to find herself, a piece of her was still lost.

CHAPTER 15

THE LAUNCH PARTY WAS IN FULL swing that Friday when Simone headed to the lobby, pausing to grab two flutes of prosecco along the way. When the door slid open, Erica was there waiting for her, looking as dazzling as ever in a long velvet dress and with her voluminous waves in a high ponytail. Her face lit up when she saw Simone. "Oh my goodness, did you bring me a glass of prosecco?"

"How could I not?"

"I love that you remembered my favorite drink."

"I try."

She really had been trying. Trying not to cry at the wine bar. Trying to stay present, grateful, and focused as she and Erica had gotten to know each other. Eventually, she'd noticed her efforts starting to pay off. She'd felt butterflies—real ones—when they'd hugged goodbye at the end of the night. She was pretty sure she felt them again when she hugged Erica now, in the lobby of the Rainbow Museum, and Erica planted a soft kiss on Simone's cheek. *Do not think about Ryan Foley.*

At least he was in Barrie this weekend, too busy being a good son to come to the launch party.

Erica's eyes went wide as Simone led her through the sliding door and into the atrium. Even Simone, who was here every day, was amazed by how far the Rainbow Museum had come. When she'd started her job at the beginning of January, the place had still been a construction zone, with tarps and ladders and the scents of sawdust and fresh paint in the air. Now, it wasn't just finished—it was *dazzling*. Billie Eilish played from the speakers, metallic balloons floated above the ball pit, and servers in sequined tuxes held trays of prosecco and multicolored Jell-O shots. The place was packed with journalists, influencers, and other VIPs. Frankie, who'd been bouncing around the party like a ping-pong ball, had a permanent grin on his face.

After showing her date around the first floor, Simone introduced Erica to Seth, Lucy, Nina, and their partners. Sweet, bubbly Erica hit it off with her colleagues right away, whipping out photos of her dog, Greta, in the Hanukkah sweater she'd knit her by hand. "She's half-Chihuahua, half-dachshund," Erica explained, "also known as a chiweenie."

"Stop." Seth was cackling. "I'm obsessed." Lucy's wife, Holly, was already pulling up photos of Cheddar, Gouda, and Blue in Santa costumes.

Meanwhile, Lucy sidled over to Simone. "What's wrong?" she whispered.

"Nothing," Simone said quickly. "Why?"

"You seem stressed out."

No shit I'm stressed out! I was on a quest to live my best queer life when I ended up having the hottest sex ever with a straight, IPA-drinking, flannel-wearing carpenter man, and now he's all I can think about.

Simone had texted Lucy from Whistler when she and Ryan finally started getting along, but she'd intentionally kept their hookup a secret, and she had no plans to change that. Yes, Lucy had lovingly supported her through tough stuff before, but that was exactly why Simone *didn't* want to tell her the truth. Lucy had put so much time and energy into guiding her through the aftermath of coming out. Simone feared it would feel like a slap in the face for her to turn around and suddenly admit she was lusting after a straight guy. Worse, Lucy might start to wonder whether Simone was genuinely queer, or if she'd only claimed the bisexual label to fit in at her new job. Or to seem edgy. And what if those things were actually *true*, and Simone wasn't even bi to begin with? She looked at Erica. Her date was kind, and outgoing, and beautiful, and yet . . .

Her pulse pounded as she cast around for something to say to her friend. "It's just a little warm in here." Lucy arched an eyebrow, but Simone wasn't going to crack. "I'm gonna grab some water. Erica, you want me to grab you a water?"

Erica turned to her, smiled, and looped an arm through Simone's. "I'll come with."

"We'll be back in a minute."

"All righty then," Lucy said.

Erica hugged Simone close to her side as they navigated their way around the ball pit to the makeshift bar. She smelled like rose petals again. Simone reminded herself it was normal not to be totally head over heels for someone right away. She'd straight-up despised Ryan when she'd first met him, and look where *they'd* ended up.

Great. Now she was thinking about Ryan again.

She and Erica were waiting for their waters when someone else placed an order from behind Simone.

"Can I get the IPA please? Thanks."

She knew that deep voice. Knew the way it reverberated in her chest and turned her insides to molten lava.

Simone spun around—and thought she might pass out. She hadn't been prepared for the life-altering experience that was seeing Ryan Foley in semiformal attire. He'd swapped his usual flannel and denim for a wool sports coat and slacks; under the jacket, he wore a white shirt with no tie and the top two buttons undone. As if she'd needed a reminder that she'd seen and touched his spectacular bare chest.

"Simone—hey." She caught the way his eyes flitted down her body and back up again.

"Ryan. Oh my God." Suddenly, she really *was* too hot. "I thought you were in Barrie this weekend."

"My moms both woke up with sore throats today, so we had to postpone."

"Oh! I'm sorry to hear that." *Was* she, though? No, she was not—that is, until she snapped back to reality and remembered she was here with a date.

Erica turned around with their water glasses in hand. She handed one to Simone, then looked at Ryan, then looked back at Simone, like she was waiting for an introduction. Simone suddenly wished her water glass was full of vodka. Or bleach. "Erica, this is Ryan, the Rainbow Museum's head carpenter. He and his team built pretty much everything you see here . . . and he was with me on that Whistler Pride trip I was telling you about." Simone turned to Ryan, dying on the inside. "Ryan, this is Erica, my . . ."

Her words got stuck in her throat, but Erica swooped in. "It's our second date," she said brightly.

Simone saw it: the exact millisecond when Erica's words hit

Ryan. He quickly regained his composure, but she hadn't missed the way his jaw had tensed, as though the news had physically stung. "Oh," he said. "Nice."

Erica plowed onward, evidently oblivious to the charge crackling in the air. "How did you like Whistler?" she asked Ryan. "Simone said the trip was absolutely amazing."

"It was," Ryan replied, but not to Erica. His eyes were locked on Simone's. Simone stared back, convinced she saw a longing there that matched hers. A longing with a heavy dose of hurt. She wondered if he'd been thinking of her the way she'd been thinking of him. If he'd come with her face in his mind, her name on his lips.

"I'm from LA, so I didn't grow up skiing," Erica went on. "I'd love to learn at some point. Simone, maybe you could teach me."

"Sure," Simone said, but a second too late and an octave too high. Erica shot a curious glance at Simone, then at Ryan, then at Simone again.

Ryan cleared his throat. "Well, I see a few other people I know, so I'm gonna go and say hi. Erica, it was nice to meet you, and Simone . . . it was great to see you."

She knew what Ryan's real smile looked like. She'd seen it in Whistler a handful of times, like when they'd both fallen into the tree well. This was not Ryan's real smile: an expression so pinched it was almost a grimace. She couldn't bear to look at him any longer, so she spoke to her water glass instead.

"It was great to see you, too!" Simone was so tightly wound that her voice came out as a squeak. She looked up and watched him go, waiting for a wave of relief that never came. Her eyes glued to Ryan's back, she wasn't aware of the chasm of awkward silence stretching between her and Erica until her date attempted to fill it.

"This water was much needed."

"Mm-hmm." Simone drained the rest of her glass.

"Um . . . do you want to keep hanging out here? Or should we go back to your friends?"

Simone wanted option C: Chase after Ryan. But she would never—not with Erica here as her date. Instead, she chose option D: space. "Actually, would you mind hanging with Lucy and Seth for a few minutes while I run to the washroom? I won't be long."

"Are you okay?" Erica was looking at her curiously again.

"Yeah, totally. Just—water!" She held up her empty glass. "Sometimes my bladder is teeny-tiny." Who was she and where were these words coming from?

Erica arched an eyebrow. "Okay."

Simone stormed past the mirror with its positive affirmations and locked herself in a stall. She sat on the crinkly seat cover, staring at the door, hating her life. The point of sleeping with him in Whistler had been to get him out of her system, not to wind up aching for him every second of every day since. How had a single hookup made her *this* obsessed with Ryan Foley, to the point where she didn't want to open herself up to anyone else?

And then the reality dawned on her—or maybe, like the fact of her queerness, it already had, and she was just now admitting it to herself. The truth was, there was so much more she wanted to explore with Ryan Foley. More than a single night of sex could possibly satisfy.

She was just starting to register the depth of her desire when the washroom door swung open and shut. "Simone?" It was Lucy. Better than Erica, but still not someone she was ready to talk to about everything she was feeling.

"Hey," she called back. "What's up?"

"I came to check on you."

"I'm fine."

"You don't sound fine. Will you come out and talk to me? I'm worried about you."

She knew Lucy wouldn't back down. Simone could either talk to her friend or avoid the conversation and live in a toilet stall for the rest of her life. She flushed and opened the door. Lucy was facing her, leaning against the counter with her arms crossed. "Hi," she said pointedly.

"Hi," Simone murmured as she slunk to the counter and turned on the faucet.

Lucy ducked to make sure the other stalls were empty before she carried on. "With all due respect, what is going *on* with you? You were acting weird before you went to the bar, and now I have Erica telling me you've been in the washroom for a long time, and she doesn't know what's up." Lucy turned around so she could see Simone's face in the mirror. Their eyes met in the glass, and Lucy lowered her voice. "Erica also said the two of you had a super awkward interaction with Ryan."

Simone peered down at her soapy hands. Her neck and ears were on fire, which meant she must be turning red.

"Is this about Ryan?" Lucy asked.

Reluctantly, Simone nodded.

Lucy sighed. "I thought you guys had been getting along."

"We have."

"Then what's going—"

"Luce, we hooked up."

When Simone found Lucy in the mirror again, her friend's jaw was hanging open. "Excuse me? You hooked up? Where? When? How was it? Oh my God, I have forty gazillion questions."

"Isn't Erica wondering where the heck I am?"

"She was, but then she and Holly started nerding out *hard* on pet sweaters, so I feel like she's probably okay for a little while longer."

"Okay, that's good."

"So, you and Ryan."

"Me and Ryan."

"I need to know everything, please."

Simone hoisted herself onto the counter, legs dangling off the edge, the way she and her friends would sit and gossip in the washroom between classes. She told Lucy everything—or *almost* everything, sparing her the more graphic details of their night in Vancouver. "It was the best sex I've ever had in my life, Luce," she whispered, "and now I can't stop thinking about him."

Lucy clutched her chest. "Simone Whitaker, why are you only telling me this now?"

She gazed up at the ceiling and sighed. At this point, she might as well be honest. "I was scared."

"Of what?"

"I didn't want you to think I was secretly straight." When she looked at Lucy again, her friend was staring at her like she'd just said something utterly absurd, which—now that Simone had spoken the words out loud—maybe she had.

"Believe it or not, I'm aware that 'bisexual' means 'attracted to multiple genders,' which includes men." Lucy smiled sympathetically and squeezed Simone's shoulder. "I know you, Simone, and I know you're queer. I'd never question that for a second. I mean, look at you, torn between a hot guy and a gorgeous woman at the same party. Pure bisexual chaos right there."

Simone let out a laugh that was closely followed by a groan. "Luce, Erica's amazing, and I *wanted* it to work out with her. I really did." She paused. "But I don't think I'm done with Ryan yet."

"Oh, Simone."

"I don't know what I should do, though. I just came out. My whole mission was to be with women—not a straight guy." She slumped against the wall.

Lucy put a hand on her knee. "If Ryan feels the same way, you should go for it."

"You think so?" Simone was more tentative. "I literally just came out—"

"Simone, the magical thing about being queer is that you don't have to follow the rules. You get to invent them. You get to follow your heart."

Simone laughed weakly. "Even if my heart wants a straight guy?"

"Yes, Simone: even if your queer little heart wants a straight guy."

~

ERICA AND HOLLY WERE DEEP IN an animated conversation when Simone and Lucy returned to the party. *At least Erica got a new friend out of tonight*, Simone thought, but it still didn't ease her guilt. When Erica noticed her making her way through the crowd, she frowned, as though she already had a sense of what was about to transpire.

"There you are," Erica said.

"Can we talk for a minute?" Simone nodded to the side, indicating they should go someplace quieter than the lively atrium.

"That sounds like a good idea."

Simone led her to the hallway with the rainbow stripes and the timeline of queer history on the walls, stopping in front of the plaque for the Brunswick Four, a group of lesbians who, in 1974, were kicked out of a Toronto bar and eventually arrested after they performed a song at amateur night called "I Enjoy Being a

Dyke." What a place to be breaking things off with a woman so she could go and pursue a straight guy. It seemed absurd to be doing this, after everything she'd been through to get here—like she was coming up on the finish line of a marathon, and she was randomly deciding to peel off the path. But it also felt like the right thing to do—like she would always regret not exploring what was down this way, even if it led her nowhere.

Simone took a deep breath. "Sorry I disappeared for so long back there. I've been going through some emotional stuff and I feel really bad for dragging you into it."

Erica crossed her arms. "Is everything okay?"

"It's been really nice getting to know you, but I don't think I feel that romantic connection I'm looking for. I'm so sorry."

"Simone, it's fine." She shrugged. "I mean, yeah, it sucks, but it's okay if you're not into me."

"You're an awesome person," Simone said reassuringly.

"I know—and you're missing out," Erica fired back. But then she cracked a smile, and Simone realized she wasn't mad. "Seriously, it's okay. I'm still happy I came tonight. I think Holly and I are gonna meet up and knit together."

"I love that."

"One door closes, another opens, right? Anyway, good luck with finding what you're looking for."

"You, too."

They exchanged a polite hug goodbye, and then Erica was gone. Simone breathed a sigh of relief, only to tense up again as she pulled out her phone. The most nerve-wracking part of her evening hadn't even begun. She called Ryan's number, praying he was still at the party. She hadn't spotted him since she'd emerged from the washroom, and Ryan Foley was hard to miss.

He answered on the first ring. "Simone."

"Are you still here?" she asked.

"Yeah."

"Can we talk?"

"About what?"

"I want to do it in person."

He paused. "I'm in the workshop."

"I'm coming."

She made a beeline for the elevator and jabbed the button for the basement. When she got off, she was briefly disoriented by the fact that the lights were off, but she remembered where she'd gone that one day with Frankie, and hurried around the corner to the workshop.

It was dark in there, too, but a single lamp cast a warm circle of light over the wooden table in the center of the room. Ryan leaned back against the table in his crisp white button-down, his jacket cast to the side, with his head hanging low and his hands clasped behind his neck, like he couldn't bear the weight of his own thoughts.

"Hey," she said.

Ryan glanced up, moved his hands from the back of his neck to the tops of his thighs, then looked back down at the floor. She could see from the doorway that his quads were braced—that every muscle in his body was taut. "Hey."

"What are you doing down here?"

"Nothing. I just needed space."

"Can I . . . come in?"

"Sure."

With shallow breaths, she treaded lightly toward the table, stopping an arm's length from Ryan.

"What did you want to talk about?" he asked.

"I have a problem," she said.

"What is it?"

"I can't stop thinking about you."

Ryan was quiet, and it was hard to read his expression in the dim light of the workshop. *Shit*. She was probably making him uncomfortable. "Actually, never mind," she backpedaled, flailing her hands as she talked. "I shouldn't have even brought it up. We agreed to make this a one-night thing 'cause it's better for both of us and—"

He caught one of her wrists in midair. "Simone."

"What?"

She heard him swallow. "There is no world in which seeing you on a date with someone else is 'better' for me."

"What do you mean?" she asked, her voice raspy all of a sudden.

"I mean . . ." Ryan paused. "I can't stop thinking about you, either." For a moment, they stood there in charged silence. He was still holding her wrist. "Your heart," he whispered.

"I know." Every cell in her body throbbed for him, begging for release. With her eyes locked on Ryan's, she took a step closer, silently daring him to do the same.

"Simone." His voice was deeper than she'd ever heard it. A warning. "I'm not going to do this with your date upstairs."

"She isn't here anymore. I told her I didn't think we should keep seeing each other."

"What? When?"

"Just now. I didn't want to lead her on when the truth is, I can't stop thinking about you."

She inched forward again, and now she was close enough to hear his ragged breathing, to know for certain that he was as desperate for her as she was for him. "I don't know if this is a good idea," Ryan said, and Simone froze.

"Why not?"

Now that she was closer, she could see the helplessness in his eyes, too. "Because the more I'm with you, the more I fucking want you. I can't have another—another life-changing fucking night and just go back to normal."

She'd never ached for him the way she did on the word *life-changing*. "And what if you could have me?" she whispered. She moved closer again. "What if we didn't *have* to go back to normal the next day?"

He furrowed his brow. "What are you saying?"

"I'm saying . . . what if we actually tried seeing where this goes?"

The lines in his forehead disappeared, and he blew out a long jet of air. Her own breaths were quick and shallow, like rocks skipping on the surface of a lake.

"The more I'm with you, the more I want you, too, but being without you isn't any easier," she went on. *I literally had to leave the gym for fear of orgasming on the stationary bike.* Now they were close enough that she could smell the pine needles.

"You really want to try this?" he asked quietly. "Because if we do—I need to know you mean it. I trusted someone before, thought it meant something—and it didn't. I can't do that again."

"I really do."

His palm found its way to her cheek, and he kissed her. Softly at first. Simone put her hands in his hair, knotting them into his curls, and pulled him in, deepening the kiss. A fire burned in her core and Ryan was the kindling, the oxygen, all of it. She needed more of him. She parted her lips. When their tongues met, she could *feel* his low moan of relief. The vibrations filled her mouth, awakened her whole being.

After a minute or two or ten—what was time when she was kissing Ryan?—she pulled back, gasping for air.

"Is everything okay?" he asked.

"If we don't stop now, I'm worried I'll make you lay me down on this table and go to work."

He cocked an eyebrow. "Would that be so bad?"

"I'd like to not get fired for having sex at the office," she teased. He smiled and leaned his forehead against hers.

"I was thinking," she mused. "Would you want to go out on a date?"

"Oh wow. We've never done that before."

"Wild."

"I'd love to," he said. "When were you thinking?"

It was only nine o'clock on a Friday night, and the launch party had to be winding down soon. "How's now?"

~

THE CAR DROPPED THEM OFF OUTSIDE a freestanding brick building near the lake. There was an empty patio out front with picnic tables and string lights, but Simone could hear voices and soft folk music coming from inside. A Canadian flag and a Pride flag hung in the window. "What is this place?" she asked. Ryan had called the car for them, insisting he knew the perfect spot for them to go.

"The best brewery in the city," he answered.

Simone smiled and rolled her eyes as they crunched across the gravel. "Of *course* you brought me to a brewery."

Ryan smirked back at her, his face glowing in the string lights. Simone wondered how it was scientifically possible for a human to be that handsome. He opened the door for her. "Welcome to the Common Loon."

They were in a warm, bright space that was all wood inside, like a cabin. The air smelled like pine and fresh bread. There was a long wooden bar with a dozen or so taps, and a chalkboard with the names of the beers written out by hand. People were wearing sweaters and jeans, sneakers and baseball caps. Simone and Ryan stood out in their party attire, and it wasn't long before they were spotted by the bartender, who wore a toque and a T-shirt that said COMMON LOON BREWERY.

The man's face lit up. "Hey, buddy! I didn't think I'd see you tonight. Thought you were gonna be in Barrie."

"The moms got colds." Ryan led Simone to the other end of the bar, nodding and waving to a few patrons along the way. They grabbed two stools and shimmied up to the bar as the bartender slid two coasters in front of them. "Simone, this is Dom," Ryan said. "We went to high school together and now he owns the brewery. Dom, this is Simone. We went to Whistler together."

Dom raised his eyebrows knowingly. He had a firm handshake and a bunch of tattoos climbing up the medium-brown skin of his arm. "Dom," Simone repeated. The name had jogged something in her memory. "He mentioned you the first day we skied together."

"Good things, I hope."

She smirked. "He assured me you'd *also* been calling him out for acting like a miserable gargoyle of late."

Dom turned to Ryan, grinning. "You were right. I *do* like her."

Simone blushed. "You told him about me?" she asked Ryan.

Now Ryan looked embarrassed, too. "I might have called him from Whistler for help with my apology."

"I heard the first couple of tries didn't go so well," Dom said.

Ryan shook his head. "No, no they did not."

Simone squeezed his shoulder. "You got there in the end. Thank you, Dom, for your service." Dom jokingly saluted her. "This place is amazing," she added, gesturing around at the cozy interior of the brewery.

Dom waggled his eyebrows. "Guess who did all the carpentry?"

She turned back to Ryan, impressed. "No way."

He nodded humbly at Dom. "Anything for this guy."

"Oh, stop, you just wanted a lifetime of free beer," Dom teased. "Speaking of which, what are you guys drinking tonight?"

They placed their orders and Dom returned with their drinks. "Cheers," he said, before dashing off to the other end of the bar, where a large group had just walked in.

"You wanna try the IPA?" Ryan asked. "It's my favorite of all time."

"Your favorite IPA of all the IPAs? That's saying something."

He slid his pint glass across the lacquered wooden bar that he'd built for Dom. She took a sip and wrinkled her nose. Ryan chuckled.

"It's so bitter." She preferred the wheat beer she'd ordered—sweeter, with a hint of banana—but what she liked best of all was that Ryan had offered her a taste. All of a sudden, Simone gasped and nearly fell off her metal barstool. A giant orange furball had just leapt onto the bar, landing inches from where they were sitting. "Um . . ." She whipped her head toward Dom, but he didn't seem remotely alarmed that a cat had just materialized in front of them.

Ryan laughed again. "Don't worry, that's just Loonie. He lives here."

"Really?"

"Dom found him in the basement when he bought the building. Now the whole staff takes care of him. I'm sure it's against some health code, but no one seems to care. C'mere, Loons." He held out a hand, and Loonie strutted over. Ryan scratched the spot between the cat's ears. Loonie closed his eyes and purred like a lawnmower. When Simone first met Ryan, she never would have believed he had a gentle side. A side that loved animals, and took his moms out to birthday dinners, and did massive carpentry projects out of love for his friend.

The brewery closed at midnight. When Dom announced last call at eleven thirty, Simone turned to Ryan and said, "I don't want this night to be over."

"It doesn't have to be," he told her.

Dom refused to let them pay, but Ryan covertly stuffed a handful of cash into the tip jar on their way out. He held the door open for Simone, and they walked outside to the porch. Their driver was a minute away.

Simone shivered in the February air. She'd worn her black leather jacket tonight, which was a lot more fashionable than her parka, but nowhere near as warm.

"Come," Ryan said, opening his arms. She walked straight into his chest, pressed her cheek to the soft wool of his coat. Beneath the fabric, she felt the firm rise and fall of his pecs. He wrapped her in a warm hug, pulling her in close as she threaded her arms around his waist. Ryan kissed the top of her head. "I can make you some tea when we get home, if you want."

Simone nodded. She wanted that very much.

Ryan's place was closer, so that was where they went. He lived on the top floor of a taxpayer building on Queen Street East, above a bakery with a pink-and-white-striped awning.

"Is this a constant thing? The chocolate chip cookie smell?" she asked as they climbed the staircase.

"Sometimes it's more of a cinnamon roll vibe."

"Wow, lucky you." Simone lived in a sterile new build that smelled like whatever they used to clean the carpets.

Ryan took out his key. "Just so you know, it's still a work in progress."

"Did you move in recently?"

"After the breakup."

Duh. "Sorry—right. I didn't realize you and your ex had been living together."

"Yeah."

Simone felt a sudden pang of jealousy—sharp, irrational, and totally unwelcome. She hated the idea of him living with someone else. The feeling caught her off guard, but it quickly gave way to sadness for Ryan. She couldn't begin to imagine how awful it would feel to be betrayed by someone you loved enough to move in with. She felt bad that she'd darkened the mood, so she went on her tiptoes and kissed him right there on the landing. "Well, I'm excited to see your new space."

When he opened the door, she smelled sawdust instead of chocolate chip cookies, and when he flicked on the light, she understood why.

He'd turned his entire living space into a woodworking shop. Where there could have been a dining area, he'd instead put a wooden worktable and a single metal stool. An elaborate wooden storage unit spanned the length of an exposed-brick wall, with designated spots for saws, wrenches, pliers, hammers, drills, and other tools she didn't know the names of. On a different wall, rulers and levels hung neatly from a pegboard, beneath which sat a bright orange shop vacuum. The only surfaces not occupied by carpentry-related items were the kitchen countertops and the windowsills, where different plants grew in no-frills terra-cotta pots. She liked the controlled chaos of it all, whereas her own apartment was neat but also kind of sparse. Ryan's home felt more lived-in than hers did, even though he'd only actually lived here for a couple of months.

"This is so cool," she said as she took off her leather jacket. "It never would have even occurred to me that you could do this with an apartment."

"Thanks." He took her coat and hung it on a standing wooden coatrack.

"Let me guess, you built that?"

Ryan smirked.

"You really are impressive."

"What kind of tea can I make you?"

"Anything herbal would be great."

"How's peppermint?"

"Peppermint's perfect."

While Simone grabbed a stool at the kitchen counter, Ryan grabbed a kettle and filled it. It wasn't the plug-in kind, like Simone had, but an old-fashioned-looking metal one that went on the stove.

"I'll do peppermint, too," he said, fishing the teabags from the pantry and dropping them into two ceramic mugs. While they waited for the water to boil, Ryan disappeared to the bedroom to put away his shoes and hang up his jacket, while Simone scanned the room for more details that she hadn't noticed yet. A spice rack that appeared to be handcrafted (of course) held dozens of little jars, some with names she'd never heard before, like nigella seed and fennel pollen. Next to the spice rack were a knife block and a utensil holder with a whisk, tongs, spoons, and a spatula.

"You cook," she said when he returned to the room.

"I do."

"What do you like to make?"

"Honestly, I like experimenting. It's like carpentry, where I get to be creative and make stuff by hand."

"Meanwhile, I make the same five recipes on repeat."

"Whoa. They must be good ones."

She snorted. "Not even. It's like, chicken and fish with different combinations of rice, pasta, and vegetables. Boring."

He laughed. "Then why do you keep making them?"

"Because I know I won't screw them up."

Ryan stroked his chin. "I think you should cook with me sometime. Let me take you out of your comfort zone."

"Oh yeah? You'll teach me your chaotic ways?"

"It would be my pleasure." The kettle whistled. He filled their mugs and passed one to Simone, who cupped it in her chilly palms.

She sipped her tea. It warmed her from the inside out, and her body relaxed in a way it hadn't since she'd woken up this morning. She felt like she'd lived a whole week in a day. A yawn came on so suddenly that she didn't even have time to cover her mouth.

"Tired?"

"Extremely." She loved how honest she could be with Ryan. He, of all people, would understand if she wasn't in a perfect mood all the time. Although she *was* happy—just exhausted.

"You're welcome to sleep here, just so you know."

Simone smiled. "Good, 'cause I was planning on it." She yawned again, this one so big it made her eyes water. "The only thing is, I don't know how much fun I'm going to be tonight," she said as an apology in advance. She wanted so badly to have sex with him again, but she also wanted to have enough energy to enjoy it.

"We don't have to have sex," Ryan said matter-of-factly. Simone's cheeks flushed hotter than the tea. Ryan talking about *not* having sex was somehow just as hot as if he'd talked about having it. *Because it's hot that he wants to take care of you*, Simone realized. "I just want you to be comfortable here," he said.

They carried their mugs into the bedroom, where Ryan went to the dresser. "Lemme find you something to sleep in." While Ryan dug through his T-shirt collection, Simone peered around his cozy den of a bedroom. The queen-size bed had a brown tufted quilt with a plaid wool throw, and Simone had a feeling she would never want to get out once she burrowed beneath the blankets.

He handed her an old T-shirt and a pair of shorts, and she carried them into the bathroom to get changed. Yes, they'd already seen each other naked, but that was when they'd thought they'd never see each other naked again; naturally, they'd ripped each other's clothes off. Now, there was no time limit on exploring their feelings. It made her want to take her time. She took off the dress she'd worn to the launch party and pulled Ryan's T-shirt over her head. It was impossibly soft and smelled like him.

Back in the bedroom, Ryan had swapped the overhead light for the soft glow of the bedside lamp. He'd changed into boxers and nothing else. "If I wasn't so tired, I would . . . I would . . ." She covered her mouth with the back of her hand to suppress another enormous yawn.

"You would . . . ?"

When she'd recovered, she finished: "I would climb you like a tree."

"Don't worry," he said, smirking, "we'll have plenty more time for tree climbing later."

She grabbed a scrunchie from her bag and wound her curls

into a loose topknot. Then they wriggled under the covers, and Simone realized she'd been right: She never wanted to leave this bed for as long as she lived. Ryan turned off the bedside lamp. She moved over to him, and he lifted his arm, and she wriggled into his side. She yawned again. She fell asleep in what felt like a matter of seconds, with her cheek to Ryan's chest.

CHAPTER 16

SHE AWOKE TO HIS LIPS ON the back of her neck.

She'd gotten up to use the washroom a couple of times during the night—the perils of having a hot man make you peppermint tea before bed. Every time she'd crawled back under the covers, Ryan had reached through the fog of sleep to pull her close to him again, as though his body knew it needed her on some instinctive, subconscious level. Most recently, when she'd come back to bed around six, he'd rolled onto his side and made her his little spoon. Evidently, neither of them had moved as dawn became morning and sunlight started to peek through the slats of the blinds.

"Mmmmm." Simone hadn't woken up enough to form coherent words, but she wanted to let him know that his mouth back there felt divine, and actually, if he could keep on doing that for the rest of time, she'd really appreciate it.

Ryan exhaled with his own sigh of pleasure, then returned his lips to her neck. Every kiss was featherlight but made her core ache with pleasure, and she pressed herself into the curve of his body, begging for more.

The hard ridge pressing back told her exactly what Ryan wanted. It would have been easy for Simone to reach back and wrap her hand around his cock. Too easy. She'd learned in Vancouver that Ryan liked to work for his reward, and she rather enjoyed telling him just what he had to do to get it.

This morning, she would show him. She rolled over and put a hand on the solid mass of his shoulder, guiding him onto his back. They locked eyes at her touch—a wordless exchange that made electricity zip down her spine. How many times in the past few weeks had she fantasized about Ryan being at her mercy again?

She pushed the quilt below their waists, revealing the bulge in Ryan's boxers that was begging to be free. *Not yet.* She wriggled out of her own shorts, Ryan watching reverently as she bared herself in the morning light. She slowly pulled her T-shirt off next.

He let out a sigh as she straddled him—a breathy tangle of pleasure and want. His cock was still restrained by the fabric of his boxers, and when she lowered her hips to graze his bulge, his sigh deepened to a full-body groan. She moved herself along his firm ridge again, teasing him more. She slowly increased the pressure, rubbing her clit against his erection, using him for her pleasure, the way she knew he wanted to be used.

When her clit couldn't take the teasing anymore, she knew what she had to do next. She slowly crawled forward. Grabbing the wooden headboard, she raised her upper body and knelt over his mouth. He wet his lips, hungry for her, and stared up from between her thighs as if to say, *Please*.

She was already close to coming from the look on his face alone. His vulnerability unleashed a power between her legs she'd never known was there. She gingerly lowered herself onto his eager mouth, and gasped with pleasure as his hot tongue slipped inside her. *Oh . . . my . . . God*. Pleasure rolling through her, she realized just how much of a shame it would have been to go the rest of her life without experiencing Ryan's oral skills again. Talk about depriving herself.

She was hesitant to put her full weight on him at first, until he asked her for it, taking hold of her ass and pulling her all the way down, so he could press his tongue deeper inside her when he wanted to—when he wasn't doing otherworldly things to her clit . . .

When she knew she was close to the edge, she leaned back, reaching for his waistband. She caught it and gave it a tug. *"Off,"* she whispered. In one swift motion, he let go of her ass, pulled off his boxers, and returned his hands to where they'd just been—all without stopping his tongue. "You're so good," she said, stroking his hair.

Now, at last, was the time. Ryan had earned it. Simone reached back and found his cock, so hard she could feel it throbbing when she gripped it in her palm. He moaned when she finally touched him there, moaned into her pussy, so she felt the vibrations in her core. Oh God, she was so close.

Some men might have stopped working the moment their cock was in her hand, but not Ryan. He ate her out with renewed fervor, every swirl of his tongue a thank-you for the work she was doing on him . . .

"I'm right there," she whispered.

As she tipped over the edge, she felt the muscles tense in his shaft, and he moaned into her again. Ryan was coming, too—coming with his cock in her hand and his face in her pussy—and Simone was dizzy from the power and pleasure of it all.

She let Ryan shower first, given the mess he'd made of his chest. When it was Simone's turn, Ryan popped downstairs to the bakery and returned with coffees and croissants. Wait, no—this wasn't just a regular coffee, Simone realized as she raised the cup to her lips and caught a whiff of the warm beverage within.

"Did you get us . . ."

Ryan's lips quirked into that signature smirk that drove her wild. "Maple spice lattes? Yes, I did."

She could have dragged him back to bed then and there.

Instead, they had their breakfast at the kitchen counter that doubled as a dining table, and *then* she dragged him back to bed.

Simone had always liked sex, but until Ryan, she hadn't known just how spectacular it could be. Ryan seemed to be his most satisfied when he was giving Simone pleasure—when he was proving himself useful to her. And Simone would never get tired of being his proving ground. She reveled in it, even, tapping into the dominant side she hadn't even known she had until she hooked up with Ryan that first time in Vancouver. For all the time they spent in bed, they still hadn't had penetrative sex. Simone was enjoying taking things slowly, making him work for his prize, and Ryan was evidently enjoying it, too. She'd never been with a man who'd gotten hard from the mere taste of her. Even Bree had been a bit of a pillow princess, if Simone was being honest.

They spent the whole weekend at Ryan's, moving between the bedroom and the kitchen. When they were hungry again, he improvised the perfect wintry stew using frozen ground turkey, a butternut squash, and an assortment of beans from the pantry. Simone zipped down to the bakery to get some bread to go with it, and ended up returning with four different varieties of rolls and baguettes. She fanned them out on the counter while Ryan ladled stew into bowls. "They all looked so good," she said. "I couldn't choose."

"Who said you had to choose?"

Simone grinned.

They ate them all.

~

ON MARCH ELEVENTH, SIMONE TURNED THIRTY. It was a Wednesday, and her parents called her first thing in the morning, before work. Simone was in her bedroom, inspecting her outfit in the full-length mirror, when she answered the phone.

"Happy birthday, darling," her mother simpered.

"Thanks, Mom."

"Thirty! Wow. I can't believe it. I remember when you were just a baby. Simone, one second. Your father's here, too. George—George, Simone's on the phone. Yes, right now."

"SIMONE?"

"You don't need to yell, George. She's on speakerphone."

"HAPPY BIRTHDAY," George yelled. "THIRTY'S A BIG ONE."

"Thanks, Dad," Simone said, laughing.

Ever since Kathy's low-key homophobic reaction to Simone's coming-out post, her parents had been engaging in the time-honored WASP tradition of not discussing feelings whatsoever, and Simone had to say, she wasn't mad about it. This morning, they talked about the weather down in Florida, then the weather in Toronto, then how the overall climates of Florida and Toronto compared to each other. Then they moved on to pickleball. Was it boring small talk? Sure! But at least no one was sobbing over the "hard life" she was doomed to live as a queer woman.

After precisely ten minutes, Kathy started to wrap things up. "Well, darling, we'll let you get back to your day! Are you off to work?"

"Yep."

"Things at the . . . at the museum—they're going well?"

Simone's heart skipped a beat. "They are," she said brightly, surprised her mother had ventured anywhere near the subject of Simone's identity. "They're going really well. We're open to the public now, and there's been a line down the block every day."

"Wonderful! George, isn't that great?"

"THAT'S GREAT, HON."

"George, you're going to give me a headache," her mother hissed. "Anyway, darling, we just wanted to tell you . . ." Kathy paused, and Simone thought, *Oh no, here it comes*. ". . . we're very proud of you," her mother finished.

Wait, what? "Thanks, Mom," Simone said softly. When she looked at herself in the mirror again, her eyes were glassy.

Today was going to be a good day.

She could feel it.

At work, Lucy surprised Simone by coming in early and decorating her desk with balloons, Seth brought in homemade black sesame Rice Krispies squares, and Nina got everyone in the office to sign a card with a picture of a skiing penguin on the front. Simone felt so lucky to have them all as friends.

Most of all, she felt lucky to have Ryan. At six o'clock on the dot, she closed her laptop, put on her coat, and hurried downstairs. Ryan was standing outside the Rainbow Museum in his Carhartt jacket, holding a bouquet of pink peonies. Her favorite.

"Hey, you. Happy bir—" He didn't finish getting the words out before Simone threw her arms around his neck and kissed him. His arms encircled her waist, pulling her as close to his chest as their bulky outerwear would allow.

Simone thanked him for the beautiful peonies, and they walked arm in arm to a Greek restaurant that Ryan had picked out for them. The place was small and cozy, with white stucco walls and candlelit wooden tables painted blue. When they sat down, she caught Ryan studying the shape of the table legs.

"You want to know something I really like about you?"

He looked up, cocked an eyebrow. "What?"

"The way you appreciate tiny artistic details I would never even *think* to notice." Ryan's expression melted into a smile. "It's why you're so good at what you do."

"That's really nice of you."

"It's the truth," she insisted. "How was school today?"

"School" was the new project Ryan had recently begun at a private school in the Beaches. Between that and the custom furniture orders he'd been taking, Ryan's carpentry business was booming, and she couldn't have been happier for him. They caught each other up on work that day and ordered a carafe of white wine.

They held up their glasses.

"To a delightful fucking sunflower," he teased.

"Damn right," she said, laughing.

They clinked glasses.

"So," Ryan said, his voice becoming more serious, "there's something I've been wanting to talk about." Her heart jumped into her throat like it had been launched out of a catapult. "Something good," he added quickly.

She watched the bob of his Adam's apple and tried to swallow, herself. It was impossible.

"I really like you, Simone."

"I really like you, too."

"The past few weeks have been incredible."

"I know."

Ryan looked deep into her eyes. The candle that flickered between them made the green around his irises look more like gold. Every inch of Simone's body pulsed with the beat of her heart. Ryan took one slow, steady breath. "I want you to be my girlfriend."

Simone didn't have to think twice about how to respond. She reached across the table and squeezed his hand. "YES. A thousand times yes." She was grinning so hard that her cheeks hurt.

Ryan's gaze lingered on her face. "You have the most beautiful eyes in the world."

"In the *world*?" she teased. "What if there's some girl out there with eyes like curly maple?"

He shook his head definitively. "In the world."

At the end of the meal, when Ryan fished out his phone to calculate the tip, Simone noticed something on his screen. "Wait," she said, grabbing his wrist, "did you change your wallpaper?"

Ryan smirked. "Maybe."

He passed it across the table so she could take a closer look. Instead of the wavy, orangey wood she'd seen in Whistler, Ryan's background was now a dark brown wood with the slightest hint of purple. "Is this . . . ?"

He nodded. "Walnut."

~

BY FRIDAY MORNING, SIMONE STILL COULDN'T get her dinner with Ryan out of her head. Not that she wanted to. She was a kaleidoscope of butterflies, floating a foot off the ground everywhere she went. Ryan was her boyfriend. She was his girlfriend. *You have the most beautiful eyes in the world.*

"Simone."

Sitting at her desk, she looked up from her phone. She'd been swooning over Ryan's good-morning text and apparently hadn't heard whatever question Seth had just asked her. "Sorry, what was that?"

"I asked if you knew what this all-hands meeting with Frankie was about. The one at ten."

She shook her head. "Not sure." All she knew was that the meeting was titled "PRIDE!!!," which was why she wasn't freaking out about a mysterious all-hands meeting on a Friday. That and the fact that the Rainbow Museum had been killing it since opening its doors to the public, and it seemed highly unlikely that anyone was about to lose their job.

Seth nodded at her phone. "You're texting your *boyfriend*, aren't you?" Simone didn't even have to respond out loud; when her cheeks went hot, she knew her fair-skinned ginger genes were doing it for her. Sure enough, Seth flashed a triumphant smile. "You're blushing so hard right now. Are you sexting?"

"NO."

"Because if you are, let me just say, the lighting in the bathroom stalls is surprisingly—"

"Oh my God, we're not sexting."

Seth grinned again. "But you *are* texting him."

Simone broke down and smiled, too. "He's so sweet," she said with a sigh. "He randomly woke up an hour before his alarm and went for a run on the boardwalk, and he took all these amazing photos of the sunrise over the lake."

"I love this slightly chaotic artistic energy for you."

She cocked an eyebrow. "Are you saying I'm uptight?"

"I'm saying I'm pretty sure I've seen you get hives from not being at inbox zero."

Simone laughed, and so did Seth.

"You're bringing him to my party next weekend, right?"

She nodded. "I ordered him a floral-print T-shirt and everything."

"Obsessed."

A week from tomorrow, Seth and his roommate were hosting a house party in honor of the vernal equinox, and the dress code was "spring vibes." Simone didn't know much about astrology, but she *did* know that she was a Pisces and Ryan was a Scorpio, and according to Google, Pisces and Scorpio were "highly compatible signs." Hmm. Maybe she should get more into astrology.

"I'm meeting his moms tonight," she told Seth, whose jaw dropped.

"Way to bury the lede," he shot back. "Since when?"

"Since yesterday." A bolt of nervous energy shot down her spine. "His moms wanted matching tattoos for their fortieth anniversary, and—"

"Oh my God, relationship goals."

"I know."

"I'm telling Claude. Sorry, I interrupted."

She laughed. "It's okay. This tattoo artist they like in Toronto had a last-minute cancellation, and said she could squeeze them in this afternoon. They don't come into the city that much, so Ryan asked if I wanted to meet them, and I said yes."

"Do you really want to?"

"I do," she answered honestly. "I know it's kind of soon, but . . . I don't know. Everything just feels really good."

Seth poked her in the arm. "You're totally obsessed with him."

Simone smirked back but said nothing. She couldn't deny it.

At ten, they joined the rest of the management team around the conference table in Cher. Frankie sat at the head, chugging a

Red Bull and shooting off texts at the same time. When everyone was seated, he put down his phone, shot the empty Red Bull can into the nearest wastebasket, and got down to business. "Good morning, you wonderful people, and happy Friday. I wanted to get us all together so I could share some exciting news about a plan I have in the works for Pride Month."

A current of excitement buzzed around the room.

"So, I think we can all attest to how important it is for queer people to present themselves in a way that matches who they are on the inside."

Several people around the room nodded, Simone included. She'd never felt quite like *herself* in the preppy clothes she'd grown up wearing.

"*Queer expression matters*. That's why, to kick off Pride Month, the Rainbow Museum is going to be hosting"—he drummed his index fingers on the edge of the table—"a queer makeover extravaganza! Picture this." Now he waved his hands around like he was conjuring the event in midair. "We'll offer haircuts. Makeup tutorials. Style consultations. Tattoos. Piercings. Whatever we can do to help guests look as queer as humanly possible. And then we'll have photographers take their portraits around the Rainbow Museum, because there's obviously no better backdrop than here. I'll be following up with each department next week to talk specifics. In the meantime, start thinking about what we can do to make this epic."

They all replied with obedient nods, although Simone wasn't exactly sure what it meant to "look as queer as humanly possible." Someone made a joke that they should exclusively offer septum rings in the piercing department, and laughter rippled around the room. Simone smiled along, but she was suddenly feeling uneasy, wondering if she herself needed some kind of queer makeover.

She pushed the thought from her mind and carried on with her day, focusing instead on how excited she was to see Ryan that night. He would be picking her up from the Rainbow Museum at six, and together they'd head to the Common Loon to meet his moms.

When six o'clock rolled around, the Rainbow Museum was still packed with visitors. They stayed open until nine every day, thanks to the team of guest experience specialists who worked the late shift. When Simone got outside, there was a line of guests stretching down the block, but her eyes went straight to one person.

Her boyfriend spread his arms, beckoning her in for a hug. But Simone wanted more than a hug; it had been over twenty-four hours since she'd last seen Ryan. She approached him at a run and then she leapt onto him, wrapping her arms around his neck and her legs around his waist the way couples always greeted each other on *The Bachelor*. Ryan caught her and held her there like it was no big deal, and Simone kissed him as a means of hello.

Then she heard faint voices coming from behind her:

"It should be illegal for straights to make out here."

"Seriously. It's, like, a hate crime."

The words zipped through Simone's chest like a laser beam. She pulled out of the kiss and lowered herself to the ground, her body suddenly heavy with shame. She heard the same people snickering and peered over her shoulder to see who it was. A gaggle of twentysomething guys who were attractive in an identical Ken-doll kind of way. As they sneered at Simone, they reminded her of the awful men on Crushr Seth had told her about—the ones who listed so-called sexual preferences on their profiles that were actually straight-up discriminatory, and who'd ultimately driven him off the app entirely. (He and Claude had met the old-fashioned way: by sliding into each other's DMs.)

"Why are those guys looking at us like that?" Ryan asked.

She turned back to Ryan. "I dunno," she lied. "Maybe they're weird about PDA." Simone looped her arm through Ryan's and tugged him down the sidewalk as quickly as possible, away from the line of Rainbow Museum visitors.

She pulled herself tight to his side as they walked to the next block, where his truck was parked. Ryan steered one-handed, the other hand resting on Simone's thigh. His relaxed, confident driving posture usually turned her on, but right now, she just felt jittery. *Everything's fine*, she mentally hissed at herself.

"I'm excited for you to meet my moms," Ryan said.

"Me, too," Simone answered decisively.

She wasn't going to let a few judgmental strangers ruin her night.

CHAPTER 17

SIMONE SCRATCHED THE HEAD OF THE plump orange cat who was curled up on the bar. "Thanks for guarding my seat, Loonie."

Before she plopped down on the stool she now thought of as "hers," she walked to the end of the bar, where Dom waited to give her a hug. "Loonie's genuinely been guarding that seat. A guy sat down there about an hour ago and got hissed at."

"Loonie!" She feigned disapproval in the brewery cat's direction, but the truth was she loved the idea that Loonie was becoming attached to her, whether or not it was actually true. (Loonie liked anyone who gave him head scratches and snubbed anyone who didn't.) It was another small sign of her life and Ryan's becoming enmeshed, like the toothbrushes and comfy clothes they'd recently started leaving at each other's apartments.

Simone walked back to her stool. The moms were still on their way, and Ryan had run across the street to pick up pizza for the group.

"Got something I want you to try," Dom said, stooping to open the fridge beneath the bar. He emerged holding a can with a dark brown label. "I know you're not usually a stout person, but we're trying out this new one with coffee and orange zest."

"I do love coffee," Simone said.

"That's why I have a feeling you're gonna be into this."

Simone loved that she and Dom were getting closer, too. Over the past few weeks, she'd learned the origin story of Dom and Ryan's friendship. They'd both gone to an expensive private boys' school in the city: Ryan because one of his moms—Claire—was an art teacher there and got a significant discount on tuition; Dom because his parents were loaded ophthalmologists who dreamed of him and his sister following in their footsteps. They bonded in part because they both played baseball, and in part because they both were outsiders in their own way: Ryan was the scholarship kid with lesbian moms, and Dom was one of the only Black kids at a school that skewed awfully white for being in a city as diverse as Toronto. After high school, they lived together in their first year at Queen's University, where Ryan soon realized he had no idea what he was doing pursuing a general arts degree, and that he'd much rather go to carpentry school—which he did the year after. Dom stuck it out for three more years, but when it came time to consider the next steps in his medical career, he confessed to his parents that his *true* dream was to open a brewery. With his sister already in med school, his parents were at least one for two, so they relented and gave their son a small business loan. Ten years later, the Common Loon was doing better than ever. Dom and Ryan were still best friends.

Dom cracked open the can and poured some of the velvety stout into two five-ounce glasses, one for each of them.

"Cheers," he said, passing her a glass.

"Cheers." She took a sip, then raised her eyebrows. It tasted a lot like coffee, but the orange zest made it surprisingly refreshing, too.

"Was I right?" he asked.

"You were *very* right. This is awesome."

"Speaking of awesome . . ." Dom rested his tattooed forearms on the bar and leaned in. "I heard you guys made it official."

Simone grinned and nodded. "He asked me on Wednesday. My birthday."

With a rueful smile, Dom shook his head. "I told him to do it this weekend so that your birthday and anniversary wouldn't be on the same day, and you'd have more days to celebrate. But my boy couldn't wait."

Simone grinned even wider.

Dom went off to serve another customer, then came back her way to continue the conversation. "In all seriousness, though, I just wanna say thank you for everything you've done for him. I didn't know if I'd ever see him this happy again—and definitely not this soon after the shit that went down."

"You don't have to thank me. He makes me just as happy."

"I know, I know, but damn, it was rough watching him go through all that. Losing your girlfriend *and* one of your closest friends at the same time? Just . . . brutal."

Simone paused with her stout halfway to her lips. "Wait, I know about Victoria and the finance bro, but who was the friend?"

"Oh, shit. He said he'd told you about Victoria, so I assumed you knew."

Her heart lurched. She put down the glass without taking a sip. "Knew what?"

Dom's eyes darted to the window and back again. "I don't

know if it's technically my story to share, but I'll tell you this: I lost a close friend last year, too."

She watched him go off to greet another regular, his words churning in her head. It had sounded like the finance bro—the guy Victoria cheated on Ryan with—was one of Ryan and Dom's *close friends*.

Oh God.

She spun her glass in circles, her stomach doing the same. It was bad enough to be betrayed by one person you cared about, but two? No wonder the man had his walls up when they first met.

Her mind flashed to the way she'd reacted to the jerks outside the Rainbow Museum—how she'd practically dragged him down the sidewalk, ashamed to be seen with him. Ryan deserved better. He deserved someone steady. Simone could not, *would* not, be betrayal number three.

A spasm of pain in her temples told her she was clenching her jaw with the force of a trash compactor, so she did one of her go-to stretches to relax it. Sliding a hand through the collar of her shirt, she pressed down on the skin below her collarbone and craned her neck in the opposite direction. She most definitely looked like she was experiencing an exorcism, but whatever. She needed to pull it together and get back to being the bubbly Simone who'd gushed to Seth about her plans tonight.

She turned at the sound of the brewery doors opening. If there were ever a time to get her bubbliness back, it was now. There was Ryan, carrying two pizza boxes, and behind him were two women: one short and sturdy with an edgy silver faux-hawk, the other tall and willowy with elbow-length ash-brown hair. She slapped on a smile and bounced over to meet the moms.

"Hi!" she squealed.

Ryan set the boxes on the corner of the bar. "Mom, Mum, this is Simone. Simone, these are my moms."

The woman with the faux-hawk immediately stepped forward. "Paula," she said in a booming voice, and pulled Simone in for a one-armed hug. "I'd hug ya with both, but . . ." She showed off the clear bandage covering the inside of her forearm.

"The tattoos!" Simone cried. "How did it go?"

"Fantastic. It's hard to see it through the bandage, but she did a phenomenal job. And Claire made the design."

Paula looked at her wife, who stepped forward, holding out a hand to Simone. "It's lovely to meet you, dear. We've heard so much about you from Ry." Her smile was polite, if a bit restrained. Simone felt a flicker of nerves that Claire could somehow see right through her bubbly facade to the writhing bisexual chaos within.

Simone shook her hand, still smiling. "I've heard so much about you, too. Including the fact that you call him Ry, which is adorable."

Simone had expected a laugh, or at least a chuckle, but instead, all she got from Claire was a thank-you. *Tough crowd.* The woman put her hand on Ryan's shoulder. "Should we sit down?"

"Yeah, let's do it," Ryan replied, and led them to one of the round tables.

Simone sat between Ryan and Paula and across from Claire, who thoughtfully nibbled at her pizza while Paula peppered Simone with friendly questions. Simone couldn't help but notice that Claire opened up when *Dom* came over to say hi and grab a slice. She even stood to give him a one-armed hug, like the one Paula had given Simone.

While the moms were busy catching up with Dom, Ryan slid a hand onto Simone's leg. "Is everything okay?"

"Yeah! Why wouldn't it be?"

"You seem . . . chipper."

She knew this was his polite way of saying that something seemed off. "I just want your moms to like me!"

"Simone, of course they do!"

Simone let out a small laugh. "Not sure I'm your mum's cup of tea."

He gave her a small smile. "I think she's just being protective. Especially after . . . you know."

After Victoria cheated on you with one of your closest friends, she thought miserably. She wanted to ask him about it, but not here.

"Stop worrying and just be *you*," he said, and kissed her on the forehead.

Tell that to my spiraling brain.

"Aww, would ya look at these two lovebirds?" Dom teased them from across the table. "Aren't they cute?"

"Adorable," Paula confirmed.

Claire sipped her drink as Dom walked back to the bar.

Under the table, Ryan gave Simone's leg a reassuring squeeze. "Mum," he said to Claire, "you should show Simone the tattoo design."

"Oh. Sure." She pulled up an image on her phone and slid it across the table.

Simone peered at the intricate line drawing and gasped with recognition. "She took me on a picnic for our first date," Paula explained, leaning in to appreciate the drawing, too. "We were down by the lake, and these giant green dragonflies were just . . . everywhere. Landing on our food, on us . . . It was actually a bit creepy."

"Oh, stop, it was romantic," Claire countered, flashing a loving smile at her wife.

Simone turned to Ryan, her heart swelling. "Was this your inspiration for the dragonfly at the Rainbow Museum?"

He nodded.

Claire reached over and squeezed her son's wrist. "We were touched that he gave us a shout-out."

"I bawled when he sent us a photo," Paula said.

"He's the best son in the world," Claire added.

"Okay, okay, that's enough." Ryan chuckled as he rose from his chair. "I'm going to run to the washroom. Be right back."

When he was gone, Simone turned to Paula and Claire. "I don't know if he told you, but that giant dragonfly was the reason we met."

"Yes, he told us," Claire said pointedly.

"Speaking of which, congrats on coming out." Paula patted the back of Simone's hand.

"Thank you," she said, trying to steady her voice as her annoying insecurities reared their heads. A part of her couldn't help wondering if Ryan's moms secretly saw her the way she sometimes feared she was: someone playing at being queer, and not really living it. She was happy with Ryan, but she hadn't yet had the kind of visibly queer relationship she'd dreamed about when she came out, and some days, that felt like a loss. She hated how easily the doubt crept in. And what kind of monster was she anyway, having these thoughts now of all times?

"I'm sure you know this, but he was going through a really tough time when you met," Claire said. Her eyes flitted to Ryan's empty chair. "We weren't sure how he'd pull through."

Guilt clawed at Simone's insides. She nodded solemnly.

Paula patted her hand again. "Don't be sad. He's doing so much better now, thanks to you."

Simone wasn't sure she deserved any thanks at all.

~

RYAN CARESSED HER LEG ON THE drive back to his apartment. "I thought that went well, didn't you?"

"I did, yeah."

Ryan glanced sideways and cocked an eyebrow. "Something on your mind?"

You don't want to know, she thought, chewing her bottom lip. After everything he'd been through, she refused to let him down. "Actually, there *is* something," she said. "When you were out getting pizza, Dom was saying how good it was to see you happy after everything you went through last year. And he mentioned you lost a girlfriend and a good friend at the same time."

The corners of Ryan's mouth wilted.

"I'm sorry," she said quickly. "If you don't want to talk about it—"

"It's okay. It's not some big secret or anything. It just makes me really fucking mad, and—" He cut himself off by clenching his teeth. She saw his jaw muscles bulging in the orange glow of the streetlights.

"We really don't have to talk about it . . ."

Ryan sighed. "No, it's probably good for me. What I was saying before: It makes me really fucking mad, and also . . . humiliated." He paused, stole a sideways glance at Simone. "I told you Victoria cheated on me with a finance bro, right?"

"Yeah."

"Well, that finance bro was this guy Travis. Our best friend—well, *former* best friend—from high school."

"No," she groaned.

He nodded grimly, his eyes on the road. "Victoria and I met

on Hinge around four years ago, I guess? We moved in together around the two-year mark, and I guess it was a year after that when she and Travis started hooking up."

"Did you ever suspect anything?"

"I had no idea. It never would have remotely occurred me, since a) we were living together, so I was under the impression we were both serious about each other; and b) she was doing her residency at the hospital, so she barely had time for *one* relationship.

"So this one night at the start of December, Dom was doing a special event at the brewery—a fundraiser for the food bank." Now that Ryan had started the story, he seemed intent on getting it all out. "Victoria said she couldn't go because she had to cover a shift at the hospital for a friend who'd gotten sick. Then, at the last minute, Travis says he can't make it, either, 'cause he's stuck at some client dinner that's running late.

"Well, the next week, I'm waiting to meet Victoria near the hospital, and I randomly run into her friend—the one who'd supposedly been sick—and I ask how she's feeling, because apparently it was bad enough that Victoria had to cover for her."

"Let me guess," Simone interjected. "She had no idea what the hell you were talking about."

"Worse," Ryan answered. "She was like, 'Wait, what? Victoria was the one who was sick. I covered for *her*.'"

Simone clapped a hand over her open mouth.

"So then the question was: Where had Victoria actually been on the night of Dom's fundraiser?"

She was nauseated. "How did you figure it out?"

"I just asked her, plain and simple. And she came out with it."

"Oh, Ryan."

He was quiet for a moment as he turned onto the side street

where he parked his truck. "In a way, what Travis did was the worst part of it. At the end of the day, I'd known Victoria for a few years, but Travis and I had been friends since we were kids. We were a little trio in high school: me, him, and Dom. We'd go to his family's cottage in the summer, go skiing with Dom's family in the winter. We all lived together that one year I was at Queen's, and he and Dom stayed housemates the whole way through." Ryan pulled up to the curb and shifted into park. "The whole time he and Victoria were seeing each other, he was still texting me and Dom every day, like normal."

"Oh God."

"Yeah."

He turned off the car, and they lapsed into silence, neither of them making a move to get out yet.

"Anyway," he said after a moment, "thank you."

"For what?"

"For making me feel safe enough to give this a chance."

There was the clawing guilt again, its talons even sharper than before. "Of course," she whispered, taking his hand. She was glad it was dark as she did her best impression of a sincere smile.

CHAPTER 18

THE SKY WAS DARK, AND RAIN pelted the windows. It was the following Friday, and Simone was perched on a stool in Ryan's kitchen. Her boyfriend stood on the other side of the counter with the sleeves of his flannel shirt rolled up to his elbows and his hands in a large metal bowl. The muscles of his forearms flexed as he worked the beef, egg, onion, cheese, and breadcrumb mixture. He'd decided to make spaghetti and meatballs for dinner on this blustery almost-spring evening.

Simone looked away from Ryan's forearms and turned back to the images on her phone. Women with shags, mullets, wolf cuts, and under cuts. While Ryan was preparing their dinner, Simone had secretly googled "curly queer hairstyles for women." She'd been to the hair salon last month and probably didn't need another cut until August, but still—she wanted to see what would come up. As she pictured herself with short bangs or a part of her head buzzed, she couldn't help but wonder: Maybe if she'd had one of *these* hairstyles, those jerks outside the Rainbow Museum would have recognized her as one of their own.

Funny how she'd spent so long trying to convince the world she was straight, and now she was sitting here worried that she didn't seem queer enough. Whenever she'd been out with Ryan in the past week and they'd encountered a visibly queer couple, Simone had resisted the bizarre and overwhelming urge to shout that she was bi. The urge felt something like panic—a desperate need to belong *somewhere*. Simone wasn't straight, and if queer people didn't want her, either, then who did she have?

She'd started to find herself envious of Lucy and Holly, and Seth and Claude, and Nina and her partner Dani, who was a lesbian trans woman. Not to mention Ryan's moms, with their fortieth-anniversary dragonfly tattoos. No one who saw any of *them* together would ever question whether they were queer, but when people saw her and Ryan together, they automatically assumed she was straight. Of course, if they saw her with a woman, they'd probably assume she was a lesbian, which wasn't true either—but at least they'd still assume she was a part of the community.

Ryan muttered under his breath that he'd forgotten to add parsley. He washed his hands, grabbed a pair of scissors, and went to the little herb garden he nursed on the windowsill. *Why did I have to be attracted to men in the first place?* she thought to herself. *My life would be so much easier if I were a lesbian.*

Shame consumed her as soon as the thought crossed her mind. Simone knew she was privileged to be able to pass for straight. Sure, those guys outside the Rainbow Museum had been jerks, but she didn't have to worry about homophobic aggression when she was out in public with Ryan. If she wanted to get pregnant, she didn't have to worry about a sperm donor; all she had to do was stop taking her birth control pills and let Ryan come inside her. Simone knew it obviously wasn't *easier* to be a lesbian. But passing for straight meant she also lived with the constant pain of not being seen for who she really was.

The following evening, Simone stood in front of the full-length mirror in her bedroom, running her hands down the sides of her pastel floral sundress. She was attempting to scrutinize herself through the eyes of Seth's party guests later tonight, when Ryan came up behind her and put his hands on top of hers.

His eyes lingered on the hint of her cleavage visible above the scalloped neckline. "You look so fucking good in this dress."

She responded with a wishy-washy "Hmm." She hadn't worn this dress since her sister-in-law's baby shower last spring, which had been held under a tent in the rose garden at her parents' country club. She remembered standing in a circle with her mother and some of her mother's friends, who were gossiping—as always—about the members of their social circle who weren't present that day. At one point, Kathy leaned in closer to the other ladies with raised eyebrows, a signal that she was about to launch into something especially juicy. "Did you hear about Marcy's daughter?"

"The one in high school or university?"

"University. She broke up with that boyfriend of hers, and now she's decided to become a"—Kathy lowered her voice to a whisper, like she was uttering a curse word—"*lesbian*."

"Oh, that poor boyfriend. She brought him to the club a few times. He was lovely."

"Poor Marcy, too. She thought they were going to get married."

At this point, Simone knew she liked women but didn't want to admit it. These ladies had no idea what was going on beneath her pretty pastels. This was a dress that screamed straightness, and Simone was about to wear it to an astrology-themed party at the home of her Rainbow Museum colleague—with her straight boyfriend on her arm, no less.

Ryan surveyed her face in the mirror. "You don't think you look good?"

I don't think I look queer, she wanted to say, but she didn't want him to think she was trying to impress other women. And besides, her dress matched the floral T-shirt she'd gotten him, and Seth had been adamant that everyone take the vernal equinox theme seriously. "I was worried the dress didn't fit quite right," she said instead. "I've started doing those lifting classes at the gym, so I'm a little more muscular that I was before, and—"

"It fits you perfectly." He bent down and kissed the side of her neck, sending shivers down her spine. "I'll go put on my shoes, and then we'll head out?"

Simone swallowed. "Sounds good."

Seth lived with a roommate on the top floor of an old Victorian house in the Annex. As they climbed the rickety stairs, Simone could hear the din of voices. What would she say when she met Seth's friends?

I'm Simone, and this is my boyfriend, Ryan.

I'm bisexual, though.

Just for the record.

At the top of the stairs, Ryan held the apartment door open for Simone, who led the way inside. It was crowded with people in flower crowns, sundresses, linens, and, in Seth's case, a gauzy green robe that billowed behind him everywhere he moved.

Seth glided over and welcomed them both with hugs. Then he stepped back to admire their outfits. "Okay, power couple in matching florals!" He leaned closer to Ryan and lowered his voice. "I heard you two made it official. Congrats."

"Thanks, man." Ryan then performed the staggeringly bro-y gesture of shaking Seth's hand and clapping him on the back.

"Lucy and Holly have a wedding tonight, but Nina and Dani are on their way. C'mon, I'll show you around." Seth gave them a quick tour of the apartment, pointing out the bathroom, the snack table, and the makeshift bar in the corner where his roommate, a woman with short blond hair named Vanessa, had taken on the role of mixologist. "She's a teacher now, but she misses her old bartending days," Seth explained. "Whenever we do a party like this, she spends weeks testing recipes and coming up with a menu. You *have* to try her cocktails. But there's also beer and club soda in the fridge, if that's more your thing."

When Seth got pulled into a neighboring conversation, Simone suggested they make their way to the bar. "No beer tonight," she said, nudging him with her elbow. It was half a joke and half a warning.

While they were in line for drinks, someone passed them a printed-out menu to peruse. There were four drinks to choose from: Water Sign, which was gin-based and clear; Fire Sign, made with a smoky mezcal; Earth Sign, which had "mushroom-infused bourbon"; and Air Sign, a bubbly prosecco-based drink. Simone had now studied enough queer hairstyles to know that Seth's former-bartender roommate, Vanessa, was sporting the shag-mullet hybrid known as a wolf cut. She had an eyebrow ring, too. Simone was instantly self-conscious again in her baby-shower dress.

Vanessa greeted them with a friendly smile. "I haven't seen you two before! Are you friends with Seth?"

"I'm Simone—I work with Seth at the Rainbow Museum. And this is my boyfriend, Ryan." She felt ashamed when she said the word *boyfriend*. Then she was ashamed for being ashamed, because Ryan was the best, standing proudly beside her in his floral T-shirt.

"Aww, that's awesome!"

Simone couldn't tell what, exactly, Vanessa thought was "awesome." That she worked at the Rainbow Museum? That she and Ryan were a couple? Or that Seth's token "straight" friends had shown up in costume to his very queer, astrology-themed house party? She glanced over her shoulder and saw there was no one else in line for drinks, so there was no rush to put in an order.

She reached across the bar and touched Vanessa's wrist. "I am *obsessed* with this menu. Seth said you spent weeks on it."

"The mushroom-infused bourbon took me a while to perfect."

"You're so impressive."

Vanessa smiled demurely. "Well, you haven't tasted anything yet."

Simone smirked. "I can't wait to."

For some reason, it had suddenly felt urgent that she signal to Seth's roommate that she, Simone Whitaker, was Also Attracted to Women™. Explaining that she was a Pisces, she ordered the Water Sign, to make Vanessa think she knew more about astrology than she actually did. Ryan ordered the Earth Sign so they could both try the mushroom-infused bourbon. Vanessa nodded and got to work.

Ryan turned to Simone and tucked a stray curl behind her ear. "Are you okay?" There was that crease between his eyebrows.

"I'm great," she lied, because the truth was something she couldn't possibly admit: that she hadn't been able to stop herself from flirting with Vanessa right in front of him.

"You're . . . chipper again. Are you still worried about the dress?"

"I said I'm great," she insisted, and poked him in the arm.

Vanessa passed them their cocktails, and they migrated into the center of the living room. Nina and Dani had just arrived, so they talked to them for a bit. Then, when Nina and Dani set off to order cocktails, they found Claude, who introduced them to a bunch of Seth's other friends. With every new person she and Ryan met, Simone fought the urge to randomly announce she was bi.

But when the playlist threw it back to 2008 with Katy Perry's "I Kissed a Girl," Simone saw an opportunity. She interrupted one of Seth's friends to squeal, "Oh my God, who else had a total queer awakening when this song came out?"

Technically, Simone hadn't thought twice about the song when it came out, and her most profound queer awakening had occurred last fall, when she was sobbing uncontrollably in the shower after her breakup with Bree, but who really cared about historical accuracy?

Oh right: her boyfriend.

"Didn't this come out when we were in, like, middle school?" Ryan asked her, when no one else could hear. "I thought you didn't know you were bi back then."

She made up a rambling story, something about how she'd always been secretly obsessed with the song but didn't know why, and then she'd finally put two and two together years later. She could tell Ryan didn't quite believe her, but what else could she say? That she was embarrassed to be seen with him? She put what was left of her Water Sign on a side table, slid a hand into his curls, and pulled him down for a kiss, hoping it would be enough to quell whatever suspicions might be swirling around in his mind. As she kissed him, she abruptly thought of the guys outside the Rainbow

Museum and pulled back, bumping into the side table and sending her drink tumbling to the floor.

Thankfully, the liquid was clear, and the cup was plastic, but Ryan was even more unsettled than before. "Simone, why are you being weird?" he asked, grabbing a handful of napkins from the table and stooping to wipe up the spilled drink and collect the empty cup. Standing again, he looked at her like he didn't recognize her. In his defense, Simone didn't recognize herself, but she was in too deep to turn back now.

"Nothing," she insisted. And then, to stop the line of questioning in its tracks: "C'mon, let's get more drinks."

Simone was tipsy after consuming ninety percent of her first drink, which had also tasted like it was ninety-percent hard liquor. "I *love* your hair," she gushed at Vanessa, as the woman mixed them another round. "It's *sooo* pretty. Isn't Vanessa's hair *so* pretty, Ryan?"

"Oh, yeah—um, really pretty," Ryan stammered, clearly not wanting to offend Vanessa but also baffled by the words that were tumbling out of his girlfriend's lips.

Vanessa paused what she was doing and looked back and forth between the two of them, her face slowly contorting into a grimace. "Listen, you guys, I'm just gonna put this out there. Yes, I'm bi, but that's not really up my alley."

Simone had no idea what she was talking about. "Sorry, what do you mean?"

Vanessa gave her a look like it should have been obvious, and then, suddenly, it *was* obvious, and Simone had never wanted the floor to open up as badly as she did right now.

"Oh my God. Vanessa, no. I'm so sorry. I—" Simone looked to Ryan, hoping he would swoop in and save her from what was fast becoming the single most awkward experience of her life, but he wasn't there.

He was walking away.

He was headed for the door.

Shit.

"Ryan, wait!" She frantically apologized to Vanessa one more time, then took off after her boyfriend. That is, if he even wanted to *be* her boyfriend anymore. She caught him by the sleeve of his floral T-shirt. The one that totally wasn't his style, but that he'd worn anyway, because it made her happy. When he turned around, she saw how tightly he was clenching his jaw. "I'm so sorry," she blurted at him. "I've been an absolute nightmare this whole time."

The muscles of his jaw relaxed, but not all the way.

"Can we go somewhere and talk?" she pleaded.

Ryan breathed out a jet of air. "Fine."

They went into Seth's bedroom, which was empty, and closed the door behind them. If anyone assumed the straights were off to bang each other in missionary, well, Simone would just have to let them think that.

She sat on the edge of the bed. She waited for Ryan to come and join her, but he remained standing six feet away with his arms crossed. "Mind telling me why you made it sound like we were trying to have a threesome with Seth's roommate?"

Simone was so embarrassed she could die. "For the record, I wasn't trying to have a threesome with anyone."

"What *were* you trying to do, then?"

"I don't know." She was still too ashamed to tell him the truth.

Ryan let out an exasperated sigh. He reminded her of the Ryan she used to know, back when they were still enemies. "You're the one who wanted to talk. So talk."

She pressed the heels of her palms into her eyes. Why did this have to be so hard?

Now, instead of crossing his arms, Ryan was raking his hands through his hair. He looked almost desperate—frantic. "Listen, Simone. You know what I went through with Travis and Victoria. I can't handle you keeping secrets like this. It's killing me. If you'd rather go be with Vanessa, or anyone—"

"NO." She leapt to her feet and closed the distance between them. She wrapped her arms around his torso, pressed her cheek to his chest. "Ryan, I swear, I want to be with you."

He didn't pull away, but he didn't hug her back, either. "Then why have you been so off all night?"

Simone's voice was small. "Because I don't want people to think I'm straight."

"What?"

Now she was crying, her tears soaking his floral T-shirt. She told him about the guys outside the Rainbow Museum and the real reason she felt so weird in the dress. By the time she was done explaining herself, Ryan was holding her with one arm and rubbing her back with the other.

"Simone, why didn't you just tell me?"

She sniffed.

"Simone?"

"Because I didn't want to let you down. I didn't want to make you think I have doubts."

She noticed his hand slowing down. "*Do* you have doubts?"

"Not about you as a person, or a partner," she whispered.

"What are you worried about, then?" he asked.

A new wave of tears welled in her eyes. "That as amazing

as you are—and as much I like you—that this is how I'm always gonna feel when we're together."

"Like you're coming off as straight?"

"Like I don't belong anywhere," she sobbed, the tears plummeting down her cheeks and into his shirt. "Like I'm too queer for straight people like my parents, but too 'straight' for queer people who don't know I'm bi. And sometimes I wonder if I'd be happier if I just had a girlfriend, but then—" Another sob wracked her throat, cutting her off.

"Then what?" Ryan whispered.

She looked up at him. Even in the midst of a total emotional breakdown, she could still get lost in his eyes. "Then I wouldn't get to be with you," she answered. "And you're the best person I've ever met."

"Oh, Simone." He cupped her tearstained cheeks and kissed her hard—kissed her like he wanted to take away her pain. Then he held her to his chest, so close she could feel his heartbeat. "You're the best person I've ever met, too," he said.

She nuzzled against him. "Maybe I need to stop caring what everyone else thinks," she mused. "If you're my favorite person, and I'm yours, then—"

"Who else matters?"

He kissed the top of her head.

For a while, they held each other. Then Simone sniffed. "Sorry I made it seem like I was soliciting that woman for a threesome."

Ryan snorted. "Yeah, I'm not sure how we're gonna show our faces out there again."

"Oh, we're not," she said. "We're getting out of here as fast as humanly possible."

Simone felt better, more sure of herself, than she had all week. They slithered out of the bedroom, bursting out laughing like high schoolers who'd just snuck out of detention. She called them an Uber and they went back to her place, where Ryan carried her straight to bed. He ate her out with the floral sundress pushed up to her waist.

Simone woke up in the middle of the night needing to pee. That's what she got for hydrating after sex. She tiptoed to and from the washroom, careful not to wake Ryan as she slipped back under the covers. He was sleeping on his side like an angel, hands folded beneath his cheek.

She tapped her phone on the bedside table to see how much time she still had to sleep. Phew, it was only a little after three. But her heart jolted into her throat when she saw the little green notification underneath: a new text message—from Bree Park.

CHAPTER 19

"DO YOU THINK YOUR PARENTS ARE gonna like me?" Ryan asked as they sat in northbound traffic on the Don Valley Parkway.

Simone inched the car forward. The traffic in Toronto was truly abysmal. "Um, they're gonna *love* you. Do you know how happy they're gonna be that their deviant bisexual daughter is in a 'normal' hetero relationship? They're probably going to take one look at you and weep with relief. Oh, wait, just kidding. Weeping with relief would require acknowledging that I'm bi, and we both know that's not gonna happen."

Ryan reached across the center console and caressed Simone's leg. She knew she was rambling, but she was nervous. It was the first time she'd be seeing her parents in person since coming out.

"Didn't you say they were surprisingly supportive when they called for your birthday?" he asked.

"I guess so," she admitted. "My mom randomly said she was proud of me."

"And she was good when you talked the other day," he reminded her.

Now that it was April, her parents were back from Florida, and Kathy had called Simone to invite her for family brunch. When Simone asked if she could bring someone, Kathy hadn't just sounded okay with it; she'd actually sounded excited—like she'd completely forgotten that "someone" could theoretically be a woman. "Maybe she got hit in the head on the pickleball court," Simone reasoned.

"Or *maybe*," Ryan said, pausing for emphasis, "she realized she fucked up, and she's actually coming around."

Simone sighed. "You just never know."

"Well, whatever happens, I'll be with you the whole way."

"Thanks," she murmured. It made her feel like a terrible person that she still couldn't stop thinking about Bree's text message. It was still sitting there on Simone's phone, unanswered—but also undeleted. It was short enough that Simone had it memorized. (Okay, fine: She'd also read it more times than she cared to admit.) Bree had opened with a link to Simone's coming-out post, then said: "Hey, I heard about this at dinner with a few old Sharpe friends tonight. FUCKING FINALLY. For real, though, I'm proud of you, and I hope you're living your best queer life. Let me know if you ever wanna hang out. I'd love to catch up :)"

It wasn't that Simone was still interested in Bree or anything like that. It was just that she'd come to assume they'd never talk to each other again, and that she'd never have the chance to properly apologize. A part of her *did* want to catch up with Bree, but the other part of her knew that after everything that had happened at the vernal equinox party—and in Ryan's last relationship—it would be a catastrophic mistake to start messaging her ex.

At long last, she steered the car off the DVP and onto York Mills Road. The street had felt like the universe's main artery when she was little and she barely left the confines of her insular suburban neighborhood. Her school, her friends, her family's country club—even those godforsaken dance classes—had all been within walking distance of her house. It was no wonder she'd grown up sheltered from the queer, wide world.

She made the familiar turn onto Jacqueline Boulevard. ("Like 'Jackie O.,'" Kathy always said when she wanted to make sure someone had the spelling right—as if every twenty-first-century Canadian knew how the former American first lady spelled her full Christian name.) The Whitakers lived on a spacious corner lot, where there used to be a cluster of big, shaggy spruce trees in the yard. When Simone was little, her parents had them cut down so they could plant prim little shrubs in their place. Kathy, the gardener in chief, said she didn't like the look of all the spruce cones littering the lawn, but Simone now suspected the perfectly cube-shaped shrubs were also a power move. If Kathy couldn't control everything in her personal life, at least she could tell nature exactly what she wanted it to do. Looming over the lawn was a two-story house made of pinkish brick, its color reminding Simone of raw ground turkey. It had five bedrooms, a two-car garage, and a picture window.

She pulled into the driveway and put the car in park.

Ryan squeezed her leg. His hand was still there, from before. "Ready?"

"Not really."

"Kiss me, then."

She turned to him and smiled. He'd shaved this morning, and he looked so handsome, she could have climbed over the center console and straddled him. Instead, she settled for a kiss. "All right," she said, taking one last deep inhale of the side of his neck, "let's do this."

Simone led the way up the front walk and rang the bell. She could hear it echoing in the spacious foyer on the other side of the door.

"Coming!" Kathy called in an oddly singsong voice.

"At least she sounds happy," Simone muttered to Ryan, who was standing off to the side, clutching the neck of the wine bottle he'd brought as a gift.

The lock clicked, the door swung open, and there was Kathy Whitaker with her perfectly made-up face—more tanned than when she'd left in November—her platinum-blond blowout, and her diamond earrings. "There's my darling daughter!" she cried in that same singsong voice. Behind her, George sidled into the foyer looking a bit like a lost beagle.

"Hi, guys . . ."

Simone's voice trailed off when she noticed their outfits. Kathy, who'd evidently noticed Simone noticing, struck a pose in the fitted white T-shirt she wore tucked into jeans. Emblazoned across her chest, in rainbow block letters, were the words PROUD MOM.

George's T-shirt said PROUD DAD.

"We couldn't wait to show you our new shirts," Kathy announced brightly.

Simone stood on the doorstep, blinking at her parents in shock. She'd imagined so many things that could happen at this brunch, from mind-numbing conversations about Florida humidity to offensive tirades about her sexuality, but never in a million years would Simone have predicted this.

She wondered if she was dreaming. But no, her parents really were wearing those shirts, and her mother really was staring at her with hope in her eyes.

And then Simone was wiping away tears.

"Are those happy tears or sad tears, darling?" her mother ventured.

"Happy," Simone choked out.

"Oh, darling." Kathy walked to Simone with open arms and wrapped her in a hug, filling Simone's nose with the scent of her Chanel perfume. "We may be straight, but we're not narrow. Right, George?"

"That's right."

Simone hugged her father, too.

"Now, who's this?" Kathy asked, apparently just having noticed Ryan hovering outside on the front walk.

With the shock of her parents' change of heart, Simone had almost forgotten she had a surprise of her own. She waved Ryan through the door. "Mom, Dad, this is Ryan. My boyfriend."

Now, Kathy was the one blinking in shock. She turned to Ryan and proceeded to survey him with narrowed eyes that were all-too-familiar to Simone. Ryan, who was still untrained in the art of recognizing Kathy's disapproval, smiled back at her.

"It's so nice to meet you, Mr. and Mrs. Whitaker. Thank you for having me."

While George shook Ryan's hand, Kathy turned back to Simone as though she hadn't even heard the greeting. "You brought . . . a boyfriend?" she asked quietly, so that only Simone could hear. The singsong quality had slipped from her voice.

Panic simmered in Simone's chest. "You said it was okay for me to bring someone, didn't you?"

"I did, yes, but I was under the impression . . ." She trailed off, smoothing her manicured hands down the sides of torso.

Simone's shoulders drooped as she realized what was happening.

"You thought I was bringing someone else." *A woman*, she wanted to say. *You thought I was bringing a woman*.

"Well," Kathy said, "when you make such a big announcement on social media . . ."

Her panic was reaching a boil. She was back in Seth's building in her baby-shower dress, climbing the steps to the vernal equinox party. Feeling painfully—*devastatingly*—heterosexual. "I'm bi," she hissed, but Kathy didn't hear. George had put a hand on his wife's shoulder.

"Ryan brought us a very nice bottle of wine."

"Thank you, dear." Kathy graciously accepted the bottle. "What's this, chardonnay?"

"Simone said you're a fan of white."

"Usually pinot grigio, but you know what?" She looked up from the label and flashed him what could loosely be described as a smile. "I can handle a surprise."

Simone winced. Ryan chuckled obliviously. "I'll remember pinot for next time."

"I'll go put this in the wine fridge," Kathy said. "George, you come with me to the kitchen, and Simone, why don't you show Ryan to the family room? Your brothers and the girls are there. Can we bring you anything to drink? Coffee? Tea?"

"Coffee would be great, thanks," Ryan said.

"I'm good with water," Simone squeaked. As soon as her parents had marched off to the kitchen, she turned to Ryan, who was still smiling, and said, "Well, this is officially a disaster."

His face fell. "What do you mean? This is amazing. Their shirts . . ."

"They wore those shirts because they thought I was bringing a *girlfriend*."

"Wait . . . what?"

"Yes." She repeated exactly what her mother had said to her when Ryan and George were talking. As she did, she wanted to cry again—and not happy tears—because it hit her just how fleeting that magical moment had been, when Kathy had looked at her with eyes full of hope . . .

"But why would she hope you were specifically bringing home a woman?" asked Ryan, who'd pulled Simone into a hug.

"I don't know," she whimpered into his shirt. "I just hate that I disappointed her."

"No way." Ryan moved his hands to the tops of Simone's shoulders. "Whatever she's trying to do, you are *not* going to let it get to you. Remember in Whistler, when you told me I was a miserable gargoyle and you were a delightful fucking sunflower?" Simone nodded weakly. "*That* is the attitude you're going to bring to this brunch."

She sighed. "I don't know if I have it in me."

Ryan kissed her forehead, then whispered in her ear: "I do."

She led him through the house to the family room. Before her nieces came along, they would have used the formal living room, but Kathy didn't want almost-four-year-old Cecilia or eight-month-old Phoebe going anywhere near her white couches. Channeling as much VFE—Venus flytrap energy—as she could, she looped her arm through Ryan's and marched through the archway.

Oh, lord.

There were garlands of rainbow flags taped to the ceiling; one giant rainbow flag draped over the coffee table; rainbow streamers hanging over the windows; and three sequined throw pillows on the sectional, which together spelled out LOVE IS LOVE.

Simone cleared her throat. Her brothers and sisters-in-law looked up from the floor, where they'd all been helping her nieces solve a puzzle. Matt and Jason both had the same ginger curls as Simone, which Matt kept short and Jason wore in a medium-length flow, parted down the middle. "Everyone, this is my boyfriend, Ryan," she announced. "Ryan, this is Matt; his wife, Megan; Jason; his wife, Callie; and those are my nieces, Cecilia and Phoebe—they're Matt and Megan's daughters."

Matt got to his feet and walked over, Jason following closely behind. "Nice to meet you, man," Matt said.

Ryan shook hands with her brothers and sisters-in-law—none of whom wore T-shirts that proclaimed them a PROUD anything.

Matt must have noticed the way Simone was eyeing the sequined pillows. "For the record, I told Mom that all this Pride stuff was a little over-the-top."

"Not that we're *anti*-Pride," Megan chimed in.

"It just seemed like it might be whiplash after the way she first reacted," Matt said.

Not only was it whiplash, but there was something hollow about it, too. Her brothers and their wives had sent her sweet, supportive texts in the wake of her coming-out post. Matt had even had that nice conversation with her on the drive up to Whistler. Those things meant more to Simone than T-shirts and sequined pillows.

"I just don't get where it's all coming from," she confided in the group. "What made her go from one end of the spectrum to . . ." She gestured around at the cheesily decorated family room.

Her brothers looked at each other and shook their heads. Jason shrugged. "Better late than never, though, right?"

~

SIMONE WASN'T SURE. SHE HATED THE thought, but some twisted part of her—one she could recognize was steeped in privilege—wished her mother had been spewing homophobic nonsense. At least then Simone would have felt queer in her mother's eyes. Now, sitting next to her straight boyfriend at the dining room table, she just felt like rain on Kathy's Pride parade.

"So, how'd the two of you meet?" George asked.

Simone and Ryan took turns telling a G-rated version of the story as they passed around quiche, corn muffins, salad, and roasted vegetables. They explained how they'd gotten off on the wrong foot, only to end up spending a week together in Whistler. They talked about their guide group; about Simone dropping her phone off a chairlift; about Ryan breaking it down at drag bingo. Eventually, Ryan took Simone's hand and told her family how he'd asked her to be his girlfriend.

While Megan and Callie swooned, Simone's mother dabbed at the corners of her downturned mouth with a napkin. "Well, darling, it's lovely to see you in such a nice relationship. I just wish I could have had a heads-up before I went and bought all these decorations!"

Simone's vision went blurry, and she looked at her plate, tried to focus on the half-eaten food. "I'm sorry," she said, because that was what she'd *always* said when other people were upset—until she'd met Ryan, and she'd realized how good it felt to stand up for herself. At the moment, under her mother's withering gaze, she couldn't remember how to do that.

But then Ryan stepped in. "What do you wish you had a heads-up about?"

Simone looked up in time to see her mother arching her eyebrows. Kathy clearly hadn't been prepared to be challenged. "What I meant," Kathy said slowly, "is that it sounds like Simone has decided she's going to be straight now."

Simone sank so low in her chair that she could have slid right under the table, but Ryan sat up even taller. "Simone's still bi."

"But now she has a boyfriend."

"So?"

"So she's chosen men, hasn't she?"

Then Matt and Jason piped up.

"She doesn't have to 'choose' anything."

"Yeah, that's not how it works, Mom."

Simone had never loved her brothers as much as she did right now. She'd never loved *Ryan* as much as she did right now. Her heart was a red balloon inflating with air . . .

. . . until it was punctured by her mother's next words.

"Be that as it may, if I were the one who'd just come out in such a public way, I'd care about the way things looked."

Simone was flailing and falling at the same time—which perhaps explained why she made the split-second decision to defensively blurt out: "Ryan has lesbian moms!"

Everyone fell silent, presumably as they tried to work out what Ryan's lesbian moms had to do with Simone's bisexuality. The answer, of course, was nothing; but for some reason, Simone had still felt the need to scream it out of nowhere, and now her boyfriend was looking at her with a mix of bewilderment and horror.

"Why don't I get started on these dishes?" George suggested.

Simone was on fire with shame. She needed to get as far as humanly possible from this cursed conversation, so she jumped to her feet. "I'll help, Dad."

They gathered the empty plates, Simone making it her mission not to make eye contact with Ryan. In the kitchen, George washed and Simone dried, while in the dining room, Kathy could be heard saying: "Two mothers? How fascinating. Tell me about *that*."

"Sorry your mother was giving you a hard time in there," George muttered. "For the record, I don't care who you date, as long as you're happy."

Would have been nice if you'd said so in the moment, Simone thought bitterly, but she knew George would never be so bold. She'd gotten her aversion to conflict from someone, and it certainly hadn't been Kathy. Instead, Simone asked her father: "Why's Mom suddenly so obsessed with having a queer daughter?"

"Well, let's see. I think it might have had something to do with some neighbors of ours down in Florida—the Murrays."

Ah. Simone had heard plenty about the Murrays, a wealthy family from Manhattan who'd recently purchased a condo in Naples in the same gated community as her parents. Her mother had referred to the Murrays as "new friends of ours," but Simone was pretty sure that Kathy saw the Murray family matriarch, Joan, as more of a rival than an ally. She hadn't met the Murrays when she was in Florida over the holidays, but she'd felt their presence in her mother's offhand comments: about how owning a speedboat, like the Murrays did, would be "more trouble than it was worth"; how it was *good* that they didn't own a golf cart, either, because Kathy liked to get her steps in, and she was probably in better shape than Joan.

"What happened with the Murrays?" Simone asked warily.

"Their kids were down visiting in February, and we spent a bit of time with the whole family. They have a son and a daughter around your age, and the son is, uh . . ." He gestured at the nearest rainbow flag.

"Queer?"

"Yes." In true Whitaker fashion, his ears had turned red. "He brought his, uh—his husband." The redness deepened.

Simone was beginning to sense what was going on here. Kathy

might not have had a speedboat, or even a golf cart, but she *did* have a queer child to rival the Murrays'.

And then Simone had shown up with Ryan, and Kathy had presumably wondered what good it was having a queer daughter if the whole world saw her as straight.

If I were the one who'd just come out in such a public way, I'd care about the way things looked.

Simone imagined what Lucy would say if she were here. She'd probably accuse Kathy of performative allyship, a phrase Simone had learned from her Rainbow Museum colleagues. Kathy had shelled out for T-shirts and decorations, but she hadn't even learned what bisexuality meant. Case in point, she seemed to think you were only bi until you decided what you really were—that bisexuality was just a stepping stone on the way to being gay or straight.

Simone wasn't gay, and she wasn't straight, either. But even though she logically knew that her mother was wrong, there was still a vulnerable little girl inside her—one who trembled in the wings before her dance recital, afraid to go onstage, but even more afraid to disappoint her mother.

When Simone reentered the dining room, Ryan was explaining to Kathy that yes, he knew the identity of the man who'd donated sperm to his mothers, and in fact, they still caught up once a year around Ryan's birthday, but no, he didn't think of the man as his "father," nor did the man think of Ryan as his "son." It seemed like an awfully invasive line of questioning between people who'd just met. But Ryan was still gamely responding to Kathy, and Kathy was nodding, wide-eyed, like he was the most fascinating person she'd ever encountered, so Simone didn't interrupt them as she returned to her seat. But when she put a hand on Ryan's knee, he tensed. She took it away.

An hour later, they pulled out of the Whitakers' driveway without speaking. When Simone glanced at Ryan from the driver's seat, his jaw was clenched, and his gray-green eyes were staring straight ahead, yet oddly unfocused. She finally worked up the courage to say something. "Sorry my mom was asking such personal questions." God, she was acting exactly like her father.

Ryan didn't respond right away. Simone swore she could hear her heartbeat in the charged silence. When he finally did open his mouth, his voice was eerily quiet. "Your mom wasn't the problem, Simone."

"Seriously? She was being so nosy! Also, that stuff she said about me being straight now, just because—"

Ryan cut Simone off with a deep breath and a sharp exhale. "Simone, I don't *care* that your mom is totally ignorant. I mean, I *do* care, obviously—those things are bad—but they just don't faze me anymore. Growing up, I was the kid with lesbian moms; it's not news to me that the world is full of people who make offensive comments and ask inappropriate questions. I know how to deal with that shit. But what I *can't* deal with is my own girlfriend not having my fucking back. I was sitting there, defending you—calling out your mom on her performative ally bullshit—and then you make this big announcement that I have two queer moms. And you say it like my parents are some kind of currency you can use to show your mom that you *are* still queer, even though you brought home a boyfriend."

By the time Ryan stopped to breathe, the blood had fully drained from Simone's face. She was ashamed because he was right: That was exactly why she'd blurted out that information. "I'm sorry," she whispered. What else was there to say?

Ryan scoffed.

"You don't believe me?"

He shrugged. "I mean, you said you were sorry at Seth's party, too. You can only leave me stranded so many times . . ."

. . . *before I stop trusting you*, Simone finished in her head. She hated herself for disappointing Ryan; hated herself for disappointing her mother; hated herself for failing to find a version of Simone Whitaker that made everyone happy. "I don't know what else to say," she said, her voice wavering.

"I'm not just looking for you to *say* something, Simone. I want to *feel* like we're actually on the same team here—not like I'm some baggage you're ashamed of hauling around."

"I'm not ashamed of you," she said defensively, but even to her ears the words sounded hollow. Hadn't she been ashamed when those strangers had ridiculed her for kissing Ryan? When they'd shown up at Seth's party? When her mother had put it together that she wasn't dating a woman?

"Well, it definitely feels that way," Ryan muttered.

Simone groaned. At this point, she would take being straight if it meant she could just exist peacefully in this relationship. "Ryan, I have no clue what I'm doing. I'm so used to feeling either too queer or not queer enough, and I have no idea how to just *exist normally* as a bisexual human. And it's even harder to figure it out when I'm also navigating a brand-new relationship."

When Ryan didn't respond, she turned her head and found him pressing the heels of his palms into his eyes.

"Ryan?"

When he finally spoke, his voice was thicker, raspier—like he was on the verge of tears. "Simone, I need you to listen to me."

"I *am* listening."

"I need you to be honest with me if you don't want to do this."

"Do what?"

"This relationship."

"Wait, Ryan, that's not what I said at all. I *do* want this. I'm just saying it's a lot to get used to at once. I'm sure I'll be way more settled a year from now, when—"

"A *year* from now?"

Her pulse shot up. "I—I don't know. Maybe it'll only be a few more months . . . ?"

"I can't wait that long to find out if my girlfriend really wants to be with me or not." Ryan pushed his hands into his hair and made fists around his curls. They lapsed into silence as they made their way downtown.

She pulled into her parking space underneath her building and turned off the ignition. In the passenger seat, Ryan unbuckled his seat belt but made no other moves to get out of the car. Simone did the same. They sat there in the chilly parking garage, staring through the windshield at the white cinder block wall, until Simone worked up the courage to ask her next question. "Well, what are we supposed to do now?"

Ryan let out the longest, saddest sigh she'd ever heard. "I don't know," he replied in a low, defeated voice. Like his entire soul had gone flat. "At this point, I think I might need a break."

"We can talk more later," she offered. "Let's go upstairs and—"

"That's not what I meant."

"What do you mean?"

Ryan paused, then said slowly: "I don't just mean a break from this conversation."

Simone was confused. Then, when she realized what he was saying, a lump rose in her throat. Her voice was thin and strangled. "You think we should break up?" Just saying it out loud brought tears to her eyes.

"For a bit," he answered in that same defeated tone. "So that we can both decide if this is really what we want."

A hot tear trickled down Simone's cheek. She hated the thought of being away from him. At the same time, maybe he had a point. Maybe they both needed to do some soul-searching if they wanted to give their relationship a fair shot. "Okay," Simone whispered. "How long?"

"Two weeks?"

She nodded despondently, barely able to process what was happening: that she and Ryan would be broken up for the next fourteen days, and somehow, in that time, she was supposed to find answers to impossible questions. Two weeks was an eternity and no time at all. "Do you want me to drive you home?" she asked softly.

"No."

"You sure?"

"Yeah, I'm good."

Simone couldn't bear to leave on such sad terms. "Are we allowed to hug goodbye?" she asked, sniffling.

At that, Ryan softened. "C'mere."

Simone dove across the center console and buried her face in his massive shoulder. She cried into the fabric of his Carhartt jacket while Ryan rubbed her back in slow circles. After a minute or so, Ryan's hand stopped moving, and Simone pulled back and wiped her eyes. They both climbed out of the old Volvo. With a heavy heart, Simone watched as Ryan shoved his hands in his pockets and trudged up the ramp to the street.

CHAPTER 20

SIMONE SCREAMED LIKE A BANSHEE INTO her pink velvet throw pillow. After watching Ryan leave, she'd trudged to her apartment and collapsed face-first onto the couch, where she planned to stay for the next two weeks—or, quite possibly, until the end of time.

The question she needed to answer wasn't how she felt about Ryan. She obviously still had feelings for him—was obviously still attracted to him. The question was whether she was ready to commit to a relationship with a straight guy so soon after coming out as bi. What if she committed to Ryan, and they got married, and then she realized, too late, that she actually *should* have explored more with women before settling down? Or what if she walked away, and Ryan met someone else, and then she realized, too late, that she'd never want anyone the way she wanted him? This decision could very well dictate the rest of her life, and she only had fourteen days to make it.

She was running low on oxygen with her face jammed in the pillow. Rolling onto her side, she grabbed her phone and dragged it off the coffee table. Maybe the internet could assure her that everything would be okay. *Said no one ever*, she thought, as she opened her browser and searched "bisexual woman in heterosexual relationship." If she could just read about bi women who were perfectly happy to be in relationships with men, maybe she would feel more optimistic.

The first thing that popped up was a personal essay in *The Guardian*: "I'm a bisexual woman stuck in a heterosexual relationship." *She sounds like she could be happier*, Simone thought, clicking a Reddit post instead. A bi woman explained that she'd recently come out to a seemingly supportive queer coworker, but when she'd mentioned that she had a boyfriend, the coworker had replied, "Well, that's disappointing."

"That's why I never tell people I'm bi anymore," someone else wrote in the comments.

Much like whenever she googled her random aches and pains, Simone desperately wished she could unsee these search results. With a shudder, she exited the browser.

Maybe what she actually needed was therapy. Simone had never done it before, although from what she understood, didn't it usually take people a while to find a provider they liked? And after that, to make actual progress? What were Simone's chances of achieving *both* of those things in the next two weeks? She didn't know, but she would try. She went and got her laptop, searched "queer-friendly therapists Toronto," and scrolled through the results.

Private therapists weren't covered under OHIP, Ontario's public health insurance, so she went to her email and pulled up the documents she'd gotten from the Rainbow Museum when she was first hired—the ones that had all the benefits listed, and that she'd merely skimmed in her eagerness to be gainfully employed again. Simone furrowed her brow. Surely a company whose entire identity was focused on supporting the 2SLGBTQIA+ community would offer robust mental health coverage to its employees—nearly all of whom were queer themselves.

She grabbed her phone and texted Lucy, Seth, and Nina: "Just looking at our health benefits—is it true we only get $300 a year for therapy?" While she waited for a response, she searched for the price of an average therapy appointment in Toronto. Her stomach dropped. Three hundred bucks was *not* going to get her far.

"YUP, it sucks," Lucy wrote back. "I've been pestering Frankie about it for a while now."

"What does he say??" Nina asked.

"That it's hard to get good benefits when your employee base is on the smaller side like ours, which is fair, TBH. But I still think he could be doing a way better job of negotiating with the provider—or finding a new provider."

"I'm guessing that's not super high on his priority list," Nina wrote.

"Correct," Lucy replied.

Seth chimed in with three pill emojis. "At least OHIP covers psych visits!!!"

Simone didn't have it in her to laugh. Who did Frankie think he was, offering such stingy mental health benefits when he claimed to support the queer community? Simone was a bisexual in distress! She needed to talk to someone!

Let me know if you ever wanna hang out. I'd love to catch up. Suddenly, Simone had an idea. She navigated out of her Rainbow Museum group chat and opened the still-unanswered message from Bree.

What if she did have lingering feelings for Bree after all, and it was the reason she couldn't quite commit to Ryan?

Simone must have read the message at least twenty times in the past two weeks, but she'd never had it in her to respond. Too risky. But now, things were different. Not only were she and Ryan on a break, but he'd *encouraged* her to use this time to figure out what she really wanted in her love life. Biting her bottom lip, Simone read the message one more time. Then, at last, she typed a response.

~

AS SIMONE RODE THE ELEVATOR TO the rooftop bar at the Ace Hotel the following Friday, she had the feeling she was doing something wrong. *You're allowed to have cocktails with Bree*, she reminded herself again, as the floors ticked higher and higher.

In no way was she cheating on Ryan, because for starters, this wasn't a date. And even if it *had* been, she and Ryan were on a break—a no-contact break, at that. The day after their fight, she'd texted to say good morning and ask how he was doing. "To be honest, I need space," he'd written back. "I think not talking for the time being would be best for both of us."

Coming from someone who lately had made her feel so safe, the words were like a current carrying her out to sea alone on a life raft. Without him, she was unmoored, but she guessed that was the whole idea. To use her time at sea to find answers. Therefore, when she really thought about it, it would have been irresponsible of Simone *not* to meet up with Bree.

And it wasn't as though she was being unfair to Bree, luring her ex out for drinks just for her own selfish soul-searching. Bree was the one who'd asked *Simone* to meet up.

The doors opened with a ding, and Simone's heart rocketed into her throat as she stepped out into the bar. The vibe was industrial and cozy at the same time: concrete floors and pillars with sumptuous leather furniture and Oriental rugs. Bree was already there, sipping her go-to dirty martini on a love seat by the lit fireplace. The flames glistened in her black hair, which she'd cropped into a sleek bob since Simone had last seen her.

When Bree spotted Simone weaving her way over, she set down her cocktail with a grin. She stood up in her heeled ankle boots, which she'd paired with black leather pants and a sequined top. "Hey, you."

Hugging Bree was a disorienting experience, as the last time they'd seen each other, she'd been banishing Simone from her apartment. Bree was wearing her usual rose-scented perfume, and as Simone breathed it in, she vividly remembered being in Bree's bedroom, playing Good Girl as they applied to jobs. Her cheeks flushed.

"Come, sit." Bree gestured to the love seat. Simone sat, and Bree settled in next to her, their knees touching. And then Bree's slender fingers were on her arm. "It's good to see you."

"It's good to see you, too." Simone was trying to remember how to talk. Bree had a commanding presence as it was, and seeing her now, after everything that had happened, was frankly overwhelming.

"I was so happy you got back to me."

"Sorry it took me so long."

"Don't worry," Bree said, rolling her eyes teasingly. "I'm well aware that you do things at your own pace." She plucked a piece of paper off the table. "Here's the menu, by the way. I already ordered us fries."

Simone scanned the cocktail list, but her brain couldn't compute what she was reading. When the waiter came by, she ordered the same thing as Bree. The waiter whisked the menu away and left the two women alone by the fire.

"So," Bree began, with a knowing waggle of her eyebrows, "you're a whole new woman, huh?"

Simone laughed nervously. "I guess so?"

"I'm proud of you."

Simone relaxed into the love seat. "Honestly, it was all because of you."

Bree arched an eyebrow. "Was it, now?"

"Do you remember the last thing you said to me before I left?"

Bree smirked. "Remind me."

"'You're the one who's gonna spend the rest of her life lying to herself.'"

"Ah, yes." Bree sipped her martini.

The fries came, along with Simone's dirty martini. Bree raised her own glass. "Cheers to me being right all along."

"Cheers to me being a raging bisexual," Simone conceded. She took a sip of her drink, wincing as she forced it down. She liked the buzz she got from a dirty martini, but she'd never gotten used to the brininess—it was like sipping salt water.

She set it down. "Joking aside, I'm so embarrassed about everything I said that day. I was terrified to admit that I was queer, so instead, I tried to gaslight you into believing I was straight. I'm so sorry."

Bree snorted as she bit off the top half of a French fry. "As if I ever would have believed you were straight. But thank you," she added. "I do appreciate the apology."

"You must have been so mad at me. *I'm* so mad at me, just remembering it all."

Bree thoughtfully nibbled the remaining half of her fry. "Yeah, I was pretty fucking pissed off. But honestly, once I cooled off, I mostly just felt sorry for you. The fact that we were basically in a relationship, but you still couldn't admit that you were queer? That must have been really painful." Her honey-brown eyes were full of sincerity.

"It was awful," Simone admitted, reaching for her martini again. "And when you said you wanted me to be your girlfriend—"

"I really meant it," Bree said matter-of-factly. Heat crept up Simone's neck and into her cheeks, which might have been from the gin but also might not have been. "But listen, I'm just glad you're doing better now. I've seen a bunch of posts about the Rainbow Museum. Seems cool."

"It's all right." Simone was still bitter about the lackluster health benefits. "What about you? What have you been up to since the fall?"

They sipped their drinks, ate fries, and chatted about Bree's life. She'd gotten an offer on one of the software engineering jobs she'd applied to after the layoffs, but she'd ultimately turned it down in favor of going freelance. Now she was making more money and working fewer hours, which gave her the freedom to pursue more hobbies. She was taking a pottery class, doing yoga, getting lessons on making Korean food from her eighty-five-year-old grandma.

"Ooh, what have you learned to make so far?"

"*Learned* is a strong word," Bree said, laughing. They were both starting in on their second martinis, and had ordered a second basket of fries. "I can only really do it when she's yelling at me in Korean. Otherwise, I forget all the steps. When you come over, we'll order takeout."

Not "if" you come over. "When." A shiver went down Simone's spine. She'd already been covered in a thin sheen of sweat, so now she felt sort of clammy.

Bree touched her arm again. "Hey, Simone?"

"Hmm?" Simone's heart thudded against her rib cage.

"I've always thought you were really cool." Bree set her martini on the table. She seemed to be choosing her words carefully. "Yes, I was hurt by everything that happened between us, but like I said, I mostly just felt sad that such a wonderful person was so repressed. And now that you're out"— she briefly bit her perfect Cupid's bow lip—"well, what I'm trying to say is: I'd be into potentially exploring things again." Bree shifted closer on the love seat.

Her rose-scented perfume was making Simone dizzy, and the one and a half martinis weren't helping, either. She forced herself to think rationally: She'd come here tonight to find out if deep down, her heart still wanted Bree. And now Bree was mere inches from her, lips plump and red, waiting to see what Simone would do next.

Simone's stomach was twisting in knots, while her armpits prickled with sweat. The closer Bree shifted on the love seat, the more Simone thought of Ryan.

Ryan standing up to her mother at brunch, insisting Simone was still bi no matter who she was dating; Ryan holding her as she cried in Seth's bedroom; Ryan proudly introducing her to his moms; Ryan buying her maple spice lattes and making her homemade meatballs; Ryan dancing onstage at drag bingo and helping her find her phone in the woods. She thought of big things and little things—all things she didn't want to live without for a day longer.

Simone jerked backward into the armrest, sloshing dirty martini onto her lap. "I'm so sorry," she blurted. "I just realized . . ." *I love Ryan*, she thought. "I don't have the same feelings that I used to."

Bree passed her a napkin from the table. "It's fine," she said, then slumped against the back of the love seat. "If I'm being honest, I was forcing it a little, too."

Simone looked up from pressing the napkin into the damp fabric of her dress. "Wait, really?"

Bree reached for her martini again. "Can I be totally honest? You have to promise not to think I'm a jerk."

"Like I've never been a jerk to you."

"Ha." A smile flickered across Bree's face. "The truth is, I really did want to see you tonight . . . but part of the reason I reached out is that I've been trying really hard to get over someone."

"Who?"

"This woman I started seeing in December. Gabi." She paused. "You're not mad, are you?"

"Not at all." And it was true. Simone grabbed two fries at once and dipped them in mayo, suddenly ravenous. "Did you guys break up?"

"Not by choice," Bree said, gazing into the fireplace. "She accepted a two-year job posting in Paris—"

"—and didn't want to do long-distance?" Simone guessed.

"No, Gabi *did*." Bree's voice lowered in pitch. "I was the one who freaked out."

"*You* did?"

"I don't know why." Bree swirled her martini around in her glass. "A part of me wanted to, but then a part of me got scared that it was a really big commitment so early in the relationship."

"But you're lesbians," Simone teased.

"Look at you, with the queer jokes." Bree smirked.

"Is there something about Gabi that makes you scared to commit?"

"No, Gabi's amazing," Bree answered immediately. "Sorry, is it weird that I'm telling you this?"

"No! Please, keep going. It's actually nice."

Bree spent the next few minutes gushing about Gabi, a Brazilian Canadian climate scientist who spoke four languages and loved doing yoga and crossword puzzles in her spare time. It sounded like Bree was obsessed with this woman, and Simone told her so.

"I *am* pretty obsessed with her," Bree admitted.

"And although you've attempted to move on . . ." Simone gestured at herself.

". . . I just can't stop thinking about her," Bree finished.

"Are you worried about the actual experience of long-distance? Like, the loneliness? Or the time difference?"

"Not really," Bree said with a shrug. "Now that I'm freelance, I'd be able to visit whenever I wanted."

"Then what are you so worried about?"

Bree appeared to mull it over. "I guess that . . ." She sighed. "I dunno. Some of my friends think we're being ridiculous for even considering this after like four months of dating. And what if they're right? What if we *do* end up regretting making such a big commitment so early on?"

Simone almost laughed. Suddenly, from her perspective, the solution to Bree's problem couldn't have been clearer. "Let's say you *do* regret long-distance. You follow your heart, and then you regret it. What then?"

Bree looked up at the ceiling and took a deep breath, like she was bracing herself for impact. "Then I guess we'd have to break up, and it would be really fucking awful."

Tell me about it, Simone thought. "You're right. It would. But you know what's way worse? Spending the rest of your life lying to yourself that you didn't really want to give things a shot with Gabi, who sounds like the literal woman of your dreams."

Bree's jaw dropped. "Simone Whitaker, did you just use my own line against me?"

Simone shrugged innocently, her own heart filling with hope for the first time all week.

"You really think I should do it?" Bree asked softly.

"Has she left for Paris yet?"

Bree shook her head. "She flies out tomorrow."

Simone tapped the top of her wrist like Judge Judy in that meme. "What the hell are you waiting for?" She flailed her arm toward the elevators. "Bree Park, go get your girl! Drinks are on me."

Bree jumped to her feet and grabbed her jacket off the arm of the love seat. "We didn't even get to talk about *your* love life."

"It's okay, we'll hang out again."

"Takeout at my place?"

"Done." Simone grinned—not just because she'd fixed things with Bree, but because she knew exactly what she needed to do next.

CHAPTER 21

SIMONE PACED ON THE SIDEWALK AS she waited for the eastbound Queen streetcar, whispering the truth that had dawned on her as she'd pulled away from Bree. "I love Ryan. I . . . love . . . Ryan." She even loved the way it sounded, loved the way it felt as it passed through her lips. She knew she needed to take the same advice she'd just given Bree. She had to tell him how she felt.

She boarded the streetcar and grabbed a pole by an empty chair. She was too antsy to sit. As they trundled east, she took out her phone and pulled up Ryan's number. They were supposed to be no-contact, but she figured that didn't matter now that she knew exactly what she wanted. She would see if he was free to meet up. Then she would tell him how she felt.

The phone rang . . . and rang . . . and rang. It dawned on Simone that maybe Ryan didn't want *her*—that he'd used their time apart to reach the opposite conclusion. Simone was about to give up when she finally heard the deep rumble of his voice. "Simone?"

"Ryan."

"Are you okay?"

Through the phone, she heard the ticking of a turn signal. Ryan must have been in his truck. What if he was driving up to Barrie? What if he wasn't free to meet up all weekend?

"I love you," she blurted out. "I don't need another week to think about it. I love you and I want to be with you and I—"

Ryan cut her off mid-sentence. "Where are you right now?"

"On the streetcar. I'll be home in about fifteen."

"I'll meet you there."

Ryan must have been downtown already, because Simone had only just taken off her shoes when there was a knock on her apartment door. The urgent rap sent her heart shooting into her throat, and she lunged for the handle like it was her husband returning from war. She yanked open the door, and there he was—all six glorious feet and two inches of him—dressed in that gray crewneck that made her ache to cozy up with him on a normal day. Tonight, she couldn't keep her hands off him for another second. She didn't even wait to say hello. Still in her jacket, Simone leapt into Ryan's arms, wrapped her legs around his waist, and pressed her lips against his, like it was their very first kiss in Vancouver. In a way, this felt like a first kiss, too.

He squeezed her ass and pulled her close, anchoring her to his body. Normally, he was a strict no-shoes-in-the-house sort of person, but he could apparently make an exception for carrying her into the kitchen in his work boots and setting her down on the peninsula. Simone didn't want to stop kissing him, but she had to say it in person, so she pulled back and looked into his eyes—gray and green, like moss on a rock. "I love you," she said, the words electrifying every cell in her body.

"I love you, too," he said back.

They kissed some more, the heat of Ryan's tongue matched only by the heat between Simone's legs. Maybe today, she'd finally take him inside her. She shifted to the very edge of the countertop, craving as much contact between their bodies as she could get. She wriggled out of her jacket, too, so Ryan could run his hands along the contours of her body in her tight black dress. As he teasingly traced the sides of her breasts, Simone could feel his erection straining against his jeans.

"I know we should probably be talking," he whispered in her ear, sending shivers down her spine, "but I really, really want to make you come right now."

She nodded desperately, moaned the word *"Please."*

"One sec." While Ryan washed his hands in the kitchen sink, Simone attempted to shimmy out of her nylons without getting off the counter. Ryan saw her struggling and darted over. "Lemme help you." Simone lifted herself up so Ryan could roll the nylons over the curve of her ass and down her legs. He moved slowly, like he was savoring every newly revealed inch of her skin. "Jesus. I didn't know I had a thing for stockings until right now."

She smirked. "Oh yeah?"

"I don't think I've seen you wear them before." He bent and kissed her bare inner thigh, sending a shiver down her spine. "Where were you tonight, dressed up like this?"

Simone froze. She reminded herself for the millionth time that she hadn't done anything wrong by meeting up with Bree. It still felt that way, though—because she loved him. And she didn't want to hurt him. But she didn't want to lie to him, either. Doing everything in her power to keep her voice from wavering, she said: "I met up with Bree."

Ryan froze, too. He was kneeling on the tile floor, trailing kisses down Simone's calf. Her skin was sensitive there, and she could feel the exact moment when his lips stiffened, then drew back. "Bree?"

"Yeah."

"Which Bree?"

There was only one Bree and they both knew it. "Bree Park. The woman I sort of dated last year." The countertop under Simone's bare ass cheeks felt unbearably cold all of a sudden. Her nylons were still around her ankles, binding them together. Sensing that she and Ryan weren't going back to sex anytime soon, Simone slid off the counter and tugged them back up. She did it clumsily, and her thumbnail pierced the fabric, creating a hole and a massive run up her shin. She swore under her breath.

Meanwhile, Ryan sat back on his heels, a deep crease down the center of his brow. "You met up with Bree." He didn't phrase it as a question, but rather as a statement he was still trying to process. Simone didn't say anything as Ryan slowly got to his feet. His eyes were pointed at the floor, but they had a faraway look to them.

With a sickening lurch, she imagined the worst-case scenarios that might be playing through his mind. Scenarios as bad as what happened with Victoria and Travis. "It really wasn't a big deal," she said quietly. He walked out of the kitchen and into the living room with no indication of having heard her. Panicked, she followed in his wake, looking pathetic in her ripped nylons. "Ryan?"

He stopped walking when he reached the coffee table. Folded his hands behind his neck. Seemed to stare out the window at the pitch-black sky for a long time without breathing.

"Ryan, say something."

"I can't."

"Why not?"

"Because I'm trying not to freak out."

"Ryan."

When he finally turned around, his eyes were glassy. She'd

known that it would be hard to tell him the truth, but she hadn't predicted that it would be *this* hard. "Why did you meet up with her?"

Simone took a deep, steadying breath. "She reached out a few weeks ago after seeing my coming-out post—"

"You've been messaging her for *a few weeks?!*"

"No!" she cried. "*No*. I didn't even reply to her until the other day—when we were on a break."

"Because you wanted to date her instead?"

"No!" she cried again. He hadn't even let her finish explaining. "She saw my coming-out post and asked if I wanted to catch up."

His wounded eyes scanned her little black dress, her now-ripped nylons. "You were on a date tonight. With your ex."

"I was *not*. But even if I had been—Ryan, we decided together to officially break up for two weeks, so I don't need to justify who I saw during that period." Her panic was morphing into frustration.

"Did anything happen?" he asked.

Simone answered him honestly. "After I apologized for the way I treated her last year, there was a point where she was leaning in to kiss me, but before anything happened, I realized the only person I love—the only person in the world I want to be with—is you."

He didn't speak, letting a bone-deep iciness pass between them instead. Simone could tell right away that her words had meant nothing to him—that he'd effectively stopped listening as soon as she'd said the word *kiss*.

"Fuck," he growled, pinching the bridge of nose as tears finally sprang from his eyes. He swore again, louder this time, and spun around to face the window.

"Ryan, listen to me—"

"Oh, I'm listening." His harsh, sarcastic tone made Simone want to scream and cry at the same time. It was his Mr. Actual Hard Work voice—the voice of someone who wanted absolutely nothing to do with her, despite having declared his love for her mere minutes ago.

She gathered whatever strength she had left and continued. "I didn't do anything wrong, Ryan. I'm not Victoria. I'm not Trav—"

"Will you stop talking about them?"

"I don't know what you want me to say right now!" She threw her arms up in the air. Now she *was* screaming and crying at the same time. "I don't know what you want from me at all. When I act like everything's all sunshine and rainbows, it makes you miserable, but when I'm totally honest with you—like right now—you're miserable, too. I can't win. It's not fair."

Ryan sank into the armchair, his elbows on his knees and his head in his hands. A part of her wanted to go over there and comfort him, but a larger part didn't want to take one step closer to a man who might never be able to trust her. She'd dated insecure men before: men who always wanted to know who she was texting, and talking to, and hanging out with. She didn't want to repeat those experiences with Ryan. With a lightning bolt of clarity, she remembered something else—something Lucy had helped her realize that night at the Rainbow Museum's launch party: that queerness was all about freedom.

"I feel trapped," she murmured, more to herself than to Ryan.

He glanced up at the sound of her voice. "What?"

"I said I feel trapped." Simone crossed her arms and backed farther away from him.

Ryan watched, his face crumpling—but then it hardened, like water becoming ice. Gripping the armrests, he abruptly pushed himself to standing. "If that's how you feel, I'll leave. You never have to see me again."

"Ryan, wait. I never said I—"

"You said I make you feel trapped."

"No, I didn't say *you* make me feel trapped. I said I feel trapped, and I meant right now, in this argument. You're not being rational."

"How am I supposed to be rational when I find out and you and your ex—"

"*—did nothing wrong*, Ryan. You have trust issues! And if we're ever gonna make this work, you need to deal with them. I know you've been talking to Dom, and Dom's great, but I feel like you might need a little extra support . . ."

Ryan narrowed his eyes at Simone. "I know what you're doing."

"What am I doing?"

"You want this break to go on longer so you can keep hooking up with your ex."

Simone jerked her head back. "Are you kidding me right now? If that's what you think, then you don't understand me at all. I'm not over here trying to 'hook up with my ex.' I met up with her because I was genuinely struggling with my own identity."

"Oh, sure."

"I'm not bullshitting you, Ryan. You don't know what it's like to be bi. You just don't."

"I know what it's like to be loyal to someone you love."

She was starting to second-guess whether she was actually in love with the man standing before her. How had she been so sure of it less than an hour ago? Their passionate reunion seemed like it had happened in another lifetime, to different people.

"You don't love me," Ryan muttered. When Simone didn't respond right away, he let out a harsh laugh, like the gust of an ice storm. "No one fucking does."

She thought about countering the absurd claim, but what good would it do to keep arguing?

"There you go," scoffed Ryan, who'd seemingly registered her silence. "Glad we're finally on the same page about something." He patted his pockets, checking for his wallet and keys. "I'm gonna leave," he said, shattering every piece of her already-shattered heart before he made for the door.

He was gone before she could say goodbye. He hadn't even taken his boots off when he'd carried her into the kitchen.

When Ryan was gone, and she was alone in the quiet apartment, she collapsed onto the couch and sobbed. She should probably get a new throw pillow, given how much she'd been using the current one as a Kleenex lately. Then, when she'd run out of tears, she went to her bag and took out her phone to message Lucy, who always knew what to say when Simone was falling apart.

The first thing she saw when she tapped the screen was a message from Bree. It was a slightly blurry selfie of her and a gorgeous bronze-skinned woman, both of them grinning deliriously, with splotches around their eyes like they'd been crying happy tears. Simone read the message underneath: "We're doing long-distance!!! Thank you for helping me see the light!!!" Simone hearted the message, but really, she wanted to throw her phone through the wall.

CHAPTER 22

BARISTA JOE COULD TELL RIGHT AWAY that something was off. It was Monday morning, and Simone had just trudged up to the counter and ordered a good old-fashioned vat of cold brew. Joe leaned in and whispered to her like they were spies exchanging crucial information: "Keep it on the DL, but I can still make you a maple spice latte even though we've switched to the spring menu."

Actually, no! My ex-boyfriend loves those and I'm trying not to think about the complete and utter implosion of our relationship! If she said that out loud, she'd end up having a full emotional breakdown in the coffee shop and scaring away customers. She shook her head at Joe. "I appreciate it, but I need the strongest stuff you've got."

Barista Joe leaned in even closer and lowered his voice even more. "Listen, if you need something *really* strong, I can hook you up . . ."

Simone's eyebrows shot up her forehead. "Oh! Oh, no, but thank you so much, Joe," she stammered awkwardly. "I should be all set with the cold brew."

With a quick nod, he snapped back to his usual professional demeanor. "Room for milk?"

"No, thank you."

"Coming right up."

She shuffled to the end of the bar, wishing she could text Ryan and tell him about the absurd interaction she'd just had. *"Um, I think Barista Joe just offered to sell me drugs?!"* But she and Ryan were broken up now, and hadn't spoken since he'd stormed out of her apartment on Friday night. She'd spent the weekend crying, moping, and doing random tasks around the apartment in an attempt to distract herself from crying and moping even more. She'd slept terribly, tortured by nightmares involving Ryan: There'd been one where she'd had to confess to him that she and Bree had gotten married; another where Ryan had told her he'd gotten a carpentry job in France, but he didn't trust her enough to do long-distance. Her pillow had been soaked with tears every time she'd woken up.

At least the cold brew would give her the energy jolt she needed . . . even if it also reminded her of Ryan. She would go back in time if she could, to spilling her cold brew all over his white T-shirt, if it meant she could do things differently the second time around. She stared at her feet as she walked into the Rainbow Museum. It was another form of torture to have to work among sets that Ryan had built by hand. There was no escaping him when he was literally all around her.

Upstairs, she dropped her bag and made a tired beeline for Lucy, who was already at her desk. She'd bought her a chocolate chip cookie to say thank you for comforting her over FaceTime on Friday night. She wished she'd picked another kind of baked good, because the sweet smell coming from the paper bag was reminding her way too much of the stairwell leading up to Ryan's apartment.

As Simone approached the finance team's desks, Lucy's eyes stayed glued to her laptop screen. Her shoulders were up by her ears, and she was frowning.

"Hey, you," Simone ventured, as cheerfully as she could when she also wanted to collapse. Lucy waited a beat before glancing up. When she did, she looked murderous. "Luce, what's wrong?"

Lucy exhaled a jet of air through flared nostrils, like a fire-breathing dragon. "Frankie."

"What's he doing now?"

Lucy peered around to make sure the coast was clear, then lowered her voice. "We're figuring out the staffing budget for the Queer Makeover Extravaganza. Obviously, we'll need all hands on deck when it comes to the guest experience team, but he's throwing a fit about having to pay them any overtime. Like, I'm sorry, do you expect these hourly workers to volunteer for you out of the goodness of their hearts?"

Simone was confused. "We can afford it, can't we?" The Rainbow Museum had been killing it since opening its doors in February. Frankie had now been a guest on several morning shows, radio shows, and podcasts, insisting that if you loved and supported the 2SLGBTQIA+ community, you *had* to come visit the Rainbow Museum. There was a permanent line down the block of people desperate to come inside, pose for photos, and splurge in the gift shop.

"Of course we can afford it," Lucy muttered. "It doesn't make any sense."

"Well, here. I brought you a cookie to say thanks for the other night." She placed the paper bag on Lucy's desk.

Lucy furrowed her brow. "The other night?"

"Our FaceTime."

"Oh! Right. Of course."

"I really appreciated it."

"No prob—and thanks so much for the cookie." Lucy's eyes darted back to her screen.

Simone had the sense that she was distracting her. With a wave, she said, "Talk to you later," and returned to her desk, where Seth was unpacking his things. Simone, Seth, and Nina had a check-in with Frankie in a few minutes to discuss influencer marketing plans for the Queer Makeover Extravaganza. Simone hoped their boss would be less of an asshole about *this* than about paying his workers what they deserved.

In the conference room, Frankie paired his laptop to the giant monitor on the wall, so he could show them the accounts of influencers he wanted to work with, and what kind of promotional content he wanted to them to create. Simone looked at the posts and captions, but she was too exhausted to really see any of it. Words, shapes, and colors blurred together before her eyes. All she *really* saw was Ryan—the pain on his face when she'd told him she felt trapped. She nodded at every slide—at every idea Frankie suggested. It all seemed fine compared to the actual disaster she was dealing with.

The next time Simone nodded her head wordlessly, Frankie squinted at her suspiciously. "Really? Nothing you want to contribute?"

"All of this seems perfect."

"Is that so?" he pressed, his tone eerily calm.

"Mm-hmm," Simone squeaked, recalling her Cardinal Rule of Working for Frankie Marlow: Don't get on his bad side.

But it would seem that ship was already setting sail. "Simone, I need you to listen to me." Frankie tented his fingers on the tabletop. Then, with Seth and Nina sitting right there, he continued: "I am not paying you an above-market-rate salary so you can sit there like a bobblehead, telling me everything seems perfect."

Whatever Barista Joe had tried to hook her up with earlier, there was no way it could have jolted her awake the way Frankie's words had just done. "Um . . . uh . . ." She was sputtering like an overheating engine, her mind casting around for something insightful to say. Anything. Across the table, Seth gave her a look that said, *You got this. Think*. But all she'd been thinking about since the meeting began was Ryan.

And then it came to her: something she'd talked about with Ryan and his moms when they met at the Common Loon that night. She stopped sputtering and cleared her throat. "Actually, um—on the general topic of promoting the event—one thing we might want to consider is the actual name of it."

"Oh yeah?" Frankie countered. "You have a problem with 'Queer Makeover Extravaganza'?"

Good lord, he was really on a tear today. Did he want feedback, or did he just want to butt heads? "I don't, personally," Simone said slowly, "but I know there are still some people in the community, especially in the older generations, who think of the word *queer* as a slur. And I wonder if it might be more inclusive to call it something like the Pride Makeover Extravaganza, or the Rainbow Make—"

"Got it—thanks," Frankie said curtly. Seth closed his eyes and grimaced. Simone's face was on fire, which meant she must be turning the color of a ripe tomato. "In the future," Frankie continued, "the time to bring up an issue with the event name is not *weeks* into planning, when I already have Phillip's team designing assets with *this* name."

"Sorry," Simone said, trying not to cry.

"In any case, I think the name's fine," Frankie muttered. "We're not catering to old people anyway. Nina, Seth: do you agree?"

"Totally," Seth replied, then shot Simone a desperate, apologetic look.

"I can see Simone's point—I also know people who don't love the label—but I agree it might be challenging to rebrand the event when we're this far along in the process," Nina answered diplomatically.

"Great," Frankie said.

"Sorry," Nina whispered to Simone.

Frankie snapped his fingers, like he was remembering something. "Oh, Seth—I had an idea I wanted to run by you. We're going to be bringing in a photographer to take people's portraits after their makeovers, and I was thinking we could have you there helping people post them. And, you know, giving expert consultations on how to make sure your social media is giving off maximum queer vibes."

Seth looked a little confused, but gave Frankie a thumbs-up anyway. "Love it," Seth said.

"Great. I gotta run. Nina, send me the names we have on the invite list so far, and Seth, Slack Simone the rest of the design notes we had for Kiera, so she can send them off to her ASAP."

Seth nodded.

"And Simone," Frankie added, "look alive."

While Frankie, Nina, and Seth stood up and carried their laptops out of the room—Seth mouthing *I'm sorry* on his way to the door—Simone stayed where she was, her face on fire, wishing she'd called out sick today. Only then she'd be home, crying and moping like she'd done all weekend. There was nowhere Simone could be at peace. Not when the pain was in her heart.

She looked up to make sure no one was waiting to claim the conference room. She wanted to sit here, alone, until she was confident that she wasn't about to burst into tears. One of the promotional graphics for the event was still blown up on the monitor. Though her point about the event title hadn't occurred to her until she'd been put on the spot, she still stood by it. Not everyone had reclaimed the word *queer*, and sure, while younger people accounted for the vast majority of their paying guests, she still thought they should be as inclusive as possible, especially given how hard the previous generations had fought for 2SLGBTQIA+ rights. The Brunswick Four and the Operation Soap protesters in Toronto; the Stonewall Uprising leaders in New York City; all the HIV/AIDS activists—the Rainbow Museum never would have *existed* without the very people Frankie had just dismissed. Simone was getting more and more upset about this, when she realized that Frankie hadn't remembered to disconnect his laptop from the conference room monitor. She could see his cursor moving around. He must have just gotten back to his office.

She watched as he closed the presentation deck and opened Slack. Oh no. As upset as she was with her boss, she still felt uncomfortable spying on his private conversations. She scrambled to reach the iPad in the middle of the table so she could disconnect Frankie from the display. *How is it that we can shoot rockets into space, and yet we can't make conference room technology that doesn't require a PhD in electrical engineering to figure out?* She was jabbing the iPad and watching the monitor when suddenly, she froze. Her own name had just appeared on the screen . . . in a private conversation between Frankie and Seth.

Frankie: Ummm can we talk about Simone trying to change the event name lol

Frankie: Don't tell me I'm not allowed to use the word queer when you've been out for like 5 minutes

Frankie: and you're dating a guy lmao

Frankie: girl, you are basically straight

Seth: 🤣

Seth: I think they broke up though

Frankie: RIP

Frankie: whatever, she's still bi, aka 50% straight

Seth: 🤣

Simone watched the conversation play out, the blood rushing from her head. Her boss and one of her new best friends—they were both making fun of her behind her back. She ran over to the monitor, groped around back for anything that felt like a power button. At last, she found it. She quickly snapped a photo of the screen, then turned it off. The monitor mercifully went black, but her body still trembled with shock. She looked out at the office, wondering what she should do—where she should go. Certainly not back to her desk, where Seth would be sitting right next to her. She could tell Lucy what happened, but Lucy was dealing with her own Frankie-related issues today. Nina was there too, but the thought of approaching her made Simone feel embarrassed. What if she secretly harbored the same feelings as Seth? What if *everyone* did?

So much for trying not to cry. As pressure mounted behind her eyes, she grabbed her laptop and darted to her desk, head down.

Without a word to Seth, she deposited her computer, snatched her jacket off the back of her chair, and bolted for the elevator. She needed space. Fresh air. Possibly a whole new life.

Simone stumbled outside, randomly picked a direction, and walked. She tried to appreciate that it was finally feeling like spring in Toronto. The trees had leaves again, and the air smelled faintly of grass and dirt and other things that came from the earth. The temperature was cold in the shade but warm in the sun.

She couldn't have cared less about the weather. She was still crying.

She walked past the spot on the sidewalk where the strangers had made fun of her for kissing Ryan. She thought she'd been ashamed then, but that was nothing compared to the vortex of emotions she felt after seeing her boss's words on the monitor. With all his press appearances in recent months, Frankie had become a recognizable figure in Toronto's queer community. Something of a leader, even. And he thought of Simone as a fraud.

She walked down Church Street, past Dorothy and Friends, the dive bar where she'd gone to karaoke night with her colleagues. Where she'd danced onstage to "Mamma Mia" with Seth—back when she thought Seth was her real friend—and Lucy had gotten strangers at the bar to chant her name. She remembered the electrifying feeling of fitting in for the first time in her life. Now she had the sickening hunch that everyone in her newfound community saw her the same way Frankie did: as a queer imposter. Even Lucy probably thought so. Simone replayed their stilted interaction from earlier, when Lucy had seemed to be distracted by work. What if the real reason for her standoffishness hadn't been Frankie, but Simone? What if on Friday night, on the other end of the phone, Lucy had secretly been rolling her eyes at the supposedly queer woman who couldn't stop sobbing over a guy? She imagined what Lucy must have told Holly when she'd gotten off the phone. Oh God, they were still friendly with Erica, too. The three of them had probably sat in a knitting circle, making pet sweaters and talking about how annoying that queer wannabe Simone Whitaker was.

She walked past the Toronto Metropolitan University campus, all the way down to Queen Street, where she paused at the corner. The Rainbow Museum was back the way she'd come, but the thought of returning to the office today was unbearable. Instead, she turned left, toward Leslieville. She could do her job from her personal laptop. If Frankie had an issue with her working from home, that was fine. He was already fed up with her.

Lately, it seemed like everyone was: Frankie, Seth, Lucy, probably the rest of her colleagues, her mother, maybe her father, too, since he bore the brunt of Kathy's moods. And then there was Ryan, who'd stormed angrily out of her apartment Friday night, after an argument that had been worse than any of the ones they'd had when they were still nemeses. She'd blamed their fight on his trust issues, but what the hell did she know? Maybe Simone had been the problem all along, the way she'd always been the problem with Bree. The way she'd always been the problem in every goddamn relationship in her life. She used to wish for a seemingly simpler life as a lesbian. Now she wished for a life where she was straight—not closeted, but really and truly straight, where she could have Ryan, but none of the weird identity issues that came with being bi.

She crossed the bridge over the Don River, remembering the split second she'd once contemplated how it would feel to let the water claim her. That had been the day she'd come out, after her phone call with Kathy. Three months later, why did she still feel hopeless? This wasn't how coming out was supposed to work.

Somehow, she'd screwed up, and the worst part was that she didn't even know where, which meant she had no idea how to fix what was wrong.

Lucy had tried teaching her to knit one time: a basic square, with thirty stitches per row. Simone thought she'd gotten the hang of it, until she realized her square looked more like a lumpy trapezoid. Because she couldn't pinpoint where the problem was, the only way to fix her square was to unravel the whole thing. That's what Simone was doing now. Unraveling. She picked up her pace as she entered Leslieville, hoping to make it back home before she fully came apart.

CHAPTER 23

ON SUNDAY, SIMONE GRABBED THE LAST can of black beans from the pantry and the remaining wisps of shredded cheddar cheese from the fridge. She pulled out the only flour tortilla left in the bag and slapped it half-heartedly into the frying pan, where it landed with a familiar sizzle. She'd lost count of how many quesadillas she'd made for herself this week, but this would evidently be the last one.

She'd have to go to the grocery store at some point, but that would mean leaving her apartment, which she'd managed to avoid doing since Monday. She'd told her colleagues she'd come down with "that upper respiratory thing that's been going around," and had been working from home ever since. Lucy had messaged Simone a few times to see how she was doing, but Simone hadn't written back, convinced Lucy would be happier not having to deal with her at all. By Thursday, Lucy had stopped texting.

Simone always kept a well-stocked pantry, so she'd been able to feed herself all week. She slid the quesadilla onto a plate and cut it into quarters. She picked up one of the slices, blew on it, and took a bite. It was hot, bland, and a little soggy. Whatever. She was not in the mood to treat herself.

As she chewed the lackluster quesadilla, she wandered over to the pantry to see what supplies she had left. Vanilla protein powder, slivered almonds, raisins, breadcrumbs. Ugh. She would have to go to the grocery store today. She finished eating and got in the car without bothering to shower or change out of her sweats. She wasn't trying to impress the staff or clientele at Loblaws.

Simone pushed her shopping cart down the aisles like a zombie, wondering how she would ever show her face at work again, when everyone probably thought of her the way Frankie did. *Girl, you are basically straight.* She grabbed another bag of flour tortillas and dropped them into the cart.

She was so lost in her own despair that she didn't initially realize that someone was calling her name from behind her. Not until that someone strode around to the front of her cart, so that she couldn't take another step without running him over. She clocked his bald head, his bushy white mustache, his whimsical round glasses. *Total cool grandpa vibes*.

"Glen!" she exclaimed.

Her Whistler ski buddy beamed at her. "I thought that was you! I saw you from over in the produce section, and said, 'I know those ginger curls!'" She swept them over her shoulders, worried they looked more like a rat's nest than anything else. "You didn't hear me the first few times I called your name," Glen went on. "The people in the store must think I'm senile."

"Sorry, I was totally distracted," Simone said. "It's good to see you! How are you?"

"Oh, you know, I'm fine," he answered. She thought she detected a hint of sadness on his face, but maybe that was just her own misery tainting her view of the world. "Enjoying the spring weather!" He gestured at his outfit: He was wearing a fun floral shirt under a denim jacket.

"Me, too," she lied, hoping it wasn't terribly obvious that she hadn't been outside in almost a week.

They briefly caught up in the grocery aisle: Glen asked how the Rainbow Museum had been faring in its first few months, and she told him about the company's success; she asked how work was going at Loving Minds—his queer mental health nonprofit, which he'd told her about in Whistler—and he confessed they'd been having some fundraising challenges lately.

Simone remembered the chairlift ride when Glen had first told her about Loving Minds. How she'd instantly connected to the mission on a soul-deep level, having recently gone through the mental agony of her breakup with Bree, her decision to come out, and her mother's unhappy response. No queer person should ever have to feel the way she did when she'd gazed over the railing into the icy water of the Don River. Hell, no queer person should ever have to feel the way Simone was feeling *now*, like there was nowhere on earth she belonged. So when she heard that Loving Minds was having financial issues, she raised her eyebrows in concern. "Oh no! I wonder if there's some way the Rainbow Museum could help support you."

Glen's eyes widened behind his circular frames. "You think so?"

"I don't know for sure, but the Rainbow Museum's whole mission is supporting the queer community. We should talk."

"That would be amazing." Glen checked his watch, then flashed her a hopeful smile. "If you're not in a rush, maybe we could grab a quick coffee or tea after this? There's a place around the corner. My treat."

Because Simonè adored Glen—and also because she couldn't bear the thought of turning another person against her—she agreed.

They met up again in the parking lot, then drove caravan-style to the coffee shop Glen had mentioned. It was warm enough to sit outside, so they grabbed seats in the peaceful back garden, under a blossoming cherry tree whose buds were just beginning to open. As they sipped lavender-hibiscus tea in the mottled sunlight, Glen explained how Loving Minds had relied heavily on funding from a certain corporate sponsor, but that sponsor had recently been acquired, and its new owners had different plans for charitable donations. Simone had heard Frankie say that once the Rainbow Museum was turning a profit, he would donate a portion of its proceeds to 2SLGBTQIA+ charities. She promised Glen that she'd see what she could do.

"Simone, thank you," he said sincerely, cupping his warm mug. "You're the best."

You're the only one who thinks so, she thought darkly.

"Enough about me, though. How are you?"

"Oh, I'm all right," she said vaguely. "Work's been busy."

"And how's our dancing queen?"

It took Simone a second to realize he was talking about Ryan, and when she did, her heart gave a painful throb. "Good," she said, looking at a spot on the wooden fence over Glen's shoulder. "He's done with everything at the Rainbow Museum and moved on to other projects."

"Aww. I liked him a lot. Good egg, that one."

"Yeah," she whispered, her throat suddenly tight.

"Can I tell you something? I hope this doesn't sound weird—please forgive me, if so—but I always sensed"—he wiggled his fingers in the air—"a sort of *vibe* between the two of you."

Simone closed her eyes.

"I'm sorry," Glen said quickly. "Maybe that *was* a weird thing to say."

When she opened her eyes again, they were wet with tears.

Glen's face fell. "Oh no. Honey, what happened?"

She hadn't intended to spill her guts to Glen from her Whistler guide group, but at this point, she could either tell him the truth or sit here sobbing at him with no explanation, the latter of which seemed way more awkward for Glen. So she told him the truth. "We just broke up," she confessed. "We got together after Whistler, and everything was great, and we were in love, and then I went and ruined it all."

Glen leaned forward with an understanding look and reached a weathered hand across the table. "I didn't buy anything frozen at the store."

Simone sniffed. "What?"

He gave her a sad smile. "If you want to talk, I have plenty of time to listen."

"Oh." His kindness had brought on a fresh wave of tears.

"Hang on one sec," he said, getting up and darting inside as fast as his legs could carry him. He returned with a wad of napkins for Simone to dry her eyes with. She dabbed at her face, spewing out a jumble of thank-yous and apologies. Glen waved them all off.

When Simone had collected herself, she shared more. "You know how I came out as bi a few weeks before Whistler?" Glen nodded. "Well, I had it in my head that I was finally going to live my best queer life. And then I fell in love with a guy."

"Ah." A knowing smirk played across his face.

"I know, I know," she went on. "Being with Ryan doesn't

make me any less queer, but honestly, that's what it feels like, since everyone sees you together and assumes you're straight, which is really uncomfortable. So then you feel this pressure to constantly declare your sexuality, which is also really uncomfortable, and it's like, *ugh*—you can't win. And *then* I feel like a privileged asshole for getting frustrated, 'cause in the grand scheme of things, I'm an able-bodied cis white woman in a heterosexual relationship! My life is like, ridiculously easy, relatively speaking—you know?!"

As she paused to catch her breath, Glen said: "I do."

She furrowed her brow, then thought about the knowing smirk he'd given her a minute ago. "You do?"

Glen replied with a slow nod. He was silent for a moment, as though debating how much to share.

"I didn't buy anything frozen, either," she said.

That brought a smile to Glen's face—but with a hint of sadness, like she'd thought she noticed in the grocery aisle. "In Whistler, I think I told you about my current boyfriend, yes?" Simone nodded. *Byron*, she remembered. "What I don't think I mentioned," Glen continued slowly, "is that I was happily married to a woman for twenty-one years."

Simone's eyes widened. "You *were*?"

"Let me guess: You assumed I was gay?"

Simone's cheeks went as hot as her tea as she realized she herself had made an incorrect assumption about a fellow bisexual. "I did," she admitted, wincing. "I'd, um—I'd love to hear more about your wife. Or, ex-wife?"

Glen gazed at the pink petal of a cherry blossom that had just fallen onto their table. "Rose passed away nine years ago. She had breast cancer."

"Oh, Glen." Simone put a hand on top of his. "I'm so sorry."

"I appreciate that," he said sincerely. "I think about Rose every day. Rose, and Jeff."

Simone didn't know who Jeff was, either, but she waited for Glen to tell her.

"Jeff was the first love of my life. We were young when we met, at U of T, in the fall of eighty-one." When he named the year, a shadow seemed to pass over his eyes. "At that point, AIDS just seemed like a rumor coming out of the States. Oh, you're telling me gay men in San Francisco and New York are getting some mysterious 'cancer'? Sounds to me like ultra-conservative propaganda. But then in eighty-two, we had the first reported case in Canada. Jeff got sick in eighty-three, and he passed away a few months later."

"Oh my God," she whispered, horrified. "Glen, I am so, so—"

He slid his hand out from under Simone's and held it up, gently cutting her off. "I really do appreciate your sympathy, but that's not the reason I'm sharing all this. I'm sharing this because I know what it's like to be bisexual but to feel like you're not 'enough' for your own community."

Simone swallowed hard.

Glen returned his hand to the table, laying it next to Simone's. "When I lost Jeff, I thought I'd never love anyone like that again. And for years, I didn't. Then, in ninety-two, I met Rose at an AIDS activists' meeting in the Village. She was straight, but she'd lost a dear friend around the same time I lost Jeff. When we started to fall in love . . . jeez, it's hard to explain all the things I was feeling at once. One, I felt like I was betraying Jeff by moving on with someone else; and two, I felt like I was betraying the whole community by moving on with a straight woman. Regardless of her being this radical, outspoken ally—I still felt like I was abandoning a piece of my own identity."

"I get that—the identity part." In fact, Simone got it all too well. A strange mix of feelings came over her as she realized they'd had parallel experiences, decades apart: There was frustration, sure, but there was also this strange sense of belonging. Like Simone was part of a queer narrative that was bigger than herself. "But despite all that, you and Rose ended up happily married for a really long time."

"That we did," he said proudly.

"How?"

Glen smirked. "How did I stay in touch with my queerness while married to a straight woman for twenty-one years?"

"Yes!" she cried.

He chuckled. "Oh, Simone, there were so many ways. I mean, for starters, I chose a partner who knew and respected the fact that I was bisexual, so I never felt like I had to hide around her."

"Right," Simone said, nodding. She thought of Ryan schooling her mother at the performative Pride-themed brunch.

"Having queer friends was important, too—*true* friends, who knew my heart, so I never felt like I had to prove anything to them." Now, Simone thought of Lucy, who'd talked her through too many identity crises to count; who'd brought her to queer karaoke night; who'd texted her nearly every day this past week, checking in.

"I found other ways to stay connected to the community, too," Glen went on. "I volunteered, I marched, I started working in the nonprofit world."

Simone nodded even harder, a warmth like a fire spreading in her belly.

"*But*," he said, holding up his index finger, "I do want to be very clear about something. Those things were fulfilling for me, personally, but even if I hadn't done any of them, I still would have been queer. And my marriage to Rose still would have been queer, too. Listen to me, Simone: Queerness isn't about what you do, or who your friends are, or who you love. Queerness is who you *are*. Which means that any relationship you're in, Simone, will be a queer relationship, because *you're queer*."

Tears sprang to her eyes, and her bottom lip trembled. "Glen, I might need you to repeat that to me for the rest of my life."

He smiled. "It would be my pleasure. And speaking of relationships," Glen went on, and here he let out a wistful sigh, "if there's one thing I've learned in my sixty-three years—losing Jeff, and then Rose—it's that nothing in the universe is more important than love. Whether that love is romantic or platonic, what have you—what matters is that we soak in every last drop of it that we can, because we don't know how much time we're gonna get." Glen took a final sip of tea, his eyes on the cherry blossom petal. He put down his mug and picked up the petal, twirling it between his thumb and forefinger. Simone noticed he had that melancholy smile again. "Rose adored cherry blossoms, and Jeff's birthday was in April," he mused. "I always miss them extra this time of year." Glen turned back to Simone, glassy-eyed. "Thank you for the opportunity to remember them."

"Thank *you*," she whispered, wiping her own eyes. "For everything."

They sat in silence for a minute or so, Glen thoughtfully twirling the cherry blossom, and Simone thinking about Ryan. She'd been so down on herself this past week that she'd reverted to blaming herself for their breakup. She'd forgotten how irrationally angry he'd been, how suffocated she'd felt by his trust issues. She wanted to do what Glen said, to soak in every last drop of love that she could, but she also deserved a love that made her feel free. Freedom was the whole point of being queer, was it not?

Simone and Glen hugged goodbye on the sidewalk, promising to talk soon. "Remember," Glen said before they parted ways, "being bi isn't about who you date—it's who you are. And you *are* one of us. You hear me?"

"I hear you," she promised.

"Loud and clear?"

"Loud and clear."

She was walking back to her car when Glen called her name, and she turned around. "One more thing!" he said, hurrying over. "I forget if I mentioned it, but one of the things we do at Loving Minds is facilitate free support groups for different subsets of the community. We do one for people under the bisexual and pansexual umbrella. You're welcome to come check it out sometime. It might be helpful to meet other people in the same situation."

Simone grinned. "I'd love that."

CHAPTER 24

AS SOON AS SHE WAS DONE unpacking her groceries, Simone made herself another mug of tea and plopped onto the couch to begin stitching her life back together. There were so many problems she still didn't know how to solve: the fact that Frankie had made the Rainbow Museum a hostile workplace; the fact that Seth was just pretending to be her friend; the fact that Ryan was gone from her life and might not ever return. But there was one step she could take right now to make things better.

"Well, well, well," Lucy said when she answered the FaceTime. Her blond hair was in a messy bun, and she was wearing a sheet mask.

"Sorry to disturb your Sunday Scaries ritual."

"Hey, at least I'm hearing from you for the first time in *seventeen years*. Are you okay?" She sounded concerned, but also peeved, which was fair.

"I'm fine—health-wise." Simone glanced away, ashamed that she'd lied about having a plague to Lucy, who'd shown her nothing but steadfast support since they'd met. She looked back at her friend, who was squinting at her suspiciously through the slits in her sheet mask. The absurdity of her appearance took the edge off Simone's nerves. "I was never sick," she admitted. "I haven't been coming into the office because something really fucked-up happened, and it made me feel like no one actually wanted me around, which I now realize was an extreme reaction, but—"

Lucy's eyes softened. "Wait, what happened?"

Simone told Lucy about the meeting where Frankie had forgotten to disconnect his laptop from the monitor. Then she texted Lucy the photo she'd snapped of Frankie and Seth's Slack conversation. The FaceTime video paused when Lucy opened the photo on her end, but Simone could still hear her reaction. "Oh my God. Oh. My. God."

When Lucy reappeared, she'd taken off the sheet mask. Her dewy face was scrunched in a mixture of sympathy and indignation. "I don't even know where to start," she said, shaking her head.

"I know."

"It's bad enough that Frankie's shit-talking an employee to another direct report, but the raging biphobia on top of it? From the founder of the *Rainbow Museum*?"

"And Seth just went along with it," Simone lamented.

Lucy sighed. "It's really disappointing."

"It's really humiliating."

"Yeah, for *them*. You don't have anything to be ashamed of. But listen, I still completely understand why you reacted the way you did." She closed her eyes for a moment. "This one time, before I met Holly, I went on a date with someone who teased me for not being a 'gold-star lesbian.' Let me tell you, I *spiraled*."

"Oh God."

"Right? Like, way to make me feel not gay enough because I hooked up with guys in university, when I was still figuring shit out."

"That's so messed up."

"And so's this," Lucy demanded. "Ugh, Simone, I'm sorry they said this stuff, and I'm sorry you had to see it."

"Thanks," Simone whispered. "But Luce, I'm still sorry that I lied about being sick and ignored your texts. You were checking in to see if I was okay, which is like, so nice of you. You're an amazing friend, and I'm so lucky to know you."

"Stop, you're gonna make me cry."

"It's true."

"I feel lucky to know you, too."

"I wish we could hug right now," Simone said.

"What if we both nuzzle our phones, like cats?" Lucy suggested.

Simone snorted. "Anything for you."

When they were done nuzzling, Lucy pushed the flyaway hair off her face. "So, about these Slacks. What do you think you're going to do?"

Simone mulled it over. There was still a small part of her that didn't know how she'd ever look Frankie or Seth in the eye again. But now that she'd talked to Glen and Lucy, there was a much larger part of her that felt brave, and bold, and determined to stand up for herself. "I'm gonna be Simone 2.0," she said.

~

SIMONE KEPT HER CHIN UP AS she marched into the Rainbow Museum on Monday morning, even though her palms were clammy and her heart was a jackhammer. Upstairs, in the office, she immediately spotted Seth, who was dressed in the same neon windbreaker he'd been wearing on her first day. He was in the kitchen.

She went to her desk and took off her coat. She could wait for Seth to come back to the chair next to hers—or she could go straight to him. She knew what Simone 2.0 would do.

"Hey," she said to his back, as he filled his Stanley at the sink. Seth spun around at the sound of her voice. She would have assumed his smile was genuine had she not seen the Slacks and learned he was totally fake.

"Oh my God, you're back! Finally!" He put down his water bottle and wrapped her in a hug. It would have been so easy to hug him back—to pretend that nothing was wrong—but today, she kept her arms down at her sides. Seth let go of her and stepped back, pouting. "Are you okay?"

She swallowed. "Do you have a minute to talk?"

"Of course." He reached for a stool at the kitchen island. Phillip was standing behind them, grabbing oat milk from the fridge.

"Actually, do you mind if we go somewhere private?"

She led him to Ru Paul, where she perched on the edge of a beanbag with her back straight. She couldn't let herself sink into the fabric.

Seth plopped into the beanbag next to her. "Simone, what's wrong?"

You can do this, she told herself as she took a deep breath. "You remember that marketing meeting the other day, when I suggested we change the name of the Queer Makeover Extravaganza?"

Seth rolled his eyes. "Frankie was being such an asshole that day."

Anger rose inside of her like water reaching a rolling boil. "You both were. After the meeting, Frankie forgot to disconnect his laptop, and I saw what you guys were Slacking about me behind my back."

Seth's face fell. The rest of his body froze.

"Frankie said I'm 'basically straight,' and that I shouldn't be taken seriously because I've only been out for 'like five minutes,' and you just laughed along with all of it. Do you know how much it hurt to see that? Not just from my boss, but also from someone I considered a friend?"

He buried his face in his hands, and when he looked up again, his eyes were bloodshot. "Simone." His voice was husky. "I am so, so sorry." He blinked as though something had dawned on him. "Is that why you stopped coming into work?"

She nodded.

"Oh, Simone." He leaned forward and put a hand on her knee, which made her flinch, so he retracted it, his expression full of shame. "I know I should have defended you, or at least ignored his evil messages, but sometimes it's just so hard to push back, and I hate myself for not being stronger."

She wasn't sure if she could trust him. Not after seeing those Slacks. "How do I know you're not just saying that?"

"Simone, please believe me: Frankie says shit like that about everyone, and it makes me so fucking uncomfortable. It's like he's trying to start some 'boys' club' with the only other cis guy around his age at the company. I'd show you the Slacks, but I don't want to share all the fucked-up things he's said about people."

His voice cracked, and something at the bottom of her heart told her Seth was being sincere. Simone leaned forward and put a hand on his knee. "I believe you."

Seth's lower lip trembled. "You do?"

She nodded.

He let out a sigh of relief. "I still feel awful that I hurt you. I need therapy so I can work on setting boundaries with him. I can't afford therapy, obviously, 'cause our health plan sucks, but if I could, please know I would totally be working on it, and in the meantime, I'll be watching a shit ton of therapists on Instagram who talk about setting social boundaries with your manager."

"Trust me," she said, "I know how scary it is to push back against people whose opinions you care about. There's a reason I didn't come out until I was twenty-nine. And you're what, twenty-four? In your first job out of university?" Seth nodded. "I bet that's *really* freaking scary."

"Thanks," he murmured at the ground. "But I just want you to know"—he slowly looked up again—"that I don't believe any of that ignorant shit Frankie said about you, and about bi people in general."

"I know you don't," she promised.

"Frankie, on the other hand . . ." He glanced over Simone's shoulder, as though checking to see if their boss was anywhere close to the conference room. "You don't even know how much of an asshole he is. This is just the tip of the iceberg."

Simone frowned. "What do you mean?"

Seth peered over her shoulder again, looking nervous. "Shit, he just came out of his office. Let's talk later."

Simone remembered they had a meeting with Frankie first thing this morning. They clambered out of the beanbag chairs and hurried to Lil Nas X. Simone had been dreading having to see her boss again, but she hadn't anticipated the righteous fury that coursed through her now, as they took their seats around the table.

Frankie nodded at Simone. "Glad to see you back. How're you feeling?"

As if you care. "Better," she said, and it was true. She'd smoothed things over with Lucy and Seth, two true friends who knew her heart, and had a life-changing run-in with Glen, the bisexual elder she hadn't known she'd needed. The only thing still missing from her life was Ryan, whose absence was still a gaping wound in her chest. It ached all the time: whenever she walked through the Rainbow Museum; whenever she saw other couples holding hands and kissing; whenever she saw his toothbrush in her bathroom or his comfy clothes folded neatly under her bed, because she still couldn't bring herself to give them back. She wanted him in her life again, wanted to give their love an actual chance to blossom, but she also knew that Ryan had trust issues, and if he wasn't willing to work on himself, there was nothing she could do.

Once Nina had arrived, they ran through the agenda items Frankie had sent over in advance, Simone making sure to be extra vocal with her feedback this week. She didn't care about impressing her asshole of a boss, but she did need the aforementioned asshole of a boss to listen when she brought up Glen's charity.

"Anything else?" Frankie asked, a little impatiently, when they'd reached the end of the agenda.

"Actually, yes." Simone sat up straighter in her chair. Her heart was thumping, but she tried not to let it shake her voice. "There's one more thing I wanted to run by you. A possible charitable side to the event."

"Oh." He blatantly glanced at the clock on the wall. *Asshole*. "What did you have in mind?"

As Simone spoke, she could already tell her pitch was doomed by the expression on Frankie's face. He was half smiling, half grimacing, like a wedding guest enduring a drunk groomsman's ten-minute-long toast. The old Simone, who twisted herself into pretzels to make other people comfortable, would have cut herself off by now. Instead, she did what any drunk groomsman would do—hell, what any confident man would do. She kept talking.

"On a personal note, being bi, I've had straight people *and* queer people say mean stuff about me, and it's definitely taken a toll on my mental health." She looked pointedly at Frankie, and then at Seth, who gave her a supportive nod. "I think of all the other queer people who could be feeling the same way, and how awesome it would be for the Rainbow Museum to help them."

"Thanks for that, Simone." Frankie still had on that infuriating pained smile. "We certainly *do* want to support the 2SLGBTQIA+ community in everything we do. However, given how new we still are as a business, and where we're at revenue-wise, the finance team has unfortunately advised that we hold off on making significant charitable contributions at this point in our journey."

"But we sponsored Whistler Pride," she pointed out.

"Well, *technically*, we provided a service in exchange for an incredibly valuable advertising opportunity. It was more of a mutually beneficial scenario than what you're describing. Listen, I know it's disappointing. I wish we could donate to charities left and right! But look at it this way: Running the Queer Makeover Extravaganza as a strictly for-profit event will help bring in the kind of money we need to support philanthropic initiatives in the future. Does that make sense?"

Simone wanted to push back, but Seth was giving her a wide-eyed look that said, *Wait*. That's when she remembered there was something he still had to tell her about their boss. "Yep, that makes sense," she replied, feigning obedience.

After the meeting, she and Seth went straight to Lucy's desk. When Lucy saw the two of them together, she furrowed her brow at Simone as if to ask, *Do you need me to rip him a new one?* "We talked it out," Simone said, before Lucy could go into mama bear mode. "It's all good."

"Well, not *good*, per se," Seth chimed in. He turned to Lucy and whispered, "Frankie's been shit-talking everyone to me, trying to make me his little partner in crime. It's been awful, but I was just telling Simone, I think I know why he's been doing it."

The three of them took the elevator downstairs and slipped through the employees-only side door. They went around to the alley behind the building where people sometimes took smoke breaks, and where they could talk in private without risk of being overheard. They checked to make sure that no one was lurking in any of the nooks in the brickwork, then stood in a tight circle with their heads together.

Seth spoke first. "So, Frankie's even more fucked-up than I realized." He told Lucy how Frankie had just shot down Simone's idea on the grounds that the Rainbow Museum couldn't afford to launch any philanthropic initiatives that weren't "mutually beneficial" in some way. He made air quotes with his fingers and rolled his eyes. "He claims this is all on the advice of the finance department."

Lucy's jaw dropped. "Are you kidding me?"

"Apparently, your department said we're still not in a place revenue-wise to make any significant charitable contributions."

Lucy pinched the bridge of her nose. "What. The actual. Fuck. As I've been telling him literally forever, we have money for all of it: paying the staff overtime, charitable donations . . ."

"And what does he say?" Simone asked.

"He always blames someone else—like, 'Well, we can't spend that money without the board's approval . . .'"

"So with us, he blames the finance department, and with the finance department, he blames the board," Seth recapped. "When the board asks what he's doing with all that revenue, he probably blames someone else for why he can't give them a straight answer."

Simone had a feeling *this* was what Seth had tried to tell her earlier. "And what's the actual reason he's being so shady about money?" she whispered.

Seth looked up and down the alley, making sure they were still alone, and pulled his phone from the pocket of his windbreaker. Wincing, he opened his messaging app. "Before I show you this," he said warily, "please keep in mind, once again, that I'm going to work on setting social boundaries with my boss." Seth scrolled back through his text message history with Frankie, to an exchange from the week before last. He handed the phone to Simone, and the two women huddled over the screen to read the conversation. When they were finished, they looked up, and Simone saw her own shock and dismay reflected in Lucy's face.

"He's secretly investing in *Crushr*?" Lucy's voice dripped with disdain. They'd both heard Seth's horror stories about the popular queer hookup app, where racism, fatphobia, transphobia, and other forms of hatred were permitted under the guise of "sexual preferences."

"That's right," Seth said, "you know, the app I literally had to delete because of how many guys wrote 'no Asians' on their profiles."

Simone reread his messages with Frankie, shaking her head the whole time. "Frankie says he knows the app is 'super problematic,' but he doesn't care because he's making a shit ton of money?"

"Correct," Seth replied.

"And he's promising you a raise at the end of the year as long as you keep it on the DL."

"Also correct."

"And *beyond* fucked-up," Lucy added. "You should take this straight to HR—oh wait! We don't have HR, because of course we don't." She craned her neck, looking up at the building that loomed over them in the alley. "Why the hell did we decide to work here again?"

"Because you were traumatized from Bay Street, I'd just graduated, and Simone had just been laid off, so we all desperately needed jobs," Seth reminder her. "Also, we're all higher than a zero on the Kinsey scale."

Simone looked up at the building, too. Wistfully, she added, "It seemed like a good place at first." *A queer oasis*. Those were the words she'd thought of when she'd first toured the office. When she'd seen all the bright colors, and the conference rooms named after queer icons, and the company-wide Slack messages about the bisexual giant tortoise in Ecuador. She realized now that those were all surface-level expressions of queerness. That when it came to actually supporting their community, Frankie Marlow talked the talk, but he didn't walk the walk. Simone saw now that there had never been any hope of convincing Frankie to partner with Glen's nonprofit out of the goodness of his heart. He supported the queer community insofar as doing so made him money.

How fitting that when it came to the Queer Makeover Extravaganza, Frankie seemed to be sending the message that your outside appearance could dictate exactly how queer you were. He wanted Seth giving consultations on how to make sure your social media was giving off "maximum queer vibes," for God's sake! Yes, presentation was obviously important—she could still remember the joy in Phoenix's voice, back in Whistler, when they'd talked about the euphoria of chopping off their hair—but it wasn't what *made* you queer. Phoenix would have been nonbinary regardless of how their hair looked, the same way trans people were still trans regardless of whether they medically transitioned. The same way gay people were still gay if they'd never had a partner before. The same way bisexual people were still bi, regardless of their partner's gender. In a way, Frankie reminded her of her mother, eternally fretting about the way things looked to outside observers.

Glen's words from the day before came back to her now: "My

dear, bisexuality isn't about who you date—it's who you are." Simone thought about who she'd been, who she was now, and who she wanted to become.

Simone had always believed she wasn't a big ideas person. That she was born to make other people's visions come to life. The truth was, she could make big ideas of her own. She'd just never been brave enough to try.

"We should probably start looking for new jobs, 'cause this place sort of sucks," she said. Seth and Lucy both nodded. "But in the meantime, how would you feel about helping me plan a Pride event?"

CHAPTER 25

IT WAS THE LAST DAY OF May, a Sunday, and Simone had just returned from her Loving Minds support group meeting, which had evolved into post-support-group brunch. Full of love, hope, and an exceptional stack of pancakes, she dove back into the project she'd been working on for the past six weeks. With the help of Lucy, Seth, and Glen and his team, she was throwing a charity karaoke night to benefit Loving Minds and kick off Pride Month in the best way possible.

She was emailing back Barista Joe, whose coffee shop was generously donating desserts, when her phone rang. It was Letty, the woman who owned Dorothy and Friends. Simone hit send on her email, then picked up the phone. "Hey, Letty."

"Simone—hey." Letty didn't sound like her usual laid-back self. "We have a bit of a problem."

Letty explained what had happened that morning. She'd arrived at Dorothy and Friends to open the bar, turned on one of the taps, and noticed something strange about the water. It was brown, and not in the way a single faucet sometimes coughed up a bit of rust from the old pipes. It was brown in the sense that every single plumbing fixture in the dive bar—including the toilets—was spewing water that looked like a medium-roast coffee. "I realized we're probably dealing with a water main issue, so I called my plumber, and she's on her way. I figured I should let you know as soon as possible, since we're supposed to be hosting your event tomorrow night."

"Supposed to be"? Simone didn't like the sound of that. "How long do you think it'll take to fix?" she asked Letty.

"I'll have a better idea once the plumber gets here . . . but you might want to start thinking about potential contingency plans."

"What kind of contingency plans?"

There was a long pause on Letty's end, during which, Simone googled "how long do water main breaks take to fix." She scanned the top result: "A simple water main repair can be completed in six to eight hours, but large or complicated repairs may take several days to a week." *No, no, no, no, NO*. Simone's heart shot into her throat as Letty finally answered: "Contingency plans either for rescheduling the event or finding a different venue. I'm so sorry, Simone."

"Okay," she said numbly, then remembered Letty was having just as bad a day as she was. "I'm sorry you have to deal with this, too."

"I'll update you as soon as she checks it out, but again, I just wanted to keep you in the loop."

"Sounds good," she said before hanging up, even though everything sounded very, very bad. For the past six weeks, she'd spent nearly every minute of her spare time planning this charity event to help queer Torontonians access mental health care. She'd come up with the karaoke night concept; she'd booked the venue; she'd found local businesses to donate food and prizes; and she'd developed a whole marketing plan to get the word out. Over a hundred people had RSVP'd. She couldn't reschedule the event *this* last-minute. It was Pride Month, and people were busy. Plus, she knew for a fact—from the blissfully ignorant emails she'd just been exchanging with Barista Joe—that her donated food was already being prepared. If she postponed the event, she could lose sponsors.

Simone felt like Ryan would know something about water main breaks. Even if he couldn't personally fix it, he could at least give her a helpful prognosis. But Ryan still hadn't reached out since the breakup, and Simone certainly hadn't reached out to him. Not even to try and return his clothes, which annoyingly still smelled like him.

As for the fundraiser, she would just have to look into finding another venue. That could hold over a hundred people. And support a karaoke machine . . . which she would also have to buy. All with one day's notice.

Simone saw the past six weeks of her life sliding down the drain. Sure, she'd also been spending her working hours planning the Queer Makeover Extravaganza, which was slated for the following weekend, but her heart wasn't tied to Frankie's Pride-themed money grab the way it was tied to this charity event she'd put together.

With a sickening mix of panic and dread, Simone messaged her group text with Lucy, Seth, and Glen, relaying the bad news about the water main break at Dorothy and Friends. They all agreed their best course of action was to immediately start asking around about alternate venue possibilities. Hopefully, it wouldn't come to that. Hopefully, it would turn out to be the simple kind of water main break you could fix in six to eight hours, and not the extremely rude kind that took several days to a week.

Letty called back later that afternoon with the verdict. "It's gonna take several days," she said. "Maybe even a week."

NO, NO, NO, NO, NO.

They wished each other good luck and hung up. Simone, who was sitting on the couch, grabbed the pink velvet throw pillow she still hadn't replaced and screamed into it for old time's sake. Except today, she allowed herself no more than a minute to wallow in despair before grabbing her phone again, alerting the group text, and getting to work. They drafted a message explaining their plight, which they posted on social media and sent to anyone in their contact lists who might be able to help, or at least point them in the right direction. It wasn't long before Glen heard back from an old classmate with a huge backyard, and Lucy got a lead from her cousin who worked at a progressive Jewish community center. They were briefly hopeful, until they found out the old classmate lived close to an hour outside the city—not ideal—and the Jewish community center had a strict maximum capacity of a hundred people, which would mean they'd have to turn away guests who'd already RSVP'd yes. Also not ideal. Simone half wondered if Frankie would grow a heart and offer them space in the Rainbow Museum, but her boss remained silent.

Simone and Seth decamped to Lucy's, where they'd set up a war room at the kitchen table. Holly supplied them with tea and snacks while they desperately sent messages and made phone calls. Cheddar, Gouda, and Blue wandered beneath them, rubbing their furry faces against their ankles as if for good luck, but by early evening, it was starting to seem like all the luck in the world wouldn't solve their problem. They had no more leads. It didn't help that it was now Sunday night, and a lot of businesses were closed until tomorrow.

"Just throwing this out there: Maybe we *should* just do it in

Glen's friend's backyard," Seth ventured. "Maybe people won't mind driving to Ajax . . . on a Monday night . . . to sing karaoke in some guy's backyard . . . okay, fuck, nobody in the world is gonna want to do that." With a groan, he scooped up another handful of the pretzels he'd been stress-eating.

Lucy held up her phone to show them the weather app. "It's also supposed to rain in Ajax tomorrow."

"We're so screwed." Simone flopped over and put her forehead on the table, her curls going everywhere. They'd have to email their sponsors and say thanks but no thanks. Then they'd have to email everyone who'd RSVP'd, saying the event had been postponed indefinitely, and they were very sorry, and they hoped people would still find it in their hearts to donate to Loving Minds. How incredibly disappointing. How incredibly *humiliating*.

"What even *is* a water main?" Seth grumbled. "Why do you only ever hear about them breaking? What good are they doing for the world?"

Partway through his grumbling, Simone's phone rang. She lifted her head. The call was from a Toronto number she didn't have in her contacts. It didn't look familiar, either. Normally, she'd assume a call like this was spam, but tonight she was willing to risk it. She picked up. "Hello?"

"Hey! Um—is that Simone?"

The man's voice was stilted. She recognized it, but couldn't quite place it. "This is Simone—who's this?"

"It's Dom."

"Dom!" Simone instantly went from dead to alert, but also a little flustered. She hadn't heard from him since the breakup.

"I, um—I saw you're in need of a venue. And that it's urgent."

The pounding of her pulse intensified. She waved to get Seth and Lucy's attention. "Yes, but more like *extremely* urgent," she replied, fumbling to put him on speakerphone. "It would be for tomorrow night, at seven, for like a hundred and fifty people? The bar in the Village where we were supposed to host our Pride fundraiser had a water main break."

"Oh, damn."

"It's a mess." Simone exchanged wide-eyed, desperate looks with Seth and Lucy, who were currently clutching each other's hands like two finalists at a beauty pageant.

"So, yeah. The reason I called"—they all leaned closer to the phone—"was to see if you wanted to host your event at the Common Loon. We're usually closed on Mondays, but I'd be down to open up and let you—"

He hadn't even finished speaking before Simone screamed, "YES!" and started thanking him profusely. Seth and Lucy shrieked with glee, which made the cats bolt from the kitchen in terror, and Holly went chasing after them, shouting their names.

"What did you say?" Dom asked Simone. "It just got very loud on your end."

"Quiet," Simone hissed at her friends, but her grin was as wide as theirs. "I said thank you, and we would absolutely love that so much. You have no idea. Dom, *thank you*."

"You're welcome," he said casually. "Oh, no—Loonie, get out of there! That was *my* water cup. Bad brewery cat. Sorry, you know how Loonie loves making himself at home on the bar."

Simone's smile faltered. For a second there, it had felt like old times. "Yes, I'm well aware."

Dom cleared his throat. "Anyway, I'm just about to close up for the night. Can I call you back when I'm home to talk logistics?"

"Of course," Simone said. She unleashed a string of thank-yous before they said goodbye. The moment she ended the call, she, Seth, and Lucy leapt to their feet and cheered. Holly skipped back into the room doing a celebratory dance with the grumpy-looking cat she was holding in the air. When they finally calmed down, they called Glen to deliver the good news, and proceeded to freak out all over again.

Which was why it wasn't until later, when Simone was driving home and waiting at a red light, that she thought about Dom's phone call and realized something that made her breath catch in her throat.

"I saw you're in need of a venue. And that it's urgent," Dom had said. But Dom didn't have Instagram. He paid one of his bartenders to manage the Common Loon's account, but it wasn't as though that person would have seen her post and sent it to Dom. Wasn't there only one mutual friend between them? Only one person who could have seen her plea on Instagram, passed it along to Dom, and given him Simone's number?

There was a part of her that still hoped they could make up. It was the same part of her that still reached for his T-shirt underneath the bed to smell it every so often. Maybe sending the post to Dom was Ryan's way of signaling that he was ready to try again, too.

But she refused to get her hopes up. As far as she knew, Ryan was still irrationally angry at her.

The light turned green. She shook off the ridiculous thought and hit the gas.

CHAPTER 26

"COME SEE ME."

They were arguably the most ominous three words a boss could send their employee, and they were the three words Simone saw in her Slack DMs from Frankie when she sat down at her desk the next morning.

She could have been petrified, but instead, she walked to his office with her shoulders back and her head held high. She knocked on the glass door, and he waved her in. There was no EDM blasting from the speakers. There was no music at all.

"Grab a seat," he said.

She did.

He folded his hands behind his head and leaned back in his chair, the picture of someone pretending to be cool, calm, and collected. "I saw your Instagram post last night. The one about this . . . charity event you're throwing. I know you've been promoting it for a while now, but I didn't know until last night that you were personally in charge."

She lifted her chin. "Is there a problem with me supporting a charity?"

"With you supporting a charity? No. But I'll tell you what *is* a problem: that your performance has been pretty damn disappointing lately, and I suspect it's because you're prioritizing your own event over the one that I'm paying you to plan."

On the wall behind his chair, there was a neon sign that said HUSTLE in cursive letters. She stared at the sign as she considered how to respond. If this had been at her old job—hell, if this had been a few months ago—she'd have been spewing out a string of apologies by now. But when she thought about why Frankie was mad at her, she realized she didn't feel bad at all. In fact, she was *happy* she'd made the choice to prioritize the fundraiser, and if she had to go back in time, she would make the same choice again. And suddenly, she knew what she had to do. She looked Frankie dead in the eyes. "You're absolutely right. I do care more about the Loving Minds fundraiser than the Queer Makeover Extravaganza."

Frankie arched a brow. "And . . . ?"

It was her last chance to say she was sorry, to beg for her boss's forgiveness. She knew the words would come easily if she let them, like muscle memory. Then she remembered something Frankie himself had said a long time ago: *"We don't make decisions because they're easy."* She thought of the options she could take from here, and landed on the one that scared her the most. If there was one thing she'd learned on her coming-out journey, it was that the scariest option was usually right.

"And I think it would be best for both of us if we parted ways," Simone said.

Frankie jerked his head back. "You what?"

She sat up straighter in her chair, feeling lighter than before. "I quit."

"You're not serious."

"I am." She stood up. "And by the way, if this is our exit interview? Let me give you a bit of feedback. Remember to disconnect your laptop from the conference room monitor before you spew a bunch of biphobia on Slack. Better yet, try *actually* supporting the community for once, instead of making us more insecure than we already were to begin with."

He blinked at her, speechless.

With that, she said, "Happy Pride," and marched out of his office for the last time.

When she got back to her desk, Seth was there. "So, what's the plan for later?" he asked without looking up from his laptop, oblivious to the fact that she was packing up her things. "I figure we'll sneak out around four and—"

"That's what you and Lucy will do. I'm leaving now. I just quit."

He abandoned whatever he was typing and spun around in his chair. "Simone Whitaker, what did you just say?!"

"I said I quit." She stuffed the bisexual hydrangeas into her tote bag. "So you guys can meet me at the brewery whenever you're able to get there."

"Um, I have like seventy billion questions."

"Questions about what?" asked Lucy, who'd just wandered over to their desks. She saw what Simone was doing and cocked her head to the side. "Wait, what's going on?"

"This bitch just *quit*," Seth said with admiration in his voice.

"Oh my God!" Lucy clapped a hand over her open mouth. "Tell us everything."

"I will tonight," Simone promised, and stuffed the last of her desk decor into her bag. "Right now, I just want to get the hell out of here before I take any of it back."

~

SIMONE WAS TRYING NOT TO TOTALLY freak out that she'd just quit her job without having another one lined up. She'd managed to find a new job last year, and she'd be able to do it again—or so she was telling herself, so she could make her way home without imploding from panic. Quitting a toxic job felt a lot like coming out, she realized: liberating and downright terrifying at the same time.

At least she had the fundraiser to distract her—not to mention the fact that she was throwing an event with the help of her ex-boyfriend's best friend.

"Loonie won't mind if I put these on the bar?" It was five thirty that evening, and Simone was at the Common Loon, arranging placards with instructions on how to donate to Loving Minds. On the other side of the bar, Dom was polishing beer glasses, his tattooed arms moving with a practiced ease.

"I think you're good," he said in that same awkward tone he'd been using with her since yesterday.

In Dom's defense, it *was* awkward that the two of them were spending any kind of time together, given that she and his best friend had just been through an acrimonious breakup. Neither of them had brought up the topic of Ryan, and Simone wanted to keep it that way—for now, at least. She was still reeling from quitting her job that morning, and with doors opening in thirty minutes, she had neither the time nor the emotional capacity to delve into the absolute mess that was her relationship with Ryan. She had a big idea to finish bringing to life.

Simone, Glen, and their colleagues were scrambling to prepare the taproom for the fundraiser. Simone had spent the day with Glen, running around, gathering supplies, and rehashing her dramatic showdown with Frankie. At five o'clock, they'd met up with Seth and Lucy at the brewery, rehashed the dramatic showdown again, and then started setting up the taproom for the seven o'clock event. So far, the setup was going smoothly. Smoothly in a "controlled chaos" sort of way, which was the best you could possibly expect for an event that didn't have a venue less than twenty-four hours before.

Against the long wall opposite the bar, there was a table full of desserts she and Glen had picked up from Barista Joe, and beside it, another table of prizes they'd be raffling off later. But the real pièce de résistance was over by the shorter wall, where there now hung a projector screen—on which Simone could make out the lyrics to "Mamma Mia." Seth crouched on the hardwood floor, fiddling with the dials on the karaoke machine they'd ordered last night, which had thankfully come with a next-day delivery option.

With ten minutes until showtime, Lucy found Simone straightening chairs around the tables. The chairs didn't need to be straightened, but everything else was done—the room was ready—and Simone's body was still crackling with energy.

"How're you feeling?" Lucy asked.

"Fine," Simone lied. She was nervous about her speech, but talking about it would make her even more nervous.

As Simone positioned a chair *just so*, Lucy squinted her eyes and studied her. "You're nervous about your speech," she declared.

Why did Lucy always have to be so incredibly perceptive? *Because she cares about you*, Simone reminded herself. She couldn't believe she'd ever doubted it. "Maybe a little," she admitted.

"What the heck do *you* have to be nervous about? You called out Frankie Marlow straight to his face today. You can do anything. I know it."

Simone let go of the chair, darted around the table, and threw her arms around Lucy, who stumbled backward, laughed as she regained her balance, and hugged Simone back. "Thank you for everything you've done for me," Simone said, her face full of Lucy's shiny blond hair.

"You know you don't have to thank me." Lucy gave her a squeeze, then stepped back to look her in the eye. "That's just what we do. We take care of each other."

"Yeah, but I feel like the care has been a bit . . . one-directional." Simone gestured from Lucy to herself. "If you know what I mean."

"And you don't think I was a needy bitch when I first came out? Please." Lucy rolled her eyes. "I was the babyest gay who ever baby-gayed."

"Well, I promise I won't be a baby bi forever."

Lucy looked around the taproom at Simone's big idea brought to life. "You know, between this and you quitting the Rainbow Museum, I think you've officially graduated to badass bi."

Simone beamed at her. "I love you, Luce."

"I love you, too." She pointed over Simone's shoulder. "Also, um, holy shit?"

"What?" Simone asked, suddenly panicking that the step-and-repeat banner had collapsed, or that Loonie had jumped up on the dessert table and started licking the cupcakes. But then Lucy spun her around by the shoulders so she could see what the fuss was.

"We already have a crowd," Lucy announced.

She was right. Simone grinned when she saw the guests already queueing outside on the porch, relieved they'd seen the texts, emails, and social media posts about the last-minute location change.

"Everyone okay if I let 'em in?" Dom asked.

Across the taproom, the ragtag team of organizers clapped, cheered, and gave thumbs-ups. Simone issued a rallying cry: "Let's have a great night, everyone!" Glen caught her eye and winked as he cupped his mouth and whooped.

It was surreal that after weeks of planning, not to mention a last-minute water main fiasco, guests were streaming into Simone's charity karaoke night. She'd gone from believing she was worthless—from barely holding herself together—to building something so much bigger than herself. Her fingertips tingled with pent-up potential as she dreamed of what *else* she was capable of. She was a badass bisexual and her future was limitless.

Simone went to the door to welcome guests, guide them into the taproom, and warn them not to be alarmed by the giant orange cat prowling back and forth along the bar. Holly, Nina, and Nina's partner Dani were there, along with some more of their Rainbow Museum colleagues. They were followed by a gaggle of Simone's support-group friends.

Bree had messaged Simone to say she sadly couldn't make it tonight, since she was visiting Gabi in Paris—but she'd sent Simone screenshots of the donations they'd both made to Loving Minds.

Claude was here, clinging lovingly to Seth's arm, as was Byron, clinging lovingly to Glen's. Simone grasped her elbow with the opposite hand, wishing there were someone clinging to hers like that.

Wishing that *someone* were Ryan.

Or . . . not quite. She did wish that someone were Ryan, but a version of Ryan that had worked on his trust issues, the way she'd been working through her own identity issues in her Loving Minds support group.

"Simone," said a familiar man's voice. When she whirled around, she saw two heads of ginger hair in the exact same shade as hers.

Her brothers had come to support her.

"You guys!" she squealed, pulling Matt and Jason in for a clumsy group hug. Nestling her head between theirs, she looked behind them and saw that Callie, Megan, and Simone's two nieces had come, too.

"We're super proud of you," Matt said, clapping Simone on the shoulder, while Jason peered around the taproom.

"Yeah, this is seriously impressive," he agreed.

"I love you guys," she said, for the first time she could remember.

"Love you, too," they both said.

Now all three Whitaker siblings were turning red, but Simone didn't regret a thing. "I better see both of you doing karaoke later," she teased.

Matt turned to Jason. "We should probably head to the bar, then."

Before they walked away, Jason asked, "Is Ryan coming?"

The question hit Simone like a punch to the gut. She hadn't told her family about the breakup, and now wasn't the time—not when she was minutes away from having to speak in front of the whole room. "He couldn't make it tonight," was all she replied, her tone clipped.

Jason frowned, but before he could say anything else, Glen tapped Simone on the shoulder, a microphone in his hand. "You ready?" he asked, holding it out to her. The plan was for Simone to speak first, then introduce Glen, who would go into more detail about all the ways Loving Minds supported queer mental health.

She nodded and took the mic, wondering if it was possible for the pounding of your own heart to crack a rib. Well, there was only one way to find out. Glen placed his thumb and index finger in his mouth and did one of those absurdly loud whistles to get people's attention. As the lively chatter petered out, Dom jogged around the bar and set down a plastic milk crate for Simone to stand on.

She tapped the mic to make sure it was working. Seth flashed her a thumbs-up as the *thunk, thunk, thunk* reverberated around the taproom. Simone climbed onto the milk crate, so she was at least a head taller than the rest of the crowd. Surveying the sea of people who'd filled the Common Loon on a Monday night—the first night of Pride Month—Simone felt dizzyingly proud . . . and also straight-up dizzy. She took a deep breath.

"Hey everyone! I'm Simone Whitaker. You may remember me from the seven thousand emails reminding you about the change of location for tonight's event." There was laughter—praise the lord. Simone felt herself relax. "I want to thank you all so much for coming out on the first day of Pride Month to show some love for an organization that's doing amazing work for the queer community here in Toronto."

There was a creak from the front door, and her eyes instinctively darted to the source of the noise.

Simone was about to find out if heartbeats really could crack ribs, because the person who'd just walked in was wearing a white T-shirt, worn-in jeans, and a pair of leather work boots she'd recognize anywhere. Suddenly, she had tunnel vision, the whole room going black except for the pinprick that was Ryan's gorgeous face. His square jaw, dotted with stubble; his shaggy mahogany-brown curls; his magical gray-green eyes. Like moss on a rock.

Then she remembered that she was still holding a microphone—that every set of eyes in the Common Loon was on her. Even Loonie's. What the hell had she just been saying? Oh. Right. With the deepest breath she could manage now that Ryan had entered the room, she continued.

"I first learned about Loving Minds in January, when I met its founder, Glen, at the Whistler Pride and Ski Festival. At the time, I'd been out publicly as bisexual for all of"—she pretended to check her watch—"three weeks?" Another smattering of knowing laughter helped her relax again. "Before I came out, I spent years repressing my queerness, which took a serious toll on my mental health." *Cue the flashback to her sobbing in the shower*. "I thought my mental health would get better after I finally came out, but honestly, it was still pretty rough. When you're bi, you sometimes feel like you're too queer for straight people, but not queer *enough* for other queer people. There are definitely some people in the audience who know what I'm talking about."

Sure enough, there were whoops of solidarity from her new support-group friends. Simone referenced a stat she'd learned at one of her very first meetings.

"Research actually shows that bi people are at a greater risk of having poor mental health than lesbians and gay men. Personally, I've gone through some pretty dark times, but with the help of my family and friends—including the folks at Loving Minds—I can now say with total confidence that I am not only a proud queer woman, but a woman who's queer *enough*. And I want to—"

She was cut off by a holler of support from someone in the crowd, and the next thing Simone knew, the whole taproom was cheering for her. It was a tidal wave of sound that rivaled the support for Tiny Tank Top at the drag bingo dance-off. Simone's cheeks hurt from smiling as she took in the room, soaking up every last drop of love.

In the sea of eyes locked on Simone, there were two she could feel more than all the rest. They belonged to Ryan, who'd moved farther into the room and was now standing with an elbow on the bar. His pose might have been casual, but the look on his face was anything but: an intense, smoldering gaze that made the muscles in her core tighten, that tugged on the invisible string connecting them through the crowd. *Gah*. She was still supposed to resent him for the way things had ended between them. Also, she had a speech to finish.

"As I was saying," she went on as the applause quieted down, "I want to do everything in my power to make sure other queer people can take care of their mental health, too. Which is why it's now my absolute pleasure to introduce you to Glen Tully, a wise man who once told me that bisexuality isn't about who you date." She looked down at Glen, who was beaming up at her. "It's who you *are*. He's helped countless members of the queer community—myself included—with his nonprofit, Loving Minds . . ."

As another round of applause filled the Common Loon, Simone handed off the microphone to Glen, who took her place on the milk crate. As her feet carried her toward the bar, she was vaguely aware of people congratulating her on a job well done, of people patting her on the back and clapping her on the shoulders. There was only one thing, one person, she could truly focus on, and it was the six-foot-two straight man who still hadn't taken his eyes off her. Like he was scared that if he looked away, he'd lose her forever.

"Simone. That was . . . amazing."

His deep voice, the way it reverberated in her chest—she was already turning to liquid. Then she remembered what a complete and utter mess their relationship was. "Thank you," she said, and crossed her arms.

Ryan rubbed the back of his neck, his biceps flexing. *Stop staring at his arm muscles, Simone*. "I know you're gonna be busy tonight, but I was hoping you'd have a few minutes to talk at some point."

"Let's go after Glen's speech."

When the crowd burst into applause, Simone and Ryan went to the door and slipped out into the warm late-spring evening. The sun was back out following an afternoon rainstorm, and the air had a fresh, earthy scent.

Ryan led her down the porch steps to one of the picnic tables positioned under the string lights, their shoes crunching on the gravel. He stooped to lay a hand on the bench. "It's dry."

She sat down with her back against the tabletop. "Did you make this?" she asked, caressing the smooth wooden surface of the bench. Ryan nodded. "It's . . . nice."

"Thanks." He sat down beside her, leaving space between their bodies. "I'm just gonna get right into it, if that's okay."

"Okay."

"I'm sorry," he blurted, like the words had been clawing to get out. "The last time we saw each other—when you told me what happened with Bree—I was an insecure asshole, and I'm ashamed of how terribly I treated you."

Simone raised her eyebrows, surprised he could even say Bree's name without losing his cool.

"I realized I'd made a fucking colossal mistake pretty much as soon as I left your apartment that night, but the thought of turning around freaked me out, too, 'cause I knew I had a problem when it came to trusting people, and I couldn't just switch that off, even if I'd wanted to. I thought about what you said, that I should talk to someone other than Dom. So, I did."

"You talked to a therapist?"

"I talked to two."

"Two?!"

"The first person figured out that I was dealing with something called betrayal trauma, so then she referred me to a colleague who specializes in treating it. He's been great."

"Betrayal trauma," Simone repeated, mulling over the words. "What is that, exactly?"

"It's basically when your trust is violated by someone really significant in your life. In my case, by *two* really significant people. It can show up in a bunch of different ways, like emotional dysregulation."

"Yeah, that tracks with our first few meetings."

"No kidding." He laughed softly, then sighed. "Another big way it shows up is with trust issues in relationships."

"Yeah, that tracks, too." She nodded slowly, thinking about Ryan's behavior in the five months she'd known him through this new lens. It all added up. "And it definitely didn't help that while you were dealing with that, I was over here going through a whole identity crisis." They both chuckled, easing some of the tension between them. "Luckily, I was able to join this support group that's been super helpful. I can't tell you how nice it is to have friends who are bi, who can totally validate what I'm going through."

"It sounds like you've come a long way," he said sincerely.

"I have." She turned to Ryan with a tentative smile. "It sounds like you have, too."

Ryan lifted the foot that was closer to Simone. She panicked that he was going to get up and walk away for some reason, but instead, Ryan shifted so that he was straddling the bench, facing her.

The sight of his legs spread open like that stirred the desire deep in her core. Even after all this time, she still wanted him so badly she ached. "Simone," he said, and she couldn't resist the urge to be closer. She swung her own leg over the bench, so that now they were face-to-face. Eye-to-eye. Heart-to-heart. "I didn't just come here tonight to apologize. I came here because I want to try again. I've wanted it from the second I walked out of your apartment, but I refused to waste your time until I knew for a fact that I could be the kind of partner you deserve. Because, Simone, you're the most amazing woman I've ever met."

"Oh, Ryan . . ." she whispered, but trailed off because he looked like he had more to say.

"We've both been through hard shit, but you've been through a kind that I'll never have to experience, and I don't know how I'd handle it if I did. And somehow, you still show up for everyone else with a smile. Like a delightful fucking sunflower."

Right on cue, Simone started to smile.

"I felt worthless for a really long time."

"Oh, Ryan, that's not—"

"I know it's not true," he said emphatically, "because I met you. You reminded me that I'm good at what I do. That I should actually be proud of myself once in a while."

"More than once in a while."

"Thank you." Ryan shifted closer to her on the bench, narrowing the space between them. "I've come so far from the person I was six months ago. When you first met me, I was this heartbroken wreck. I hated myself and anyone who wasn't miserable like me. Then you came along—you and your *chipperness*," he teased, "and you showed me that I was worthy of being happy. That I was worthy of love."

He moved even closer. Their knees touched, and the sparks sent a fire roaring through Simone's body.

"You made me a better person, too," she said. "Six months ago, I was this insecure ball of anxiety. All I ever did was twist myself into knots to make other people comfortable. I didn't care how badly it hurt me, as long as it kept the peace. I reached the point where I'd twisted myself so many times that I lost sight of the real me. I forgot that I could be confident—that I could be brave. With you, I found myself again."

Cupping her cheek with his callused palm, he gazed into her eyes. "I love you," Ryan whispered.

"I love you, too," she said, and kissed him.

~

SIMONE AND RYAN WALKED HAND IN hand up the porch steps and into the brewery, where Seth and Claude were boldly kicking off karaoke with a rendition of "Don't Go Breaking My Heart"—interpretive dance moves and all.

"You're going to make me get up there, aren't you?" Ryan asked.

"Oh, don't pretend you don't love putting on a show." She nudged him playfully in the ribs. "Maybe you should sing 'Pony.'" He snorted with laughter, and she patted him on the arm. "Don't worry, I'll buy you an IPA first."

They made their way over to the bar, where Dom took one look at their entwined fingers and grinned at Simone for the first time all night. "Now this is what I was hoping to see!"

Simone narrowed her eyes at him teasingly. "This whole time, you knew he was going to show up, didn't you?"

Dom looked at Ryan. "Did you tell her that you saved the whole fundraiser?"

Simone rounded on Ryan. "It *was* you."

"He sent me a screenshot of your Instagram post, asking if there was anything I could do to help," Dom said.

"I was following along with all the updates about the event," Ryan admitted. "I was planning to come support you no matter what."

Simone's heart swelled.

The evening went by in a happy blur, but Simone tried to soak in as much as she could. Her brothers performing a Celine Dion ballad with a truly impressive level of commitment; her niece Cecilia bonding with Loonie; Dom hitting it off with one of Simone's support-group friends; Ryan telling Glen that he'd spoken to people at the private school where he'd been doing his latest project, and that they might be interested in partnering with Loving Minds on some kind of youth mental health initiative. At this last piece of news, Simone genuinely thought her heart might explode.

"I really can't thank you both enough," Glen said, a hand on each of their arms.

Simone shook her head. "I think we've all helped each other in our own ways." She caught Ryan smiling at her, and she smiled back.

Glen must have clocked the exchange, because he smirked before turning to Simone. "I'm curious, now that you're a free agent, would you ever consider nonprofit work?"

"Wait." Ryan looked confused. "Are you not at the Rainbow Museum anymore?"

Simone smacked her forehead and laughed. "Oh my God, I've been so distracted, I forgot to tell you: I quit."

"She put that toxic asshole in his place," Glen added proudly. Simone blushed.

"Holy shit," Ryan said. "Sounds like I should say . . . congrats?"

"Absolutely," Glen said, patting Simone on the back.

"I never liked that guy," Ryan said with a shake of his head. "Honestly, I was happy to be out of there, too." His eyes found Simone's, and he lowered his voice. "Except that it meant I wouldn't get to see you."

When Ryan excused himself to grab something from the dessert table, Glen sidled up to Simone and spoke in a knowing whisper. "Now, is it just me, or am I detecting a vibe between the two of you again?"

She grinned. "I took your advice."

"Oh yes?"

"About soaking in every last drop of love. We talked tonight, and we decided to give our relationship another try. We both figured out what was holding us back last time, and now I think we can make it work."

Glen grinned back at her. "I'm proud of you."

"I'm proud of me, too."

Beyoncé's "Love on Top" started to play, and someone tapped the mic to get the audience's attention. Simone and Glen looked over—and found Byron getting ready to sing. "This next one goes out to a man who always puts my love on top." He spotted Glen and pointed at him. "Baby, you're the one I love." Simone and everyone around them cheered.

While Glen moved closer to watch the performance, Ryan wandered back over with a glazed donut for them to share. "Guess what flavor it is?"

She considered the beige icing. "Caramel?"

"Try again."

He gave her half. She smelled it—and beamed at him. "Maple?"

"That's the one."

"I'll try not to get icing on my nose this time."

"If you do, I'll lick it off."

She feigned shock. "Ryan Foley offering to eat icing off my face? You must really love me."

"I really do."

They tapped their maple donuts together like they were toasting with champagne. "Happy Pride," she said.

Ryan leaned down and kissed her. "Happy Pride, Simone."

CHAPTER 27

RYAN'S APARTMENT WAS THE SAME AS she remembered, the aroma of chocolate chip cookies from the bakery downstairs mingling with the scent of sawdust to make something sweet, warm, and earthy—a smell as delightfully unique as Ryan himself. Without even turning on the lights, they kicked off their shoes. Simone grabbed Ryan by the hand and led him into the bedroom like it belonged to the both of them. The curtains were open, letting in silvery-blue moonlight.

They'd already done enough talking tonight. Standing at the side of the bed, she gingerly lifted his white cotton T-shirt over his head. His skin was hot to the touch when she ran her fingertips over his smooth chest, down his strong arms. She planted a soft kiss on his sternum and felt his torso shiver in her hands. She felt powerful, the way she always did during sex with Ryan, and *God*, it turned her on.

"You've missed me, haven't you?"

Ryan watched reverently as she took off her own shirt. "More than you could possibly imagine," he said in a low growl, easing one of her bra straps over the curve of her shoulder. She reached behind her, unhooked it, and took the whole damn thing off. "God, I missed you so much." He grazed the sensitive underside of her breast with the pad of his thumb, then rubbed it across her taut nipple. Now Simone was the one shivering. Ryan leaned in to whisper in her ear. "I missed showing you how good I can make you feel."

"Good," she whispered back, "because there's something I want you to do for me tonight."

"What's that?"

With a sly smirk, she ran her hands through his thick curls and caressed the back of his neck. Cupping the sides of his head, making it so that he couldn't look anywhere else but down into her eyes, she said, "I want you to fuck me, Ryan."

He swore under his breath, and she felt his muscles go taut. "I can do that for you, baby," he said. "Let me grab a condom."

She perched on the edge of the mattress as he went to the bedside table and opened the lower drawer. Simone had never seen inside it. "You have lube," she noticed.

"What, is that weird?"

"No—it's hot. Most straight guys don't realize how much it can help."

"We can use as much as you want." Ryan grabbed a couple of condoms and placed them next to the bed. "I also use it on my own," he added.

"Like, instead of lotion?"

"Not exactly." He bit his bottom lip. "Do you know about prostate massage?"

The mere thought of Ryan exploring his own pleasure made her core clench with desire. "Do *you* know you're the hottest person on Planet Earth?"

She stood up and eagerly unbuttoned her jeans. Ryan did the same with his, and soon they were both naked on the bed, Simone on her back and Ryan on top of her, his lips working their way down from her jaw, to her neck, to her collarbone. "Wait," Simone breathed before he went any further. Ryan paused, looking up at her with concern. "Everything's fine," she said with a reassuring smile. "I just want to feel you first."

She motioned for him to come back up, then pulled him in for a deep kiss while his body sank onto hers. She'd missed him so much, she needed to feel him in as many places as she could: his curls grazing her cheek; his tongue gently sweeping the inside of her mouth; his heavy torso grounding her like a weighted blanket. He moaned into the kiss, and she felt his erection heavy on her thigh.

"Are you hard for me already?" she whispered.

"I can't control myself around you." He pushed himself up to a high kneeling position, unwrapped the condom, and rolled it down his stiff cock. Then he lowered himself back onto her, pressing his shaft against her swollen clit, and Simone let out a gasp that was equal parts surprise and satisfaction.

"Does that feel good?" he asked.

"Now I'm the one who can't control myself," she rasped, grabbing his ass and pulling his body as close to hers as she could. His bulge flush against her clit, he massaged her with a calculated rhythm, sending waves of pleasure cascading up and down her spine. Ryan whispered in her ear, his words punctuated by the pulsing of his hips: "I'll give you . . . whatever . . . you want . . . baby."

Her clit throbbed against his cock. "I want you to taste me. But only if you promise to fuck me when you're done."

He swore again. "You're going to be the death of me."

Simone moaned with relief when Ryan's face disappeared

between her legs, and it wasn't long before she could feel herself nearing the edge of delicious oblivion. "I'm getting close," she said, her voice raspy. He slipped a finger inside her and hooked it forward, massaging her front wall while his tongue continued circling her clit. *Fuck*. She was tipping over the edge—there was no stopping it now— "I want you to fuck me," she told him with a desperate urgency. "I want you to make me come with your cock. Now—*please*."

He immediately obliged, cursing under his breath. His wet fingers moving to her clit, he knelt between her legs and pressed into her, filled her up so that every last one of the thousands of nerve endings in and around her core erupted in fireworks of pleasure. She was weightless, her orgasm carrying her up to another galaxy and refusing to bring her back down again—not while Ryan's cock was thrusting into her and his fingers rubbed small circles over her clit. Her pussy clenched around him, showing his body exactly what she needed it to do.

Simone laughed softly, a little deliriously, as she drifted back to the bed, where Ryan was still inside her, rock hard, as deep as he could go. She lay there, catching her breath, reveling in the way he stretched and filled her, like he needed to reach as much of her as he could. Ryan's cock inside her had been *entirely* worth the wait, and they weren't even done yet. "I love you," she said. "Every inch of you. You're perfect."

"I love you, too." He kissed her softly on the lips. "And I love making you come."

She smirked up at him. "Well, now you're going to let me do the same thing for you."

With Ryan still inside her, she reached for the open bedside drawer and seized the bottle of lube she'd seen earlier. She hadn't tried this before, but she'd read about it: how you could use your fingers to find someone's prostate, and how stimulating it could feel really good for them. Supposedly, straight men tended to shy away from anything anal, as though touching a certain part of your body said *anything* about your sexuality. The notion had always struck Simone as ridiculous—as ridiculous as the idea that a certain haircut or piercing could make her queerer than she already was. Ryan, of course, was not one of these sexually repressed straight men. He was like no other straight man she'd ever met.

Like no other person she'd ever met, period.

With Ryan lying on top of her, his hips between her legs, she reached around to his ass. "Is this okay?" she asked.

He nodded, sucking in a sharp breath of anticipation as she traced the line between his cheeks. "Just go slow."

She nodded back. With their eyes locked on each other's, she gingerly put a finger inside him. Shuddering with pleasure, he released the breath he'd been holding.

"Simone." He sighed, thrusting into her again. His movements were slower but more intense at the same time. She loved feeling him clench around her finger, loved that she was inside of him while *he* was inside of *her*—that they were both fucking each other and dizzy with the pleasure of it all.

"Holy shit," she breathed. Between the waves of pleasure from his thrusting cock and the erotic idea that she was deep inside him, too, Simone realized she was on the verge of another orgasm. "I think I'm going to come again."

"*Fuck*, me, too."

She fucked him faster, and he thrust deeper into her, the two of them matching each other's intensity as they both got closer to climax.

"Don't stop. Ryan, I'm . . ." she gasped.

He growled out a string of profanities and praises in answer, his body tensing.

And then they unraveled, their bodies arching and shuddering as one. Like an island in a storm, they held each other as the waves crashed over them. Together at last, they could withstand anything.

Ryan lay with his head on Simone's chest. They were both damp with sweat, both breathing heavily, both in a state of exhaustion and sheer bliss. Ryan murmured, "That was the best sex—"

"—we've ever had?" Simone asked.

"I was actually going to say it was the best sex I've ever had in my life."

"Okay, good," she said, chuckling, "because I was just thinking the same thing."

He kissed the tops of her breasts. "And it'll just keep getting better from here."

~

SIMONE FOLLOWED RYAN TO THE SHOWER, admiring his glorious naked body from behind. He turned on the faucet, and they both got in together, Simone facing the water and Ryan standing behind her. She closed her eyes, relaxing in the warm spray that splashed onto her breasts.

"You're so beautiful," he said, his lips by her ear. Then she smelled his evergreen-scented soap, felt his hands on her skin, and moaned as she melted under his touch. He washed her and massaged her at the same time, starting with her neck and shoulders and making his way down her back.

"Turn around," Ryan whispered.

He covered her torso in soapy lather, devoting extra time to her breasts. Her nipples were hard by the time he was done with them. He knelt to wash her thighs, her calves, and her feet. When he was finished, he placed a reverent kiss on her clit. With a moan, she sank her fingers into his damp curls. He looked up at her. "Can I keep going?"

"Please," she begged, and spread her legs wider, craving so much more than the brush of his lips.

She placed a foot on the edge of the tub, granting him easier access to the parts of her he wanted to taste again. Her hands still in his hair, she guided his face to her pussy and let him devour her, but it wasn't long before she looked down, saw his stiffening cock, and knew she'd need him inside of her again as soon as humanly possible. It was a good thing she'd thought to leave a condom on the counter by the sink.

The jet of water pelting the back of her neck gave Simone an idea. "Ryan," she breathed. He pulled back and looked up at her. "I need you to turn me around and fuck me."

"Let me get—"

"I brought one." She reached around the curtain and grabbed the foil wrapper.

"Have I mentioned how much I love you?" he asked as he climbed to his feet. His hard cock was ready for another round.

"Not as much as I love you." Smirking, she handed him the condom and reached for the removable shower head. She took it off its holder and twisted the nozzle so that the jet narrowed and became more powerful. "Perfect," she murmured.

Ryan turned her around again. With one hand gripping the shower head and the other splayed on the tile, she leaned forward and arched her back. He traced his swollen head around her slick opening, until Simone couldn't stand the ache of desire for one more second. "Please," she moaned, arching her back even more.

Ryan's cock filling her from behind was a whole new sensation—deeper and more intense than when he'd entered from on top. "Oh my God," she gasped.

He paused with his hands on her hips. "Is this okay?"

"Ryan, it's unbelievable." She rocked back against his pelvis, taking every last inch of him inside her. Ryan swore, tightening his hold on her hips. "Is it okay for you?" she asked.

"Baby, it's so fucking good." She rocked into him again, and he breathed out a sharp jet of air. "You're making it hard for me to control myself."

She smirked. "I'm not going to apologize for that."

"You shouldn't. You're fucking perfect."

Simone aimed the shower head between her legs and cried out in ecstasy when the gush of water hit her clit. Ryan this deep inside her was one thing, but Ryan this deep inside her with the shower head acting as a vibrator was something else entirely, something deeper and sweeter than she'd ever felt in her life.

She heard him take a ragged breath. "You clenching around me like that—I'm already so fucking close."

"Hold still inside me while I get there, too."

Relishing the feeling of being stretched—of being filled—she used the jet of water to bring herself closer to climax. "It feels so good," she breathed—and then, "I'm almost there."

"Tell me when you're about to come."

"I'm there," she answered desperately, "*now.*"

On her cue, he fucked her over the edge—sent her hurtling into new depths of pleasure. She cried out his name as she came around his cock.

"So . . . fucking . . . hot." With three more deep thrusts, he was passing his own point of no return. Shuddering, he bit the back of her shoulder to stifle his groans. The pain sent another wave of pleasure down her spine.

Ryan pulled out, and Simone returned the shower head to its cradle. She turned, looped her arms around his neck, and kissed him softly on the mouth. "You were right," she said, smiling up at him.

He furrowed his brow. "About what?"

She stood on tiptoe and kissed him again. "That it'll just keep getting better."

After they dried off, Simone went to the dresser and chose one of his soft cotton T-shirts to sleep in. Ryan pulled on some cozy-looking shorts, went to the kitchen, and made them tea. It didn't matter that it was June; Simone relished the hot mug cupped between her palms as they cuddled under the thin summer quilt in the moonlit bedroom. It brought back memories of Whistler, of warming up by the bonfire after a long day of skiing. Of falling head over heels for Ryan, even though she hadn't been ready to accept it at the time. How far she'd come since then. How far they'd *both* come.

"What do you think you'll do, now that you're free?" Ryan asked. She'd just finished telling him the full story of quitting the Rainbow Museum.

"I dunno yet. I think I might look into some nonprofit jobs."

"That would be awesome."

"And in the meantime, maybe you could teach me a few things about carpentry. And cooking. And in exchange, I'll take you to Pilates." He chuckled. "You know, strengthening your core is apparently good for sex," she pointed out.

"In that case, it sounds like a fair trade."

Simone nuzzled into Ryan's bare shoulder. "Remember in Whistler, when I said that being with a guy would feel like a wasted opportunity?"

Ryan laughed softly. "I was trying to be so supportive because you were talking about coming out, but I was secretly like . . . damn. There goes that."

"Well, when I said it, I didn't know how amazing you were. How free I could feel with you as my partner."

He kissed the top of her head. "Does this mean you're amending your statement?"

"A wasted opportunity would have been never falling in love with you." Simone took another sip of tea, thinking maybe they'd make Whistler Pride an annual tradition. "And Ryan," she added, "being with you now feels like *infinite* opportunity."

EPILOGUE

The following January

SIMONE WAS ABOUT TO TAKE A major risk, and she knew it.

She yanked off her mitten and reached into the pocket of her parka, where she gripped her phone with her bare hand. Squeezing it like her life depended on it, she brought it out into the open air and turned on the camera.

"Put that away," Ryan demanded.

"Just one photo."

"Simone, do you realize where we are?" He flailed his gloved hands at the winter wonderland around them—or rather, beneath them. Fifty feet below, skiers and snowboarders glided through the fresh blanket of snow that had fallen on the mountain overnight.

"Yes, I do realize we're on a Whistler chairlift."

"Do you remember what happened the last time you took out your phone on a Whistler chairlift?"

"Hmm." She pretended to have to think about it. "I seem to remember us having a very romantic foray in the snowy woods."

"After we both nearly died on a double black diamond."

"But we got to share a beaver tail afterward, which was also very romantic," she pointed out. "Come on. The longer you protest, the longer my phone is hovering dangerously over this very high drop . . ."

"Okay, *fine*."

She'd been with Ryan long enough to know he wasn't really upset. He was just her moody gargoyle, doing his best to ward off any dangers that might befall her. They pressed their helmets together, and Simone quickly snapped a selfie.

"Luis, Roberto: You guys wanna squeeze in?"

The middle-aged Ecuadorian couple paused their conversation in Spanish and scooted in for a smiling group photo. The sky behind them was a vivid blue.

"I can't believe how perfect the weather is," Simone said to Ryan as she tucked her phone back inside her parka.

He prodded her pocket himself to make sure it was secure. Only when he was satisfied that they wouldn't be repeating last year's phone-dropping fiasco did he say, "They really lucked out."

"So did I." She snuggled into her boyfriend's side. They were on the Peak Express—the chairlift that ferried riders to the summit of Whistler Mountain. A year ago, they'd taken this route to watch Margot propose to Thea. Today, they were headed back to the Top of the World to watch the couple get married.

It had been easy for Simone to get the time off work to come to the Whistler Pride and Ski Festival again. Her boss, after all, was Glen, who was seated on the chair ahead of them, along with Byron, Phoenix, and Phoenix's new partner, Orla. In spite of the water main shit show, the Loving Minds fundraiser had been a huge success—and when Glen's longtime program manager had announced her retirement a few weeks later, he'd offered the job to Simone.

Seth and Lucy were still at the Rainbow Museum, and she still talked to them all the time, which was how she'd stayed on top of all the drama that had transpired since she'd left—or really, *because* she'd left. Seth had been so inspired by Simone taking a stand against Frankie that he'd worked up the courage to send screenshots of their former boss's messages to the Rainbow Museum's board of directors. Frankie had given up his majority stake in the company in exchange for all the capital he'd raised, which meant the board had possessed the power to strip him of his CEO title—and that was exactly what they'd done. They'd recently hired someone new in his place: a woman with a vision of building out the educational sections of the museum, and, yes, giving a portion of the proceeds to charity. Simone was holding out hope that a Loving Minds partnership might actually come to fruition.

Her relationships with Ryan's moms were also on the up. She'd opened up to them about the reasons for her and Ryan's tumultuous start, and she'd been relieved when Paula and Claire had responded with understanding. Claire had even asked Simone to forgive her for being so guarded the first time they met, and Simone had said she understood—after all, she loved Ryan, too—and then both of them had hugged, and laughed, and hugged some more, and long story short, they now texted each other about the addictive, low-budget queer dating shows that Paula and Ryan refused to watch. Simone and Ryan had split the holidays between Florida and Barrie, meaning less time with the Whitakers and more time with the in-laws she was growing to love as much as Ryan.

Not that she didn't love her own parents—nor did she think they didn't love her. Like Lucy had once told her, it was just that her parents were too scared to change the world, so instead they wanted Simone to do the changing. Lately, Kathy had pivoted to badgering Simone and Ryan about when they were getting married, since they were both in their thirties, after all, and did Simone really want to have a geriatric pregnancy? How Kathy had decided Simone wanted kids—when Simone wasn't even sure herself—was beyond her. George was as unhelpful as ever, preferring to keep the peace with Kathy rather than rock the boat. Simone was working with her new therapist on setting boundaries, because she didn't want to tie herself in knots anymore to make her parents more comfortable. She didn't want to do that for anyone.

Of course, with Ryan, she knew she would never have to.

With him, she knew she could be her truest self, and he would love her—not *in spite* of who she was, but *because* of who she was.

The brides wore white ski suits. Simone, Ryan, and around thirty of Margot and Thea's friends and family members gathered at the summit and cheered as the women sealed their vows with a kiss. Simone wiped away heartfelt tears, remembering how she'd also felt like crying a year ago in this very spot, when she was falling for the man standing next to her, but scared that she was wasting an opportunity. She still stood by what she'd told him the night they got back together: that being with Ryan felt like infinite opportunity.

The plan was for the wedding party to follow the brides down the mountain in the world's most on-brand wedding procession, which would lead to a casual après-ski reception. But right before they took off down the slope, Simone tugged on the sleeve of Ryan's parka. He turned to her and lifted his goggles, looking concerned. "Are you okay?"

She lifted her own goggles and looked up at him with a blissful smile. "Kiss me on top of the world."

The lines disappeared from his forehead, and he smiled back

at her, his gray-green eyes sparkling in the midday sun. "There's nothing I'd like to do more."

As he kissed her on the snowy summit, warming her from the inside out, Simone knew she wanted to soak in Ryan's love forever—or as long as the universe would let her.

And until then, her queer little heart would love him more every day.

ACKNOWLEDGMENTS

In the spring of 2024, after years of working in journalism and writing books at the same time, I decided to quit my magazine job and go all in on my career as an author. I had an idea for a queer romance novel about a woman who comes out as bi, then reluctantly falls for a straight guy, and I couldn't wait any longer to explore it. I am incredibly grateful to everyone who played a role in bringing that book idea to life.

Thank you to my agent, Danielle Burby, who encouraged me to make the leap and boldly advocated for this book from the moment I pitched it. (You were right: *Ain't No Mountain Bi Enough* was not the correct title.) Thank you to my international dream team of editors, Ghjulia Romiti and Brittany Lavery, who shared my vision for Simone's story on a truly mind-melding level. And thank you to editorial assistant and romance connoisseur Muna Hussein, who contributed brilliant notes to the revision process.

Thank you to the teams at Gallery Books and Simon & Schuster Canada who helped create this book and share it with readers: Jennifer Bergstrom, Sally Marvin, Fallon McKnight, Sarah Westergren,

Christine Masters, Polly Watson, Caroline Pallotta, Emily Arzeno, Angel Musyimi, Kaitlyn Lonnee, Hope Herr-Cardillo, Lisa Litwack, Kelli McAdams, Kristen Solecki, Jane Phan, Brigid Black, Rebecca Snoddon, and Natasha Kempnich.

Finally, thank you to all the family and friends who have lovingly supported me as I've recognized and embraced my own queerness over the years. I am extraordinarily lucky to be surrounded by your love, and without you, I never could have written this story.

Keep an eye out for Jordyn Taylor's next novel—
a second-chance sapphic romance.

She got the girl, the ring, and the viral proposal . . .
so why is she spiraling?

Coming in early 2027

© Chad Johnson

ABOUT THE AUTHOR

JORDYN TAYLOR is the *USA Today* bestselling and award-winning author of the young adult novels *The Rebel Girls of Rome*, *The Paper Girl of Paris*, *Wicked Darlings*, *Don't Breathe a Word*, and *The Revenge Game*. She is a former executive editor at *Men's Health* and an adjunct professor of journalism at New York University's Arthur L. Carter Journalism Institute. Jordyn was born and raised in Toronto, Canada, and now lives in New York City. *See You at the Summit* is her adult debut.